Baroness Orczy

EMMA MAGDALENA ROSALIA MARIE JOSEPHA BARBARA ORCZY, Baroness Orczy, was born in Hungary in 1865. Her father abandoned his family's estate when the peasants working it refused to accept modern farming methods. The Orczy family settled in London, and Emma studied art. Following her marriage to the illustrator Montague Barstow, Emma Orczy and her husband produced several children's books before the Baroness turned to writing historical novels.

Completed in 1902, *The Scarlet Pimpernel* was turned down by every publisher to whom it was submitted. Not until a play based on it proved to be an enormous success did the novel finally get published, and its hero become one of the most popular characters in English fiction.

Baroness Orczy wrote several more books about the Scarlet Pimpernel's adventures, as well as numerous other historical novels. She died in 1947.

YEARLING CLASSICS

Works of lasting literary merit by English and American classic and contemporary writers

EIGHT COUSINS, OR THE AUNT HILL, *Louisa May Alcott*

AN OLD-FASHIONED GIRL, *Louisa May Alcott*

LITTLE WOMEN, *Louisa May Alcott*

CARRIE'S WAR, *Nina Bawden*

THE SECRET GARDEN, *Frances Hodgson Burnett*

THE DANCING BEAR, *Peter Dickinson*

SMITH, *Leon Garfield*

LASSIE COME-HOME, *Eric Knight*

DR. DOLITTLE: A TREASURY, *Hugh Lofting*

WINNIE-THE-POOH, *A. A. Milne*

POLLYANNA, *Eleanor H. Porter*

A GIRL OF THE LIMBERLOST, *Gene Stratton Porter*

FIVE LITTLE PEPPERS AND HOW THEY GREW, *Margaret Sidney*

FIVE LITTLE PEPPERS MIDWAY, *Margaret Sidney*

HEIDI GROWS UP, *Charles Tritten*

DADDY-LONG-LEGS, *Jean Webster*

THE BIRDS' CHRISTMAS CAROL, *Kate Douglas Wiggin*

YEARLING BOOKS/YOUNG YEARLINGS/YEARLING CLASSICS are designed especially to entertain and enlighten young people. Patricia Reilly Giff, consultant to this series, received the bachelor's degree from Marymount College. She holds the master's degree in history from St. John's University, and a Professional Diploma in Reading from Hofstra University. She was a teacher and reading consultant for many years, and is the author of numerous books for young readers.

For a complete listing of all Yearling titles, write to
Dell Readers Service, P.O. Box 1045,
South Holland, IL 60473.

The Scarlet Pimpernel

Baroness Orczy

With an Afterword by Kathryn Lasky

A DELL YEARLING CLASSIC

Published by
Dell Publishing
a division of
Bantam Doubleday Dell Publishing Group, Inc.
666 Fifth Avenue
New York, New York 10103

ISBN: 0-440-40220-4

Printed in the United States of America

September 1989

10 9 8 7 6 5 4 3 2 1

OPM

Contents

1	Paris: September, 1792	1
2	Dover: "The Fisherman's Rest"	12
3	The Refugees	25
4	The League of the Scarlet Pimpernel	35
5	Marguerite	45
6	An Exquisite of '92	53
7	The Secret Orchard	66
8	The Accredited Agent	74
9	The Outrage	89
10	In the Opera Box	98
11	Lord Grenville's Ball	117
12	The Scrap of Paper	126
13	Either—Or?	137
14	One o'Clock Precisely!	141
15	Doubt	152
16	Richmond	159
17	Farewell	177
18	The Mysterious Device	187
19	The Scarlet Pimpernel	193
20	The Friend	205
21	Suspense	214
22	Calais	225
23	Hope	238
24	The Death-Trap	247
25	The Eagle and the Fox	256
26	The Jew	267

27   On the Track   280
28   The Père Blanchard's Hut   290
29   Trapped   302
30   The Schooner   308
31   The Escape   324
     Afterword   338

Chapter 1

Paris:
September, 1792

A surging, seething, murmuring crowd of beings that are human only in name, for to the eye and ear they seem naught but savage creatures, animated by vile passions and by the lust of vengeance and of hate. The hour, some little time before sunset, and the place, the West Barricade, at the very spot where, a decade later, a proud tyrant raised an undying monument to the nation's glory and his own vanity.

During the greater part of the day the guillotine had been kept busy at its ghastly work: all that France had boasted of in the past centuries, of ancient names, and blue blood, had paid toll to her desire for liberty and for fraternity. The carnage had only ceased at this late hour of the day because there were other more interesting sights for the people to witness, a little while before the final closing of the barricades for the night.

1

And so the crowd rushed away from the Place de la
Grève and made for the various barricades in order to
watch this interesting and amusing sight.

It was to be seen every day, for those aristos were such
fools! They were traitors to the people of course, all of
them, men, women, and children, who happened to be
descendants of the great men who since the Crusades had
made the glory of France: her old *noblesse*. Their ancestors
had oppressed the people, had crushed them under the
scarlet heels of their dainty buckled shoes, and now the
people had become the rulers of France and crushed their
former masters—not beneath their heels, for they went
shoeless mostly in these days—but beneath a more effectual weight, the knife of the guillotine.

And daily, hourly, the hideous instrument of torture
claimed its many victims—old men, young women, tiny
children, even until the day when it would finally demand
the head of a King and of a beautiful young Queen.

But this was as it should be: were not the people now
the rulers of France? Every aristocrat was a traitor, as his
ancestors had been before him: for two hundred years now
the people had sweated, and toiled, and starved, to keep a
lustful court in lavish extravagance; now the descendants
of those who had helped to make those courts brilliant
had to hide for their lives—to fly, if they wished to avoid
the tardy vengeance of the people.

And they did try to hide, and tried to fly: that was just
the fun of the whole thing. Every afternoon before the
gates closed and the market carts went out in procession
by the various barricades, some fool of an aristo endeavoured to evade the clutches of the Committee of Public

Safety. In various disguises, under various pretexts, they tried to slip through the barriers which were so well guarded by citizen soldiers of the Republic. Men in women's clothes, women in male attire, children disguised in beggars' rags: there were some of all sorts: ci-devant counts, marquises, even dukes, who wanted to fly from France, reach England or some other equally accursed country, and there try to rouse foreign feeling against the glorious Revolution, or to raise an army in order to liberate the wretched prisoners in the Temple, who had once called themselves sovereigns of France.

But they were nearly always caught at the barricades. Sergeant Bibot especially at the West Gate had a wonderful nose for scenting an aristo in the most perfect disguise. Then, of course, the fun began. Bibot would look at his prey as a cat looks upon the mouse, play with him, sometimes for quite a quarter of an hour, pretend to be hoodwinked by the disguise, by the wigs and other bits of theatrical make-up which hid the identity of a ci-devant noble marquise or count.

Oh! Bibot had a keen sense of humour, and it was well worth hanging round that West Barricade, in order to see him catch an aristo in the very act of trying to flee from the vengeance of the people.

Sometimes Bibot would let his prey actually out by the gates, allowing him to think for the space of two minutes at least that he really had escaped out of Paris, and might even manage to reach the coast of England in safety: but Bibot would let the unfortunate wretch walk about ten meters towards the open country, then he would send two men after him and bring him back, stripped of his disguise.

Oh! that was extremely funny, for as often as not the fugitive would prove to be a woman, some proud marchioness, who looked terribly comical when she found herself in Bibot's clutches after all, and knew that a summary trial would await her the next day and after that, the fond embrace of Madame la Guillotine.

No wonder that on this fine afternoon in September the crowd round Bibot's gate was eager and excited. The lust of blood grows with its satisfaction, there is no satiety: the crowd had seen a hundred noble heads fall beneath the guillotine to-day, it wanted to make sure that it would see another hundred fall on the morrow.

Bibot was sitting on an overturned and empty cask close by the gate of the barricade; a small detachment of citoyen soldiers was under his command. The work had been very hot lately. Those cursed aristos were becoming terrified and tried their hardest to slip out of Paris: men, women and children, whose ancestors, even in remote ages, had served those traitorous Bourbons, were all traitors themselves and right food for the guillotine. Every day Bibot had had the satisfaction of unmasking some fugitive royalists and sending them back to be tried by the Committee of Public Safety, presided over by that good patriot, Citoyen Foucquier-Tinville.

Robespierre and Danton both had commended Bibot for his zeal and Bibot was proud of the fact that he on his own initiative had sent at least fifty aristos to the guillotine.

But to-day all the sergeants in command at the various barricades had had special orders. Recently a very great number of aristos had succeeded in escaping out of France and in reaching England safely. There were curious rumours about these escapes; they had become very frequent and singularly daring; the people's minds were becoming strangely excited about it all. Sergeant Grospierre had been sent to the guillotine for allowing a whole family of aristos to slip out of the North Gate under his very nose.

It was asserted that these escapes were organised by a band of Englishmen, whose daring seemed to be unparalleled, and who, from sheer desire to meddle in what did not concern them, spent their spare time in snatching away lawful victims destined for Madame la Guillotine. These rumours soon grew in extravagance; there was no doubt that this band of meddlesome Englishmen did exist; moreover, they seemed to be under the leadership of a man whose pluck and audacity were almost fabulous. Strange stories were afloat of how he and those aristos whom he rescued became suddenly invisible as they reached the barricades and escaped out of the gates by sheer supernatural agency.

No one had seen these mysterious Englishmen; as for their leader, he was never spoken of, save with a superstitious shudder. Citoyen Foucquier-Tinville would in the course of the day receive a scrap of paper from some mysterious source; sometimes he would find it in the pocket of his coat, at others it would be handed to him by someone in the crowd, whilst he was on his way to the sitting of the Committee of Public Safety. The paper always contained a brief notice that the band of meddlesome Englishmen were at work, and it was always signed with a device drawn in red—a little star-shaped flower, which we in England call the Scarlet Pimpernel. Within a few hours of the receipt of this impudent notice, the citoyens of the Committee of Public Safety would hear that so many royalists and aristocrats had succeeded in reaching the coast, and were on their way to England and safety.

The guards at the gates had been doubled, the sergeants in command had been threatened with death, whilst liberal rewards were offered for the capture of these daring and impudent Englishmen. There was a sum of five thousand francs promised to the man who laid hands on the mysterious and elusive Scarlet Pimpernel.

Everyone felt that Bibot would be that man, and Bibot allowed that belief to take firm root in everybody's mind; and so, day after day, people came to watch him at the West Gate, so as to be present when he laid hands on any fugitive aristo who perhaps might be accompanied by that mysterious Englishman.

"Bah!" he said to his trusted corporal, "Citoyen Grospierre was a fool! Had it been me now, at that North Gate last week . . ."

Citoyen Bibot spat on the ground to express his contempt for his comrade's stupidity.

"How did it happen, citoyen?" asked the corporal.

"Grospierre was at the gate, keeping good watch," began Bibot, pompously, as the crowd closed in round him, listening eagerly to his narrative. "We've all heard of this meddlesome Englishman, this accursed Scarlet Pimpernel. He won't get through *my* gate, *morbleu!* unless he be the devil himself. But Grospierre was a fool. The market carts were going through the gates; there was one laden with casks, and driven by an old man, with a boy beside him. Grospierre was a bit drunk, but he thought himself very

clever; he looked into the casks—most of them, at least—
and saw they were empty, and let the cart go through."

A murmur of wrath and contempt went round the group
of ill-clad wretches, who crowded round Citoyen Bibot.

"Half an hour later," continued the sergeant, "up comes
a captain of the guard with a squad of some dozen soldiers
with him. 'Has a cart gone through?' he asks of Grospierre,
breathlessly. 'Yes,' says Grospierre, 'not half an hour ago.'
'And you have let them escape,' shouts the captain furi-
ously. 'You'll go to the guillotine for this, citoyen sergeant! that cart held concealed the *ci-devant* Duc de Chalis
and all his family!' 'What!' thunders Grospierre, aghast.
'Aye! and the driver was none other than that cursed
Englishman, the Scarlet Pimpernel.' "

A howl of execration greeted this tale. Citoyen Grospierre
had paid for his blunder on the guillotine, but what a fool!
oh! what a fool!

Bibot was laughing so much at his own tale that it was
some time before he could continue.

" 'After them, my men,' shouts the captain," he said
after a while, " 'remember the reward; after them, they
cannot have gone far!' And with that he rushes through
the gate, followed by his dozen soldiers."

"But it was too late!" shouted the crowd, excitedly.

"They never got them!"

"Curse that Grospierre for his folly!"

"He deserved his fate!"

"Fancy not examining those casks properly!"

But these sallies seemed to amuse Citoyen Bibot exceedingly; he laughed until his sides ached, and the tears
streamed down his cheeks.

"Nay, nay!" he said at last, "those aristos weren't in the cart; the driver was not the Scarlet Pimpernel!"

"What?"

"No! The captain of the guard was that cursed Englishman in disguise, and everyone of his soldiers aristos!"

The crowd this time said nothing: the story certainly savoured of the supernatural, and though the Republic had abolished God, it had not quite succeeded in killing the fear of the supernatural in the hearts of the people. Truly that Englishman must be the devil himself.

The sun was sinking low down in the west. Bibot prepared himself to close the gates.

"*En avant* the carts," he said.

Some dozen covered carts were drawn up in a row, ready to leave town, in order to fetch the produce from the country close by, for market the next morning. They were mostly well known to Bibot, as they went through his gate twice every day on their way to and from the town. He spoke to one or two of their drivers—mostly women—and was at great pains to examine the inside of the carts.

"You never know," he would say, "and I'm not going to be caught like that fool Grospierre."

The women who drove the carts usually spent their day on the Place de la Grève, beneath the platform of the guillotine, knitting and gossiping, whilst they watched the rows of tumbrils arriving with the victims the Reign of Terror claimed every day. It was great fun to see the aristos arriving for the reception of Madame la Guillotine, and the places close by the platform were very much sought after. Bibot, during the day, had been on duty on the Place. He recognized most of the old hags, "tricoteuses," as they were called, who sat there and knitted, whilst head after head fell beneath the knife, and they themselves got quite bespattered with the blood of those cursed aristos.

"Hé! la mère!" said Bibot to one of these horrible hags, "what have you got there?"

He had seen her earlier in the day, with her knitting and the whip of her cart close beside her. Now she had fastened a row of curly locks to the whip handle, all colours, from gold to silver, fair to dark, and she stroked them with her huge, bony fingers as she laughed at Bibot.

"I made friends with Madame Guillotine's lover," she said with a coarse laugh, "he cut these off for me from the heads as they rolled down. He has promised me some more to-morrow, but I don't know if I shall be at my usual place."

"Ah! how is that, la mère?" asked Bibot, who, hardened soldier though he was, could not help shuddering at the awful loathsomeness of this semblance of a woman, with her ghastly trophy on the handle of her whip.

"My grandson has got the small-pox," she said with a jerk of her thumb towards the inside of her cart, "some say it's the plague! If it is, I sha'n't be allowed to come into Paris to-morrow."

At the first mention of the word small-pox, Bibot had stepped hastily backwards, and when the old hag spoke of the plague, he retreated from her as fast as he could.

"Curse you!" he muttered, whilst the whole crowd hastily avoided the cart, leaving it standing all alone in the midst of the place.

The old hag laughed.

"Curse you, citoyen, for being a coward," she said. "Bah! what a man to be afraid of sickness."

"*Morbleu!* the plague!"

Everyone was awe-struck and silent, filled with horror for the loathsome malady, the one thing which still had the power to arouse terror and disgust in these savage, brutalised creatures.

"Get out with you and with your plague-stricken brood!" shouted Bibot, hoarsely.

And with another rough laugh and coarse jest, the old hag whipped up her lean nag and drove her cart out of the gate.

This incident had spoilt the afternoon. The people were terrified of these two horrible curses, the two maladies which nothing could cure, and which were the precursors of an awful and lonely death. They hung about the barricades, silent and sullen for a while, eyeing one another suspiciously, avoiding each other as if by instinct, lest the plague lurked already in their midst. Presently, as in the case of Grospierre, a captain of the guard appeared suddenly. But he was known to Bibot, and there was no fear of his turning out to be a sly Englishman in disguise.

"A cart, . . ." he shouted breathlessly, even before he had reached the gates.

"What cart?" asked Bibot, roughly.

"Driven by an old hag. . . . A covered cart . . ."

"There were a dozen . . ."

"An old hag who said her son had the plague?"

"Yes . . ."

"You have not let them go?"

"Morbleu!" said Bibot, whose purple cheeks had suddenly become white with fear.

"The cart contained the *ci-devant* Comtesse de Tournay and her two children, all of them traitors and condemned to death."

"And their driver?" muttered Bibot, as a superstitious shudder ran down his spine.

"Sacré tonnerre," said the captain, "but it is feared that it was that accursed Englishman himself—the Scarlet Pimpernel."

Chapter 2

Dover:
"The Fisherman's Rest"

*I*n the kitchen Sally was extremely busy—saucepans and frying pans were standing in rows on the gigantic hearth, the huge stock-pot stood in a corner, and the jack turned with slow deliberation, and presented alternately to the glow every side of a noble sirloin of beef. The two little kitchen-maids bustled around, eager to help, hot and panting, with cotton sleeves well tucked up above the dimpled elbows, and giggling over some private jokes of their own, whenever Miss Sally's back was turned for a moment. And old Jemima, stolid in temper and solid in bulk, kept up a long and subdued grumble, while she stirred the stock-pot methodically over the fire.

"What ho! Sally!" came in cheerful if none too melodious accents from the coffee-room close by.

"Lud bless my soul!" exclaimed Sally, with a good-humoured laugh, "what be they all wanting now, I wonder!"

"Beer, of course," grumbled Jemima, "you don't 'xpect Jimmy Pitkin to 'ave done with one tankard, do ye?"

"Mr. 'Arry, 'e looked uncommon thirsty too," simpered Martha, one of the little kitchen-maids; and her beady black eyes twinkled as they met those of her companion, whereupon both started on a round of short and suppressed giggles.

Sally looked across for a moment, and thoughtfully rubbed her hands against her shapely hips; her palms were itching, evidently, to come in contact with Martha's rosy cheeks—but inherent good-humour prevailed, and with a pout and a shrug of the shoulders, she turned her attention to the fried potatoes.

"What ho, Sally! hey, Sally!"

And a chorus of pewter mugs, tapped with impatient hands against the oak tables of the coffee-room, accompanied the shouts for mine host's buxom daughter.

"Sally!" shouted a more persistent voice, "are ye goin' to be all night with that there beer?"

"I do think father might get the beer for them," muttered Sally, as Jemima, stolidly and without further comment, took a couple of foam-crowned jugs from the shelf, and began filling a number of pewter tankards with some of that home-brewed ale for which "The Fisherman's Rest" had been famous since the days of King Charles. " 'E knows 'ow busy we are in 'ere."

"Your father is too busy discussing politics with Mr. 'Empseed to worry 'isself about you and the kitchen," grumbled Jemima under her breath.

Sally had gone to the small mirror which hung in a

corner of the kitchen, and was hastily smoothing her hair and setting her frilled cap at its most becoming angle over her dark curls; then she took up the tankards by their handles, three in each strong, brown hand, and laughing, grumbling, blushing, carried them through into the coffee-room.

There, there was certainly no sign of that bustle and activity which kept four women busy and hot in the glowing kitchen beyond.

The coffee-room of "The Fisherman's Rest" is a show place now at the beginning of the twentieth century. At the end of the eighteenth, in the year of grace 1792, it had not yet gained that notoriety and importance which a hundred additional years and the craze of the age have since bestowed upon it. Yet it was an old place, even then, for the oak rafters and beams were already black with age—as were the panelled seats, with their tall backs, and the long polished tables between, on which innumerable pewter tankards had left fantastic patterns of many-sized rings. In the leaded window, high up, a row of pots of scarlet geraniums and blue larkspur gave the bright note of colour against the dull background of the oak.

That Mr. Jellyband, landlord of "The Fisherman's Rest" at Dover, was a prosperous man, was of course clear to the most casual observer. The pewter on the fine old dressers, the brass above the gigantic hearth, shone like silver and gold—the red-tiled floor was as brilliant as the scarlet geranium on the window sill—this meant that his servants were good and plentiful, that the custom was constant, and of that order which necessitated the keeping up of the coffee-room to a high standard of elegance and order.

As Sally came in, laughing through her frowns, and displaying a row of dazzling white teeth, she was greeted with shouts and a chorus of applause.

"Why, here's Sally! What ho, Sally! Hurrah for pretty Sally!"

"I thought you'd grown deaf in that kitchen of yours," muttered Jimmy Pitkin, as he passed the back of his hand across his very dry lips.

"All ri'! all ri'!" laughed Sally, as she deposited the freshly-filled tankards upon the tables, "why, what a 'urry, to be sure! And is your gran'mother a-dyin' an' you wantin' to see the pore soul afore she'm gone! I never see'd such a mighty rushin'!"

A chorus of good-humoured laughter greeted this witticism, which gave the company there present food for many jokes, for some considerable time. Sally now seemed in less of a hurry to get back to her pots and pans. A young man with fair curly hair, and eager, bright blue eyes, was engaging most of her attention and the whole of her time, whilst broad witticisms anent Jimmy Pitkin's fictitious grandmother flew from mouth to mouth, mixed with heavy puffs of pungent tobacco smoke.

Facing the hearth, his legs wide apart, a long clay pipe in his mouth, stood mine host himself, worthy Mr. Jellyband, landlord of "The Fisherman's Rest," as his father had been before him, aye, and his grandfather and great-grandfather too, for that matter. Portly in build, jovial in countenance and somewhat bald of pate, Mr. Jellyband was indeed a typical rural John Bull of those days—the days when our prejudiced insularity was at its height, when to an Englishman, be he lord, yeoman, or peasant, the whole of the continent of Europe was a den of immorality, and the rest of the world an unexploited land of savages and cannibals.

There he stood, mine worthy host, firm and well set up on his limbs, smoking his long churchwarden and caring nothing for nobody at home, and despising everybody abroad. He wore the typical scarlet waistcoat, with shiny brass buttons, the corduroy breeches, the grey worsted stockings and smart buckled shoes, that characterised every self-respecting innkeeper in Great Britain in these days—and while pretty, motherless Sally had need of four pairs of brown hands to do all the work that fell on her shapely shoulders, worthy Jellyband discussed the affairs of nations with his most privileged guests.

The coffee-room indeed, lighted by two well-polished lamps, which hung from the raftered ceiling, looked cheerful and cosy in the extreme. Through the dense clouds of tobacco smoke that hung about in every corner, the faces of Mr. Jellyband's customers appeared red and pleasant to look at, and on good terms with themselves, their host and all the world; from every side of the room loud guffaws accompanied pleasant, if not highly intellectual, conversation—while Sally's repeated giggles testified to the good use Mr. Harry Waite was making of the short time she seemed inclined to spare him.

They were mostly fisher-folk who patronised Mr. Jellyband's coffee-room, but fishermen are known to be very thirsty people; the salt which they breathe in, when they are on the sea, accounts for their parched throats when on shore. But "The Fisherman's Rest" was something more than a rendezvous for these humble folk. The London and Dover coach started from the hostel daily, and passengers who had come across the Channel, and those who started for the "grand tour," all became acquainted with Mr. Jellyband, his French wines and his home-brewed ales.

It was towards the close of September, 1792, and the weather which had been brilliant and hot throughout the month had suddenly broken up; for two days torrents of rain had deluged the south of England, doing its level best to ruin what chances the apples and pears and late plums had of becoming really fine, self-respecting fruit. Even now it was beating against the leaded windows, and tumbling down the chimney, making the cheerful wood fire sizzle in the hearth.

"Lud! did you ever see such a wet September, Mr. Jellyband?" asked Mr. Hempseed.

He sat in one of the seats inside the hearth, did Mr. Hempseed, for he was an authority and an important personage not only at "The Fisherman's Rest," where Mr. Jellyband always made a special selection of him as a foil for political arguments, but throughout the neighbourhood, where his learning and notably his knowledge of the Scriptures was held in the most profound awe and respect. With one hand buried in the capacious pockets of his corduroys underneath his elaborately-worked, well-worn smock, the other holding his long clay pipe, Mr. Hempseed sat there looking dejectedly across the room at the rivulets of moisture which trickled down the window panes.

"No," replied Mr. Jellyband, sententiously, "I dunno,

Mr. 'Empseed, as I ever did. An' I've been in these parts nigh on sixty years."

"Aye! you wouldn't rec'llect the first three years of them sixty, Mr. Jellyband," quietly interposed Mr, Hempseed. "I dunno as I ever see'd an infant take much note of the weather, leastways not in these parts, an' *I*'ve lived 'ere nigh on seventy-five years, Mr. Jellyband."

The superiority of this wisdom was so incontestable that for the moment Mr. Jellyband was not ready with his usual flow of argument.

"It do seem more like April than September, don't it?" continued Mr. Hempseed, dolefully, as a shower of rain-drops fell with a sizzle upon the fire.

"Aye! that it do," assented the worthy host, "but then what can you 'xpect, Mr. 'Empseed, I says, with sich a government as we've got?"

Mr. Hempseed shook his head with an infinity of wisdom, tempered by deeply-rooted mistrust of the British climate and the British Government.

"I don't 'xpect nothing, Mr. Jellyband," he said. "Pore folks like us is of no account up there in Lunnon, I knows that, and it's not often as I do complain. But when it comes to sich wet weather in September, and all me fruit a-rottin' and a-dyin' like the 'Guptian mother's first-born, and doin' no more good than they did, pore dears, save to a lot of Jews, pedlars and sich, with their oranges and sich like foreign ungodly fruit, which nobody'd buy if English apples and pears was nicely swelled. As the Scriptures say—"

"That's quite right, Mr. 'Empseed," retorted Jellyband, "and as I says, what can you 'xpect? There's all them

Frenchy devils over the Channel yonder a-murderin' their king and nobility, and Mr. Pitt and Mr. Fox and Mr. Burke a-fightin' and a-wranglin' between them, if we Englishmen should 'low them to go on in their ungodly way. 'Let 'em murder!' says Mr. Pitt. 'Stop 'em!' says Mr. Burke."

"And let 'em murder, says I, and be demmed to 'em," said Mr. Hempseed, emphatically, for he had but little liking for his friend Jellyband's political arguments, wherein he always got out of his depth, and had but little chance for displaying those pearls of wisdom which had earned for him so high a reputation in the neighbourhood and so many free tankards of ale at "The Fisherman's Rest."

"Let 'em murder," he repeated again, "but don't let's 'ave sich rain in September, for that is agin the law and the Scriptures which says—"

"Lud! Mr. 'Arry, 'ow you made me jump!"

It was unfortunate for Sally and her flirtation that this remark of hers should have occurred at the precise moment when Mr. Hempseed was collecting his breath, in order to deliver himself of one of those Scriptural utterances which had made him famous, for it brought down upon her pretty head the full flood of her father's wrath.

"Now then, Sally, me girl, now then!" he said, trying to force a frown upon his good-humoured face, "stop that fooling with them young jackanapes and get on with the work."

"The work's gettin' on all ri', father."

But Mr. Jellyband was peremptory. He had other views for his buxom daughter, his only child, who would in God's good time become the owner of "The Fisherman's

Rest," than to see her married to one of these young fellows who earned but a precarious livelihood with their net.

"Did ye hear me speak, me girl?" he said in that quiet tone, which no one inside the inn dared to disobey. "Get on with Lord Tony's supper, for, if it ain't the best we can do, and 'e not satisfied, see what you'll get, that's all."

Reluctantly Sally obeyed.

"Is you 'xpecting special guests then to-night, Mr. Jellyband?" asked Jimmy Pitkin, in a loyal attempt to divert his host's attention from the circumstances connected with Sally's exit from the room.

"Aye! that I be," replied Jellyband, "friends of my Lord Tony hisself. Dukes and duchesses from over the water yonder, whom the young lord and his friend, Sir Andrew Ffoulkes, and other young noblemen have helped out of the clutches of them murderin' devils."

But this was too much for Mr. Hempseed's querulous philosophy.

"Lud!" he said, "what they do that for, I wonder? I don't 'old not with interferin' in other folks' ways. As the Scriptures say—"

"Maybe, Mr. 'Empseed," interrupted Jellyband, with biting sarcasm, "as you're a personal friend of Mr. Pitt, and as you says along with Mr. Fox: 'Let 'em murder!' says you."

"Pardon me, Mr. Jellyband," feebly protested Mr. Hempseed, "I dunno as I ever did."

But Mr. Jellyband had at last succeeded in getting upon his favourite hobby-horse, and had no intention of dismounting in any hurry.

"Or maybe you've made friends with some of them French chaps 'oo they do say have come over here o' purpose to make us Englishmen agree with their murderin' ways."

"I dunno what you mean, Mr. Jellyband," suggested Mr. Hempseed, "all I know is—"

"All I know is," loudly asserted mine host, "that there was my friend Peppercorn, 'oo owns the 'Blue-Faced Boar,' an' as true and loyal an Englishman as you'd see in the land. And now look at 'im—'E made friends with some o' them frog-eaters, 'obnobbed with them just as if they was Englishmen, and not just a lot of immoral, God-forsaking furrin' spies. Well! and what happened? Peppercorn 'e now ups and talks of revolutions, and liberty, and down with the aristocrats, just like Mr. 'Empseed over 'ere!"

"Pardon me, Mr. Jellyband," again interposed Mr. Hempseed feebly, "I dunno as I ever did—"

Mr. Jellyband had appealed to the company in general, who were listening awe-struck and open-mouthed at the recital of Mr. Peppercorn's defalcations. At one table two customers—gentlemen apparently by their clothes—had pushed aside their half-finished game of dominoes, and had been listening for some time, and evidently with much amusement at Mr. Jellyband's international opinions. One of them now, with a quiet, sarcastic smile still lurking round the corners of his mobile mouth, turned towards the centre of the room where Mr. Jellyband was standing.

"You seem to think, mine honest friend," he said quietly, "that these Frenchmen—spies I think you called them—are mighty clever fellows to have made mincemeat so to speak of your friend Mr. Peppercorn's opinions, How did they accomplish that now, think you?"

"Lud! sir, I suppose they talked 'im over. Those Frenchies, I've 'eard it said, 'ave got the gift of the gab—and Mr. 'Empseed 'ere will tell you 'ow it is that they just twist some people round their little finger like."

"Indeed, and is that so, Mr. Hempseed?" inquired the stranger politely.

"Nay, sir!" replied Mr. Hempseed, much irritated, "I dunno as I can give you the information you require."

"Faith, then," said the stranger, "let us hope, my worthy host, that these clever spies will not succeed in upsetting your extremely loyal opinions."

But this was too much for Mr. Jellyband's pleasant equanimity. He burst into an uproarious fit of laughter, which was soon echoed by those who happened to be in his debt.

"Hahaha! hohoho! hehehe!" He laughed in every key, did my worthy host, and laughed until his sides ached, and his eyes streamed. "At me! hark at that! Did ye 'ear 'im say that they'd be upsettin' my opinions?—Eh?—Lud love you, sir, but you do say some queer things."

"Well, Mr. Jellyband," said Mr. Hempseed, sententiously, "you know what the Scriptures say: 'Let 'im 'oo stands take 'eed lest 'e fall.' "

"But then hark'ee, Mr. 'Empseed," retorted Jellyband, still holding his sides with laughter, "the Scriptures didn't know me. Why, I wouldn't so much as drink a glass of ale with one o' them murderin' Frenchmen, and nothin' 'd make me change my opinions. Why! I've 'eard it said that them frog-eaters can't even speak the King's English, so, of course, if any of 'em tried to speak their God-forsaken lingo to me, why, I should spot them directly, see!—and forewarned is forearmed, as the saying goes."

"Aye! my honest friend," assented the stranger cheerfully, "I see that you are much too sharp, and a match for any twenty Frenchmen, and here's to your very good health, my worthy host, if you'll do me the honor to finish this bottle of mine with me."

"I am sure you're very polite, sir," said Mr. Jellyband, wiping his eyes which were still streaming with the abundance of his laughter, "and I don't mind if I do."

The stranger poured out a couple of tankards full of wine, and having offered one to mine host, he took the other himself.

"Loyal Englishmen as we all are," he said, whilst the same humorous smile played round the corners of his thin lips—"loyal as we are, we must admit that this at least is one good thing which comes to us from France."

"Aye! we'll none of us deny that, sir," assented mine host.

"And here's to the best landlord in England, our worthy host, Mr. Jellyband," said the stranger in a loud tone of voice.

"Hip, hip, hurrah!" retorted the whole company present. Then there was loud clapping of hands, and mugs and tankards made a rattling music upon the tables to the accompaniment of loud laughter at nothing in particular, and of Mr. Jellyband's muttered exclamations:

"Just fancy *me* bein' talked over by any God-forsaken furriner!—What?—Lud love you, sir, but you do say some queer things."

To which obvious fact the stranger heartily assented. It was certainly a preposterous suggestion that anyone could ever upset Mr. Jellyband's firmly-rooted opinions anent the utter worthlessness of the inhabitants of the whole continent of Europe.

Chapter 3

The Refugees

*F*eeling in every part of England certainly ran very high at this time against the French and their doings. Smugglers and legitimate traders between the French and English coasts brought snatches of news from over the water, which made every honest Englishman's blood boil, and made him long to have "a good go" at those murderers, who had imprisoned their king and all his family, subjected the queen and the royal children to every species of indignity, and were even now loudly demanding the blood of the whole Bourbon family and of every one of its adherents.

The execution of the Princesse de Lamballe, Marie Antoinette's young and charming friend, had filled every one in England with unspeakable horror, the daily execution of scores of royalists of good family, whose only sin was their aristocratic name, seemed to cry for vengeance to the whole of civilised Europe.

Yet, with all that, no one dared to interfere. Burke had exhausted all his eloquence in trying to induce the British Government to fight the revolutionary government of France, but Mr. Pitt, with characteristic prudence, did not feel that this country was fit yet to embark on another arduous and costly war. It was for Austria to take the initiative; Austria, whose fairest daughter was even now a dethroned queen, imprisoned and insulted by a howling mob; and surely 'twas not—so argued Mr. Fox—for the whole of England to take up arms, because one set of Frenchmen chose to murder another.

As for Mr. Jellyband and his fellow John Bulls, though they looked upon all foreigners with withering contempt, they were royalist and anti-revolutionists to a man, and at this present moment were furious with Pitt for his caution and moderation, although they naturally understood nothing of the diplomatic reasons which guided that great man's policy.

But now Sally came running back, very excited and very eager. The joyous company in the coffee-room had heard nothing of the noise outside, but she had spied a dripping horse and rider who had stopped at the door of "The Fisherman's Rest," and while the stable boy ran forward to take charge of the horse, pretty Miss Sally went to the front door to greet the welcome visitor.

"I think I see'd my Lord Antony's horse out in the yard, father," she said, as she ran across the coffee-room.

But already the door had been thrown open from outside, and the next moment an arm, covered in drab cloth and dripping with the heavy rain, was round pretty Sally's waist, while a hearty voice echoed along the polished rafters of the coffee-room.

"Aye, and bless your brown eyes for being so sharp, my pretty Sally," said the man who had just entered, whilst worthy Mr. Jellyband came bustling forward, eager, alert and fussy, as became the advent of one of the most favoured guests of his hostel.

"Lud, I protest, Sally," added Lord Antony, as he deposited a kiss on Miss Sally's blooming cheeks, "but you are growing prettier and prettier every time I see you—and my honest friend, Jellyband here, must have hard work to keep the fellows off that slim waist of yours. What say you, Mr. Waite?"

Mr. Waite—torn between his respect for my lord and his dislike of that particular type of joke—only replied with a doubtful grunt.

Lord Antony Dewhurst, one of the sons of the Duke of Exeter, was in those days a very perfect type of a young English gentleman—tall, well set-up, broad of shoulders and merry of face, his laughter rang loudly wherever he went. A good sportsman, a lively companion, a courteous, well-bred man of the world, with not too much brains to spoil his temper, he was a universal favourite in London drawing-rooms or in the coffee-rooms of village inns. At "The Fisherman's Rest" everyone knew him—for he was fond of a trip across to France, and always spent a night under worthy Mr. Jellyband's roof on his way there or back.

He nodded to Waite, Pitkin and the others as he at last released Sally's waist, and crossed over to the hearth to warm and dry himself: as he did so, he cast a quick, somewhat suspicious glance at the two strangers, who had quietly resumed their game of dominoes, and for a moment a look of deep earnestness, even of anxiety, clouded his jovial face.

But only for a moment; the next he had turned to Mr. Hempseed, who was respectfully touching his forelock.

"Well, Mr. Hempseed, and how is the fruit?"

"Badly, my lord, badly," replied Mr. Hempseed, dolefully, "but what can you 'xpect with this 'ere government favourin' them rascals over in France, who would murder their king and all their nobility."

"Odd's life!" retorted Lord Antony; "so they would, honest Hempseed,—at least those they can get hold of, worse luck! But we have got some friends coming here to-night, who at any rate have evaded their clutches."

It almost seemed, when the young man said these words, as if he threw a defiant look towards the quiet strangers in the corner.

"Thanks to you, my lord, and to your friends, so I've heard it said," said Mr. Jellyband.

But in a moment Lord Antony's hand fell warningly on mine host's arm.

"Hush!" he said peremptorily, and instinctively once again looked towards the strangers.

"Oh! Lud love you, they are all right, my lord," retorted Jellyband; "don't you be afraid. I wouldn't have spoken, only I knew we were among friends. That gentleman over there is as true and loyal a subject of King George as you are yourself, my lord, saving your presence. He is but lately arrived in Dover, and is settling down in business in these parts."

"In business? Faith, then, it must be as an undertaker, for I vow I never beheld a more rueful countenance."

"Nay, my lord, I believe that the gentleman is a wid-
ower, which no doubt would account for the melancholy
of his bearing—but he is a friend, nevertheless, I'll vouch
for that—and you will own, my lord, that who should
judge of a face better than the landlord of a popular
inn—"

"Oh, that's all right, then, if we are among friends,"
said Lord Antony, who evidently did not care to discuss
the subject with his host. "But, tell me, you have no one
else staying here, have you?"

"No one, my lord, and no one coming, either, leastways—"

"Leastways?"

"No one your lordship would object to, I know."

"Who is it?"

"Well, my lord, Sir Percy Blakeney and his lady will be
here presently, but they ain't a-goin' to stay—"

"Lady Blakeney?" queried Lord Antony, in some
astonishment.

"Aye, my lord. Sir Percy's skipper was here just now.
He says that my lady's brother is crossing over to France
to-day in the *Day Dream*, which is Sir Percy's yacht, and
Sir Percy and my lady will come with him as far as here to
see the last of him. It don't put you out, do it, my lord?"

"No, no, it doesn't put me out, friend; nothing will put
me out, unless that supper is not the very best which Miss
Sally can cook, and which has ever been served in 'The
Fisherman's Rest.' "

"You need have no fear of that, my lord," said Sally,
who all this while had been busy setting the table for
supper. And very gay and inviting it looked, with a large
bunch of brilliantly coloured dahlias in the centre, and the
bright pewter goblets and blue china about.

"How many shall I lay for, my lord?"

"Five places, pretty Sally, but let the supper be enough for ten at least—our friends will be tired, and, I hope, hungry. As for me, I vow I could demolish a baron of beef to-night."

"Here they are, I do believe," said Sally, excitedly, as a distant clatter of horses and wheels could now be distinctly heard, drawing rapidly nearer.

There was general commotion in the coffee-room. Everyone was curious to see my Lord Antony's swell friends from over the water. Miss Sally cast one or two quick glances at the little bit of mirror which hung on the wall, and worthy Mr. Jellyband bustled out in order to give the first welcome himself to his distinguished guests. Only the two strangers in the corner did not participate in the general excitement. They were calmly finishing their game of dominoes, and did not even look once towards the door.

"Straight ahead, Comtesse, the door on your right," said a pleasant voice outside.

"Aye! there they are, all right enough," said Lord Antony, joyfully; "off with you, my pretty Sally, and see how quickly you can dish up the soup."

The door was thrown wide open, and, preceded by Mr. Jellyband, who was profuse in his bows and welcomes, a party of four—two ladies and two gentlemen—entered the coffee-room.

"Welcome! Welcome to old England!" said Lord Antony, effusively, as he came eagerly forward with both hands outstretched towards the newcomers.

"Ah, you are Lord Antony Dewhurst, I think," said one of the ladies, speaking with a strong foreign accent.

"At your service, Madame," he replied, as he ceremoniously kissed the hands of both the ladies, then turned to the men and shook them both warmly by the hand.

Sally was already helping the ladies to take off their travelling cloaks, and both turned, with a shiver, towards the brightly-blazing hearth.

There was a general movement among the company in the coffee-room. Sally had bustled off to her kitchen, whilst Jellyband, still profuse with his respectful salutations, arranged one or two chairs around the fire. Mr. Hempseed, touching his forelock, was quietly vacating the seat in the hearth. Everyone was staring curiously, yet deferentially, at the foreigners.

"Ah, Messieurs! what can I say?" said the elder of the two ladies, as she stretched a pair of fine, aristocratic hands to the warmth of the blaze, and looked with unspeakable gratitude first at Lord Antony, then at one of the young men who had accompanied her party, and who was busy divesting himself of his heavy, caped coat.

"Only that you are glad to be in England, Comtesse," replied Lord Antony, "and that you have not suffered too much from your trying voyage."

"Indeed, indeed, we are glad to be in England," she said, while her eyes filled with tears, "and we have already forgotten all that we have suffered."

Her voice was musical and low, and there was a great deal of calm dignity and of many sufferings nobly endured marked in the handsome, aristrocratic face, with its wealth of snow-white hair dressed high above the forehead, after the fashion of the times.

"I hope my friend, Sir Andrew Ffoulkes, proved an entertaining travelling companion, madame?"

"Ah, indeed, Sir Andrew was kindness itself. How could my children and I ever show enough gratitude to you all, Messieurs?"

Her companion, a dainty, girlish figure, childlike and pathetic in its look of fatigue and of sorrow, had said nothing as yet, but her eyes, large, brown, and full of tears, looked up from the fire and sought those of Sir Andrew Ffoulkes, who had drawn near to the hearth and to her; then, as they met his, which were fixed with unconcealed admiration upon the sweet face before him, a thought of warmer colour rushed up to her pale cheeks.

"So this is England," she said, as she looked round with childlike curiosity at the great open hearth, the oak rafters, and the yokels with their elaborate smocks and jovial, rubicund, British countenances.

"A bit of it, Mademoiselle," replied Sir Andrew, smiling, "but all of it, at your service."

The young girl blushed again, but this time a bright smile, fleet and sweet, illumined her dainty face. She said nothing, and Sir Andrew too, was silent, yet those two young people understood one another, as young people have a way of doing all the world over, and have done since the world began.

"But, I say, supper!" here broke in Lord Antony's jovial voice, "supper, honest Jellyband. Where is that pretty wench of yours and the dish of soup? Zooks, man, while you stand there gaping at the ladies, they will faint with hunger."

"One moment! one moment, my lord," said Jellyband, as he threw open the door that led to the kitchen and shouted lustily: "Sally! Hey, Sally there, are ye ready, my girl?"

Sally was ready, and the next moment she appeared in the doorway carrying a gigantic tureen, from which rose a cloud of steam and an abundance of savoury odour.

"Odd's my life, supper at last!" ejaculated Lord Antony, merrily, as he gallantly offered his arm to the Comtesse.

"May I have the honour?" he added ceremoniously, as he led her towards the supper table.

There was general bustle in the coffee-room: Mr. Hempseed and most of the yokels and fisher-folk had gone to make way for "the quality," and to finish smoking their pipes elsewhere. Only the two strangers stayed on, quietly and unconcernedly playing their game of dominoes and sipping their wine; whilst at another table Harry Waite, who was fast losing his temper, watched pretty Sally bustling round the table.

She looked a very dainty picture of English rural life, and no wonder that the susceptible young Frenchman could scarce take his eyes off her pretty face. The Vicomte de Tournay was scarce nineteen, a beardless boy, on whom the terrible tragedies which were being enacted in his own country had made but little impression. He was elegantly, and even foppishly dressed, and once safely landed in England he was evidently ready to forget the horrors of the Revolution in the delights of English life.

"Pardi, if zis is England," he said as he continued to ogle Sally with marked satisfaction, "I am of it satisfied."

It would be impossible at this point to record the exact exclamation which escaped through Mr. Harry Waite's clenched teeth. Only respect for "the quality," and notably for my Lord Antony, kept his marked disapproval of the young foreigner in check.

"Nay, but this *is* England, you abandoned young reprobate," interposed Lord Antony with a laugh, "and do not, I pray, bring your loose foreign ways into this most moral country."

Lord Antony had already sat down at the head of the table with the Comtesse on his right. Jellyband was bustling round, filling glasses and putting chairs straight, Sally waited, ready to hand round the soup. Mr. Harry Waite's friends had at last succeeded in taking him out of the room, for his temper was growing more and more violent under the Vicomte's obvious admiration for Sally.

"Suzanne," came in stern, commanding accents from the rigid Comtesse.

Suzanne blushed again; she had lost count of time and of place, whilst she had stood beside the fire, allowing the handsome young Englishman's eyes to dwell upon her sweet face, and his hand, as if unconsciously, to rest upon hers. Her mother's voice brought her back to reality once more, and with a submissive "Yes, Mama," she too took her place at the supper table.

Chapter 4

The League
of the
Scarlet Pimpernel

*T*hey all looked a merry, even a happy party, as they sat round the table; Sir Andrew Ffoulkes and Lord Antony Dewhurst, two typical good-looking, well-born and well-bred Englishmen of that year of grace 1792, and the aristocratic French comtesse with her two children, who had just escaped from such dire perils, and found a safe retreat at last on the shores of protecting England.

In the corner the two strangers had apparently finished their game; one of them arose, and standing with his back to the merry company at the table, he adjusted with much deliberation his large triple caped coat. As he did so, he gave one quick glance all around him. Everyone was busy laughing and chatting, and he murmured the words "All safe!": his companion then, with the alertness born of long practice, slipped on to his knees in a moment, and the next had crept noiselessly under the oak bench. The stranger then with a loud "Good-night," quietly walked out of the coffee-room.

Not one of those at the supper table had noticed this curious and silent manœuvre, but when the stranger finally closed the door of the coffee-room behind him, they all instinctively sighed a sigh of relief.

"Alone, at last!" said Lord Antony, jovially.

Then the young Vicomte de Tournay rose, glass in hand, and with the graceful affectation peculiar to the times, he raised it aloft, and said in broken English,—

"To His Majesty George Three of England. God bless him for his hospitality to us all, poor exiles from France."

"His Majesty the King!" echoed Lord Antony and Sir Andrew as they drank loyally to the toast.

"To His Majesty King Louis of France," added Sir Andrew, with solemnity. "May God protect him, and give him victory over his enemies."

Everyone rose and drank this toast in silence. The fate of the unfortunate King of France, then a prisoner of his own people, seemed to cast a gloom even over Mr. Jellyband's pleasant countenance.

"And to Monsieur le Comte de Tournay de Basserive," said Lord Antony, merrily. "May we welcome him in England before many days are over."

"Ah, Monsieur," said the Comtesse, as with a slightly trembling hand she conveyed her glass to her lips, "I scarcely dare to hope."

But already Lord Antony had served out the soup, and for the next few moments all conversation ceased, while Jellyband and Sally handed round the plates and everyone began to eat.

"Faith, Madame!" said Lord Antony, after a while, "mine was no idle toast; seeing yourself, Mademoiselle Suzanne and my friend the Vicomte safely in England now, surely you must feel reassured as to the fate of Monsieur le Comte."

"Ah, Monsieur," replied the Comtesse, with a heavy sigh, "I trust in God—I can but pray—and hope . . . "

"Aye, Madame!" here interposed Sir Andrew Ffoulkes, "trust in God by all means, but believe also a little in your English friends, who have sworn to bring the Count safely across the Channel, even as they have brought you to-day."

"Indeed, indeed, Monsieur," she replied, "I have the fullest confidence in you and in your friends. Your fame, I assure you, has spread throughout the whole of France. The way some of my own friends have escaped from the clutches of that awful revolutionary tribunal was nothing short of a miracle—and all done by you and your friends—"

"We were but the hands, Madame la Comtesse . . ."

"But my husband, Monsieur," said the Comtesse, whilst unshed tears seemed to veil her voice, "he is in such deadly peril—I would never have left him, only . . . there were my children . . . I was torn between my duty to him, and to them. They refused to go without me . . . and you and your friends assured me so solemnly that my husband would be safe. But, oh! now that I am here—amongst you all—in this beautiful, free England—I think of him, flying for his life, hunted like a poor beast . . . in such peril. . . . Ah! I should not have left him . . . I should not have left him! . . ."

The poor woman had completely broken down; fatigue, sorrow and emotion had overmastered her rigid, aristo-

cratic bearing. She was crying gently to herself, whilst
Suzanne ran up to her and tried to kiss away her tears.

Lord Antony and Sir Andrew had said nothing to inter-
rupt the Comtesse whilst she was speaking. There was no
doubt that they felt deeply for her; their very silence
testified to that—but in every century, and ever since
England has been what it is, an Englishman has always felt
somewhat ashamed of his own emotion and of his own
sympathy. And so the two young men said nothing, and
busied themselves in trying to hide their feelings, only
succeeding in looking immeasurably sheepish.

"As for me, Monsieur," said Suzanne, suddenly, as she
looked through a wealth of brown curls across at Sir
Andrew, "I trust you absolutely, and I *know* that you will
bring my dear father safely to England, just as you brought
us to-day."

This was said with so much confidence, such unuttered
hope and belief, that it seemed as if by magic to dry the
mother's eyes, and to bring a smile upon everybody's lips.

"Nay! You shame me, Mademoiselle," replied Sir Andrew; "though my life is at your service, I have been but a
humble tool in the hands of our great leader, who organised and effected your escape."

He had spoken with so much warmth and vehemence
that Suzanne's eyes fastened upon him in undisguised
wonder.

"Your leader, Monsieur?" said the Comtesse, eagerly.
"Ah! of course, you must have a leader. And I did not
think of that before! But tell me where is he? I must go to
him at once, and I and my children must throw ourselves
at his feet, and thank him for all that he has done for us."

"Alas, Madame!" said Lord Antony, "that is impossible."

"Impossible? Why?"

"Because the Scarlet Pimpernel works in the dark, and his identity is only known under a solemn oath of secrecy to his immediate followers."

"The Scarlet Pimpernel?" said Suzanne, with a merry laugh. "Why! what a droll name! What is the Scarlet Pimpernel, Monsieur?"

She looked at Sir Andrew with eager curiosity. The young man's face had become almost transfigured. His eyes shone with enthusiasm; hero-worship, love, admiration for his leader seemed literally to glow upon his face. "The Scarlet Pimpernel, Mademoiselle," he said at last, "is the name of a humble English wayside flower; but it is also the name chosen to hide the identity of the best and bravest man in all the world, so that he may better succeed in accomplishing the noble task he has set himself to do."

"Ah, yes," here interposed the young Vicomte, "I have heard speak of this Scarlet Pimpernel. A little flower—red?— yes! They say in Paris that every time a royalist escapes to England that devil, Foucquier-Tinville, the Public Prose-cutor, receives a paper with that little flower dessinated in red upon it. . . . Yes?"

"Yes, that is so," assented Lord Antony.

"Then he will have received one such paper to-day?"

"Undoubtedly."

"Oh! I wonder what he will say!" said Suzanne, merrily. "I have heard that the picture of that little red flower is the only thing that frightens him."

"Faith, then," said Sir Andrew, "he will have many

more opportunities of studying the shape of that small scarlet flower."

"Ah! Monsieur," sighed the Comtesse, "it all sounds like a romance, and I cannot understand it all."

"Why should you try, Madame?"

"But, tell me, why should your leader—why should you all—spend your money and risk your lives—for it is your lives you risk, Messieurs, when you set foot in France—and all for us French men and women, who are nothing to you?"

"Sport, Madame la Comtesse, sport," asserted Lord Antony, with his jovial, loud and pleasant voice; "we are a nation of sportsmen, you know, and just now it is the fashion to pull the hare from between the teeth of the hound."

"Ah, no, no, not sport only, Monsieur . . . you have a more noble motive, I am sure, for the good work you do."

"Faith, Madame, I would like you to find it then . . . as for me, I vow, I love the game, for this is the finest sport I have yet encountered.—Hair-breadth escapes . . . the devil's own risks!—Tally ho!—and away we go!"

But the Comtesse shook her head, still incredulously. To her it seemed preposterous that these young men and their great leader, all of them rich, probably well-born, and young, should for no other motive than sport, run the terrible risks, which she knew they were constantly doing. Their nationality, once they had set foot in France, would be no safeguard to them. Anyone found harbouring or assisting suspected royalists would be ruthlessly condemned and summarily executed, whatever his nationality might be. And this band of young Englishmen had, to her own knowledge, bearded the implacable and bloodthirsty tribunal of the Revolution, within the very walls of Paris itself, and had snatched away condemned victims, almost from the very foot of the guillotine. With a shudder, she recalled the events of the last few days, her escape from Paris with her two children, all three of them hidden beneath the hood of a rickety cart, and lying amidst a heap of turnips and cabbages, not daring to breathe, whilst the mob howled "Á la lanterne les aristos!" at that awful West Barricade.

It had all occurred in such a miraculous way; she and her husband had understood that they had been placed on the list of "suspected persons," which meant that their trial and death was but a matter of days—of hours, perhaps.

Then came the hope of salvation; the mysterious epistle, signed with the enigmatical scarlet device; the clear, peremptory directions; the parting from the Comte de Tournay, which had torn the poor wife's heart in two; the hope of reunion; the flight with her two children; the covered cart; that awful hag driving it, who looked like some horrible evil demon, with the ghastly trophy on her whip handle!

The Comtesse looked round at the quaint, old-fashioned English inn, the peace of this land of civil and religious liberty, and she closed her eyes to shut out the haunting vision of that West Barricade, and of the mob retreating panic-stricken when the old hag spoke of the plague.

Every moment under that cart she expected recognition, arrest, herself and her children tried and condemned, and these young Englishmen, under the guidance of their brave and mysterious leader, had risked their lives to save

them all, as they had already saved scores of other innocent people.

And all only for sport? Impossible! Suzanne's eyes as she
sought those of Sir Andrew plainly told him that she
thought that *he* at any rate rescued his fellowmen from
terrible and unmerited death, through a higher and nobler
motive than his friend would have her believe.

"How many are there in your brave league, Monsieur?"
she asked timidly.

"Twenty all told, Mademoiselle," he replied, "one to
command, and nineteen to obey. All of us Englishmen,
and all pledged to the same cause—to obey our leader
and to rescue the innocent."

"May God protect you all, Messieurs," said the Comtesse,
fervently.

"He has done that so far, Madame."

"It is wonderful to me, wonderful!—That you should all
be so brave, so devoted to your fellowmen—yet you are
English!—and in France treachery is rife—all in the name
of liberty and fraternity."

"The women even, in France, have been more bitter
against us aristocrats than the men," said the Vicomte,
with a sigh.

"Ah, yes," added the Comtesse, while a look of haughty
disdain and intense bitterness shot through her melancholy eyes. "There was that woman, Marguerite St. Just,
for instance. She denounced the Marquis de St. Cyr and
all his family to the awful tribunal of the Terror."

"Marguerite St. Just?" said Lord Antony, as he shot a
quick and apprehensive glance across at Sir Andrew.

"Marguerite St. Just?—Surely . . ."

"Yes!" replied the Comtesse, "surely you know her. She was a leading actress of the Comédie Française, and she married an Englishman lately. You must know her—"

"Know her?" said Lord Antony. "Know Lady Blakeney—the most fashionable woman in London—the wife of the richest man in England? Of course, we all know Lady Blakeney."

"She was a school-fellow of mine at the convent in Paris," interposed Suzanne, "and we came over to England together to learn your language. I was very fond of Marguerite, and I cannot believe that she ever did anything so wicked."

"It certainly seems incredible," said Sir Andrew. "You say that she actually denounced the Marquis de St. Cyr? Why should she have done such a thing? Surely there must be some mistake—"

"No mistake is possible, Monsieur," rejoined the Comtesse, coldly. "Marguerite St. Just's brother is a noted republican. There was some talk of a family feud between him and my cousin, the Marquis de St. Cyr. The St. Justs are quite plebeian, and the republican government employs many spies. I assure you there is no mistake. . . . You had not heard this story?"

"Faith, Madame, I did hear some vague rumours of it, but in England no one would credit it. . . . Sir Percy Blakeney, her husband, is a very wealthy man, of high social position, the intimate friend of the Prince of Wales . . . and Lady Blakeney leads both fashion and society in London."

"That may be, Monsieur, and we shall, of course, lead a very quiet life in England, but I pray God that while I remain in this beautiful country, I may never meet Marguerite St. Just."

The proverbial wet blanket seemed to have fallen over the merry little company gathered round the table. Suzanne looked sad and silent; Sir Andrew fidgeted uneasily with his fork, whilst the Comtesse, encased in the plate-armour of her aristocratic prejudices, sat, rigid and unbending, in her straight-backed chair. As for Lord Antony, he looked extremely uncomfortable, and glanced once or twice apprehensively towards Jellyband, who looked just as uncomfortable as himself.

"At what time do you expect Sir Percy and Lady Blakeney?" he contrived to whisper unobserved, to mine host.

"Any moment, my lord," whispered Jellyband in reply.

Even as he spoke, a distant clatter was heard of an approaching coach; louder and louder it grew, one or two shouts became distinguishable, then the rattle of horses' hoofs on the uneven cobble stones, and the next moment a stable boy had thrown open the coffee-room door and rushed in excitedly.

"Sir Percy Blakeney and my lady," he shouted at the top of his voice, "they're just arriving."

And with more shouting, jingling of harness, and iron hoofs upon the stones, a magnificent coach, drawn by four superb bays, had halted outside the porch of "The Fisherman's Rest."

Chapter 5

Marguerite

*I*n a moment the pleasant oak-raftered coffee-room of the inn became the scene of hopeless confusion and discomfort. At the first announcement made by the stable boy, Lord Antony, with a fashionable oath, had jumped up from his seat and was now giving many and confused directions to poor bewildered Jellyband, who seemed at his wits' end what to do.

"For goodness' sake, man," admonished his lordship, "try to keep Lady Blakeney talking outside for a moment, while the ladies withdraw. Zounds!" he added, with another more emphatic oath, "this is most unfortunate."

"Quick, Sally! the candles!" shouted Jellyband, as hopping about from one leg to another, he ran hither and thither, adding to the general discomfort of everybody.

The Comtesse, too, had risen to her feet: rigid and

45

erect, trying to hide her excitement beneath more becoming *sang-froid*, she repeated mechanically,—

"I will not see her!—I will not see her!"

Outside, the excitement attendant upon the arrival of very important guests grew apace.

"Good-day, Sir Percy!—Good-day to your ladyship! Your servant, Sir Percy!"—was heard in one long, continued chorus, with alternate more feeble tones of—"Remember the poor blind man! of your charity, lady and gentleman!"

Then suddenly a singularly sweet voice was heard through all the din.

"Let the poor man be—and give him some supper at my expense."

The voice was low and musical, with a slight sing-song in it, and a faint *soupçon* of foreign intonation in the pronunciation of the consonants.

Everyone in the coffee-room heard it and paused instinctively, listening to it for a moment. Sally was holding the candles by the opposite door, which led to the bedrooms upstairs, and the Comtesse was in the act of beating a hasty retreat before that enemy who owned such a sweet musical voice; Suzanne reluctantly was preparing to follow her mother, whilst casting regretful glances towards the door, where she hoped still to see her dearly beloved, erstwhile school-fellow.

Then Jellyband threw open the door, still stupidly and blindly hoping to avert the catastrophe which he felt was in the air, and the same low, musical voice said, with a merry laugh and mock consternation,—

"B-r-r-r! I am as wet as a herring! *Dieu!* has anyone ever seen such a contemptible climate?"

"Suzanne, come with me at once—I wish it," said the Comtesse, peremptorily.

"Oh! Mama!" pleaded Suzanne.

"My lady . . . er . . . h'm! . . . my lady! . . ." came in feeble accents from Jellyband, who stood clumsily trying to bar the way.

"*Pardieu*, my good man," said Lady Blakeney, with some impatience, "what are you standing in my way for, dancing about like a turkey with a sore foot? Let me get to the fire, I am perished with the cold."

And the next moment Lady Blakeney, gently pushing mine host on one side, had swept into the coffee-room.

There are many portraits and miniatures extant of Marguerite St. Just—Lady Blakeney as she was then—but it is doubtful if any of these really do her singular beauty justice. Tall, above the average, with magnificent presence and regal figure, it is small wonder that even the Comtesse paused for a moment in involuntary admiration before turning her back on so fascinating an apparition.

Marguerite Blakeney was then scarcely five-and-twenty, and her beauty was at its most dazzling stage. The large hat, with its undulating and waving plumes, threw a soft shadow across the classic brow with the aureole of auburn hair—free at the moment from any powder; the sweet, almost childlike mouth, the straight chiselled nose, round chin, and delicate throat, all seemed set off by the picturesque costume of the period. The rich blue velvet robe moulded in its every line the graceful contour of the figure, whilst one tiny hand held, with a dignity all its own, the tall stick adorned with a large bunch of ribbons which

fashionable ladies of the period had taken to carrying
recently.

With a quick glance all around the room, Marguerite
Blakeney had taken stock of every one there. She nodded
pleasantly to Sir Andrew Ffoulkes, whilst extending a
hand to Lord Antony.

"Hello! my Lord Tony, why—what are *you* doing here
in Dover?" she said merrily.

Then, without waiting for a reply, she turned and faced
the Comtesse and Suzanne. Her whole face lighted up
with additional brightness, as she stretched out both arms
towards the young girl.

"Why! if that isn't my little Suzanne over there. *Pardieu,*
little citizeness, how came you to be in England? And
Madame too?"

She went up effusively to them both, with not a single
touch of embarrassment in her manner or in her smile.
Lord Tony and Sir Andrew watched the little scene with
eager apprehension. English though they were, they had
often been in France, and had mixed sufficiently with the
French to realize the unbending hauteur, the bitter hatred with which the old *noblesse* of France viewed all those
who had helped to contribute to their downfall. Armand
St. Just, the brother of beautiful Lady Blakeney—though
known to hold moderate and conciliatory views—was an
ardent republican, his feud with the ancient family of St.
Cyr—the rights and wrongs of which no outsider ever
knew—had culminated in the downfall, the almost total
extinction, of the latter. In France, St. Just and his party
had triumphed, and here in England, face to face with

these three refugees driven from their country, flying for their lives, bereft of all which centuries of luxury had given them, there stood a fair scion of those same republican families which had hurled down a throne, and uprooted an aristocracy whose origin was lost in the dim and distant vista of bygone centuries.

She stood there before them, in all the unconscious insolence of beauty, and stretched out her dainty hand to them, as if she would, by that one act, bridge over the conflict and bloodshed of the past decade.

"Suzanne, I forbid you to speak to that woman," said the Comtesse, sternly, as she placed a restraining hand upon her daughter's arm.

She had spoken in English, so that all might hear and understand; the two young English gentlemen as well as the common innkeeper and his daughter. The latter literally gasped with horror at this foreign insolence, this impudence before her ladyship—who was English, now that she was Sir Percy's wife, and a friend of the Princess of Wales to boot.

As for Lord Antony and Sir Andrew Ffoulkes, their very hearts seemed to stand still with horror at this gratuitous insult. One of them uttered an exclamation of appeal, the other one of warning, and instinctively both glanced hurriedly towards the door, whence a slow, drawly, not unpleasant voice had already been heard.

Alone among those present Marguerite Blakeney and the Comtesse de Tournay had remained seemingly unmoved. The latter, rigid, erect and defiant, with one hand still upon her daughter's arm, seemed the very personification of unbending pride. For the moment Marguerite's sweet face had become as white as the soft fichu which swathed her throat, and a very keen observer might have noted that the hand which held the tall, be-ribboned stick was clenched, and trembled somewhat.

But this was only momentary; the next instant the delicate eyebrows were raised slightly, the lips curved sarcastically upwards, the clear blue eyes looked straight at the rigid Comtesse, and with a slight shrug of the shoulders—

"Hoity-toity, citizeness," she said gaily, "what fly stings you, pray?"

"We are in England now, Madame," rejoined the Comtesse, coldly, "and I am at liberty to forbid my daughter to touch your hand in friendship. Come, Suzanne."

She beckoned to her daughter, and without another look at Marguerite Blakeney, but with a deep, old-fashioned curtsey to the two young men, she sailed majestically out of the room.

There was silence in the old inn parlour for a moment, as the rustle of the Comtesse's skirts died away down the passage. Marguerite, rigid as a statue, followed with hard, set eyes the upright figure, as it disappeared through the doorway—but as little Suzanne, humble and obedient, was about to follow her mother, the hard, set expression suddenly vanished, and a wistful, almost pathetic and childlike look stole into Lady Blakeney's eyes.

Little Suzanne caught that look; the child's sweet nature went out to the beautiful woman, scarce older than herself; filial obedience vanished before girlish sympathy;

at the door she turned, ran back to Marguerite, and putting her arms round her, kissed her effusively; then only did she follow her mother, Sally bringing up the rear, with a pleasant smile on her dimpled face, and with a final curtsey to my lady.

Suzanne's sweet and dainty impulse had relieved the unpleasant tension. Sir Andrew's eyes followed the pretty little figure, until it had quite disappeared, then they met Lady Blakeney's with unassumed merriment.

Marguerite, with dainty affectation, had kissed her hand to the ladies, as they disappeared through the door, then a humorous smile began hovering round the corners of her mouth.

"So that's it, is it?" she said gaily. "La! Sir Andrew, did you ever see such an unpleasant person? I hope when I grow old I sha'n't look like that."

She gathered up her skirts, and assuming a majestic gait, stalked towards the fireplace.

"Suzanne," she said, mimicking the Comtesse's voice, "I forbid you to speak to that woman!"

The laugh which accompanied this sally, sounded perhaps a trifle forced and hard, but neither Sir Andrew nor Lord Tony were very keen observers. The mimicry was so perfect, the tone of the voice so accurately reproduced, that both the young men joined in a hearty cheerful "Bravo!"

"Ah! Lady Blakeney!" added Lord Tony, "how they must miss you at the Comédie Française, and how the Parisians must hate Sir Percy for having taken you away."

"Lud, man," rejoined Marguerite, with a shrug of her

graceful shoulders, " 'tis impossible to hate Sir Percy for anything; his witty sallies would disarm even Madame la Comtesse herself."

The young Vicomte, who had not elected to follow his mother in her dignified exit, now made a step forward, ready to champion the Comtesse should Lady Blakeney aim any further shafts at her. But before he could utter a preliminary word of protest, a pleasant, though distinctly inane laugh, was heard from outside, and the next moment an unusually tall and very richly dressed figure appeared in the doorway.

Chapter 6

An Exquisite of '92

Sir Percy Blakeney, as the chronicles of the time inform us, was, in this year of grace 1792, still a year or two on the right side of thirty. Tall, above the average, even for an Englishman, broad-shouldered and massively built, he would have been called unusually good-looking, but for a certain lazy expression in his deep-set blue eyes, and that perpetual inane laugh which seemed to disfigure his strong, clearly-cut mouth.

It was nearly a year ago now that Sir Percy Blakeney, Bart., one of the richest men in England, leader of all the fashions, and intimate friend of the Prince of Wales, had astonished fashionable society in London and Bath, by bringing home, from one of his journeys abroad, a beautiful, fascinating, clever, French wife. He, the sleepiest, dullest, most British Britisher that had ever set a pretty woman yawning had secured a brilliant matrimonial prize for which, as all chroniclers aver, there had been many competitors.

Marguerite St. Just had first made her *début* in artistic Parisian circles at the very moment when the greatest social upheaval the world has ever known was taking place within its very walls. Scarcely eighteen, lavishly gifted with beauty and talent, chaperoned only by a young and devoted brother, she had soon gathered round her in her charming apartment in the Rue Richelieu, a coterie which was as brilliant as it was exclusive—exclusive, that is to say, only from one point of view: Marguerite St. Just was from principle and by conviction a republican—equality of birth was her motto—inequality of fortune was in her eyes a mere untoward accident, but the only inequality she admitted was that of talent. "Money and titles may be hereditary," she would say, "but brains are not," and thus her charming salon was reserved for originality and intellect, for brilliance and wit, for clever men and talented women, and the entrance into it was soon looked upon in the world of intellect—which even in those days and in those troublous times found its pivot in Paris—as the seal to an artistic career.

Clever men, distinguished men, and even men of exalted station formed a perpetual and brilliant court round the fascinating young actress of the Comédie Française, and she glided through republican, revolutionary, bloodthirsty Paris like a shining comet with a trail behind her of all that was most distinguished, most interesting, in intellectual Europe.

Then the climax came. Some smiled indulgently and called it an artistic eccentricity, others looked upon it as a wise provision, in view of the many events which were crowding thick and fast in Paris just then, but to all, the real motive of that climax remained a puzzle and a mystery. Anyway, Marguerite St. Just married Sir Percy Blakeney one fine day, just like that, without any warning to her friends, without a *soirée de contrat*, or *dîner de fiançailles* or other appurtenances of a fashionable French wedding.

How that stupid, dull Englishman ever came to be admitted within the intellectual circle which revolved round "the cleverest woman in Europe," as her friends unanimously called her, no one ventured to guess—a golden key is said to open every door, asserted the more malignantly inclined.

Enough, she married him, and the "cleverest woman in Europe" had linked her fate to that "demmed idiot" Blakeney, and not even her most intimate friends could assign to this strange step any other motive than that of supreme eccentricity. Those friends who knew, laughed to scorn the idea that Marguerite St. Just had married a fool for the sake of the worldly advantages with which he might endow her. They knew, as a matter of fact, that Marguerite St. Just cared nothing about money, and still less about a title; moreover, there were at least half a dozen other men in the cosmopolitan world equally well-born, if not so wealthy as Blakeney, who would have been only too happy to give Marguerite St. Just any position she might choose to covet.

As for Sir Percy himself, he was universally voted to be totally unqualified for the onerous post he had taken upon himself. His chief qualifications for it seemed to consist in his blind adoration for her, his great wealth, and the high favour in which he stood at the English court; but London society thought that, taking into consideration his own intellectual limitations, it would have been wiser on his part, had he bestowed those worldly advantages upon a less brilliant and witty wife.

Although lately he had been so prominent a figure in fashionable English society, he had spent most of his early life abroad. His father, the late Sir Algernon Blakeney, had had the terrible misfortune of seeing an idolized young wife become hopelessly insane after two years of happy married life. Percy had just been born when the late Lady Blakeney fell a prey to the terrible malady which in those days was looked upon as hopelessly incurable and nothing short of a curse of God upon the entire family. Sir Algernon took his afflicted young wife abroad, and there presumably Percy was educated, and grew up between an imbecile mother and a distracted father, until he attained his majority. The death of his parents following close upon one another left him a free man, and as Sir Algernon had led a forcibly simple and retired life, the large Blakeney fortune had increased tenfold.

Sir Percy Blakeney had traveled a great deal abroad, before he brought home his beautiful, young, French wife. The fashionable circles of the time were ready to receive them both with open arms. Sir Percy was rich, his wife was accomplished, the Prince of Wales took a very great liking to them both. Within six months they were the acknowledged leaders of fashion and of style. Sir Percy's coats were the talk of the town, his inanities were quoted, his foolish laugh copied by the gilded youth at Almack's or the Mall.

Everyone knew that he was hopelessly stupid, but then that was scarcely to be wondered at, seeing that all the Blakeneys for generations had been notoriously dull, and that his mother had died an imbecile.

Thus society accepted him, petted him, made much of him, since his horses were the finest in the country, his *fêtes* and wines the most sought after. As for his marriage with "the cleverest woman in Europe," well! the inevitable came with sure and rapid footsteps. No one pitied him, since his fate was of his own making. There were plenty of young ladies in England, of high birth and good looks, who would have been quite willing to help him to spend the Blakeney fortune, whilst smiling indulgently at his inanities and his good-humoured foolishness. Moreover, Sir Percy got no pity, because he seemed to require none—he seemed very proud of his clever wife, and to care little that she took no pains to disguise that good-natured contempt which she evidently felt for him, and that she even amused herself by sharpening her ready wits at his expense.

But then Blakeney was really too stupid to notice the ridicule with which his clever wife covered him, and if his matrimonial relations with the fascinating Parisienne had not turned out all that his hopes and his dog-like devotion for her had pictured, society could never do more than vaguely guess at it.

In his beautiful house at Richmond he played second fiddle to his clever wife with imperturbable *bonhomie;* he lavished jewels and luxuries of all kinds upon her, which she took with inimitable grace, dispensing the hospitality of his superb mansion with the same graciousness with which she had welcomed the intellectual coterie of Paris.

Physically, Sir Percy Blakeney was undeniably handsome—always excepting the lazy, bored look which was habitual to him. He was always irreproachably dressed, and wore the exaggerated "Incroyable" fashions, which had just crept across from Paris to England, with the perfect good taste innate in an English gentleman. On this special afternoon in September, in spite of the long journey by coach, in spite of rain and mud, his coat set irreproachably across his fine shoulders, his hands looked almost femininely white, as they emerged through billowy frills of finest Mechlin lace: the extravagantly short-waisted satin coat, wide-lapelled waistcoat and tight-fitting striped breeches, set off his massive figure to perfection, and in repose one might have admired so fine a specimen of English manhood, until the foppish ways, the affected movements, the perpetual inane laugh, brought one's admiration of Sir Percy Blakeney to an abrupt close.

He had lolled into the old-fashioned inn parlour, shaking the wet off his fine overcoat; then, putting up a gold-rimmed eye-glass to his lazy blue eye, he surveyed the company, upon whom an embarrassed silence had suddenly fallen.

"How do, Tony? How do, Ffoulkes?" he said, recognising the two young men and shaking them by the hand. "Zounds, my dear fellow," he added, smothering a slight yawn, "did you ever see such a beastly day? Demmed climate this."

With a quaint little laugh, half of embarrassment and half of sarcasm, Marguerite had turned towards her husband, and was surveying him from head to foot, with an amused little twinkle in her merry blue eyes.

"La!" said Sir Percy, after a moment or two's silence, as no one offered any comment, "how sheepish you all look. . . . What's up?"

"Oh, nothing, Sir Percy," replied Marguerite, with a certain amount of gaiety, which, however, sounded some-what forced, "nothing to disturb your equanimity—only an insult to your wife."

The laugh which accompanied this remark was evi-dently intended to reassure Sir Percy as to the gravity of the incident. It apparently succeeded in that, for, echoing the laugh, he rejoined placidly—

"La, m'dear! you don't say so. Begad! who was the bold man who dared to tackle you—eh?"

Lord Tony tried to interpose, but had no time to do so, for the young Vicomte had already quickly stepped forward.

"Monsieur," he said, prefixing his little speech with an elaborate bow, and speaking in broken English, "my mother, the Comtesse de Tournay de Basserive, has offenced Ma-dame, who, I see, is your wife. I cannot ask your pardon for my mother; what she does is right in my eyes. But I am ready to offer you the usual reparation between men of honour."

The young man drew up his slim stature to its full height and looked very enthusiastic, very proud, and very hot as he gazed at six foot odd of gorgeousness, as repre-sented by Sir Percy Blakeney, Bart.

"Lud, Sir Andrew," said Marguerite, with one of her merry infectious laughs, "look on that pretty picture—the English turkey and the French bantam."

The simile was quite perfect, and the English turkey looked down with complete bewilderment upon the dainty little French bantam, which hovered quite threateningly around him.

"La! sir," said Sir Percy at last, putting up his eyeglass and surveying the young Frenchman with undisguised wonderment, "where, in the cuckoo's name, did you learn to speak English?"

"Monsieur!" protested the Vicomte, somewhat abashed at the way his warlike attitude had been taken by the ponderous-looking Englishman.

"I protest 'tis marvellous!" continued Sir Percy, imperturbably, "demmed marvellous! Don't you think so, Tony—eh? I vow I can't speak the French lingo like that. What?"

"Nay, I'll vouch for that!" rejoined Marguerite. "Sir Percy has a British accent you could cut with a knife."

"Monsieur," interposed the Vicomte earnestly, and in still more broken English, "I fear you have not understand. I offer you the only posseeble reparation among gentlemen."

"What the devil is that?" asked Sir Percy, blandly.

"My sword, Monsieur," replied the Vicomte, who, though still bewildered, was beginning to lose his temper.

"You are a sportsman, Lord Tony," said Marguerite, merrily; "ten to one on the little bantam."

But Sir Percy was staring sleepily at the Vicomte for a moment or two, through his partly closed heavy lids, then he smothered another yawn, stretched his long limbs, and turned leisurely away.

"Lud love you, sir," he muttered good-humouredly, "demmit, young man, what's the good of your sword to me?"

What the Vicomte thought and felt at that moment, when that long-limbed Englishman treated him with such marked insolence, might fill volumes of sound reflections. . . . What he said resolved itself into a single articulate word, for all the others were choked in his throat by his surging wrath.

"A duel, Monsieur," he stammered.

Once more Blakeney turned, and from his high altitude looked down on the choleric little man before him; but not even for a second did he seem to lose his own imperturbable good-humour. He laughed his own pleasant and inane laugh, and burying his slender, long hands into the capacious pockets of his overcoat, he said leisurely—

"A duel? La! is that what he meant? Odd's fish! you are a bloodthirsty young ruffian. Do you want to make a hole in a law-abiding man? . . . As for me, sir, I never fight duels," he added, as he placidly sat down and stretched his long, lazy legs out before him. "Demmed uncomfortable things, duels, ain't they, Tony?"

Now the Vicomte had no doubt vaguely heard that in England the fashion of dueling amongst gentlemen had been suppressed by the law with a very stern hand; still to him, a Frenchman, whose notions of bravery and honour were based upon a code that had centuries of tradition to back it, the spectacle of a gentleman actually refusing to fight a duel was little short of an enormity. In his mind he vaguely pondered whether he should strike that long-legged Englishman in the face and call him a coward, or whether such conduct in a lady's presence might be deemed ungentlemanly, when Marguerite happily interposed.

"I pray you, Lord Tony," she said in that gentle, sweet,

musical voice of hers, "I pray you play the peace-maker. The child is bursting with rage, and," she added with a *soupçon* of dry sarcasm, "might do Sir Percy an injury." She laughed a mocking little laugh, which, however, did not in the least disturb her husband's placid equanimity. "The British turkey has had the day," she said. "Sir Percy would provoke all the saints in the calendar and keep his temper the while."

But already Blakeney, good-humoured as ever, had joined in the laugh against himself.

"Demmed smart that now, wasn't it?" he said, turning pleasantly to the Vicomte. "Clever woman my wife, sir. . . . You will find *that* out if you live long enough in England."

"Sir Percy is in the right, Vicomte," here interposed Lord Antony, laying a friendly hand on the young Frenchman's shoulder. "It would hardly be fitting that you should commence your career in England by provoking him to a duel."

For a moment longer the Vicomte hesitated, then with a slight shrug of the shoulders directed against the extraordinary code of honour prevailing in this fog-ridden island, he said with becoming dignity—

"Ah, well! if Monsieur is satisfied, I have no griefs. You, mi'lor', are our protector. If I have done wrong, I withdraw myself."

"Aye, do!" rejoined Blakeney, with a long sigh of satisfaction, "withdraw yourself over there. Demmed excitable little puppy," he added under his breath. "Faith, Ffoulkes, if that's a specimen of the goods you and your friends bring over from France, my advice to you is, drop 'em 'mid Channel, my friend, or I shall have to see old Pitt about it, get him to clap on a prohibitive tariff, and put you in the stocks an you smuggle."

"La, Sir Percy, your chivalry misguides you," said Marguerite coquettishly, "you forget that you yourself have imported one bundle of goods from France."

Blakeney slowly rose to his feet, and, making a deep and elaborate bow before his wife, he said with consummate gallantry,—

"I had the pick of the market, Madame, and my taste is unerring."

"More so than your chivalry, I fear," she retorted sarcastically.

"Odd's life, m'dear! be reasonable! Do you think I am going to allow my body to be made a pincushion of, by every little frog-eater who don't like the shape of your nose?"

"Lud, Sir Percy!" laughed Lady Blakeney as she bobbed him a quaint and pretty curtsey, "you need not be afraid! 'Tis not the *men* who dislike the shape of my nose."

"Afraid be demmed! Do you impugn my bravery, Madame? I don't patronize the ring for nothing, do I, Tony? I've put up the fists with Red Sam before now, and—he didn't get it all his own way either—"

"S'faith, Sir Percy," said Marguerite, with a long and merry laugh, that went echoing along the old oak rafters of the parlour, "I would I had seen you then . . . ha! ha! ha! ha!—you must have looked a pretty picture. . . . and . . . and to be afraid of a little French boy . . . ha! ha! . . . ha! ha!"

"Ha! ha! ha! he! he! he!" echoed Sir Percy, good-humouredly. "La, Madame, you honour me! Zooks!

Ffoulkes, mark ye that! I have made my wife laugh!—The cleverest woman in Europe! . . . Odd's fish, we must have a bowl on that!" and he tapped vigorously on the table near him. "Hey! Jelly! Quick, man! Here, Jelly!"

Harmony was once more restored. Mr. Jellyband, with a mighty effort, recovered himself from the many emotions he had experienced within the last half hour. "A bowl of punch, Jelly, hot and strong, eh?" said Sir Percy. "The wits that have just made a clever woman laugh must be whetted! Ha! ha! ha! Hasten, my good Jelly!"

"Nay, there is no time, Sir Percy," interposed Marguerite. "The skipper will be here directly and my brother must get on board, or the *Day Dream* will miss the tide."

"Time, m'dear? There is plenty of time for any gentleman to get drunk and get on board before the turn of the tide."

"I think, your ladyship," said Jellyband, respectfully, "that the young gentleman is coming along now with Sir Percy's skipper."

"That's right," said Blakeney, "then Armand can join us in the merry bowl. Think you, Tony," he added, turning towards the Vicomte, "that that jackanapes of yours will join us in a glass? Tell him that we drink in token of reconciliation."

"In fact you are all such merry company," said Marguerite, "that I trust you will forgive me if I bid my brother good-bye in another room."

It would have been bad form to protest. Both Lord Antony and Sir Andrew felt that Lady Blakeney could not altogether be in tune with them at that moment. Her love for her brother, Armand St. Just, was deep and touching in the extreme. He had just spent a few weeks with her in her English home, and was going back to serve his country, at a moment when death was the usual reward for the most enduring devotion.

Sir Percy also made no attempt to detain his wife. With that perfect, somewhat affected gallantry which characterised his every movement, he opened the coffee-room door for her, and made her the most approved and elaborate bow, which the fashion of the time dictated, as she sailed out of the room without bestowing on him more than a passing, slightly contemptuous glance. Only Sir Andrew Ffoulkes, whose every thought since he had met Suzanne de Tournay seemed keener, more gentle, more innately sympathetic, noted the curious look of intense longing, of deep and hopeless passion, with which the inane and flippant Sir Percy followed the retreating figure of his brilliant wife.

Chapter 7

The Secret Orchard

*O*nce outside the noisy coffee-room, alone in the dimly-lighted passage, Marguerite Blakeney seemed to breathe more freely. She heaved a deep sigh, like one who had long been oppressed with the heavy weight of constant self-control, and she allowed a few tears to fall unheeded down her cheeks.

Outside the rain had ceased, and through the swiftly passing clouds, the pale rays of an after-storm sun shone upon the beautiful white coast of Kent and the quaint, irregular houses that clustered round the Admiralty Pier. Marguerite Blakeney stepped on to the porch and looked out to sea. Silhouetted against the ever-changing sky, a graceful schooner, with white sails set, was gently dancing in the breeze. The *Day Dream* it was, Sir Percy Blakeney's yacht, which was ready to take Armand St. Just back to France into the very midst of that seething, bloody Revo-

lution which was overthrowing a monarchy, attacking a
religion, destroying a society, in order to try and rebuild
upon the ashes of tradition a new Utopia, of which a few
men dreamed, but which none had the power to establish.

In the distance two figures were approaching "The Fisherman's Rest": one, an oldish man, with a curious fringe of
grey hairs round a rotund and massive chin, and who
walked with that peculiar rolling gait which invariably
betrays the seafaring man: the other, a young, slight figure, neatly and becomingly dressed in a dark, many caped
overcoat; he was clean-shaved, and his dark hair was
taken well back over a clear and noble forehead.

"Armand!" said Marguerite Blakeney, as soon as she
saw him approaching from the distance, and a happy smile
shone on her sweet face, even through the tears.

A minute or two later brother and sister were locked in
each other's arms, while the old skipper stood respectfully
on one side.

"How much time have we got, Briggs?" asked Lady
Blakeney, "before Monsieur St. Just need go on board?"

"We ought to weigh anchor before half an hour, your
ladyship," replied the old man, pulling at his grey forelock.

Linking her arm in his, Marguerite led her brother
towards the cliffs.

"Half an hour," she said, looking wistfully out to sea,
"half an hour more and you'll be far from me, Armand!
Oh! I can't believe that you are going, dear! These last
few days—whilst Percy has been away, and I've had you
all to myself, have slipped by like a dream."

"I am not going far, sweet one," said the young man
gently, "a narrow channel to cross—a few miles of road—
I can soon come back."

"Nay, 'tis not the distance, Armand—but that awful Paris . . . just now . . ."

They had reached the edge of the cliff. The gentle seabreeze blew Marguerite's hair about her face, and sent the ends of her soft lace fichu waving round her, like a white and supple snake. She tried to pierce the distance far away, beyond which lay the shores of France: that relentless and stern France which was exacting her pound of flesh, the blood-tax from the noblest of her sons.

"Our own beautiful country, Marguerite," said Armand, who seemed to have divined her thoughts.

"They are going too far, Armand," she said vehemently. "You are a republican, so am I . . . we have the same thoughts, the same enthusiasm for liberty and equality . . . but even *you* must think that they are going too far . . ."

"Hush!—" said Armand, instinctively, as he threw a quick, apprehensive glance around him.

"Ah! you see: you don't think yourself that it is safe even to speak of these things—here in England!" She clung to him suddenly with strong, almost motherly, passion: "Don't go, Armand!" she begged; "don't go back! What should I do if . . . if . . . if . . ."

Her voice was choked in sobs, her eyes, tender, blue and loving, gazed appealingly at the young man, who in his turn looked steadfastly into hers.

"You would in any case be my own brave sister," he said gently, "who would remember that, when France is in peril, it is not for her sons to turn their backs on her."

Even as he spoke, that sweet, childlike smile crept back into her face, pathetic in the extreme, for it seemed drowned in tears.

"Oh! Armand!" she said quaintly, "I sometimes wish you had not so many lofty virtues. . . . I assure you little sins are far less dangerous and uncomfortable. But you *will* be prudent?" she added earnestly.

"As far as possible . . . I promise you."

"Remember, dear, I have only you . . . to . . . to care for me. . . ."

"Nay, sweet one, you have other interests now. Percy cares for you. . . ."

A look of strange wistfulness crept into her eyes as she murmured,—

"He did . . . once . . ."

"But surely . . ."

"There, there, dear, don't distress yourself on my account. Percy is very good . . ."

"Nay!" he interrupted energetically, "I will distress myself on your account, my Margot. Listen, dear, I have not spoken of these things to you before; something always seemed to stop me when I wished to question you. But, somehow, I feel as if I could not go away and leave you now without asking you one question. . . . You need not answer it if you do not wish," he added, as he noted a sudden hard look, almost of apprehension, darting through her eyes.

"What is it?" she asked simply.

"Does Sir Percy Blakeney know that . . . I mean, does he know the part you played in the arrest of the Marquis de St. Cyr?"

She laughed—a mirthless, bitter, contemptuous laugh, which was like a jarring chord in the music of her voice.

"That I denounced the Marquis de St. Cyr, you mean,

to the tribunal that ultimately sent him and all his family to the guillotine? Yes, he does know. . . . I told him after I married him. . . ."

"You told him all the circumstances—which so completely exonerated you from any blame?"

"It was too late to talk of 'circumstances'; he heard the story from other sources; my confession came too tardily, it seems. I could no longer plead extenuating circumstances: I could not demean myself by trying to explain—"

"And?"

"And now I have the satisfaction, Armand, of knowing that the biggest fool in England has the most complete contempt for his wife."

She spoke with vehement bitterness this time, and Armand St. Just, who loved her so dearly, felt that he had placed a somewhat clumsy finger upon an aching wound.

"But Sir Percy loved you, Margot," he repeated gently.

"Loved me?—Well, Armand, I thought at one time that he did, or I should not have married him. I daresay," she added, speaking very rapidly, as if she were about to lay down a heavy burden, which had oppressed her for months, "I daresay that even you thought—as everybody else did—that I married Sir Percy because of his wealth—but I assure you, dear, that it was not so. He seemed to worship me with a curious intensity of concentrated passion, which went straight to my heart. I had never loved any one before, as you know, and I was four-and-twenty then—so I naturally thought that it was not in my nature to love. But it has always seemed to me that it *must* be *heavenly* to be loved blindly, passionately, wholly . . . worshipped, in fact—and the very fact that Percy was slow and stupid was an attraction for me, as I thought he would love me all the more. A clever man would naturally have other interests, an ambitious man other hopes. . . . I thought that a fool would worship, and think of nothing else. And I was ready to respond, Armand; I would have allowed myself to be worshipped, and given infinite tenderness in return. . . ."

She sighed—and there was a world of disillusionment in that sigh. Armand St. Just had allowed her to speak on without interruption: he listened to her, whilst allowing his own thoughts to run riot. It was terrible to see a young and beautiful woman—a girl in all but name—still standing almost at the threshold of her life, yet bereft of hope, bereft of illusions, bereft of those golden and fantastic dreams, which should have made her youth one long, perpetual holiday.

Yet perhaps—though he loved his sister dearly—perhaps he understood: he had studied men in many countries, men of all ages, men of every grade of social and intellectual status, and inwardly he understood what Marguerite had left unsaid. Granted that Percy Blakeney was dullwitted, but in his slow-going mind, there would still be room for that ineradicable pride of a descendant of a long line of English gentlemen. A Blakeney had died on Bosworth Field, another had sacrificed life and fortune for the sake of a treacherous Stuart: and that same pride—foolish and prejudiced as the republican Armand would call it— must have been stung to the quick on hearing of the sin which lay at Lady Blakeney's door. She had been young, misguided, ill-advised perhaps. Armand knew that· and those who took advantage of Marguerite's youth, her im-

pulses and imprudence, knew it still better; but Blakeney
was slow-witted, he would not listen to "circumstances,"
he only clung to facts, and these had shown him Lady
Blakeney denouncing a fellowman to a tribunal that knew
no pardon: and the contempt he would feel for the deed
she had done, however unwittingly, would kill that same
love in him, in which sympathy and intellectuality could
never have had a part.

Yet even now, his own sister puzzled him. Life and love
have such strange vagaries. Could it be that with the
waning of her husband's love, Marguerite's heart had awakened with love for him? Strange extremes meet in love's
pathway: this woman, who had had half intellectual Europe at her feet, might perhaps have set her affections on
a fool. Marguerite was gazing out towards the sunset.
Armand could not see her face, but presently it seemed to
him that something which glittered for a moment in the
golden evening light, fell from her eyes onto her dainty
fichu of lace.

But he could not broach that subject with her. He knew
her strange, passionate nature so well, and knew that
reserve which lurked behind her frank, open ways.

They had always been together, these two, for their
parents had died when Armand was still a youth, and
Marguerite but a child. He, some eight years her senior,
had watched over her until her marriage; had chaperoned
her during those brilliant years spent in the flat of the Rue
de Richelieu, and had seen her enter upon this new life of
hers, here in England, with much sorrow and some
foreboding.

This was his first visit to England since her marriage,

and the few months of separation had already seemed to have built up a slight, thin partition between brother and sister; the same deep, intense love was still there, on both sides, but each now seemed to have a secret orchard, into which the other dared not penetrate.

There was much Armand St. Just could not tell his sister; the political aspect of the revolution in France was changing almost every day; she might not understand how his own views and sympathies might become modified, even as the excesses, committed by those who had been his friends, grew in horror and in intensity. And Marguerite could not speak to her brother about the secrets of her heart; she hardly understood them herself; she only knew that, in the midst of luxury, she felt lonely and unhappy.

And now Armand was going away; she feared for his safety, she longed for his presence. She would not spoil these last few sadly-sweet moments by speaking about herself. She led him gently along the cliffs, then down to the beach; their arms linked in one another's, they had still so much to say, that lay just outside that secret orchard of theirs.

Chapter 8

The
Accredited Agent

*T*he afternoon was rapidly drawing to a close; and a long, chilly English summer's evening was throwing a misty pall over the green Kentish landscape.

The *Day Dream* had set sail, and Marguerite Blakeney stood alone on the edge of the cliff for over an hour, watching those white sails, which bore so swiftly away from her the only being who really cared for her, whom she dared to love, whom she knew she could trust.

Some little distance away to her left the lights from the coffee-room of "The Fisherman's Rest" glittered yellow in the gathering mist; from time to time it seemed to her aching nerves as if she could catch from thence the sound of merry-making and of jovial talk, or even that perpetual, senseless laugh of her husband's, which grated continually upon her sensitive ears.

Sir Percy had had the delicacy to leave her severely

74

alone. She supposed that, in his own stupid, good-natured
way, he may have understood that she would wish to
remain alone, while those white sails disappeared into the
vague horizon, so many miles away. He, whose notions of
propriety and decorum were supersensitive, had not suggested even that an attendant should remain within call.
Marguerite was grateful to her husband for all this; she
always tried to be grateful to him for his thoughtfulness,
which was constant, and for his generosity, which really
was boundless. She tried even at times to curb the sarcastic, bitter thoughts of him, which made her—in spite of
herself—say cruel, insulting things, which she vaguely
hoped would wound him.

Yes! she often wished to wound him, to make him feel
that she too held him in contempt, that she too had
forgotten that once she had almost loved him. Loved that
inane fop! whose thoughts seemed unable to soar beyond
the tying of a cravat or the new cut of a coat. Bah! And
yet! . . . vague memories, that were sweet and ardent and
attuned to this calm summer's evening, came wafted back
to her memory, on the invisible wings of the light seabreeze: the time when first he worshipped her; he seemed
so devoted—a very slave—and there was a certain latent
intensity in that love which had fascinated her.

Then suddenly that love, that devotion, which throughout his courtship she had looked upon as the slavish
fidelity of a dog, seemed to vanish completely. Twenty-
four hours after the simple little ceremony at old St.
Roch, she had told him the story of how, inadvertently,
she had spoken of certain matters connected with the

Marquis de St. Cyr before some men—her friends—who
had used this information against the unfortunate Marquis, and sent him and his family to the guillotine.

She hated the Marquis. Years ago, Armand, her dear
brother, had loved Angèle de St. Cyr, but St. Just was a
plebeian, and the Marquis full of the pride and arrogant
prejudices of his caste. One day Armand, the respectful,
timid lover, ventured on sending a small poem—enthusiastic,
ardent, passionate—to the idol of his dreams. The next
night he was waylaid just outside Paris by the valets of the
Marquis de St. Cyr, and ignominiously thrashed—thrashed
like a dog within an inch of his life—because he had dared
to raise his eyes to the daughter of the aristocrat. The
incident was one which, in those days, some two years
before the great Revolution, was of almost daily occur-
rence in France; incidents of that type, in fact, led to the
bloody reprisals, which a few years later sent most of those
haughty heads to the guillotine.

Marguerite remembered it all: what her brother must
have suffered in his manhood and his pride must have
been appalling; what she suffered through him and with
him she never attempted even to analyse.

Then the day of retribution came. St. Cyr and his kind
had found their masters, in those same plebeians whom
they had despised. Armand and Marguerite, both intellectual, thinking beings, adopted with the enthusiasm of
their years the Utopian doctrines of the Revolution, while
the Marquis de St. Cyr and his family fought inch by inch
for the retention of those privileges, which had placed
them socially above their fellow-men. Marguerite, impul-

sive, thoughtless, not calculating the purport of her words, still smarting under the terrible insult her brother had suffered at the Marquis' hands, happened to hear—amongst her own coterie—that the St. Cyrs were in treasonable correspondence with Austria, hoping to obtain the Emperor's support to quell the growing revolution in their own country.

In those days one denunciation was sufficient: Marguerite's few thoughtless words, anent the Marquis de St. Cyr, bore fruit within twenty-four hours. He was arrested. His papers were searched: letters from the Austrian Emperor, promising to send troops against the Paris populace, were found in his desk. He was arraigned for treason against the nation, and sent to the guillotine, whilst his family, his wife and his sons, shared this awful fate.

Marguerite, horrified at the terrible consequences of her own thoughtlessness, was powerless to save the Marquis: her own coterie, the leaders of the revolutionary movement, all proclaimed her as a heroine: and when she married Sir Percy Blakeney, she did not perhaps altogether realise how severely he would look upon the sin which she had so inadvertently committed, and which still lay heavily upon her soul. She made full confession of it to her husband, trusting to his blind love for her, her boundless power over him, to soon make him forget what might have sounded unpleasant to an English ear.

Certainly at the moment he seemed to take it very quietly; hardly, in fact, did he appear to understand the meaning of all she said; but what was more certain still, was that never after that could she detect the slightest sign of that love, which she once believed had been wholly hers. Now they had drifted quite apart, and Sir Percy seemed to have laid aside his love for her as he would an ill-fitting glove. She tried to rouse him by sharpening her ready wit against his dull intellect; endeavoured to excite his jealousy, if she could not rouse his love; tried to goad him to self-assertion, but all in vain. He remained the same, always passive, drawling, sleepy, always courteous, invariably a gentleman: she had all that the world and a wealthy husband can give to a pretty woman, yet on this beautiful summer's evening, with the white sails of the *Day Dream* finally hidden by the evening shadows, she felt more lonely than that poor tramp who plodded his way wearily along the rugged cliffs.

With another heavy sigh, Marguerite Blakeney turned her back upon the sea and cliffs, and walked slowly back towards "The Fisherman's Rest." As she drew near, the sound of revelry, of gay, jovial laughter, grew louder and more distinct. She could distinguish Sir Andrew Ffoulkes' pleasant voice, Lord Tony's boisterous guffaws, her husband's occasional, drawly, sleepy comments; then, realising the loneliness of the road and the fast gathering gloom round her, she quickened her steps . . . the next moment she perceived a stranger coming rapidly towards her. Marguerite did not look up: she was not the least nervous, and "The Fisherman's Rest" was now well within call.

The stranger paused when he saw Marguerite coming quickly towards him, and just as she was about to slip past him, he said very quietly:

"Citoyenne St. Just."

Marguerite uttered a little cry of astonishment, at thus hearing her own familiar maiden name uttered so close to her. She looked up at the stranger, and this time, with a cry of unfeigned pleasure, she put out both her hands effusively towards him.

"Chauvelin!" she exclaimed.

"Himself, citoyenne, at your service," said the stranger, gallantly kissing the tips of her fingers.

Marguerite said nothing for a moment or two, as she surveyed with obvious delight the not very prepossessing little figure before her. Chauvelin was then nearer forty than thirty—a clever, shrewd-looking personality, with a curious fox-like expression in the deep, sunken eyes. He was the same stranger who an hour or two previously had joined Mr. Jellyband in a friendly glass of wine.

"Chauvelin . . . my friend . . ." said Marguerite, with a pretty little sigh of satisfaction. "I am mightily pleased to see you."

No doubt poor Marguerite St. Just, lonely in the midst of her grandeur, and of her starchy friends, was happy to see a face that brought back memories of that happy time in Paris, when she reigned—a queen—over the intellectual coterie of the Rue de Richelieu. She did not notice the sarcastic little smile, however, that hovered round the thin lips of Chauvelin.

"But tell me," she added merrily, "what in the world, or whom in the world, are you doing here in England?"

She had resumed her walk towards the inn, and Chauvelin turned and walked beside her.

"I might return the subtle compliment, fair lady," he said. "What of yourself?"

"Oh, I?" she said, with a shrug of the shoulders. "Je m'ennuie, mon ami, that is all."

They had reached the porch of "The Fisherman's Rest," but Marguerite seemed loath to go within. The evening air was lovely after the storm, and she had found a friend who exhaled the breath of Paris, who knew Armand well, who could talk of all the merry, brilliant friends whom she had left behind. So she lingered on under the pretty porch, while through the gaily-lighted dormer-window of the coffee-room came sounds of laugher, of calls for "Sally" and for beer, of tapping of mugs, and clinking of dice, mingled with Sir Percy Blakeney's inane and mirthless laugh. Chauvelin stood beside her, his shrewd, pale, yellow eyes fixed on the pretty face, which looked so sweet and child-like in this soft English summer twilight.

"You surprise me, citoyenne," he said quietly, as he took a pinch of snuff.

"Do I now?" she retorted gaily. "Faith, my little Chauvelin, I should have thought that, with your penetration, you would have guessed that an atmosphere composed of fogs and virtues would never suit Marguerite St. Just."

"Dear me! is it as bad as that?" he asked, in mock consternation.

"Quite," she retorted, "and worse."

"Strange! Now, I thought that a pretty woman would have found English country life peculiarly attractive."

"Yes! so did I," she said with a sigh. "Pretty women," she added meditatively, "ought to have a good time in England, since all the pleasant things are forbidden them—the very things they do every day."

"Quite so!"

"You'll hardly believe it, my little Chauvelin," she said earnestly, "but I often pass a whole day—a whole day—without encountering a single temptation."

"No wonder," retorted Chauvelin, gallantly, "that the cleverest woman in Europe is troubled with *ennui*."

She laughed one of her melodious, rippling, childlike laughs.

"It must be pretty bad, mustn't it?" she said archly, "or I should not have been so pleased to see you."

"And this within a year of a romantic love match! . . ."

"Yes! . . . a year of a romantic love match . . . that's just the difficulty . . ."

"Ah! . . . that idyllic folly," said Chauvelin, with quiet sarcasm, "did not then survive the lapse of . . . weeks?" .

"Idyllic follies never last, my little Chauvelin . . . They come upon us like the measles . . . and are as easily cured."

Chauvelin took another pinch of snuff: he seemed very much addicted to that pernicious habit, so prevalent in those days; perhaps, too, he found the taking of snuff a convenient veil for disguising the quick, shrewd glances with which he strove to read the very souls of those with whom he came in contact.

"No wonder," he repeated, with the same gallantry, "that the most active brain in Europe is troubled with *ennui*."

"I was in hopes that you had a prescription against the malady, my little Chauvelin."

"How can I hope to succeed in that which Sir Percy Blakeney has failed to accomplish?"

"Shall we leave Sir Percy out of the question for the present, my dear friend?" she said drily.

"Ah! my dear lady, pardon me, but that is just what we cannot very well do," said Chauvelin, whilst once again his eyes, keen as those of a fox on the alert, darted a quick glance at Marguerite. "I have a most perfect prescription against the worst form of *ennui*, which I would have been happy to submit to you, but—"

"But what?"

"There *is* Sir Percy."

"What has he to do with it?"

"Quite a good deal, I am afraid. The prescription I would offer, fair lady, is called by a very plebeian name: Work!"

"Work?"

Chauvelin looked at Marguerite long and scrutinisingly. It seemed as if those keen, pale eyes of his were reading every one of her thoughts. They were alone together; the evening air was quite still, and their soft whispers were drowned in the noise which came from the coffee-room. Still, Chauvelin took a step or two from under the porch, looked quickly and keenly all round him, then, seeing that indeed no one was within earshot, he once more came back close to Marguerite.

"Will you render France a small service, citoyenne?" he asked, with a sudden change of manner, which lent his thin, fox-like face singular earnestness.

"La, man!" she replied flippantly, "how serious you look all of a sudden. . . . Indeed I do not know if I *would* render France a small service—at any rate, it depends upon the kind of service she—or you—want."

"Have you ever heard of the Scarlet Pimpernel, Citoyenne St. Just?" asked Chauvelin abruptly.

"Heard of the Scarlet Pimpernel?" she retorted with a long and merry laugh, "Faith, man! we talk of nothing else. . . . We have hats 'à la Scarlet Pimpernel'; our horses are called 'Scarlet Pimpernel'; at the Prince of Wales' supper party the other night we had a 'soufflé à la Scarlet Pimpernel.' . . . Lud!" she added gaily, "the other day I ordered at my milliner's a blue dress trimmed with green, and bless me, if she did not call that 'à la Scarlet Pimpernel.' "

Chauvelin had not moved while she prattled merrily along; he did not even attempt to stop her when her musical voice and her childlike laugh went echoing through the still evening air. But he remained serious and earnest whilst she laughed, and his voice, clear, incisive, and hard, was not raised above his breath as he said,—

"Then, as you have heard of that enigmatical personage, citoyenne, you must also have guessed, and known, that the man who hides his identity under that strange pseudonym, is the most bitter enemy of our republic, of France . . . of men like Armand St. Just."

"La! . . ." she said, with a quaint little sigh, "I dare swear he is. . . . France has many bitter enemies these days."

"But you, citoyenne, are a daughter of France, and should be ready to help her in a moment of deadly peril."

"My brother Armand devotes his life to France," she retorted proudly, "as for me, I can do nothing . . . here in England. . . ."

"Yes, you . . ." he urged still more earnestly, whilst his thin fox-like face seemed suddenly to have grown impressive and full of dignity, "here, in England, citoyenne . . . you alone can help us. . . . Listen!—I have been sent over here by the Republican Government as its representative: I present my credentials to Mr. Pitt in London to-morrow. One of my duties here is to find out all about this League of the Scarlet Pimpernel, which has become a standing menace to France, since it is pledged to help our cursed aristocrats—traitors to their country, and enemies of the people—to escape from the just punishment which they deserve. You know as well as I do, citoyenne, that once they are over here, those French *émigrés* try to rouse public feeling against the Republic . . . They are ready to join issue with any enemy bold enough to attack France. . . . Now, within the last month, scores of these *émigrés*, some only suspected of treason, others actually condemned by the Tribunal of Public Safety, have succeeded in crossing the Channel. Their escape in each instance was planned, organized and effected by this society of young English jackanapes, headed by a man whose brain seems as resourceful as his identity is mysterious. All the most strenuous efforts on the part of my spies have failed to discover who he is; whilst the others are the hands, he is the head, who beneath this strange anonymity calmly works at the destruction of France. I mean to strike at that head, and for this I want your help—through him afterwards I can reach the rest of the gang: he is a young buck in English society, of that I feel sure. Find that man for me, citoyenne!" he urged, "find him for France!"

Marguerite had listened to Chauvelin's impassioned speech without uttering a word, scarce making a movement, hardly daring to breathe. She had told him before, that this mysterious hero of romance was the talk of the smart set to which she belonged; already, before this, her heart and her imagination had been stirred by the thought of the brave man, who, unknown to fame, had rescued hundreds of lives from a terrible, often an unmerciful fate. She had but little real sympathy with those haughty French aristocrats, insolent in their pride of caste, of whom the Comtesse de Tournay de Basserive was so typical an example; but, republican and liberal-minded though she was from principle, she hated and loathed the methods which the young Republic had chosen for establishing itself. She had not been in Paris for some months; the horrors and bloodshed of the Reign of Terror, culminating in the September massacres, had only come across the Channel to her as a faint echo. Robespierre, Danton, Marat, she had not known in their new guise of bloody justiciaries, merciless wielders of the guillotine. Her very soul recoiled in horror from these excesses, to which she feared her brother Armand— moderate republican as he was—might become one day the holocaust.

Then, when first she heard of this band of young English enthusiasts, who, for sheer love of their fellowmen, dragged women and children, old and young men, from a horrible death, her heart had glowed with pride for them, and now, as Chauvelin spoke, her very soul went out to the gallant and mysterious leader of the reckless little band, who risked his life daily, who gave it freely and without ostentation, for the sake of humanity.

Her eyes were moist when Chauvelin had finished speaking, the lace at her bosom rose and fell with her quick, excited breathing; she no longer heard the noise of drinking from the inn, she did not heed her husband's voice or his inane laugh, her thoughts had gone wandering in search of the mysterious hero! Ah! there was a man she might have loved, had he come her way: everything in him appealed to her romantic imagination; his personality, his strength, his bravery, the loyalty of those who served under him in the same noble cause, and, above all, that anonymity which crowned him, as if with a halo of romantic glory.

"Find him for France, citoyenne!"

Chauvelin's voice close to her ear roused her from her dreams. The mysterious hero had vanished, and, not twenty yards away from her, a man was drinking and laughing, to whom she had sworn faith and loyalty.

"La! man," she said with a return of her assumed flippancy, "you are astonishing. Where in the world am I to look for him?"

"You go everywhere, citoyenne," whispered Chauvelin, insinuatingly, "Lady Blakeney is the pivot of social London, so I am told . . . you see everything, you *hear* everything."

"Easy, my friend," retorted Marguerite, drawing herself up to her full height and looking down, with a slight thought of contempt on the small, thin figure before her. "Easy! you seem to forget that there are six feet of Sir Percy Blakeney, and a long line of ancestors to stand between Lady Blakeney and such a thing as you propose."

"For the sake of France, citoyenne!" reiterated Chauvelin, earnestly.

"Tush, man, you talk nonsense anyway; for even if you did know who this Scarlet Pimpernel is, you could do nothing to him—an Englishman!"

"I'd take my chance of that," said Chauvelin, with a dry, rasping little laugh. "At any rate we could send him to the guillotine first to cool his ardour, then, when there is a diplomatic fuss about it, we can apologise—humbly—to the British Government, and, if necessary, pay compensation to the bereaved family."

"What you propose is horrible, Chauvelin," she said, drawing away from him as from some noisome insect. "Whoever the man may be, he is brave and noble, and never—do you hear me?—never would I lend a hand to such villainy."

"You prefer to be insulted by every French aristocrat who comes to this country?"

Chauvelin had taken sure aim when he shot this tiny shaft. Marguerite's fresh young cheeks became a thought more pale and she bit her under lip, for she would not let him see that the shaft had struck home.

"That is beside the question," she said at last with indifference. "I can defend myself, but I refuse to do any dirty work for you—or for France. You have other means at your disposal; you must use them, my friend."

And without another look at Chauvelin, Marguerite Blakeney turned her back on him and walked straight into the inn.

"That is not your last word, citoyenne," said Chauvelin,

as a flood of light from the passage illumined her elegant, richly-clad figure, "we meet in London, I hope!"

"We meet in London," she said, speaking over her shoulder at him, "but that is my last word."

She threw open the coffee-room door and disappeared from his view, but he remained under the porch for a moment or two, taking a pinch of snuff. He had received a rebuke and a snub, but his shrewd, fox-like face looked neither abashed nor disappointed; on the contrary, a curious smile, half sarcastic and wholly satisfied, played around the corners of his thin lips.

Chapter 9

The Outrage

A beauitful starlit night had followed on the day of incessant rain: a cool, balmy, late summer's night, essentially English in its suggestion of moisture and scent of wet earth and dripping leaves.

The magnificent coach, drawn by four of the finest thoroughbreds in England, had driven off along the London road, with Sir Percy Blakeney on the box, holding the reins in his slender feminine hands, and beside him Lady Blakeney wrapped in costly furs. A fifty-mile drive on a starlit summer's night! Marguerite had hailed the notion of it with delight. . . . Sir Percy was an enthusiastic whip; his four thoroughbreds, which had been sent down to Dover a couple of days before, were just sufficiently fresh and restive to add zest to the expedition, and Marguerite revelled in anticipation of the few hours of solitude, with the soft night breeze fanning her cheeks, her thoughts wandering, whither away? She knew from old experience that Sir Percy would speak little, if at all: he had often driven her on his beautiful coach for hours at night, from point to point, without making more than one or two casual remarks upon the weather or the state of the roads. He was very fond of driving by night, and she had very quickly adopted his fancy: as she sat next to him hour after hour, admiring the dexterous, certain way in which he handled the reins, she often wondered what went on in that slow-going head of his. He never told her, and she had never cared to ask.

At "The Fisherman's Rest" Mr. Jellyband was going the round, putting out the lights. His bar customers had all gone, but upstairs in the snug little bedrooms, Mr. Jellyband had quite a few important guests: the Comtesse de Tournay, with Suzanne, and the Vicomte, and there were two more bedrooms ready for Sir Andrew Ffoulkes and Lord Antony Dewhurst, if the two young men should elect to honor the ancient hostelry and stay the night.

For the moment these two young gallants were comfortably installed in the coffee-room, before the huge log-fire, which, in spite of the mildness of the evening, had been allowed to burn merrily.

"I say, Jelly, has everyone gone?" asked Lord Tony, as the worthy landlord still busied himself clearing away glasses and mugs.

"Everyone, as you see, my lord."

"And all your servants gone to bed?"

"All except the boy on duty in the bar, and," added Mr. Jellyband with a laugh, "I expect he'll be asleep afore long, the rascal."

"Then we can talk here undisturbed for half an hour?"

"At your service, my lord. . . . I'll leave your candles on the dresser . . . and your rooms are quite ready . . . I sleep at the top of the house myself, but if your lordship'll only call loudly enough, I daresay I shall hear."

"All right, Jelly . . . and . . . I say, put the lamp out—the fire'll give us all the light we need—and we don't want to attract the passer-by."

"All ri', my lord."

Mr. Jellyband did as he was bid—he turned out the quaint old lamp that hung from the raftered ceiling and blew out all the candles.

"Let's have a bottle of wine, Jelly," suggested Sir Andrew.

"All ri', sir!"

Jellyband went off to fetch the wine. The room now was quite dark, save for the circle of ruddy and fitful light formed by the brightly blazing logs in the hearth.

"Is that all, gentlemen?" asked Jellyband, as he returned with a bottle of wine and a couple of glasses, which he placed on the table.

"That'll do nicely, thanks, Jelly!" said Lord Tony.

"Good-night, my lord! Good-night, sir!"

"Good-night, Jelly!"

The two young men listened, whilst the heavy tread of Mr. Jellyband was heard echoing along the passage and staircase. Presently even that sound died out, and the whole of "The Fisherman's Rest" seemed wrapt in sleep, save the two young men drinking in silence beside the hearth.

For a while no sound was heard, even in the coffee-room, save the ticking of the old grandfather's clock and the crackling of the burning wood.

"All right again this time, Ffoulkes?" asked Lord Antony at last.

Sir Andrew had been dreaming evidently, gazing into the fire, and seeing therein, no doubt, a pretty, piquant face, with large brown eyes and a wealth of dark curls round a childish forehead.

"Yes!" he said, still musing, "all right!"

"No hitch?"

"None."

Lord Antony laughed pleasantly as he poured himself out another glass of wine.

"I need not ask, I suppose, whether you found the journey pleasant this time?"

"No, friend, you need not ask," replied Sir Andrew, gaily. "It was all right."

"Then here's to her very good health," said jovial Lord Tony. "She's a bonnie lass, though she is a French one. And here's to your courtship—may it flourish and prosper exceedingly."

He drained his glass to the last drop, then joined his friend beside the hearth.

"Well! you'll be doing the journey next, Tony, I expect," said Sir Andrew, rousing himself from his meditations, "you and Hastings, certainly; and I hope you may have as pleasant a task as I had, and as charming a traveling companion. You have no idea, Tony. . . ."

"No! I haven't," interrupted his friend pleasantly, "but I'll take your word for it. And now," he added, whilst a sudden earnestness crept over his jovial young face, "how about business?"

The two young men drew their chairs closer together, and instinctively, though they were alone, their voices sank to a whisper.

"I saw the Scarlet Pimpernel alone, for a few moments in Calais," said Sir Andrew, "a day or two ago. He crossed over to England two days before we did. He had escorted the party all the way from Paris, dressed—you'll never credit it!—as an old market woman, and driving—until they were safely out of the city—the covered cart, under which the Comtesse de Tournay, Mlle. Suzanne, and the Vicomte lay concealed among the turnips and cabbages. They, themselves, of course, never suspected who their driver was. He drove them right through a line of soldiery and a yelling mob, who were screaming, 'À bas les aristos!' But the market cart got through along with some others, and the Scarlet Pimpernel, in shawl, petticoat and hood, yelled 'À bas les aristos!' louder than anybody. Faith!" added the young man, as his eyes glowed with enthusiasm for the beloved leader, "that man's a marvel! His cheek is preposterous, I vow!—and that's what carries him through."

Lord Antony, whose vocabulary was more limited than that of his friend, could only find an oath or two with which to show his admiration for his leader.

"He wants you and Hastings to meet him at Calais," said Sir Andrew, more quietly, "on the second of next month. Let me see! that will be next Wednesday."

"Yes."

"It is, of course, the case of the Comte de Tournay, this time; a dangerous task, for the Comte, whose escape from his château, after he had been declared a 'suspect' by the Committee of Public Safety, was a masterpiece of the Scarlet Pimpernel's ingenuity, is now under sentence of death. It will be rare sport to get *him* out of France, and you will have a narrow escape, if you get through at all. St. Just has actually gone to meet him—of course, no one suspects St. Just as yet; but after that . . . to get them both out of the country! I'faith, 'twill be a tough job, and tax even the ingenuity of our chief. I hope I may yet have orders to be of the party."

"Have you any special instructions for me?"

"Yes! Rather more precise ones than usual. It appears that the Republican Government have sent an accredited agent over to England, a man named Chauvelin, who is said to be terribly bitter against our league, and determined to discover the identity of our leader, so that he may have him kidnapped, the next time he attempts to set foot in France. This Chauvelin has brought a whole army of spies with him, and until the chief has sampled the lot, he thinks we should meet as seldom as possible on the business of the league, and on no account should talk to each other in public places for a time. When he wants to speak to us, he will contrive to let us know."

The two young men were both bending over the fire, for the blaze had died down, and only a red glow from the dying embers cast a lurid light on a narrow semi-circle in front of the hearth. The rest of the room lay buried in complete gloom; Sir Andrew had taken a pocket-book from his pocket, and drawn therefrom a paper, which he unfolded, and together they tried to read it by the dim red firelight. So intent were they upon this, so wrapt up in the cause, the business they had so much at heart, so precious was this document which came from the very hand of their adored leader, that they had eyes and ears only for that. They lost count of the sounds around them, of the dropping of crisp ash from the grate, of the monotonous ticking of the clock, of the soft, almost imperceptible rustle of something on the floor close beside them. A figure had emerged from under one of the benches; with snake-like, noiseless movements it crept closer and closer to the two young men, not breathing, only gliding along the floor, in the inky blackness of the room.

"You are to read these instructions and commit them to memory," said Sir Andrew, "then destroy them."

He was about to replace the letter-case into his pocket, when a tiny slip of paper fluttered from it and fell on to the floor. Lord Antony stooped and picked it up.

"What's that?" he asked.

"I don't know," replied Sir Andrew.

"It dropped out of your pocket just now. It certainly did not seem to be with the other paper."

"Strange!—I wonder when it got there? It is from the chief," he added, glancing at the paper.

Both stooped to try and decipher this last tiny scrap of paper on which a few words had been hastily scrawled, when suddenly a slight noise attracted their attention, which seemed to come from the passage beyond.

"What's that?" said both instinctively. Lord Antony crossed the room towards the door, which he threw open quickly and suddenly; at that very moment he received a stunning blow between the eyes, which threw him back violently into the room. Simultaneously the crouching, snake-like figure in the gloom had jumped up and hurled itself from behind upon the unsuspecting Sir Andrew, felling him to the ground.

All this occurred within the short space of two or three seconds, and before either Lord Antony or Sir Andrew had time or chance to utter a cry or to make the faintest struggle. They were each seized by two men, a muffler was quickly tied round the mouth of each, and they were pinioned to one another back to back, their arms, hands, and legs securely fastened.

One man had in the meanwhile quietly shut the door; he wore a mask and now stood motionless while the others completed their work.

"All safe, citoyen!" said one of the men, as he took a final survey of the bonds which secured the two young men.

"Good!" replied the man at the door; "now search their pockets and give me all the papers you find."

This was promptly and quietly done. The masked man, having taken possession of all the papers, listened for a moment or two if there were any sound within "The Fisherman's Rest." Evidently satisfied that this dastardly outrage had remained unheard, he once more opened the door and pointed peremptorily down the passage. The four men lifted Sir Andrew and Lord Antony from the ground, and as quietly, as noiselessly as they had come, they bore the two pinioned young gallants out of the inn and along the Dover Road into the gloom beyond.

In the coffee-room the masked leader of this daring attempt was quickly glancing through the stolen papers.

"Not a bad day's work on the whole," he muttered, as

he quietly took off his mask, and his pale, fox-like eyes glittered in the red glow of the fire. "Not a bad day's work."

He opened one or two more letters from Sir Andrew Ffoulkes' pocket-book, noted the tiny scrap of paper which the two young men had only just had time to read; but one letter specially, signed Armand St. Just, seemed to give him strange satisfaction.

"Armand St. Just a traitor after all," he murmured. "Now, fair Marguerite Blakeney," he added viciously between his clenched teeth, "I think that you will help me to find the Scarlet Pimpernel."

Chapter 10

In the Opera Box

*I*t was one of the gala nights at Covent Garden Theatre, the first of the autumn season in this memorable year of grace 1792.

The house was packed, both in the smart orchestra boxes and the pit, as well as in the more plebeian balconies and galleries above. Glück's *Orpheus* made a strong appeal to the more intellectual portions of the house, whilst the fashionable women, the gaily-dressed and brilliant throng, spoke to the eye of those who cared but little for this "latest importation from Germany."

Selina Storace had been duly applauded after her grand aria by her numerous admirers; Benjamin Incledon, the acknowledged favourite of the ladies, had received special gracious recognition from the royal box; and now the curtain came down after the glorious finale to the second act, and the audience, which had hung spell-bound on the magic strains of the great maestro, seemed collectively to breathe a long sigh of satisfaction, previous to letting loose its hundreds of waggish and frivolous tongues.

In the smart orchestra boxes many well-known faces were to be seen. Mr. Pitt, overweighted with cares of state, was finding brief relaxation in to-night's musical treat; the Prince of Wales, jovial, rotund, somewhat coarse and commonplace in appearance, moved about from box to box, spending brief quarters of an hour with those of his more intimate friends.

In Lord Grenville's box, too, a curious, interesting personality attracted everyone's attention; a thin, small figure with shrewd, sarcastic face and deep-set eyes, attentive to the music, keenly critical of the audience, dressed in immaculate black, with dark hair free from any powder. Lord Grenville—Foreign Secretary of State—paid him marked, though frigid deference.

Here and there, dotted about among distinctly English types of beauty, one or two foreign faces stood out in marked contrast: the haughty aristocratic cast of countenance of the many French royalist *émigrés* who, persecuted by the relentless, revolutionary faction of their country, had found a peaceful refuge in England. On these faces sorrow and care were deeply writ; the women especially paid but little heed, either to the music or to the brilliant audience; no doubt their thoughts were far away with husband, brother, son maybe, still in peril, or lately succumbed to a cruel fate.

Among these the Comtesse de Tournay de Basserive, but lately arrived from France, was a most conspicuous

figure: dressed in deep, heavy black silk, with only a white
lace kerchief to relieve the aspect of mourning about her
person, she sat beside Lady Portarles, who was vainly
trying by witty sallies and somewhat broad jokes, to bring
a smile to the Comtesse's sad mouth. Behind her sat little
Suzanne and the Vicomte, both silent and somewhat shy
among so many strangers. Suzanne's eyes seemed wistful;
when she first entered the crowded house, she had looked
eagerly all around, scanned every face, scrutinised every
box. Evidently the one face she wished to see was not
there, for she settled herself down quietly behind her
mother, listened apathetically to the music, and took no
further interest in the audience itself.

"Ah, Lord Grenville," said Lady Portarles as, following
a discreet knock, the clever, interesting head of the Secretary of State appeared in the doorway of the box, "you
could not arrive more *à propos*. Here is Madame la Comtesse
de Tournay positively dying to hear the latest news from
France."

The distinguished diplomatist had come forward and
was shaking hands with the ladies.

"Alas!" he said sadly, "it is of the very worst. The
massacres continue; Paris literally reeks with blood; and
the guillotine claims a hundred victims a day."

Pale and tearful, the Comtesse was leaning back in her
chair, listening horror-struck to this brief and graphic
account of what went on in her own misguided country.

"Ah, Monsieur!" she said in broken English, "it is
dreadful to hear all that—and my poor husband still in
that awful country. It is terrible for me to be sitting here,

in a theatre, all safe and in peace, whilst he is in such peril."

"Lud, Madame!" said honest, bluff Lady Portarles, "your sitting in a convent won't make your husband safe, and you have your children to consider: they are too young to be dosed with anxiety and premature mourning."

The Comtesse smiled through her tears at the vehemence of her friend. Lady Portarles, whose voice and manner would not have misfitted a jockey, had a heart of gold, and hid the most genuine sympathy and most gentle kindliness, beneath the somewhat coarse manners affected by some ladies at that time.

"Besides which, Madame," added Lord Grenville, "did you not tell me yesterday that the League of the Scarlet Pimpernel had pledged their honour to bring Monsieur le Comte safely across the Channel?"

"Ah, yes!" replied the Comtesse, "and that is my only hope. I saw Lord Hastings yesterday . . . he reassured me again."

"Then I am sure you need have no fear. What the league have sworn, that they surely will accomplish. Ah!" added the old diplomatist with a sigh, "if I were but a few years younger . . ."

"La, man!" interrupted honest Lady Portarles, "you are still young enough to turn your back on that French scarecrow that sits enthroned in your box to-night."

"I wish I could . . . but your ladyship must remember that in serving our country we must put prejudices aside. Monsieur Chauvelin is the accredited agent of his Government . . ."

"Odd's fish, man!" she retorted, "you don't call those bloodthirsty ruffians over there a government, do you?"

"It has not been thought advisable as yet," said the Minister, guardedly, "for England to break off diplomatic relations with France, and we cannot therefore refuse to receive with courtesy the agent she wishes to send to us."

"Diplomatic relations be demmed, my lord! That sly little fox over there is nothing but a spy, I'll warrant, and you'll find—an I'm much mistaken, that he'll concern himself little with diplomacy, beyond trying to do mischief to royalist refugees—to our heroic Scarlet Pimpernel and to the members of that brave little league."

"I am sure," said the Comtesse, pursing up her thin lips, "that if this Chauvelin wishes to do us mischief, he will find a faithful ally in Lady Blakeney."

"Bless the woman!" ejaculated Lady Portarles, "did ever anyone see such perversity? My Lord Grenville, you have the gift of the gab, will you please explain to Madame la Comtesse that she is acting like a fool. In your position here in England, Madame," she added, turning a wrathful and resolute face towards the Comtesse, "you cannot afford to put on the hoity-toity airs you French aristocrats are so fond of. Lady Blakeney may or may not be in sympathy with those Ruffians in France; she may or may not have had anything to do with the arrest and condemnation of St. Cyr, or whatever the man's name is, but she is the leader of fashion in this country; Sir Percy Blakeney has more money than any half-dozen other men put together, he is hand and glove with royalty, and your trying to snub Lady Blakeney will not harm her, but will make you look a fool. Isn't that so, my lord?"

But what Lord Grenville thought of this matter, or to what reflections this homely tirade of Lady Portarles led the Comtesse de Tournay, remained unspoken, for the curtain had just risen on the third act of *Orpheus*, and admonishments to silence came from every part of the house.

Lord Grenville took a hasty farewell of the ladies and slipped back into his box, where M. Chauvelin had sat all through this *entr'acte*, with his eternal snuff-box in his hand, and with his keen pale eyes intently fixed upon a box opposite to him, where, with much frou-frou of silken skirts, much laughter and general stir of curiosity amongst the audience, Marguerite Blakeney had just entered, accompanied by her husband, and looking divinely pretty beneath the wealth of her golden, reddish curls, slightly besprinkled with powder, and tied back at the nape of her graceful neck with a gigantic black bow. Always dressed in the very latest vagary of fashion, Marguerite alone among the ladies that night had discarded the cross-over fichu and broad-lapeled over-dress, which had been in fashion for the last two or three years. She wore the short-waisted classical-shaped gown, which so soon was to become the approved mode in every country in Europe. It suited her graceful, regal figure to perfection, composed as it was of shimmering stuff which seemed a mass of rich gold embroidery.

As she entered, she leant for a moment out of the box, taking stock of all those present whom she knew. Many bowed to her as she did so, and from the royal box there came also a quick and gracious salute.

Chauvelin watched her intently all through the commence-ment of the third act, as she sat enthralled with the music, her exquisite little hand toying with a small jew-elled fan, her regal head, her throat, arms and neck, covered with magnificent diamonds and rare gems, the gift of the adoring husband who sprawled leisurely by her side.

Marguerite was passionately fond of music; *Orpheus* charmed her to-night. The very joy of living was writ plainly upon the sweet young face, it sparkled out of the merry blue eyes and lit up the smile that lurked around the lips. She was after all but five-and-twenty, in the hey day of youth, the darling of a brilliant throng, adored, *fêted*, petted, cherished. Two days ago the *Day Dream* had re-turned from Calais, bringing her news that her idolised brother had safely landed, that he thought of her, and would be prudent for her sake.

What wonder for the moment, and listening to Glück's impassioned strains, that she forgot her disillusionments, forgot her vanished love-dreams, forgot even the lazy, good-humoured nonentity who had made up for his lack of spiritual attainments by lavishing worldly advantages upon her.

He had stayed beside her in the box just as long as convention demanded, making way for His Royal High-ness, and for the host of admirers who in a continued procession came to pay homage to the queen of fashion. Sir Percy had strolled away, to talk to more congenial friends probably. Marguerite did not even wonder whither he had gone—she cared so little; she had had a little court round her, composed of the *jeunesse dorée* of London, and had just dismissed them all, wishing to be alone with Glück for a brief while.

A discreet knock at the door roused her from her enjoyment.

"Come in," she said with some impatience, without turning to look at the intruder.

Chauvelin, waiting for his opportunity, noted that she was alone, and now, without pausing for that impatient "Come in," he quietly slipped into the box, and the next moment was standing behind Marguerite's chair.

"A word with you, citoyenne," he said quietly.

Marguerite turned quickly, in alarm, which was not altogether feigned.

"Lud, man! you frightened me," she said with a forced little laugh, "your presence is entirely inopportune. I want to listen to Glück, and have no mind for talking."

"But this is my only opportunity," he said, as quietly, and without waiting for permission, he drew a chair close behind her—so close that he could whisper in her ear, without disturbing the audience, and without being seen, in the dark background of the box. "This is my only opportunity," he repeated, as she vouchsafed him no reply, "Lady Blakeney is always so surrounded, so *fêted* by her court, that a mere old friend has but very little chance."

"Faith, man!" she said impatiently, "you must seek for another opportunity then. I am going to Lord Grenville's ball tonight after the opera. So are you, probably. I'll give you five minutes then. . . ."

"Three minutes in the privacy of this box are quite sufficient for me," he rejoined placidly, "and I think that you would be wise to listen to me, Citoyenne St. Just."

Marguerite instinctively shivered. Chauvelin had not raised his voice above a whisper; he was now quietly taking a pinch of snuff, yet there was something in his attitude, something in those pale, foxy eyes, which seemed to freeze the blood in her veins, as would the sight of some deadly hitherto urguessed peril.

"Is that a threat, citoyen?" she asked at last.

"Nay, fair lady," he said gallantly, "only an arrow shot into the air."

He paused a moment, like a cat which sees a mouse running heedlessly by, ready to spring, yet waiting with that feline sense of enjoyment of mischief about to be done. Then he said quietly:

"Your brother, St. Just, is in peril."

Not a muscle moved in the beautiful face before him. He could only see it in profile, for Marguerite seemed to be watching the stage intently, but Chauvelin was a keen observer; he noticed the sudden rigidity of the eyes, the hardening of the mouth, the sharp, almost paralysed tension of the beautiful, graceful figure.

"Lud, then," she said, with affected merriment, "since 'tis one of your imaginary plots, you'd best go back to your own seat and leave me to enjoy the music."

And with her hand she began to beat time nervously against the cushion of the box. Selina Storace was singing the "Che faro" to an audience that hung spell-bound upon the prima donna's lips. Chauvelin did not move from his seat; he quietly watched that tiny nervous hand, the only indication that his shaft had indeed struck home.

"Well?" she said suddenly and irrelevantly, and with the same feigned unconcern.

"Well, citoyenne?" he rejoined placidly.

"About my brother?"

"I have news of him for you which, I think, will interest you, but first let me explain. . . . May I?"

The question was unnecessary. He felt, though Marguerite still held her head steadily averted from him, that her every nerve was strained to hear what he had to say.

"The other day, citoyenne," he said, "I asked for your help. . . . France needed it, and I thought I could rely on you, but you gave me your answer. . . . Since then the exigencies of my own affairs and your own social duties have kept us apart . . . although many things have happened. . . ."

"To the point, I pray you, citoyen," she said lightly; "the music is entrancing, and the audience will get impatient of your talk."

"One moment, citoyenne. The day on which I had the honor of meeting you at Dover, and less than an hour after I had your final answer, I obtained possession of some papers, which revealed another of those subtle schemes for the escape of a batch of French aristocrats—that traitor de Tournay amongst others—all organised by that arch-meddler, the Scarlet Pimpernel. Some of the threads, too, of this mysterious organisation have fallen into my hands, but not all, and I want you—nay! you *must* help me to gather them together."

Marguerite seemed to have listened to him with marked impatience; she now shrugged her shoulders and said gaily—

"Bah! man. Have I not already told you that I care nought about your schemes or about the Scarlet Pimpernel. And had you not spoken about my brother . . ."

"A little patience, I entreat, citoyenne," he continued imperturbably. "Two gentlemen, Lord Antony Dewhurst and Sir Andrew Ffoulkes were at 'The Fisherman's Rest' at Dover that same night."

"I know. I saw them there."

"They were already known to my spies as members of that accursed league. It was Sir Andrew Ffoulkes who escorted the Comtesse de Tournay and her children across the Channel. When the two young men were alone, my spies forced their way into the coffee-room of the inn, gagged and pinioned the two gallants, seized their papers, and brought them to me."

In a moment she had guessed the danger. Papers? . . . Had Armand been imprudent? . . . The very thought struck her with nameless terror. Still she would not let this man see that she feared; she laughed gaily and lightly.

"Faith! and your impudence passes belief," she said merrily. "Robbery and violence!—in England!—in a crowded inn! Your men might have been caught in the act!"

"What if they had? They are children of France, and have been trained by your humble servant. Had they been caught they would have gone to jail, or even to the gallows, without a word of protest or indiscretion; at any rate it was well worth the risk. A crowded inn is safer for these little operations than you think, and my men have experience."

"Well? And those papers?" she asked carelessly.

"Unfortunately, though they have given me cognisance of certain names . . . certain movements . . . enough, I think, to thwart their projected *coup* for the moment, it would only be for the moment, and still leaves me in ignorance of the identity of the Scarlet Pimpernel."

"La! my friend," she said, with the same assumed flippancy of manner, "then you are where you were before, aren't you? and you can let me enjoy the last strophe of the *aria*. Faith!" she added, ostentatiously smothering an imaginary yawn, "had you not spoken about my brother . . ."

"I am coming to him now, citoyenne. Among the papers there was a letter to Sir Andrew Ffoulkes, written by your brother, St. Just."

"Well? And?"

"That letter shows him to be not only in sympathy with the enemies of France, but actually a helper, if not a member, of the League of the Scarlet Pimpernel."

The blow had been struck at last. All along, Marguerite had been expecting it; she would not show fear, she was determined to seem unconcerned, flippant even. She wished, when the shock came, to be prepared for it, to have all her wits about her—those wits which had been nicknamed the keenest in Europe. Even now she did not flinch. She knew that Chauvelin had spoken the truth; the man was too earnest, too blindly devoted to the misguided cause he had at heart, too proud of his countrymen, of those makers of revolutions, to stoop to low, purposeless falsehoods.

That letter of Armand's—foolish, imprudent Armand— was in Chauvelin's hands. Marguerite knew that as if she had seen the letter with her own eyes; and Chauvelin would hold that letter for purposes of his own, until it suited him to destroy it or to make use of it against

Armand. All that she knew, and yet she continued to laugh more gaily, more loudly than she had done before.

"La, man!" she said, speaking over her shoulder and looking him full and squarely in the face, "did I not say it was some imaginary plot. . . . Armand in league with that enigmatic Scarlet Pimpernel! . . . Armand busy helping those French aristocrats whom he despises! . . . Faith, the tale does infinite credit to your imagination!"

"Let me make my point clear, citoyenne," said Chauvelin, with the same unruffled calm, "I must assure you that St. Just is compromised beyond the slightest hope of pardon."

Inside the orchestra box all was silent for a moment or two. Marguerite sat, straight upright, rigid and inert, trying to think, trying to face the situation, to realise what had best be done.

In the house Storace had finished the *aria*, and was even now bowing in her classic garb, but in approved eighteenth-century fashion, to the enthusiastic audience, who cheered her to the echo.

"Chauvelin," said Marguerite Blakeney at last, quietly, and without that touch of bravado which had character-ised her attitude all along, "Chauvelin, my friend, shall we try to understand one another. It seems that my wits have become rusty by contact with this damp climate. Now, tell me, you are very anxious to discover the iden-tity of the Scarlet Pimpernel, isn't that so?"

"France's most bitter enemy, citoyenne . . . all the more dangerous, as he works in the dark."

"All the more noble, you mean. . . . Well!—and you would now force me to do some spying work for you in exchange for my brother Armand's safety?—Is that it?"

"Fie! two very ugly words, fair lady," protested Chauvelin, urbanely. "There can be no question of force, and the service which I would ask of you, in the name of France, could never be called by the shocking name of spying."

"At any rate, that is what it is called over here," she said drily. "That is your intention, is it not?"

"My intention is, that you yourself win a free pardon for Armand St. Just by doing me a small service."

"What is it?"

"Only watch for me tonight, Citoyenne St. Just," he said eagerly. "Listen: among the papers which were found about the person of Sir Andrew Ffoulkes there was a tiny note. See!" he added, taking a tiny scrap of paper from his pocket-book and handing it to her.

It was the same scrap of paper which, four days ago, the two young men had been in the act of reading, at the very moment when they were attacked by Chauvelin's minions. Marguerite took it mechanically and stooped to read it. There were only two lines, written in a distorted, evidently disguised, handwriting; she read them half aloud.

" 'Remember we must not meet more often than is strictly necessary. You have all instructions for the 2nd. If you wish to speak to me again, I shall be at G.'s ball.' "

"What does it mean?" she asked.

"Look again, citoyenne, and you will understand."

"There is a device here in the corner, a small red flower . . ."

"Yes."

"The Scarlet Pimpernel," she said eagerly, "and G.'s ball means Grenville's ball. . . . He will be at my Lord Grenville's ball tonight."

"That is how I interpret the note, citoyenne," concluded Chauvelin, blandly. "Lord Antony Dewhurst and Sir Andrew Ffoulkes, after they were pinioned and searched by my spies, were carried by my orders to a lonely house on the Dover Road, which I had rented for the purpose: there they remained close prisoners until this morning. But having found this tiny scrap of paper, my intention was that they should be in London, in time to attend my Lord Grenville's ball. You see, do you not? that they must have a great deal to say to their chief . . . and thus they will have an opportunity of speaking to him to-night, just as he directed them to do. Therefore, this morning, those two young gallants found every bar and bolt open in that lonely house on the Dover Road, their jailers disappeared, and two good horses standing ready saddled and tethered in the yard. I have not seen them yet, but I think we may safely conclude that they did not draw rein until they reached London. Now you see how simple it all is, citoyenne!"

"It does seem simple, doesn't it?" she said, with a final bitter attempt at flippancy, "when you want to kill a chicken . . . you take hold of it . . . then you wring its neck . . . it's only the chicken who does not find it quite so simple. Now you hold a knife at my throat, and a hostage for my obedience. . . . You find it simple. . . . I don't."

"Nay, citoyenne, I offer you a chance of saving the brother you love from the consequences of his own folly."

Marguerite's face softened, her eyes at last grew moist, as she murmured, half to herself:

"The only being in the world who has loved me truly

and constantly. . . . But what do you want me to do, Chauvelin?" she said, with a world of despair in her tear-choked voice. "In my present position, it is well-nigh impossible!"

"Nay, citoyenne," he said drily and relentlessly, not heeding that despairing, childlike appeal, which might have melted a heart of stone, "as Lady Blakeney, no one suspects you, and with your help to-night I may—who knows?—succeed in finally establishing the identity of the Scarlet Pimpernel. . . . You are going to the ball anon. . . . Watch for me there, citoyenne, watch and listen. . . . You can tell me if you hear a chance word or whisper. . . . You can note everyone to whom Sir Andrew Ffoulkes or Lord Antony Dewhurst will speak. You are absolutely beyond suspicion now. The Scarlet Pimpernel will be at Lord Grenville's ball to-night. Find out who he is, and I will pledge the word of France that your brother shall be safe."

Chauvelin was putting the knife to her throat. Marguerite felt herself entangled in one of those webs, from which she could hope for no escape. A precious hostage was being held for her obedience: for she knew that this man would never make an empty threat. No doubt Armand was already signalled to the Committee of Public Safety as one of the "suspect"; he would not be allowed to leave France again, and would be ruthlessly struck, if she refused to obey Chauvelin. For a moment—woman-like—she still hoped to temporise. She held out her hand to this man, whom she now feared and hated.

"If I promise to help you in this matter, Chauvelin,"

she said pleasantly, "will you give me that letter of St. Just's?"

"If you render me useful assistance to-night, citoyenne," he replied with a sarcastic smile, "I will give you that letter . . . to-morrow."

"You do not trust me?"

"I trust you absolutely, dear lady, but St. Just's life is forfeit to his country . . . it rests with you to redeem it."

"I may be powerless to help you," she pleaded, "were I ever so willing."

"That would be terrible indeed," he said quietly, "for you . . . and for St. Just."

Marguerite shuddered. She felt that from this man she could expect no mercy. All-powerful, he held the beloved life in the hollow of his hand. She knew him too well not to know that, if he failed in gaining his own ends, he would be pitiless.

She felt cold in spite of the oppressive air of the opera-house. The heart-appealing strains of the music seemed to reach her, as from a distant land. She drew her costly lace scarf up around her shoulders, and sat silently watching the brilliant scene, as if in a dream.

For a moment her thoughts wandered away from the loved one who was in danger, to that other man who also had a claim on her confidence and her affection. She felt lonely, frightened for Armand's sake; she longed to seek comfort and advice from some one, who would know how to help and console. Sir Percy Blakeney had loved her once; he was her husband; why should she stand alone through this terrible ordeal? He had very little brains, it is true, but he had plenty of muscle: surely, if she provided the thought, and he the manly energy and pluck, together they could outwit the astute diplomatist, and save the hostage from his vengeful hands, without imperilling the life of the noble leader of that gallant little band of heroes. Sir Percy knew St. Just well—he seemed attached to him—she was sure that he could help.

Chauvelin was taking no further heed of her. He had said his cruel "Either—or—" and left her to decide. He, in his turn now, appeared to be absorbed in the soul-stirring melodies of *Orpheus*, and was beating time to the music with his sharp, ferret-like head.

A discreet rap at the door roused Marguerite from her thoughts. It was Sir Percy Blakeney, tall, sleepy, good-humoured, and wearing that half-shy, half-inane smile, which just now seemed to irritate her every nerve.

"Er . . . your chair is outside . . . m'dear," he said, with his most exasperating drawl, "I suppose you will want to go to that demmed ball. . . . Excuse me—er—Monsieur Chauvelin—I had not observed you. . . ."

He extended two slender, white fingers towards Chauvelin, who had risen when Sir Percy entered the box.

"Are you coming, m'dear?"

"Hush! Sh! Sh!" came in angry remonstrance from different parts of the house.

"Demmed impudence," commented Sir Percy with a good-natured smile.

Marguerite sighed impatiently. Her last hope seemed suddenly to have vanished away. She wrapped her cloak round her and without looking at her husband:

"I am ready to go," she said, taking his arm. At the door of the box she turned and looked straight at Chauvelin, who, with his *chapeau-bras* under his arm, and a curious smile round his thin lips, was preparing to follow the strangely ill-assorted couple.

"It is only *au revoir*, Chauvelin," she said pleasantly, "we shall meet at my Lord Grenville's ball, anon."

And in her eyes the astute Frenchman read, no doubt, something which caused him profound satisfaction, for, with a sarcastic smile, he took a delicate pinch of snuff, then, having dusted his dainty lace jabot, he rubbed his thin, bony hands contentedly together.

Chapter 11

Lord Grenville's Ball

*T*he historic ball given by the then Secretary of State for Foreign Affairs—Lord Grenville—was the most brilliant function of the year. Though the autumn season had only just begun, everybody who was anybody had contrived to be in London in time to be present there, and to shine at this ball, to the best of his or her respective ability.

His Royal Highness the Prince of Wales had promised to be present. He was coming on presently from the opera. Lord Grenville himself had listened to the two first acts of *Orpheus*, before preparing to receive his guests. At ten o'clock—an unusually late hour in those days—the grand rooms of the Foreign Office, exquisitely decorated with exotic palms and flowers, were filled to overflowing. One room had been set apart for dancing, and the dainty strains of the minuet made a soft accompaniment to the

gay chatter, the merry laughter of the numerous and brilliant company.

In a smaller chamber, facing the top of the fine stair-
way, the distinguished host stood ready to receive his
guests. Distinguished men, beautiful women, notabilities
from every European country had already filed past him,
had exchanged the elaborate bows and curtsies with him,
which the extravagant fashion of the time demanded, and
then, laughing and talking, had dispersed in the ball,
reception, and card rooms beyond.

Not far from Lord Grenville's elbow, leaning against
one of the console tables, Chauvelin, in his irreproachable
black costume, was taking a quiet survey of the brilliant
throng. He noted that Sir Percy and Lady Blakeney had
not yet arrived, and his keen, pale eyes glanced quickly
towards the door every time a new-comer appeared.

He stood somewhat isolated: the envoy of the Revolutionary Government of France was not likely to be very popular in England, at a time when the news of the awful
September massacres, and of the Reign of Terror and
Anarchy, had just begun to filtrate across the Channel.

In his official capacity he had been received courteously
by his English colleagues: Mr. Pitt had shaken him by the
hand; Lord Grenville had entertained him more than
once; but the more intimate circles of London society
ignored him altogether; the women openly turned their
backs upon him; the men who held no official position
refused to shake his hand.

But Chauvelin was not the man to trouble himself
about these social amenities, which he called mere incidents in his diplomatic career. He was blindly enthusiastic

for the revolutionary cause, he despised all social inequalities, and he had a burning love for his own country: these three sentiments made him supremely indifferent to the snubs he received in this fog-ridden, loyalist, old-fashioned England.

But, above all, Chauvelin had a purpose at heart. He firmly believed that the French aristocrat was the most bitter enemy of France; he would have wished to see every one of them annihilated: he was one of those who, during this awful Reign of Terror, had been the first to utter the historic and ferocious desire "that aristocrats might have but one head between them, so that it might be cut off with a single stroke of the guillotine." And thus he looked upon every French aristocrat, who had succeeded in escaping from France, as so much prey of which the guillotine had been unwarrantably cheated. There is no doubt that those royalist *émigrés*, once they had managed to cross the frontier, did their very best to stir up foreign indignation against France. Plots without end were hatched in England, in Belgium, in Holland, to try and induce some great power to send troops into revolutionary Paris, to free King Louis, and to summarily hang the bloodthirsty leaders of that monster republic.

Small wonder, therefore, that the romantic and mysterious personality of the Scarlet Pimpernel was a source of bitter hatred to Chauvelin. He and the few young jackanapes under his command, well furnished with money, armed with boundless daring and acute cunning, had succeeded in rescuing hundreds of aristocrats from France. Nine-tenths of the *émigrés*, who were *fêted* at the English court, owed their safety to that man and to his league.

Chauvelin had sworn to his colleagues in Paris that he would discover the identity of that meddlesome Englishman, entice him over to France, and then . . . Chauvelin drew a deep breath of satisfaction at the very thought of seeing that enigmatic head falling under the knife of the guillotine, as easily as that of any other man.

Suddenly there was a great stir on the handsome staircase, all conversation stopped for a moment as the major-domo's voice outside announced,—

"His Royal Highness the Prince of Wales and suite, Sir Percy Blakeney, Lady Blakeney."

Lord Grenville went quickly to the door to receive his exalted guest.

The Prince of Wales, dressed in a magnificent court suit of salmon-coloured velvet richly embroidered with gold, entered with Marguerite Blakeney on his arm; and on his left Sir Percy, in gorgeous shimmering cream satin, cut in the extravagant "Incroyable" style, his fair hair free from powder, priceless lace at his neck and wrists, and the flat *chapeau-bras* under his arm.

After the few conventional words of deferential greeting, Lord Grenville said to his royal guest,—

"Will your Highness permit me to introduce M. Chauvelin, the accredited agent of the French Government?"

Chauvelin, immediately the Prince entered, had stepped forward, expecting this introduction. He bowed very low, whilst the Prince returned his salute with a curt nod of the head.

"Monsieur," said His Royal Highness coldly, "we will try to forget the government that sent you, and look upon you merely as our guest—a private gentleman from France. As such you are welcome, Monsieur."

"Monseigneur," rejoined Chauvelin, bowing once again. "Madame," he added, bowing ceremoniously before Marguerite.

"Ah! my little Chauvelin!" she said with unconcerned gaiety, and extending her tiny hand to him. "Monsieur and I are old friends, your Royal Highness."

"Ah, then," said the Prince, this time very graciously, "you are doubly welcome, Monsieur."

"There is someone else I would crave permission to present to your Royal Highness," here interposed Lord Grenville.

"Ah! who is it?" asked the Prince.

"Madame la Comtesse de Tournay de Basserive and her family, who have but recently come from France."

"By all means!—They are among the lucky ones then!" Lord Grenville turned in search of the Comtesse, who sat at the further end of the room.

"Lud love me!" whispered his Royal Highness to Marguerite, as soon as he had caught sight of the rigid figure of the old lady; "Lud love me! she looks very virtuous and very melancholy."

"Faith, your Royal Highness," she rejoined with a smile, "virtue is like precious odours, most fragrant when it is crushed."

"Virtue, alas!" sighed the Prince, "is mostly unbecoming to your charming sex, Madame."

"Madame la Comtesse de Tournay de Basserive," said Lord Grenville, introducing the lady.

"This is a pleasure, Madame; my royal father, as you

know, is ever glad to welcome those of your compatriots whom France has driven from her shores."

"Your Royal Highness is ever gracious," replied the Comtesse with becoming dignity. Then, indicating her daughter, who stood timidly by her side: "My daughter Suzanne, Monseigneur," she said.

"Ah! charming!—charming!" said the Prince, "and now allow me, Comtesse, to introduce to you Lady Blakeney, who honours us with her friendship. You and she will have much to say to one another, I vow. Every compatriot of Lady Blakeney's is doubly welcome for her sake . . . her friends are our friends . . . her enemies, the enemies of England."

Marguerite's blue eyes had twinkled with merriment at this gracious speech from her exalted friend. The Comtesse de Tournay, who lately had so flagrantly insulted her, was here receiving a public lesson, at which Marguerite could not help but rejoice. But the Comtesse, for whom respect of royalty amounted almost to a religion, was too well-schooled in courtly etiquette to show the slightest sign of embarrassment, as the two ladies curtsied ceremoniously to one another.

"His Royal Highness is ever gracious, Madame," said Marguerite, demurely, and with a wealth of mischief in her twinkling blue eyes, "but here there is no need for his kind mediation. . . . Your amiable reception of me at our last meeting still dwells pleasantly in my memory."

"We poor exiles, Madame," rejoined the Comtesse, frigidly, "show our gratitude to England by devotion to the wishes of Monseigneur."

"Madame!" said Marguerite, with another ceremonious curtsey.

"Madame," responded the Comtesse with equal dignity.

The Prince in the meanwhile was saying a few gracious words to the young Vicomte.

"I am happy to know you, Monsieur le Vicomte," he said. "I knew your father well when he was ambassador in London."

"Ah, Monseigneur!" replied the Vicomte, "I was a leetle boy then . . . and now I owe the honour of this meeting to our protector, the Scarlet Pimpernel."

"Hush!" said the Prince, earnestly and quickly, as he indicated Chauvelin, who had stood a little on one side throughout the whole of this little scene, watching Marguerite and the Comtesse with an amused, sarcastic little smile around his thin lips.

"Nay, Monseigneur," he said now, as if in direct response to the Prince's challenge, "pray do not check this gentleman's display of gratitude; the name of that interesting red flower is well known to me—and to France."

The Prince looked at him keenly for a moment or two.

"Faith, then, Monsieur," he said, "perhaps you know more about our national hero than we do ourselves . . . perchance you know who he is. . . . See!" he added, turning to the groups round the room, "the ladies hang upon your lips . . . you would render yourself popular among the fair sex if you were to gratify their curiosity."

"Ah, Monseigneur," said Chauvelin, significantly, "rumour has it in France that your Highness could—and you would—give the truest account of that enigmatical wayside flower."

He looked quickly and keenly at Marguerite as he spoke; but she betrayed no emotion, and her eyes met his quite fearlessly.

"Nay, man," replied the Prince, "my lips are sealed! and the members of the league jealously guard the secret of their chief . . . so his fair adorers have to be content with worshipping a shadow. Here in England, Monsieur," he added, with wonderful charm and dignity, "we but name the Scarlet Pimpernel, and every fair cheek is suffused with a blush of enthusiasm. None have seen him save his faithful lieutenants. We know not if he be tall or short, fair or dark, handsome or ill-formed; but we know that he is the bravest gentleman in all the world, and we all feel a little proud, Monsieur, when we remember that he is an Englishman."

"Ah, Monsieur Chauvelin," added Marguerite, looking almost with defiance across at the placid, sphinx-like face of the Frenchman, "His Royal Highness should add that we ladies think of him as of a hero of old . . . we worship him . . . we wear his badge . . . we tremble for him when he is in danger, and exult with him in the hour of his victory."

Chauvelin did no more than bow placidly both to the Prince and to Marguerite; he felt that both speeches were intended—each in their way—to convey contempt or defiance. The pleasure-loving, idle Prince he despised: the beautiful woman, who in her golden hair wore a spray of small red flowers composed of rubies and diamonds—her he held in the hollow of his hand: he could afford to remain silent and to await events.

A long, jovial, inane laugh broke the sudden silence which had fallen over everyone.

"And we poor husbands," came in slow, affected accents from gorgeous Sir Percy, "we have to stand by . . . while they worship a demmed shadow."

Everyone laughed—the Prince more loudly than anyone. The tension of subdued excitement was relieved, and the next moment everyone was laughing and chatting merrily as the gay crowd broke up and dispersed in the adjoining rooms.

Chapter 12

The Scrap of Paper

*M*arguerite suffered intensely. Though she laughed and chatted, though she was more admired, more surrounded, more *fêted* than any woman there, she felt like one condemned to death, living her last day upon this earth.

Her nerves were in a state of painful tension, which had increased a hundredfold during that brief hour which she had spent in her husband's company, between the opera and the ball. The short ray of hope—that she might find in this good-natured, lazy individual a valuable friend and adviser—had vanished as quickly as it had come, the moment she found herself alone with him. The same feeling of good-humoured contempt which one feels for an animal or a faithful servant, made her turn away with a smile from the man who should have been her moral support in this heart-rending crisis through which she was passing: who should have been her cool-headed adviser,

126

when feminine sympathy and sentiment tossed her hither and thither, between her love for her brother, who was far away and in mortal peril, and horror of the awful service which Chauvelin had exacted from her, in exchange for Armand's safety.

There he stood, the moral support, the cool-headed adviser, surrounded by a crowd of brainless, empty-headed young fops, who were even now repeating from mouth to mouth, and with every sign of the keenest enjoyment, a doggerel couplet which he had just given forth.

Everywhere the absurd, silly words met her: people seemed to have little else to speak about, even the Prince had asked her, with a laugh, whether she appreciated her husband's latest poetic efforts.

"All done in the tying of a cravat," Sir Percy had declared to his clique of admirers.

> "We seek him here, we seek him there,
> Those Frenchies seek him everywhere.
> Is he in heaven?—Is he in hell?
> That demmed, elusive Pimpernel?"

Sir Percy's *bon mot* had gone the round of the brilliant reception-rooms. The Prince was enchanted. He vowed that life without Blakeney would be but a dreary desert. Then, taking him by the arm, had led him to the card-room, and engaged him in a long game of hazard.

Sir Percy, whose chief interest in most social gatherings seemed to centre round the card-table, usually allowed his wife to flirt, dance, to amuse or bore herself as much as she liked. And to-night, having delivered himself of his *bon mot*, he had left Marguerite surrounded by a crowd of admirers of all ages, all anxious and willing to help her to forget that somewhere in the spacious reception-rooms, there was a long, lazy being who had been fool enough to suppose that the cleverest woman in Europe would settle down to the prosaic bonds of English matrimony.

Her still overwrought nerves, her excitement and agitation, lent beautiful Marguerite Blakeney much additional charm: escorted by a veritable bevy of men of all ages and of most nationalities, she called forth many exclamations of admiration from everyone as she passed.

She would not allow herself any more time to think. Her early, somewhat Bohemian training had made her something of a fatalist. She felt that events would shape themselves, that the directing of them was not in her hands. From Chauvelin she knew that she could expect no mercy. He had set a price upon Armand's head, and left it to her to pay or not, as she chose.

Later on in the evening she caught sight of Sir Andrew Ffoulkes and Lord Antony Dewhurst, who seemingly had just arrived. She noticed at once that Sir Andrew immediately made for little Suzanne de Tournay, and that the two young people soon managed to isolate themselves in one of the deep embrasures of the mullioned windows, there to carry on a long conversation, which seemed very earnest and very pleasant on both sides.

Both the young men looked a little haggard and anxious, but otherwise they were irreproachably dressed, and there was not the slightest sign, about their courtly demeanour, of the terrible catastrophe, which they must have felt hovering round them and round their chief.

That the League of the Scarlet Pimpernel had no intention of abandoning its cause, she had gathered through
little Suzanne herself, who spoke openly of the assurance
she and her mother had had that the Comte de Tournay
would be rescued from France by the league, within the
next few days. Vaguely she began to wonder, as she
looked at the brilliant and fashionable crowd in the gaily-
lighted ball-room, which of these worldly men round her
was the mysterious "Scarlet Pimpernel," who held the
threads of such daring plots, and the fate of valuable lives
in his hands.

A burning curiosity seized her to know him: although
for months she had heard of him and had accepted his
anonymity, as everyone else in society had done; but now
she longed to know—quite impersonally, quite apart from
Armand, and oh! quite apart from Chauvelin—only for
her own sake, for the sake of the enthusiastic admiration
she had always bestowed on his bravery and cunning.

He was at the ball, of course, somewhere, since Sir
Andrew Ffoulkes and Lord Antony Dewhurst were here,
evidently expecting to meet their chief—and perhaps to
get a fresh *mot d'ordre* from him.

Marguerite looked round at everyone, at the aristocratic
high-typed Norman faces, the squarely-built, fair-haired
Saxon, the more gentle, humourous caste of the Celt,
wondering which of these betrayed the power, the energy,
the cunning which had imposed its will and its leadership
upon a number of high-born English gentlemen, among
whom rumour asserted was His Royal Highness himself.

Sir Andrew Ffoulkes? Surely not, with his gentle blue
eyes, which were looking so tenderly and longingly after

little Suzanne, who was being led away from the pleasant
tête-à-tête by her stern mother. Marguerite watched him
across the room, as he finally turned away with a sigh, and
seemed to stand, aimless and lonely, now that Suzanne's
dainty little figure had disappeared in the crowd.

She watched him as he strolled towards the doorway,
which led to a small boudoir beyond, then paused and
leaned against the framework of it, looking still anxiously
all round him.

Marguerite contrived for the moment to evade her present attentive cavalier, and she skirted the fashionable
crowd, drawing nearer to the doorway, against which Sir
Andrew was leaning. Why she wished to get closer to him,
she could not have said: perhaps she was impelled by an
all-powerful fatality, which so often seems to rule the
destinies of men.

Suddenly she stopped: her very heart seemed to stand
still, her eyes, large and excited, flashed for a moment
towards that doorway, then as quickly were turned away
again. Sir Andrew Ffoulkes was still in the same listless
position by the door, but Marguerite had distinctly seen
that Lord Hastings—a young buck, a friend of her husband's and one of the Prince's set—had, as he quickly
brushed past him, slipped something into his hand.

For one moment longer—oh! it was the merest flash—
Marguerite paused: the next she had, with admirably played
unconcern, resumed her walk across the room—but this
time more quickly towards that doorway whence Sir Andrew had now disappeared.

All this, from the moment that Marguerite had caught
sight of Sir Andrew leaning against the doorway, until she

followed him into the little boudoir beyond, had occurred in less than a minute. Fate is usually swift when she deals a blow.

Now Lady Blakeney had suddenly ceased to exist. It was Marguerite St. Just who was there only: Marguerite St. Just had passed her childhood, her early youth, in the protecting arms of her brother Armand. She had forgotten everything else—her rank, her dignity, her secret enthusiasms—everything save that Armand stood in peril of his life, and that there, not twenty feet away from her, in the small boudoir which was quite deserted, in the very hands of Sir Andrew Ffoulkes, might be the talisman which would save her brother's life.

Barely another thirty seconds had elapsed between the moment when Lord Hastings slipped the mysterious "something" into Sir Andrew's hand, and the one when she, in her turn, reached the deserted boudoir. Sir Andrew was standing with his back to her and close to a table upon which stood a massive silver candelabra. A slip of paper was in his hand, and he was in the very act of perusing its contents.

Unperceived, her soft clinging robe making not the slightest sound upon the heavy carpet, not daring to breathe until she had accomplished her purpose, Marguerite slipped close behind him. . . . At that moment he looked round and saw her; she uttered a groan, passed her hand across her forehead, and murmured faintly,—

"The heat in the room was terrible . . . I felt so faint . . . Ah! . . ."

She tottered almost as if she would fall, and Sir Andrew, quickly recovering himself, and crumpling in his hand the tiny note he had been reading, was only, apparently, just in time to support her.

"You are ill, Lady Blakeney?" he asked with much concern. "Let me . . ."

"No, no, nothing—" she interrupted quickly. "A chair—quick."

She sank into a chair close to the table, and throwing back her head, closed her eyes.

"There!" she murmured, still faintly; "the giddiness is passing off. . . . Do not heed me, Sir Andrew; I assure you I already feel better."

At moments like these there is no doubt—and psychologists actually assert it—that there is in us a sense which has absolutely nothing to do with the other five: it is not that we see, it is not that we hear or touch, yet we seem to do all three at once. Marguerite sat there with her eyes apparently closed. Sir Andrew was immediately behind her, and on her right was the table with the five-armed candelabra upon it. Before her mental vision there was absolutely nothing but Armand's face. Armand, whose life was in the most imminent danger, and who seemed to be looking at her from a background upon which were dimly painted the seething crowd of Paris, the bare walls of the Tribunal of Public Safety, with Foucquier-Tinville, the Public Prosecutor, demanding Armand's life in the name of the people of France, and the lurid guillotine with its stained knife waiting for another victim . . . Armand! . . .

For one moment there was dead silence in the little boudoir. Beyond, from the brilliant ball-room, the sweet notes of the gavotte, the frou-frou of rich dresses, the talk and laughter of a large and merry crowd, came as a strange, weird accompaniment to the drama which was being enacted here.

Sir Andrew had not uttered another word. Then it was that that extra sense became potent in Marguerite Blakeney. She could not see, for her eyes were closed, she could not hear, for the noise from the ball-room drowned the soft rustle of that momentous scrap of paper; nevertheless she knew—as if she had both seen and heard—that Sir Andrew was even now holding the paper to the flame of one of the candles.

At the exact moment that it began to catch fire, she opened her eyes, raised her hand and, with two dainty fingers had taken the burning scrap of paper from the young man's hand. Then she blew out the flame, and held the paper to her nostril with perfect unconcern.

"How thoughtful of you, Sir Andrew," she said gaily, "surely 'twas your grandmother who taught you that the smell of burnt paper was a sovereign remedy against giddiness."

She sighed with satisfaction, holding the paper tightly between her jewelled fingers; that talisman which perhaps would save her brother Armand's life. Sir Andrew was staring at her, too dazed for the moment to realise what had actually happened; he had been taken so completely by surprise, that he seemed quite unable to grasp the fact that the slip of paper, which she held in her dainty hand, was one perhaps on which the life of his comrade might depend.

Marguerite burst into a long, merry peal of laughter.

"Why do you stare at me like that?" she said playfully. "I assure you I feel much better; your remedy has proved most effectual. This room is most delightfully cool," she added, with the same perfect composure, "and the sound of the gavotte from the ball-room is fascinating and soothing."

She was prattling on in the most unconcerned and pleasant way, whilst Sir Andrew, in an agony of mind, was racking his brains as to the quickest method he could employ, to get that bit of paper out of that beautiful woman's hand. Instinctively, vague and tumultuous thoughts rushed through his mind: he suddenly remembered her nationality, and worst of all, recollected that horrible tale anent the Marquis de St. Cyr, which in England no one had credited, for the sake of Sir Percy, as well as for her own.

"What? Still dreaming and staring?" she said, with a merry laugh, "you are most ungallant, Sir Andrew; and now I come to think of it, you seemed more startled than pleased when you saw me just now. I do believe, after all, that it was not concern for my health, nor yet a remedy taught you by your grandmother that caused you to burn this tiny scrap of paper. . . . I vow it must have been your lady love's last cruel epistle you were trying to destroy. Now confess!" she added, playfully holding up the scrap of paper, "does this contain her final *congé*, or a last appeal to kiss and make friends?"

"Whichever it is, Lady Blakeney," said Sir Andrew, who was gradually recovering his self-possession, "this little note is undoubtedly mine, and . . ."

Not caring whether his action was one that would be styled ill-bred towards a lady, the young man had made a bold dash for the note; but Marguerite's thoughts flew

quicker than his own; her actions, under pressure of this
intense excitement, were swifter and more sure. She was
tall and strong; she took a quick step backwards and
knocked over the small Sheraton table which was already
top-heavy, and which fell down with a crash, together
with the massive candelabra upon it.

She gave a quick cry of alarm:

"The candles, Sir Andrew—quick!"

There was not much damage done; one or two of the
candles had blown out as the candelabra fell; others had
merely sent some grease upon the valuable carpet; one had
ignited the paper shade over it. Sir Andrew quickly and
dexterously put out the flames and replaced the candelabra
upon the table; but this had taken him a few seconds to
do, and those seconds had been all that Marguerite needed
to cast a quick glance at the paper, and to note its
contents—a dozen words in the same distorted handwriting she had seen before, and bearing the same device—a
star-shaped flower drawn in red ink.

When Sir Andrew once more looked at her, he only saw
on her face alarm at the untoward accident and relief at its
happy issue; whilst the tiny and momentous note had
apparently fluttered to the ground. Eagerly the young man
picked it up, and his face looked much relieved, as his
fingers closed tightly over it.

"For shame, Sir Andrew," she said, shaking her head
with a playful sigh, "making havoc in the heart of some
impressionable duchess, whilst conquering the affections
of my sweet little Suzanne. Well, well! I do believe it was
Cupid himself who stood by you, and threatened the
entire Foreign Office with destruction by fire, just on

purpose to make me drop love's message, before it had been polluted by my indiscreet eyes. To think that, a moment longer, and I might have known the secrets of an erring duchess."

"You will forgive me, Lady Blakeney," said Sir Andrew, now as calm as she was herself, "if I resume the interesting occupation which you had interrupted?"

"By all means, Sir Andrew! How should I venture to thwart the love-god again? Perhaps he would' mete out some terrible chastisement against my presumption. Burn your love-token, by all means!"

Sir Andrew had already twisted the paper into a long spill, and was once again holding it to the flame of the candle, which had remained alight. He did not notice the strange smile on the face of his fair *vis-à-vis*, so intent was he on the work of destruction; perhaps, had he done so, the look of relief would have faded from his face. He watched the fateful note, as it curled under the flame. Soon the last fragment fell on the floor, and he placed his heel upon the ashes.

"And now, Sir Andrew," said Marguerite Blakeney, with the pretty nonchalance peculiar to herself, and with the most winning of smiles, "will you venture to excite the jealousy of your fair lady by asking me to dance the minuet?"

Chapter 13

Either—Or?

*T*he few words which Marguerite Blakeney had managed to read on the half-scorched piece of paper, seemed literally to be the words of Fate. "Start myself to-morrow. . . ." This she had read quite distinctly; then came a blur caused by the smoke of the candle, which obliterated the next few words; but, right at the bottom, there was another sentence, which was now standing clearly and distinctly, like letters of fire, before her mental vision. "If you wish to speak to me again I shall be in the supper-room at one o'clock precisely." The whole was signed with the hastily-scrawled little device—a tiny star-shaped flower, which had become so familiar to her.

One o'clock precisely! It was now close upon eleven, the last minuet was being danced, with Sir Andrew Ffoulkes and beautiful Lady Blakeney leading the couples, through its delicate and intricate figures.

Close upon eleven! the hands of the handsome Louis
XV clock upon its ormolu bracket seemed to move along
with maddening rapidity. Two hours more, and her fate
and that of Armand would be sealed. In two hours she
must make up her mind whether she will keep the knowledge so cunningly gained to herself, and leave her brother
to his fate, or whether she will wilfully betray a brave
man, whose life was devoted to his fellow-men, who was
noble, generous, and above all, unsuspecting. It seemed a
horrible thing to do. But then, there was Armand! Armand, too, was noble and brave, Armand, too, was unsuspecting. And Armand loved her, would have willingly
trusted his life in her hands, and now, when she could
save him from death, she hesitated. Oh! it was monstrous;
her brother's kind, gentle face, so full of love for her,
seemed to be looking reproachfully at her. "You might
have saved me, Margot!" he seemed to say to her, "and
you chose the life of a stranger, a man you do not know,
whom you have never seen, and preferred that he should
be safe, whilst you sent me to the guillotine!"

All these conflicting thoughts raged through Marguerite's brain, while, with a smile upon her lips, she glided
through the graceful mazes of the minuet. She noted—
with that acute sense of hers—that she had succeeded in
completely allaying Sir Andrew's fears. Her self-control
had been absolutely perfect—she was a finer actress at this
moment, and throughout the whole of this minuet, than
she had ever been upon the boards of the Comédie
Française; but then, a beloved brother's life had not depended upon her histrionic powers.

She was too clever to overdo her part, and made no

further allusions to the supposed *billet doux,* which had
caused Sir Andrew Ffoulkes such an agonising five minutes. She watched his anxiety melting away under her
sunny smile, and soon perceived that, whatever doubt
may have crossed his mind at the moment, she had, by
the time the last bars of the minuet had been played,
succeeded in completely dispelling it; he never realised in
what a fever of excitement she was, what effort it cost her
to keep up a constant ripple of *banal* conversation.

When the minuet was over, she asked Sir Andrew to
take her into the next room.

"I have promised to go down to supper with His Royal
Highness," she said, "but before we part, tell me . . . am I
forgiven?"

"Forgiven?"

"Yes! Confess, I gave you a fright just now. . . . But,
remember, I am not an Englishwoman, and I do not look
upon the exchanging of *billet doux* as a crime, and I vow
I'll not tell my little Suzanne. But now, tell me, shall I
welcome you at my water-party on Wednesday?"

"I am not sure, Lady Blakeney," he replied evasively. "I
may have to leave London to-morrow."

"I would not do that, if I were you," she said earnestly;
then seeing the anxious look once more reappearing in his
eyes, she added gaily; "No one can throw a ball better
than you can, Sir Andrew, we should so miss you on the
bowling-green."

He had led her across the room, to one beyond, where
already His Royal Highness was waiting for the beautiful
Lady Blakeney.

"Madame, supper awaits us," said the Prince, offering

his arm to Marguerite, "and I am full of hope. The goddess Fortune has frowned so persistently on me at hazard, that I look with confidence for the smiles of the goddess of Beauty."

"Your Highness has been unfortunate at the card tables?" asked Marguerite, as she took the Prince's arm.

"Aye! most unfortunate. Blakeney, not content with being the richest among my father's subjects, has also the most outrageous luck. By the way, where is that inimitable wit? I vow, Madam, that this life would be but a dreary desert without your smiles and his sallies."

Chapter 14

One o'Clock Precisely!

*S*upper had been extremely gay. All those present declared that never had Lady Blakeney been more adorable, nor that "demmed idiot" Sir Percy more amusing.

His Royal Highness had laughed until the tears streamed down his cheeks at Blakeney's foolish yet funny repartees. His doggerel verse, "We seek him here, we seek him there," etc., was sung to the tune of "Ho! Merry Britons!" and to the accompaniment of glasses knocked loudly against the table. Lord Grenville, moreover, had a most perfect cook—some wags asserted that he was a scion of the old French *noblesse*, who having lost his fortune, had come to seek it in the *cuisine* of the Foreign Office.

Marguerite Blakeney was in her most brilliant mood, and surely not a soul in that crowded supper-room had even an inkling of the terrible struggle which was raging within her heart.

The clock was ticking so mercilessly on. It was long past midnight, and even the Prince of Wales was thinking of leaving the supper-table. Within the next half-hour the destinies of two brave men would be pitted against one another—the dearly-beloved brother and he, the un-known hero.

Marguerite had not even tried to see Chauvelin during this last hour; she knew that his keen, fox-like eyes would terrify her at once, and incline the balance of her decision towards Armand. Whilst she did not see him, there still lingered in her heart of hearts a vague, undefined hope that "something" would occur, something big, enormous, epoch-making, which would shift from her young, weak shoulders this terrible burden of responsibility, of having to choose between two such cruel alternatives.

But the minutes ticked on with that dull monotony which they invariably seem to assume when our very nerves ache with their incessant ticking.

After supper, dancing was resumed. His Royal Highness had left, and there was general talk of departing among the older guests; the young ones were indefatigable and had started on a new gavotte, which would fill the next quarter of an hour.

Marguerite did not feel equal to another dance; there is a limit to the most enduring self-control. Escorted by a Cabinet Minister, she had once more found her way to the tiny boudoir, still the most deserted among all the rooms. She knew that Chauvelin must be lying in wait for her somewhere, ready to seize the first possible opportu-nity for a *tête-à-tête*. His eyes had met hers for a moment after the 'fore-supper minuet, and she knew that the keen diplomatist, with those searching pale eyes of his, had divined that her work was accomplished.

Fate had willed it so. Marguerite, torn by the most terrible conflict heart of woman can ever know, had resigned herself to its decrees. But Armand must be saved at any cost; he, first of all, for he was her brother, had been mother, father, friend to her ever since she, a tiny babe, had lost both her parents. To think of Armand dying a traitor's death on the guillotine was too horrible even to dwell upon—impossible, in fact. That could never be, never. . . . As for the stranger, the hero . . . well! there, let Fate decide. Marguerite would redeem her brother's life at the hands of the relentless enemy, then let that cunning Scarlet Pimpernel extricate himself after that.

Perhaps—vaguely—Marguerite hoped that the daring plotter, who for so many months had baffled an army of spies, would still manage to evade Chauvelin and remain immune to the end.

She thought of all this, as she sat listening to the witty discourse of the Cabinet Minister, who, no doubt, felt that he had found in Lady Blakeney a most perfect listener. Suddenly she saw the keen, fox-like face of Chauvelin peeping through the curtained doorway.

"Lord Fancourt," she said to the Minister, "will you do me a service?"

"I am entirely at your ladyship's service," he replied gallantly.

"Will you see if my husband is still in the card-room? And if he is, will you tell him that I am very tired, and would be glad to go home soon."

The commands of a beautiful woman are binding on all

mankind, even on Cabinet Ministers. Lord Fancourt prepared to obey instantly.

"I do not like to leave your ladyship alone," he said.

"Never fear. I shall be quite safe here—and, I think, undisturbed . . . but I am really tired. You know Sir Percy will drive back to Richmond. It is a long way, and we shall not—an we do not hurry—get home before daybreak."

Lord Fancourt had perforce to go.

The moment he had disappeared, Chauvelin slipped into the room, and the next instant stood calm and impassive by her side.

"You have news for me?" he said.

An icy mantle seemed to have suddenly settled round Marguerite's shoulders; though her cheeks glowed with fire, she felt chilled and numbed. Oh, Armand! will you ever know the terrible sacrifice of pride, of dignity, of womanliness a devoted sister is making for your sake?

"Nothing of importance," she said, staring mechanically before her, "but it might prove a clue. I contrived—no matter how—to detect Sir Andrew Ffoulkes in the very act of burning a paper at one of these candles, in this very room. That paper I succeeded in holding between my fingers for the space of two minutes, and to cast my eye on it for that of ten seconds."

"Time enough to learn its contents?" asked Chauvelin, quietly.

She nodded. Then she continued in the same even, mechanical tone of voice—

"In the corner of the paper there was the usual rough device of a small star-shaped flower. Above it I read two lines, everything else was scorched and blackened by the flame."

"And what were these two lines?"

Her throat seemed suddenly to have contracted. For an instant she felt that she could not speak the words, which might send a brave man to his death.

"It is lucky that the whole paper was not burned," added Chauvelin, with dry sarcasm, "for it might have fared ill with Armand St. Just. What were the two lines, citoyenne?"

"One was, 'I start myself to-morrow,' " she said quietly; "the other—'If you wish to speak to me, I shall be in the supper-room at one o'clock precisely.' "

Chauvelin looked up at the clock just above the mantel-piece.

"Then I have plenty of time," he said placidly.

"What are you going to do?" she asked.

She was pale as a statue, her hands were icy cold, her head and heart throbbed with the awful strain upon her nerves. Oh, this was cruel! cruel! What had she done to have deserved all this? Her choice was made: had she done a vile action or one that was sublime? The recording angel, who writes in the book of gold, alone could give an answer.

"What are you going to do?" she repeated mechanically.

"Oh, nothing for the present. After that it will depend."

"On what?"

"On whom I shall see in the supper-room at one o'clock precisely."

"You will see the Scarlet Pimpernel, of course. But you do not know him."

"No. But I shall presently."

"Sir Andrew will have warned him."

"I think not. When you parted from him after the minuet he stood and watched you, for a moment or two, with a look which gave me to understand that something had happened between you. It was only natural, was it not? that I should make a shrewd guess as to the nature of that 'something.' I thereupon engaged the young gallant in a long and animated conversation—we discussed Herr Glück's singular success in London—until a lady claimed his arm for supper."

"Since then?"

"I did not lose sight of him through supper. When we all came upstairs again, Lady Portarles buttonholed him and started on the subject of pretty Mlle. Suzanne de Tournay. I knew he would not move until Lady Portarles had exhausted the subject, which will not be for another quarter of an hour at least, and it is five minutes to one now."

He was preparing to go, and went up to the doorway, where, drawing aside the curtain, he stood for a moment pointing out to Marguerite the distant figure of Sir Andrew Ffoulkes in close conversation with Lady Portarles.

"I think," he said, with a triumphant smile, "that I may safely expect to find the person I seek in the dining-room, fair lady."

"There may be more than one."

"Whoever is there, as the clock strikes one, will be shadowed by one of my men; of these, one, or perhaps two, or even three, will leave for France to-morrow. *One* of these will be the 'Scarlet Pimpernel.' "

"Yes?—And?"

"I also, fair lady, will leave for France to-morrow. The papers found at Dover upon the person of Sir Andrew Ffoulkes, speak of the neighborhood of Calais, of an inn which I know well, called 'Le Chat Gris,' of a lonely place somewhere on the coast—the Père Blanchard's hut—which I must endeavour to find. All these places are given as the point, where this meddlesome Englishman has bidden the traitor de Tournay and others to meet his emissaries. But it seems that he has decided not to send his emissaries, that 'he will start himself to-morrow.' Now, one of those persons whom I shall see anon in the supper-room, will be journeying to Calais, and I shall follow that person, until I have tracked him to where those fugitive aristocrats await him; for that person, fair lady, will be the man whom I have sought for, for nearly a year, the man whose energy has outdone me, whose ingenuity has baffled me, whose audacity has set me wondering—yes! me!—who have seen a trick or two in my time—the mysterious and elusive Scarlet Pimpernel."

"And Armand?" she pleaded.

"Have I ever broken my word? I promise you that the day the Scarlet Pimpernel and I start for France, I will send you that imprudent letter of his by special courier. More than that, I will pledge you the word of France, that the day I lay hands on that meddlesome Englishman, St. Just will be here in England, safe in the arms of his charming sister."

And with a deep and elaborate bow and another look at the clock, Chauvelin glided out of the room.

It seemed to Marguerite that through all the noise, all the din of music, dancing, and laughter, she could hear his cat-like tread, gliding through the vast reception-rooms; that she could hear him go down the massive staircase, reach the dining-room and open the door. Fate *had* decided, had made her speak, had made her do a vile and abominable thing, for the sake of the brother she loved. She lay back in her chair, passive and still, seeing the figure of her relentless enemy ever present before her aching eyes.

When Chauvelin reached the supper-room it was quite deserted. It had that woebegone, forsaken, tawdry appearance, which reminds one so much of a ball-dress, the morning after.

Half-empty glasses littered the table, unfolded napkins lay about, the chairs—turned towards one another in groups of twos and threes—seemed like the seats of ghosts, in close conversation with one another. There were sets of two chairs—very close to one another—in the far corners of the room, which spoke of recent whispered flirtations, over cold game-pie and champagne; there were sets of three and four chairs, that recalled pleasant, animated discussions over the latest scandal; there were chairs straight up in a row that still looked starchy, critical, acid, like antiquated dowagers; there were a few isolated, single chairs, close to the table, that spoke of gourmands intent on the most *recherché* dishes, and others overturned on the floor, that spoke volumes on the subject of my Lord Grenville's cellars.

It was a ghostlike replica, in fact, of that fashionable gathering upstairs; a ghost that haunts every house, where balls and good suppers are given; a picture drawn with white chalk on grey cardboard, dull and colourless, now that the bright silk dresses and gorgeously embroidered coats were no longer there to fill in the foreground, and now that the candles flickered sleepily in their sockets.

Chauvelin smiled benignly, and rubbing his long, thin hands together, he looked round the deserted supper-room, whence even the last flunkey had retired in order to join his friends in the hall below. All was silence in the dimly-lighted room, whilst the sound of the gavotte, the hum of distant talk and laughter, and the rumble of an occasional coach outside, only seemed to reach this palace of the Sleeping Beauty as the murmur of some flitting spooks far away.

It all looked so peaceful, so luxurious, and so still, that the keenest observer—a veritable prophet—could never have guessed that, at this present moment, that deserted supper-room was nothing but a trap laid for the capture of the most cunning and audacious plotter, those stirring times had ever seen.

Chauvelin pondered and tried to peer into the immediate future. What would this man be like, whom he and the leaders of a whole revolution had sworn to bring to his death? Everything about him was weird and mysterious; his personality, which he had so cunningly concealed, the power he wielded over nineteen English gentlemen who seemed to obey his every command blindly and enthusiastically, the passionate love and submission he had roused in his little trained band, and, above all, his marvellous audacity, the boundless impudence which had caused him to beard his most implacable enemies, within the very walls of Paris.

No wonder that in France the *sobriquet* of the mysterious Englishman roused in the people a superstitious shudder. Chauvelin himself as he gazed round the deserted room, where presently the weird hero would appear, felt a strange feeling of awe creeping all down his spine.

But his plans were well laid. He felt sure that the Scarlet Pimpernel had not been warned, and felt equally sure that Marguerite Blakeney had not played him false. If she had . . . a cruel look, that would have made her shudder, gleamed in Chauvelin's keen, pale eyes. If she had played him a trick, Armand St. Just would suffer the extreme penalty.

But no, no! of course she had not played him false!

Fortunately the supper-room was deserted: this would make Chauvelin's task all the easier, when presently that unsuspecting enigma would enter it alone. No one was here now save Chauvelin himself.

Stay! as he surveyed with a satisfied smile the solitude of the room, the cunning agent of the French Government became aware of the peaceful, monotonous breathing of some one of my Lord Grenville's guests, who, no doubt, had supped both wisely and well, and was enjoying a quiet sleep, away from the din of the dancing above.

Chauvelin looked round once more, and there in the corner of a sofa, in the dark angle of the room, his mouth open, his eyes shut, the sweet sounds of peaceful slumbers proceeding from his nostrils, reclined the gorgeously-apparelled, long-limbed husband of the cleverest woman in Europe.

Chauvelin looked at him as he lay there, placid, unconscious, at peace with all the world and himself, after the best of suppers, and a smile, that was almost one of pity, softened for a moment the hard lines of the Frenchman's face and the sarcastic twinkle of his pale eyes.

Evidently the slumberer, deep in dreamless sleep, would not interfere with Chauvelin's trap for catching that cunning Scarlet Pimpernel. Again he rubbed his hands together, and, following the example of Sir Percy Blakeney, he, too, stretched himself out in the corner of another sofa, shut his eyes, opened his mouth, gave forth sounds of peaceful breathing, and . . . waited!

Chapter 15

Doubt

*M*arguerite Blakeney had watched the slight sable-clad figure of Chauvelin, as he worked his way through the ball-room. Then perforce she had had to wait, while her nerves tingled with excitement.

Listlessly she sat in the small, still deserted boudoir, looking out through the curtained doorway on the dancing couples beyond: looking at them, yet seeing nothing, hearing the music, yet conscious of naught save a feeling of expectancy, of anxious, weary waiting.

Her mind conjured up before her the vision of what was, perhaps at this very moment, passing downstairs. The half-deserted dining-room, the fateful hour— Chauvelin on the watch!—then, precise to the moment, the entrance of a man, he, the Scarlet Pimpernel, the mysterious leader, who to Marguerite had become almost unreal, so strange, so weird was this hidden identity.

She wished she were in the supper-room, too, at this moment, watching him as he entered; she knew that her woman's penetration would at once recognise in the stranger's face—whoever he might be—that strong individuality which belongs to a leader of men—to a hero: to the mighty, high-soaring eagle, whose daring wings were becoming entangled in the ferret's trap.

Woman-like, she thought of him with unmixed sadness; the irony of that fate seemed so cruel which allowed the fearless lion to succumb to the gnawing of a rat! Ah! had Armand's life not been at stake! . . .

"Faith! your ladyship must have thought me very remiss," said a voice suddenly, close to her elbow. "I had a deal of difficulty in delivering your message, for I could not find Blakeney anywhere at first . . ."

Marguerite had forgotten all about her husband and her message to him; his very name, as spoken by Lord Fancourt, sounded strange and unfamiliar to her, so completely had she in the last five minutes lived her old life in the Rue de Richelieu again, with Armand always near her to love and protect her, to guard her from the many subtle intrigues which were forever raging in Paris in those days.

"I did find him at last," continued Lord Fancourt, "and gave him your message. He said that he would give orders at once for the horses to be put to."

"Ah!" she said, still very absently, "you found my husband, and gave him my message?"

"Yes; he was in the dining-room fast asleep. I could not manage to wake him up at first."

"Thank you very much," she said mechanically, trying to collect her thoughts.

"Will your ladyship honour me with the *contredanse* until your coach is ready?" asked Lord Fancourt.

"No, I thank you, my lord, but—and you will forgive me—I really am too tired, and the heat in the ball-room has become oppressive."

"The conservatory is deliciously cool; let me take you there, and then get you something. You seem ailing, Lady Blakeney."

"I am only very tired," she repeated wearily, as she allowed Lord Fancourt to lead her, where subdued lights and green plants lent coolness to the air. He got her a chair, into which she sank. This long interval of waiting was intolerable. Why did not Chauvelin come and tell her the result of his watch?

Lord Fancourt was very attentive. She scarcely heard what he said, and suddenly startled him by asking abruptly,—

"Lord Fancourt, did you perceive who was in the dining-room just now besides Sir Percy Blakeney?"

"Only the agent of the French Government, M. Chauvelin, equally fast asleep in another corner," he said. "Why does your ladyship ask?"

"I know not . . . I . . . Did you notice the time when you were there?"

"It must have been about five or ten minutes past one. . . . I wonder what your ladyship is thinking about," he added, for evidently the fair lady's thoughts were very far away, and she had not been listening to his intellectual conversation.

But indeed her thoughts were not very far away; only one storey below, in this same house, in the dining-room where sat Chauvelin still on the watch. Had he failed? For one instant that possibility rose before her as a hope—the hope that the Scarlet Pimpernel had been warned by Sir Andrew, and that Chauvelin's trap had failed to catch his bird; but that hope soon gave way to fear. Had he failed? But then—Armand!

Lord Fancourt had given up talking since he found that he had no listener. He wanted an opportunity for slipping away: for sitting opposite to a lady, however fair, who is evidently not heeding the most vigorous efforts made for her entertainment, is not exhilarating, even to a Cabinet Minister.

"Shall I find out if your ladyship's coach is ready," he said at last, tentatively.

"Oh, thank you . . . thank you . . . if you would be so kind . . . I fear I am but sorry company . . . but I am really tired . . . and, perhaps, would be best alone."

She had been longing to be rid of him, for she hoped that, like the fox he so resembled, Chauvelin would be prowling round, thinking to find her alone.

But Lord Fancourt went, and still Chauvelin did not come. Oh! what had happened? She felt Armand's fate trembling in the balance . . . she feared—now with a deadly fear—that Chauvelin *had* failed, and that the mysterious Scarlet Pimpernel had proved elusive once more; then she knew that she need hope for no pity, no mercy, from him.

He had pronounced his "Either—or—" and nothing less would content him: he was very spiteful, and would affect the belief that she had wilfully misled him, and having failed to trap the eagle once again, his revengeful mind would be content with the humble prey—Armand!

Yet she had done her best; had strained every nerve for Armand's sake. She could not bear to think that all had failed. She could not sit still; she wanted to go and hear the worst at once; she wondered even that Chauvelin had not come yet, to vent his wrath and satire upon her.

Lord Grenville himself came presently to tell her that her coach was ready, and that Sir Percy was already waiting for her—ribbons in hand. Marguerite said "Farewell" to her distinguished host; many of her friends stopped her, as she crossed the rooms, to talk to her, and exchange pleasant *au revoirs*.

The Minister only took final leave of beautiful Lady Blakeney on the top of the stairs; below, on the landing, a veritable army of gallant gentlemen were waiting to bid "Good-bye" to the queen of beauty and fashion, whilst outside, under the massive portico, Sir Percy's magnificent bays were impatiently pawing the ground.

At the top of the stairs, just after she had taken final leave of her host, she suddenly saw Chauvelin; he was coming up the stairs slowly, and rubbing his thin hands very softly together.

There was a curious look on his mobile face, partly amused and wholly puzzled, and as his keen eyes met Marguerite's they became strangely sarcastic.

"M. Chauvelin," she said, as he stopped on the top of the stairs, bowing elaborately before her, "my coach is outside; may I claim your arm?"

As gallant as ever, he offered her his arm and led her downstairs. The crowd was very great, some of the Minister's guests were departing, others were leaning against the banisters watching the throng as it filed up and down the wide staircase.

"Chauvelin," she said at last desperately, "I must know what has happened."

"What has happened, dear lady?" he said, with affected surprise. "Where? When?"

"You are torturing me, Chauvelin. I have helped you to-night . . . surely I have the right to know. What happened in the dining-room at one o'clock just now?"

She spoke in a whisper, trusting that in the general hubbub of the crowd her words would remain unheeded by all, save the man at her side.

"Quiet and peace reigned supreme, fair lady; at that hour I was asleep in the corner of one sofa and Sir Percy Blakeney in another."

"Nobody came into the room at all?"

"Nobody."

"Then we have failed, you and I? . . ."

"Yes! we have failed—perhaps . . ."

"But, Armand?" she pleaded.

"Ah! Armand St. Just's chances hang on a thread . . . pray heaven, dear lady, that that thread may not snap."

"Chauvelin, I worked for you, sincerely, earnestly . . . remember. . . ."

"I remember my promise," he said quietly; "the day that the Scarlet Pimpernel and I meet on French soil, St. Just will be in the arms of his charming sister."

"Which means that a brave man's blood will be on my hands," she said, with a shudder.

"His blood, or that of your brother. Surely at the present moment you must hope, as I do, that the enigmatical Scarlet Pimpernel will start for Calais to-day—"

"I am only conscious of one hope, citoyen."

"And that is?"

"That Satan, your master, will have need of you, else-where, before the sun rises to-day."

"You flatter me, citoyenne."

She had detained him for a while, mid-way down the stairs, trying to get at the thoughts which lay beyond that thin, fox-like mask. But Chauvelin remained urbane, sar-castic, mysterious; not a line betrayed to the poor, anxious woman whether she need fear or whether she dared to hope.

Downstairs on the landing she was soon surrounded. Lady Blakeney never stepped from any house into her coach, without an escort of fluttering human moths around the dazzling light of her beauty. But before she finally turned away from Chauvelin, she held out a tiny hand to him, with that pretty gesture of childish appeal which was so essentially her own.

"Give me some hope, my little Chauvelin," she pleaded.

With perfect gallantry he bowed over that tiny hand, which looked so dainty and white through the delicately transparent black lace mitten, and kissing the tips of the rosy fingers:—

"Pray heaven that the thread may not snap," he re-peated, with his enigmatic smile.

And stepping aside, he allowed the moths to flutter more closely round the candle, and the brilliant throng of the *jeunesse dorée*, eagerly attentive to Lady Blakeney's every movement, hid the keen, fox-like face from her view.

Chapter 16

Richmond

A few minutes later she was sitting, wrapped in cozy furs, near Sir Percy Blakeney on the box-seat of his magnificent coach, and the four splendid bays had thundered down the quiet street.

The night was warm in spite of the gentle breeze which fanned Marguerite's burning cheeks. Soon London houses were left behind, and rattling over old Hammersmith Bridge, Sir Percy was driving his bays rapidly towards Richmond.

The river wound in and out in its pretty delicate curves, looking like a silver serpent beneath the glittering rays of the moon. Long shadows from overhanging trees spread occasional deep palls right across the road. The bays were rushing along at breakneck speed, held but slightly back by Sir Percy's strong, unerring hands.

These nightly drives after balls and suppers in London

were a source of perpetual delight to Marguerite, and she appreciated her husband's eccentricity keenly, which caused him to adopt this mode of taking her home every night, to their beautiful home by the river, instead of living in a stuffy London house. He loved driving his spirited horses along the lonely, moonlit roads, and she loved to sit on the box-seat, with the soft air of an English late summer's night fanning her face after the hot atmosphere of a ball or supper-party. The drive was not a long one—less than an hour, sometimes, when the bays were very fresh, and Sir Percy gave them full rein.

To-night he seemed to have a very devil in his fingers, and the coach seemed to fly along the road, beside the river. As usual, he did not speak to her, but stared straight in front of him, the ribbons seeming to lie quite loosely in his slender, white hands. Marguerite looked at him tentatively once or twice; she could see his handsome profile, and one lazy eye, with its straight fine brow and drooping heavy lid.

The face in the moonlight looked singularly earnest, and recalled to Marguerite's aching heart those happy days of courtship, before he had become the lazy nincompoop, the effete fop, whose life seemed spent in card and supper rooms.

But now, in the moonlight, she could not catch the expression of the lazy blue eyes; she could only see the outline of the firm chin, the corner of the strong mouth, the well-cut massive shape of the forehead; truly, nature had meant well by Sir Percy; his faults must all be laid at the door of that poor, half-crazy mother, and of the distracted heart-broken father, neither of whom had cared for the young life, which was sprouting up between them, and which, perhaps, their very carelessness was already beginning to wreck.

Marguerite suddenly felt intense sympathy for her husband. The moral crisis she had just gone through made her feel indulgent towards the faults, the delinquencies, of others.

How thoroughly a human being can be buffeted and overmastered by Fate, had been borne in upon her with appalling force. Had anyone told her a week ago that she would stoop to spy upon her friends, that she would betray a brave and unsuspecting man into the hands of a relentless enemy, she would have laughed the idea to scorn.

Yet she had done these things; anon, perhaps the death of that brave man would be at her door, just as two years ago the Marquis de St. Cyr had perished through a thoughtless word of hers; but in that case she was morally innocent—she had meant no serious harm—fate merely had stepped in. But this time she had done a thing that obviously was base, had done it deliberately, for a motive which, perhaps, high moralists would not even appreciate.

And as she felt her husband's strong arm beside her, she also felt how much more he would dislike and despise her, if he knew of this night's work. Thus human beings judge of one another, superficially, casually, throwing contempt on one another, with but little reason, and no charity. She despised her husband for his inanities and vulgar, unintellectual occupations; and he, she felt, would despise her still worse, because she had not been strong enough to do right for right's sake, and to sacrifice her brother to the dictates of her conscience.

Buried in her thoughts, Marguerite had found this hour in the breezy summer night all too brief; and it was with a feeling of keen disappointment, that she suddenly realized that the bays had turned into the massive gates of her beautiful English home.

Sir Percy Blakeney's house on the river has become a historic one: palatial in its dimensions, it stands in the midst of exquisitely laid-out gardens, with a picturesque terrace and frontage to the river. Built in Tudor days, the old red brick of the walls looks eminently picturesque in the midst of a bower of green, the beautiful lawn, with its old sun-dial, adding the true note of harmony to its foreground. Great secular trees lent cool shadows to the grounds, and now, on this warm early autumn night, the leaves slightly turned to russets and gold, the old garden looked singularly poetic and peaceful in the moonlight.

With unerring precision, Sir Percy had brought the four bays to a standstill immediately in front of the fine Elizabethan entrance hall; in spite of the lateness of the hour, an army of grooms seemed to have emerged from the very ground, as the coach had thundered up, and were standing respectfully round.

Sir Percy jumped down quickly, then helped Marguerite to alight. She lingered outside for a moment, whilst he gave a few orders to one of his men. She skirted the house, and stepped on to the lawn, looking out dreamily into the silvery landscape. Nature seemed exquisitely at peace, in comparison with the tumultuous emotions she had gone through: she could faintly hear the ripple of the river and the occasional soft and ghostlike fall of a dead leaf from a tree.

All else was quiet round her. She had heard the horses prancing as they were being led away to their distant stables, the hurrying of servants' feet as they had all gone within to rest: the house also was quite still. In two separate suites of apartments, just above the magnificent reception-rooms, lights were still burning; they were her rooms, and his, well divided from each other by the whole width of the house, as far apart as their own lives had become. Involuntarily she sighed—at that moment she could really not have told why.

She was suffering from unconquerable heartache. Deeply and achingly she was sorry for herself. Never had she felt so pitiably lonely, so bitterly in want of comfort and of sympathy. With another sigh she turned away from the river towards the house, vaguely wondering if, after such a night, she could ever find rest and sleep.

Suddenly, before she reached the terrace, she heard a firm step upon the crisp gravel, and the next moment her husband's figure emerged out of the shadow. He, too, had skirted the house, and was wandering along the lawn, towards the river. He still wore his heavy driving coat with the numerous lapels and collars he himself had set in fashion, but he had thrown it well back, burying his hands as was his wont, in the deep pockets of his satin breeches: the gorgeous white costume he had worn at Lord Grenville's ball, with its jabot of priceless lace, looked strangely ghostly against the dark background of the house.

He apparently did not notice her, for, after a few moments pause, he presently turned back towards the house, and walked straight up to the terrace.

"Sir Percy!"

He already had one foot on the lowest of the terrace steps, but at her voice he started, and paused, then looked searchingly into the shadows whence she had called to him.

She came forward quickly into the moonlight, and, as soon as he saw her, he said, with that air of consummate gallantry he always wore when speaking to her,—

"At your service, Madame!"

But his foot was still on the step, and in his whole attitude there was a remote suggestion, distinctly visible to her, that he wished to go, and had no desire for a midnight interview.

"The air is deliciously cool," she said, "the moonlight peaceful and poetic, and the garden inviting. Will you not stay in it awhile; the hour is not yet late, or is my company so distasteful to you, that you are in a hurry to rid yourself of it?"

"Nay, Madame," he rejoined placidly, "but 'tis on the other foot the shoe happens to be, and I'll warrant you'll find the midnight air more poetic without my company: no doubt the sooner I remove the obstruction the better your ladyship will like it."

He turned once more to go.

"I protest you mistake me, Sir Percy," she said hurriedly, and drawing a little closer to him; "the estrangement, which, alas! has arisen between us, was none of my making, remember."

"Begad! you must pardon me there, Madame!" he protested coldly, "my memory was always of the shortest."

He looked her straight in the eyes, with that lazy nonchalance which had become second nature to him. She returned his gaze for a moment, then her eyes softened, as she came up quite close to him, to the foot of the terrace steps.

"Of the shortest, Sir Percy! Faith! how it must have altered! Was it three years ago or four that you saw me for one hour in Paris, on your way to the East. When you came back two years later you had not forgotten me."

She looked divinely pretty as she stood there in the moonlight, with the fur-cloak sliding off her beautiful shoulders, the gold embroidery on her dress shimmering around her, her childlike blue eyes turned up fully at him.

He stood for a moment, rigid and still, but for the clenching of his hand against the stone balustrade of the terrace.

"You desired my presence, Madame," he said frigidly. "I take it that it was not with a view to indulging in tender reminiscences."

His voice certainly was cold and uncompromising: his attitude before her, stiff and unbending. Womanly decorum would have suggested that Marguerite should return coldness for coldness, and should sweep past him without another word, only with a curt nod of the head: but womanly instinct suggested that she should remain—that keen instinct, which makes a beautiful woman conscious of her powers long to bring to her knees the one man who pays her no homage. She stretched out her hand to him.

"Nay, Sir Percy, why not? the present is not so glorious but that I should not wish to dwell a little in the past."

He bent his tall figure, and taking hold of the extreme tip of the fingers which she still held out to him, he kissed them ceremoniously.

"I' faith, Madame," he said, "then you will pardon me, if my dull wits cannot accompany you there."

Once again he attempted to go, once more her voice, sweet, childlike, almost tender, called him back.

"Sir Percy."

"Your servant, Madame."

"Is it possible that love can die?" she said with sudden, unreasoning vehemence. "Methought that the passion which you once felt for me would outlast the span of human life. Is there nothing left of that love, Percy . . . which might help you . . . to bridge over that sad estrangement?"

His massive figure seemed, while she spoke thus to him, to stiffen still more, the strong mouth hardened, a look of relentless obstinacy crept into the habitually lazy blue eyes.

"With what object, I pray you, Madame?" he asked coldly. "I do not understand you."

"Yet 'tis simple enough," he said with sudden bitterness, which seemed literally to surge through his words, though he was making visible efforts to suppress it, "I humbly put the question to you, for my slow wits are unable to grasp the cause of this, your ladyship's sudden new mood. Is it that you have the taste to renew the devilish sport which you played so successfully last year? Do you wish to see me once more a love-sick suppliant at your feet, so that you might again have the pleasure of kicking me aside, like a troublesome lap-dog?"

She had succeeded in rousing him for the moment: and again she looked straight at him, for it was thus she remembered him a year ago.

"Percy! I entreat you!" she whispered, "can we not bury the past?"

"Pardon me, Madame, but I understood you to say that your desire was to dwell in it."

"Nay! I spoke not of *that* past, Percy!" she said, while a tone of tenderness crept into her voice. "Rather did I speak of the time when you loved me still! and I . . . oh! I was vain and frivolous; your wealth and position allured me: I married you, hoping in my heart that your great love for me would beget in me a love for you . . . but, alas! . . ."

The moon had sunk low down behind a bank of clouds. In the east a soft grey light was beginning to chase away the heavy mantle of the night. He could only see her graceful outline now, the small queenly head, with its wealth of reddish golden curls, and the glittering gems forming the small, star-shaped, red flower which she wore as a diadem in her hair.

"Twenty-four hours after our marriage, Madame, the Marquis de St. Cyr and all his family perished on the guillotine, and the popular rumour reached me that it was the wife of Sir Percy Blakeney who helped to send them there."

"Nay! I myself told you the truth of that odious tale."

"Not till after it had been recounted to me by strangers, with all its horrible details."

"And you believed them then and there," she said with great vehemence, "without a proof or question—you believed that I, whom you vowed you loved more than life, whom you professed you worshipped, that I could do a thing so base as these *strangers* chose to recount. You

thought I meant to deceive you about it all—that I ought
to have spoken before I married you: yet, had you listened, I would have told you that up to the very morning
on which St. Cyr went to the guillotine, I was straining
every nerve, using every influence I possessed, to save him
and his family. But my pride sealed my lips, when your
love seemed to perish, as if under the knife of that same
guillotine. Yet I would have told you how I was duped!
Aye! I, whom that same popular rumour had endowed with
the sharpest wits in France! I was tricked into doing this
thing, by men who knew how to play upon my love for an
only brother, and my desire for revenge. Was it unnatural?"

Her voice became choked with tears. She paused for a
moment or two, trying to regain some sort of composure.
She looked appealingly at him, almost as if he were her
judge. He had allowed her to speak on in her own vehement, impassioned way, offering no comment, no word of
sympathy: and now, while she paused, trying to swallow
down the hot tears that gushed to her eyes, he waited,
impassive and still. The dim, grey light of early dawn
seemed to make his tall form look taller and more rigid.
The lazy, good-natured face looked strangely altered. Marguerite, excited, as she was, could see that the eyes were no
longer languid, the mouth no longer good-humored and
inane. A curious look of intense passion seemed to glow
from beneath his drooping lids, the mouth was tightly
closed, the lips compressed, as if the will alone held that
surging passion in check.

Marguerite Blakeney was, above all, a woman, with all
a woman's fascinating foibles, all a woman's most lovable
sins. She knew in a moment that for the past few months

she had been mistaken: that this man who stood here before her, cold as a statue, when her musical voice struck upon his ear, loved her, as he had loved her a year ago: that his passion might have been dormant, but that it was there, as strong, as intense, as overwhelming, as when first her lips met his in one long, maddening kiss.

Pride had kept him from her, and, woman-like, she meant to win back that conquest which had been hers before. Suddenly it seemed to her, that the only happiness life could ever hold for her again would be in feeling that man's kiss once more upon her lips.

"Listen to the tale, Sir Percy," she said, and her voice now was low, sweet, infinitely tender. "Armand was all in all to me! We had no parents, and brought one another up. He was my little father, and I, his tiny mother; we loved one another so. Then one day—do you mind me, Sir Percy? the Marquis de St. Cyr had my brother Armand thrashed—thrashed by his lacqueys—that brother whom I loved better than all the world! And his offence? That he, a plebeian, had dared to love the daughter of the aristocrat; for that he was waylaid and thrashed . . . thrashed like a dog within an inch of his life! Oh, how I suffered! his humiliation had eaten into my very soul! When the opportunity occurred, and I was able to take my revenge, I took it. But I only thought to bring that proud marquis to trouble and humiliation. He plotted with Austria against his own country. Chance gave me knowledge of this; I spoke of it, but I did not know—how could I guess? —they trapped and duped me. When I realized what I had done, it was too late."

"It is perhaps a little difficult, Madame," said Sir Percy,

after a moment of silence between them, "to go back over the past. I have confessed to you that my memory is short, but the thought certainly lingered in my mind that, at the time of the Marquis' death, I entreated you for an explanation of those same noisome popular rumours. If that same memory does not, even now, play me a trick, I fancy that you refused me *all* explanation then, and demanded of my love a humiliating allegiance it was not prepared to give."

"I wished to test your love for me, and it did not bear the test. You used to tell me that you drew the very breath of life but for me, and for love of me."

"And to probe that love, you demanded that I should forfeit mine honour," he said, whilst gradually his impassiveness seemed to leave him, his rigidity to relax; "that I should accept without murmur or question, as a dumb and submissive slave, every action of my mistress. My heart overflowing with love and passion, I *asked* for no explanation—I *waited* for one, not doubting—only hoping. Had you spoken but one word, from you I would have accepted any explanation and believed it. But you left me without a word, beyond a bald confession of the actual horrible facts; proudly you returned to your brother's house, and left me alone . . . for weeks . . . not knowing, now, in whom to believe, since the shrine, which contained my one illusion, lay shattered to earth at my feet."

She need not complain now that he was cold and impassive; his very voice shook with an intensity of passion, which he was making superhuman efforts to keep in check.

"Aye! the madness of my pride!" she said sadly. "Hardly had I gone, already I had repented. But when I returned, I found you, oh, so altered! wearing already that mask of somnolent indifference which you have never laid aside until . . . until now."

She was so close to him that her soft, loose hair was wafted against his cheek; her eyes, glowing with tears, maddened him, the music in her voice sent fire through his veins. But he would not yield to the magic charm of this woman whom he had so deeply loved, and at whose hands his pride had suffered so bitterly. He closed his eyes to shut out the dainty vision of that sweet face, of that snow-white neck and graceful figure, round which the faint rosy light of dawn was just beginning to hover playfully.

"Nay, Madame, it is no mask," he said icily; "I swore to you . . . once, that my life was yours. For months now it has been your plaything . . . it has served its purpose."

But now she knew that that very coldness was a mask. The trouble, the sorrow she had gone through last night, suddenly came back to her mind, but no longer with bitterness, rather with a feeling that this man who loved her would help her to bear the burden.

"Sir Percy," she said impulsively, "Heaven knows you have been at pains to make the task, which I had set to myself, terribly difficult to accomplish. You spoke of my mood just now; well! we will call it that, if you will. I wished to speak to you . . . because . . . because I was in trouble . . . and had need . . . of your sympathy."

"It is yours to command, Madame."

"How cold you are!" she sighed. "Faith! I can scarce believe that but a few months ago one tear in my eye had set you well-nigh crazy. Now I come to you . . . with a half-broken heart . . . and . . . and . . ."

"I pray you, Madame," he said, whilst his voice shook almost as much as hers, "in what way can I serve you?"

"Percy!—Armand is in deadly danger. A letter of his . . . rash, impetuous, as were all his actions, and written to Sir Andrew Ffoulkes, has fallen into the hands of a fanatic. Armand is hopelessly compromised . . . to-morrow, perhaps he will be arrested . . . after that the guillotine . . . unless . . . unless . . . oh! it is horrible!" . . . she said, with a sudden wail of anguish, as all the events of the past night came rushing back to her mind, "horrible! . . . and you do not understand . . . you cannot . . . and I have no one to whom I can turn . . . for help . . . or even for sympathy. . . ."

Tears now refused to be held back. All her trouble, her struggles, the awful uncertainty of Armand's fate overwhelmed her. She tottered, ready to fall, and leaning against the stone balustrade, she buried her face in her hands and sobbed bitterly.

At first mention of Armand St. Just's name and of the peril in which he stood, Sir Percy's face had become a shade more pale; and the look of determination and obstinacy appeared more marked than ever between his eyes. However, he said nothing for the moment, but watched her, as her delicate frame was shaken with sobs, watched her until unconsciously his face softened, and what looked almost like tears, seemed to glisten in his eyes.

"And so," he said with bitter sarcasm, "the murderous dog of the revolution is turning upon the very hands that fed it? . . . Begad, Madame," he added very gently, as Marguerite continued to sob hysterically, "will you dry your tears? . . . I never could bear to see a pretty woman cry, and I . . ."

Instinctly, with sudden overmastering passion, at sight of her helplessness and of her grief, he stretched out his arms, and the next, would have seized her and held her to him, protected from every evil with his very life, his very heart's blood. . . . But pride had the better of it in this struggle once again; he restrained himself with a tremendous effort of will, and said coldly, though still very gently,—

"Will you not turn to me, Madame, and tell me in what way I may have the honour to serve you?"

She made a violent effort to control herself, and turning her tear-stained face to him, she once more held out her hand, which he kissed with the same punctilious gallantry; but Marguerite's fingers, this time, lingered in his hand for a second or two longer than was absolutely necessary, and this was because she had felt that his hand trembled perceptibly and was burning hot, whilst his lips felt as cold as marble.

"Can you do ought for Anmand?" she said sweetly and simply. "You have so much influence at court . . . so many friends . . ."

"Nay, Madame, should you not rather seek the influence of your French friend, M. Chauvelin? His extends, if I mistake not, even as far as the Republican Government of France."

"I cannot ask him, Percy. . . . Oh! I wish I dared to tell you . . . but . . . but . . . he has put a price on my brother's head, which . . ."

She would have given worlds if she had felt the courage

then to tell him everything . . . all she had done that
night—how she had suffered and how her hand had been
forced. But she dared not give way to that impulse . . .
not now, when she was just beginning to feel that he still
loved her, when she hoped that she could win him back.
She dared not make another confession to him. After all,
he might not understand; he might not sympathise with
her struggles and temptation. His love still dormant might
sleep the sleep of death.

Perhaps he divined what was passing in her mind. His
whole attitude was one of intense longing—a veritable
prayer for that confidence, which her foolish pride with-
held from him. When she remained silent he sighed, and
said with marked coldness—

"Faith, Madame, since it distresses you, we will not
speak of it. . . . As for Armand, I pray you have no fear. I
pledge you my word that he shall be safe. Now, have I
your permission to go? The hour is getting late, and . . ."

"You will at least accept my gratitude?" she said, as she
drew quite close to him, and speaking with real tenderness.

With a quick, almost involuntary effort he would have
taken her then in his arms, for her eyes were swimming in
tears, which he longed to kiss away; but she had lured him
once, just like this, then cast him aside like an ill-fitting
glove. He thought this was but a mood, a caprice, and he
was too proud to lend himself to it once again.

"It is too soon, Madame!" he said quietly; "I have done
nothing as yet. The hour is late, and you must be fatigued.
Your women will be waiting for you upstairs."

He stood aside to allow her to pass. She sighed, a quick
sigh of disappointment. His pride and her beauty had been

in direct conflict, and his pride had remained the con-queror. Perhaps, after all, she had been deceived just now; what she took to be the light of love in his eyes might only have been the passion of pride or, who knows, of hatred instead of love. She stood looking at him for a moment or two longer. He was again as rigid, as impas-sive, as before. Pride had conquered, and he cared naught for her. The grey of dawn was gradually yielding to the rosy light of the rising sun. Birds began to twitter; Nature awakened, smiling in happy response to the warmth of this glorious October morning. Only between these two hearts there lay a strong, impassable barrier, built up of pride on both sides, which neither of them cared to be the first to demolish.

He had bent his tall figure in a low ceremonius bow, as she finally, with another bitter little sigh, began to mount the terrace steps.

The long train of her gold-embroidered gown swept the dead leaves off the steps, making a faint harmonious sh—sh—sh as she glided up, with one hand resting on the balustrade, the rosy light of dawn making an aureole of gold round her hair, and causing the rubies on her head and arms to sparkle. She reached the tall glass doors which led into the house. Before entering, she paused once again to look at him, hoping against hope to see his arms stretched out to her, and to hear his voice calling her back. But he had not moved; his massive figure looked the very personification of unbending pride, of fierce obstinacy.

Hot tears again surged to her eyes, and as she would not let him see them, she turned quickly within, and ran as fast as she could up to her own rooms.

Had she but turned back then, and looked out once
more on to the rose-lit garden, she would have seen that
which would have made her own sufferings seem but light
and easy to bear—a strong man, overwhelmed with his
own passion and his own despair. Pride had given way at
last, obstinacy was gone: the will was powerless. He was
but a man madly, blindly, passionately in love, and as
soon as her light footsteps had died away within the house,
he knelt down upon the terrace steps, and in the very
madness of his love he kissed one by one the places where
her small foot had trodden, and the stone balustrade
there, where her tiny hand had rested last.

Chapter 17

Farewell

When Marguerite reached her room, she found her maid terribly anxious about her.

"Your ladyship will be so tired," said the poor woman, whose own eyes were half closed with sleep. "It is past five o'clock."

"Ah, yes, Louise, I daresay I shall be tired presently," said Marguerite, kindly; "but you are very tired now, so go to bed at once. I'll get into bed alone."

"But, my lady . . ."

"Now, don't argue, Louise, but go to bed. Give me a wrap, and leave me alone."

Louise was only too glad to obey. She took off her mistress's gorgeous ball-dress, and wrapped her up in a soft billowy gown.

"Does your ladyship wish for anything else?" she asked, when that was done.

"No, nothing more. Put out the lights as you go out."

"Yes, my lady. Good-night, my lady."

"Good-night, Louise."

When the maid was gone, Marguerite drew aside the curtains and threw open the windows. The garden and the river beyond were flooded with rosy light. Far away to the east, the rays of the rising sun had changed the rose into vivid gold. The lawn was deserted now, and Marguerite looked down upon the terrace where she had stood a few moments ago trying vainly to win back a man's love, which once had been so wholly hers.

It was strange that through all her troubles, all her anxiety for Armand, she was mostly conscious at the present moment of a keen and bitter heartache.

Her very limbs seemed to ache with longing for the love of a man who had spurned her, who had resisted her tenderness, remained cold to her appeals, and had not responded to the glow of passion, which had caused her to feel and hope that those happy olden days in Paris were not all dead and forgotten.

How strange it all was! She loved him still. And now that she looked back upon the last few months of misunderstandings and of loneliness, she realised that she had never ceased to love him; that deep down in her heart she had always vaguely felt that his foolish inanities, his empty laugh, his lazy nonchalance were nothing but a mask; that the real man, strong, passionate, wilful, was there still— the man she had loved, whose intensity had fascinated her, whose personality attracted her, since she always felt that behind his apparently slow wits there was a certain something, which he kept hidden from all the world, and most especially from her.

A woman's heart is such a complex problem—the owner thereof is often most incompetent to find the solution of this puzzle.

Did Marguerite Blakeney, "the cleverest woman in Europe," really love a fool? Was it love that she had felt for him a year ago when she married him? Was it love she felt for him now that she realised that he still loved her, but that he would not become her slave, her passionate, ardent lover once again? Nay! Marguerite herself could not have told that. Not at this moment at any rate; perhaps her pride had sealed her mind against a better understanding of her own heart. But this she did know—that she meant to capture that obstinate heart back again. That she would conquer once more . . . and then, that she would never lose him. . . . She would keep him, keep his love, deserve it, and cherish it; for this much was certain, that there was no longer any happiness possible for her without that one man's love.

Thus the most contradictory thoughts and emotions rushed madly through her mind. Absorbed in them, she had allowed time to slip by; perhaps, tired out with long excitement, she had actually closed her eyes and sank into a troubled sleep, wherein quickly fleeting dreams seemed but the continuation of her anxious thoughts—when suddenly she was roused, from dream or meditation, by the noise of footsteps outside her door.

Nervously she jumped up and listened: the house itself was as still as ever; the footstep had retreated. Through her wide-open windows the brilliant rays of the morning sun were flooding her own room with light. She looked up at the clock; it was half-past six—too early for any of the household to be already astir.

She certainly must have dropped asleep, quite unconsciously. The noise of the footsteps, also of hushed, subdued voices had awakened her—what could they be?

Gently, on tip-toe, she crossed the room and opened the door to listen; not a sound—that peculiar stillness of the early morning when sleep with all mankind is at its heaviest. But the noise had made her nervous, and when, suddenly, at her feet, on the very doorstep, she saw something white lying there—a letter evidently—she hardly dared touch it. It seemed so ghostlike. It certainly was not there when she came upstairs; had Louise dropped it? or was some tantalising spook at play, showing her fairy letters where none existed?

At last she stooped to pick it up, and, amazed, puzzled beyond measure, she saw that the letter was addressed to herself in her husband's large, businesslike-looking hand. What could he have to say to her, in the middle of the night, which could not be put off until the morning?

She tore open the envelope and read:—

"A most unforeseen circumstance forces me to leave for the North immediately, so I beg your ladyship's pardon if I do not avail myself of the honour of bidding you good-bye. My business may keep me employed for about a week, so I shall not have the privilege of being present at your ladyship's water-party on Wednesday. I remain your ladyship's most humble and most obedient servant,

PERCY BLAKENEY."

Marguerite must suddenly have been imbued with her husband's slowness of intellect, for she had perforce to read the few simple lines over and over again, before she could fully grasp their meaning.

She stood on the landing, turning over and over in her hand this curt and mysterious epistle, her mind a blank, her nerves strained with agitation and a presentiment she could not very well have explained.

Sir Percy owned considerable property in the North, certainly, and he had often before gone there alone and stayed away a week at a time; but it seemed so very strange that circumstances should have arisen between five and six o'clock in the morning that compelled him to start in this extreme hurry.

Vainly she tried to shake off an unaccustomed feeling of nervousness: she was trembling from head to foot. A wild, unconquerable desire seized her to see her husband again, at once, if only he had not already started.

Forgetting the fact that she was only very lightly clad in a morning wrap, and that her hair lay loosely about her shoulders, she flew down the stairs, right through the hall towards the front door.

It was as usual barred and bolted, for the indoor servants were not yet up; but her keen ears had detected the sound of voices and the pawing of a horse's hoof against the flag-stones.

With nervous, trembling fingers Marguerite undid the bolts one by one, bruising her hands, hurting her nails, for the locks were heavy and stiff But she did not care; her whole frame shook with anxiety at the very thought that she might be too late; that he might have gone without her seeing him and bidding him "God-speed!"

At last, she had turned the key and thrown open the door. Her ears had not deceived her. A groom was standing close by holding a couple of horses; one of these was Sultan, Sir Percy's favourite and swiftest horse, saddled ready for a journey.

The next moment Sir Percy himself appeared round the further corner of the house and came quickly towards the horses. He had changed his gorgeous ball costume, but was as usual irreproachably and richly apparelled in a suit of fine cloth, with lace jabot and ruffles, high topboots, and riding breeches.

Marguerite went forward a few steps. He looked up and saw her. A slight frown appeared between his eyes.

"You are going?" she said quickly and feverishly. "Whither?"

"As I have had the honour of informing your ladyship, urgent, most unexpected business calls me to the North this morning," he said, in his usual cold, drawly manner.

"But . . . your guests to-morrow . . ."

"I have prayed your ladyship to offer my humble excuses to His Royal Highness. You are such a perfect hostess, I do not think that I shall be missed."

"But surely you might have waited for your journey . . . until after our water-party . . ." she said, still speaking quickly and nervously. "Surely the business is not so urgent . . . and you said nothing about it—just now."

"My business, as I had the honour to tell you, Madame, is as unexpected as it is urgent. . . . May I therefore crave your permission to go. . . . Can I do aught for you in town? . . . on my way back?"

"No . . . no . . . thanks . . . nothing. . . . But you will be back soon?"

"Very soon."

"Before the end of the week?"

"I cannot say."

He was evidently trying to get away, whilst she was straining every nerve to keep him back for a moment or two.

"Percy," she said, "will you not tell my why you go to-day? Surely I, as your wife, have the right to know. You have *not* been called away to the North. I know it. There were no letters, no couriers from there before we left for the opera last night, and nothing was waiting for you when we returned from the ball. . . . You are *not* going to the North, I feel convinced. . . . There is some mystery . . . and . . ."

"Nay, there is no mystery, Madame," he replied, with a slight tone of impatience. "My business has to do with Armand . . . there! Now, have I your leave to depart?"

"With Armand? . . . But you will run no danger?"

"Danger? I? . . . Nay, Madame, your solicitude does me honour. As you say, I have some influence; my intention is to exert it before it be too late."

"Will you allow me to thank you at least?"

"Nay, Madame," he said coldly, "there is no need for that. My life is at your service, and I am already more than repaid."

"And mine will be at yours, Sir Percy, if you will but accept it, in exchange for what you do for Armand," she

said, as, impulsively, she stretched out both her hands to
him. "There! I will not detain you . . . my thoughts go
with you . . . Farewell! . . ."

How lovely she looked in this morning sunlight, with
her ardent hair streaming around her shoulders. He bowed
very low and kissed her hand; she felt the burning kiss and
her heart thrilled with joy and hope.

"You will come back?" she said tenderly.

"Very soon!" he replied, looking longingly into her blue
eyes.

"And . . . you will remember? . . ." she asked, as her
eyes, in response to his look, gave him an infinity of
promise.

"I will always remember, Madame, that you have honoured me by commanding my services."

The words were cold and formal, but they did not chill
her this time. Her woman's heart had read his, beneath
the impassive mask his pride still forced him to wear.

He bowed to her again, then begged her leave to depart. She stood on one side whilst he jumped on to
Sultan's back, then, as he galloped out of the gates, she
waved him a final "Adieu."

A bend in the road soon hid him from view; his confidential groom had some difficulty in keeping pace with
him, for Sultan flew along in response to his master's
excited mood. Marguerite, with a sigh that was almost a
happy one, turned and went within. She went back to her
room, for suddenly, like a tired child, she felt quite sleepy.

Her heart seemed all at once to be in complete peace,
and, though it still ached with undefined longing, a vague
and delicious hope soothed it as with a balm.

She felt no longer anxious about Armand. The man who had just ridden away, bent on helping her brother, inspired her with complete confidence in his strength and in his power. She marvelled at herself for having ever looked upon him as an inane fool; of course, *that* was a mask worn to hide the bitter wound she had dealt to his faith and to his love. His passion would have overmastered him, and he would not let her see how much he still cared and how deeply he suffered.

But now all would be well: she would crush her own pride, humble it before him, tell him everything, trust him in everything; and those happy days would come back, when they used to wander off together in the forests of Fontainebleau, when they spoke little—for he was always a silent man—but when she felt that against that strong heart she would always find rest and happiness.

The more she thought of the events of the past night, the less fear had she of Chauvelin and his schemes. He had failed to discover the identity of the Scarlet Pimpernel, of that she felt sure. Both Lord Fancourt and Chauvelin himself had assured her that no one had been in the dining-room at one o'clock except the Frenchman himself and Percy—Yes!—Percy! she might have asked him, had she thought of it! Anyway, she had no fears that the unknown and brave hero would fall in Chauvelin's trap; his death at any rate would not be at her door.

Armand certainly was still in danger, but Percy had pledged his word that Armand would be safe, and somehow, as Marguerite had seen him riding away, the possibility that he could fail in whatever he undertook never even remotely crossed her mind. When Armand was safely

over in England she would not allow him to go back to
France.

She felt almost happy now, and, drawing the curtains
closely together again to shut out the piercing sun, she
went to bed at last, laid her head upon the pillow, and,
like a wearied child, soon fell into a peaceful and dreamless sleep.

Chapter 18

The Mysterious Device

*T*he day was well advanced when Marguerite woke, refreshed by her long sleep. Louise had brought her some fresh milk and a dish of fruit, and she partook of this frugal breakfast with hearty appetite.

Thoughts crowded thick and fast in her mind as she munched her grapes; most of them went galloping away after the tall, erect figure of her husband, whom she had watched riding out of sight more than five hours ago.

In answer to her eager inquiries, Louise brought back the news that the groom had come home with Sultan, having left Sir Percy in London. The groom thought that his master was about to get on board his schooner, which was lying off just below London Bridge. Sir Percy had ridden thus far, had then met Briggs, the skipper of the *Day Dream*, and had sent the groom back to Richmond with Sultan and the empty saddle.

This news puzzled Marguerite more than ever. Where could Sir Percy be going just now in the *Day Dream*? On Armand's behalf, he had said. Well! Sir Percy had influential friends everywhere. Perhaps he was going to Greenwich, or . . . but Marguerite ceased to conjecture; all would be explained anon: he said that he would come back, and that he would remember.

A long, idle day lay before Marguerite. She was expecting the visit of her old school-fellow, little Suzanne de Tournay. With all the merry mischief at her command, she had tendered her request for Suzanne's company to the Comtesse in the presence of the Prince of Wales last night. His Royal Highness had loudly applauded the notion, and declared that he would give himself the pleasure of calling on the two ladies in the course of the afternoon. The Comtesse had not dared to refuse, and then and there was entrapped into a promise to send little Suzanne to spend a long and happy day at Richmond with her friend.

Marguerite expected her eagerly; she longed for a chat about old schooldays with the child; she felt that she would prefer Suzanne's company to that of anyone else, and together they would roam through the fine old garden and rich deer park, or stroll along the river.

But Suzanne had not come yet, and Marguerite being dressed, prepared to go downstairs. She looked quite a girl this morning in her simple muslin frock, with a broad blue sash round her slim waist, and the dainty cross-over fichu into which, at her bosom, she had fastened a few late crimson roses.

She crossed the landing outside her own suite of apartments, and stood still for a moment at the head of the fine oak staircase, which led to the lower floor. On her left were her husband's apartments, a suite of rooms which she practically never entered.

They consisted of bedroom, dressing and reception room, and, at the extreme end of the landing, of a small study, which, when Sir Percy did not use it, was always kept locked. His own special and confidential valet, Frank, had charge of this room. No one was ever allowed to go inside. My lady had never cared to do so, and the other servants had, of course, not dared to break this hard-and-fast rule.

Marguerite had often, with that good-natured contempt which she had recently adopted towards her husband, chaffed him about this secrecy which surrounded his private study. Laughingly she had always declared that he strictly excluded all prying eyes from his sanctum for fear they should detect how very little "study" went on within its four walls: a comfortable arm-chair for Sir Percy's sweet slumbers was, no doubt, its most conspicuous piece of furniture.

Marguerite thought of all this on this bright October morning as she glanced along the corridor. Frank was evidently busy with his master's rooms, for most of the doors stood open, that of the study amongst the others.

A sudden, burning, childish curiosity seized her to have a peep at Sir Percy's sanctum. The restriction, of course, did not apply to her, and Frank would, of course, not dare to oppose her. Still, she hoped that the valet would be busy in one of the other rooms, that she might have that one quick peep in secret, and unmolested.

Gently, on tiptoe, she crossed the landing and, like

Blue Beard's wife, trembling half with excitement and wonder, she paused a moment on the threshold, strangely perturbed and irresolute.

The door was ajar, and she could not see anything within. She pushed it open tentatively: there was no sound: Frank was evidently not there, and she walked boldly in.

At once she was struck by the severe simplicity of everything around her: the dark and heavy hangings, the massive oak furniture, the one or two maps on the wall, in no way recalled to her mind the lazy man about town, the lover of race-courses, the dandified leader of fashion, that was the outward representation of Sir Percy Blakeney.

There was no sign here, at any rate, of hurried departure. Everything was in its place, not a scrap of paper littered the floor, not a cupboard or drawer was left open. The curtains were drawn aside, and through the open window the fresh morning air was streaming in.

Facing the window, and well into the centre of the room, stood a ponderous business-like desk, which looked as if it had seen much service. On the wall to the left of the desk, reaching almost from floor to ceiling, was a large full-length portrait of a woman, magnificently framed, exquisitely painted, and signed with the name of Boucher. It was Percy's mother.

Marguerite knew very little about her, except that she had died abroad, ailing in body as well as in mind, when Percy was still a lad. She must have been a very beautiful woman once, when Boucher painted her, and as Marguerite looked at the portrait, she could not but be struck by the extraordinary resemblance which must have existed between mother and son. There was the same low, square forehead, crowned with thick, fair hair, smooth and heavy; the same deep-set, somewhat lazy blue eyes, beneath firmly marked, straight brows; and in those eyes there was the same intensity behind that apparent laziness, the same latent passion which used to light up Percy's face in the olden days before his marriage, and which Marguerite had again noted, last night at dawn, when she had come quite close to him, and had allowed a note of tenderness to creep into her voice.

Marguerite studied the portrait, for it interested her: after that she turned and looked again at the ponderous desk. It was covered with a mass of papers, all neatly tied and docketed, which looked like accounts and receipts arrayed with perfect method. It had never before struck Marguerite—nor had she, alas! found it worth while to inquire—as to how Sir Percy, whom all the world had credited with a total lack of brains, administered the vast fortune which his father had left him.

Since she had entered this neat, orderly room, she had been taken so much by surprise, that this obvious proof of her husband's strong business capacities did not cause her more than a passing thought of wonder. But it also strengthened her in the now certain knowledge that, with his worldly inanities, his foppish ways, and foolish talk, he was not only wearing a mask, but was playing a deliberate and studied part.

Marguerite wondered again. Why should he take all this trouble? Why should he—who was obviously a serious, earnest man—wish to appear before his fellowmen as an empty-headed nincompoop?

He may have wished to hide his love for a wife who held him in contempt . . . but surely such an object could have been gained at less sacrifice, and with far less trouble than constant incessant acting of an unnatural part.

She looked round her quite aimlessly now: she was horribly puzzled, and a nameless dread, before all this strange, unaccountable mystery, had begun to seize upon her. She felt cold and uncomfortable suddenly in this severe and dark room. There were no pictures on the wall, save the fine Boucher portrait, only a couple of maps, both of parts of France, one of the North coast and the other of the environs of Paris. What did Sir Percy want with those? she wondered.

Her head began to ache, she turned away from this strange Blue Beard's chamber, which she had entered, and which she did not understand. She did not wish Frank to find her here, and with a last look round, she once more turned to the door. As she did so, her foot knocked against a small object, which had apparently been lying close to the desk, on the carpet, and which now went rolling, right across the room.

She stooped to pick it up. It was a solid gold ring, with a flat shield, on which was engraved a small device.

Marguerite turned it over in her fingers, and then studied the engraving on the shield. It represented a small star-shaped flower, of a shape she had seen so distinctly twice before: once at the opera, and once at Lord Grenville's ball.

Chapter 19

The
Scarlet Pimpernel

*A*t what particular moment the strange doubt first crept into Marguerite's mind, she could not herself afterwards have said. With the ring tightly clutched in her hand, she had run out of the room, down the stairs, and out into the garden, where, in complete seclusion, alone with the flowers, and the river and the birds, she could look again at the ring, and study that device more closely.

Stupidly, senselessly, now, sitting beneath the shade of an overhanging sycamore, she was looking at the plain gold shield, with the star-shaped little flower engraved upon it.

Bah! It was ridiculous! she was dreaming! her nerves were overwrought, and she saw signs and mysteries in the most trivial coincidences. Had not everybody about town recently made a point of affecting the device of that mysterious and heroic Scarlet Pimpernel?

Did she not herself wear it embroidered on her gowns?
set in gems and enamel in her hair? What was there
strange in the fact that Sir Percy should have chosen to
use the device as a seal-ring? He might easily have done
that . . . yes . . . quite easily . . . and . . . besides . . .
what connection could there be between her exquisite
dandy of a husband, with his fine clothes and refined, lazy
ways, and the daring plotter who rescued French victims
from beneath the very eyes of the leaders of a bloodthirsty
revolution?

Her thoughts were in a whirl—her mind a blank . . .
She did not see anything that was going on around her,
and was quite startled when a fresh young voice called to
her across the garden.

"*Chérie!—chérie!* where are you?" and little Suzanne,
fresh as a rosebud, with eyes dancing with glee, and brown
curls fluttering in the soft morning breeze, came running
across the lawn.

"They told me you were in the garden," she went on
prattling merrily, and throwing herself with pretty, girlish
impulse into Marguerite's arms, "so I ran out to give you a
surprise. You did not expect me quite so soon, did you, my
darling little Margot *chérie?*"

Marguerite, who had hastily concealed the ring in the
folds of her kerchief, tried to respond gaily and unconcernedly to the young girl's impulsiveness.

"Indeed, sweet one," she said with a smile, "it is delight-
ful to have you all to myself, and for a nice whole long
day. . . . You won't be bored?"

"Oh! bored! Margot, how can you say such a wicked
thing. Why! when we were in the dear old convent to-

gether, we were always happy when we were allowed to be alone together."

"And to talk secrets."

The two young girls had linked their arms in one another's and began wandering round the garden.

"Oh! how lovely your home is, Margot, darling," said little Suzanne, enthusiastically, "and how happy you must be!"

"Aye, indeed! I ought to be happy—oughtn't I, sweet one?" said Marguerite, with a wistful little sigh.

"How sadly you say it, *chérie* . . . Ah, well, I suppose now that you are a married woman you won't care to talk secrets with me any longer. Oh! what lots and lots of secrets we used to have at school! Do you remember? —some we did not even confide to Sister Theresa of the Holy Angels—though she was such a dear."

"And now you have one all-important secret, eh, little one?" said Marguerite, merrily, "which you are forthwith going to confide to me. Nay, you need not blush, *chérie*," she added, as she saw Suzanne's pretty little face crimson with blushes. "Faith, there's naught to be ashamed of! He is a noble and a true man, and one to be proud of as a lover, and . . . as a husband."

"Indeed, *chérie,* I am not ashamed," rejoined Suzanne, softly; "and it makes me very, very proud to hear you speak so well of him. I think maman will consent," she added thoughtfully, "and I shall be—oh! so happy—but, of course, nothing is to be thought of until papa is safe. . . ."

Marguerite started. Suzanne's father! the Comte de Tournay!—one of those whose life would be jeopardised if Chauvelin succeeded in establishing the identity of the Scarlet Pimpernel.

She had understood all along from the Comtesse, and also from one or two of the members of the league, that their mysterious leader had pledged his honour to bring the fugitive Comte de Tournay safely out of France. Whilst little Suzanne—unconscious of all—save her own all-important little secret, went prattling on, Marguerite's thoughts went back to the events of the past night.

Armand's peril, Chauvelin's threat, his cruel "Either —or—" which she had accepted.

And then her own work in the matter, which should have culminated at one o'clock in Lord Grenville's dining-room, when the relentless agent of the French Government would finally learn who was this mysterious Scarlet Pimpernel, who so openly defied an army of spies and placed himself so boldly, and for mere sport, on the side of the enemies of France.

Since then she had heard nothing from Chauvelin. She had concluded that he had failed, and yet, she had not felt anxious about Armand, because her husband had promised her that Armand would be safe.

But now, suddenly, as Suzanne prattled merrily along, an awful horror came upon her for what she had done. Chauvelin had told her nothing, it is true; but she remembered how sarcastic and evil he looked when she took final leave of him after the ball. Had he discovered something then? Had he already laid his plans for catching the daring plotter, red-handed, in France, and sending him to the guillotine without compunction or delay?

Marguerite turned sick with horror, and her hand convulsively clutched the ring in her dress.

"You are not listening, *chérie*," said Suzanne, reproachfully, as she paused in her long, highly interesting narrative."

"Yes, yes, darling—indeed I am," said Marguerite with an effort, forcing herself to smile. "I love to hear you talking . . . and your happiness makes me so very glad. . . . Have no fear, we will manage to propitiate maman. Sir Andrew Ffoulkes is a noble English gentleman; he has money and position, the Comtesse will not refuse her consent. . . . But . . . now, little one . . . tell me . . . what is the latest news about your father?"

"Oh!" said Suzanne, with mad glee, "the best we could possibly hear. My Lord Hastings came to see maman early this morning. He said that all is now well with dear papa, and we may safely expect him here in England in less than four days."

"Yes," said Marguerite, whose glowing eyes were fastened on Suzanne's lips, as she continued merrily:

"Oh, we have no fear now! You don't know, *chérie*, that that great and noble Scarlet Pimpernel himself, has gone to save papa. He has gone, *chérie* . . . actually gone . . ." added Suzanne excitedly. "He was in London this morning; he will be in Calais, perhaps, to-morrow . . . where he will meet papa . . . and then . . . and then . . ."

The blow had fallen. She had expected it all along, though she had tried for the last half-hour to delude herself and to cheat her fears. He had gone to Calais, had been in London this morning . . . he . . . the Scarlet Pimpernel . . . Percy Blakeney . . . her husband . . . whom she had betrayed last night to Chauvelin. . . .

Percy . . . Percy . . . her husband . . . the Scarlet Pimpernel. . . . Oh! how could she have been so blind? She understood it now—all at once . . . that part he played—the mask he wore . . . in order to throw dust in everybody's eyes.

And all for sheer sport and devilry of course!—saving
men, women and children from death, as other men
destroy and kill animals for the excitement, the love of
the thing. The idle, rich man wanted some aim in life—he,
and the few young bucks he enrolled under his banner,
had amused themselves for months in risking their lives
for the sake of an innocent few.

Perhaps he had meant to tell her when they were first
married; and then the story of the Marquis de St. Cyr had
come to his ears, and he had suddenly turned from her,
thinking, no doubt, that she might some day betray him
and his comrades, who had sworn to follow him, and so he
had tricked her, as he tricked all others, whilst hundreds
now owed their lives to him, and many families owed him
both life and happiness.

The mask of the inane fop had been a good one, and
the part consummately well played. No wonder that
Chauvelin's spies had failed to detect, in the apparently
brainless nincompoop, the man whose reckless daring and
resourceful ingenuity had baffled the keenest French spies,
both in France and in England. Even last night when
Chauvelin went to Lord Grenville's dining-room to seek
that daring Scarlet Pimpernel, he only saw that inane Sir
Percy Blakeney fast asleep in a corner of the sofa.

Had his astute mind guessed the secret, then? Here lay
the whole awful, horrible, amazing puzzle. In betraying a
nameless stranger to his fate in order to save her brother,
had Marguerite Blakeney sent her husband to his death?

No! no! no! a thousand times no! Surely Fate could not
deal a blow like that: Nature itself would rise in revolt: her
hand, when it held that tiny scrap of paper last night,

would surely have been struck numb ere it committed a deed so appalling and so terrible.

"But what is it, *chérie?*" said little Suzanne, now genuinely alarmed, for Marguerite's color had become dull and ashen. "Are you ill, Marguerite? What is it?"

"Nothing, nothing, child," she murmured, as in a dream. "Wait a moment . . . let me think . . . think! . . . You said . . . the Scarlet Pimpernel had gone to-day. . . ?"

"Marguerite, *chérie*, what is it? You frighten me. . . ."

"It is nothing, child, I tell you . . . nothing. . . . I must be alone a minute—and—dear one . . . I may have to curtail our time together to-day. . . . I may have to go away—you'll understand?"

"I understand that something has happened, *chérie*, and that you want to be alone. I won't be a hindrance to you. Don't think of me. My maid, Lucile, has not yet gone . . . we will go back together . . . don't think of me."

She threw her arms impulsively round Marguerite. Child as she was, she felt the poignancy of her friend's grief, and with the infinite tact of her girlish tenderness, she did not try to pry into it, but was ready to efface herself.

She kissed Marguerite again and again, then walked sadly back across the lawn. Marguerite did not move, she remained there, thinking . . . wondering what was to be done.

Just as little Suzanne was about to mount the terrace steps, a groom came running round the house towards his mistress. He carried a sealed letter in his hand. Suzanne instinctively turned back; her heart told her that here perhaps was further ill news for her friend, and she felt that her poor Margot was not in a fit state to bear any more.

The groom stood respectfully beside his mistress, then he handed her the sealed letter.

"What is that?" asked Marguerite.

"Just come by runner, my lady."

Marguerite took the letter mechanically, and turned it over in her trembling fingers.

"Who sent it?" she said.

"The runner said, my lady," replied the groom, "that his orders were to deliver this, and that your ladyship would understand from whom it came."

Marguerite tore open the envelope. Already her instinct had told her what it contained, and her eyes only glanced at it mechanically.

It was a letter written by Armand St. Just to Sir Andrew Ffoulkes—the letter which Chauvelin's spies had stolen at "The Fisherman's Rest," and which Chauvelin had held as a rod over her to enforce her obedience.

Now he had kept his word—he had sent her back St. Just's compromising letter . . . for he was on the track of the Scarlet Pimpernel.

Marguerite's senses reeled, her very soul seemed to be leaving her body; she tottered, and would have fallen but for Suzanne's arm round her waist. With superhuman effort she regained control over herself—there was yet much to be done.

"Bring that runner here to me," she said to the servant, with much calm. "He has not gone?"

"No, my lady."

The groom went, and Marguerite turned to Suzanne.

"And you, child, run within. Tell Lucile to get ready. I fear I must send you home, child. And—stay, tell one of the maids to prepare a traveling dress and cloak for me."

Suzanne made no reply. She kissed Marguerite tenderly, and obeyed without a word; the child was overawed by the terrible, nameless misery in her friend's face.

A minute later the groom returned, followed by the runner who had brought the letter.

"Who gave you this packet?" asked Marguerite.

"A gentleman, my lady," replied the man, "at 'The Rose and Thistle' inn opposite Charing Cross. He said you would understand."

"At 'The Rose and Thistle'? What was he doing?"

"He was waiting for the coach, your ladyship, which he had ordered."

"The coach?"

"Yes, my lady. A special coach he had ordered. I understood from his man that he was posting straight to Dover."

"That's enough. You may go." Then she turned to the groom: "My coach and the four swiftest horses in the stables, to be ready at once."

The groom and runner both went quickly off to obey. Marguerite remained standing for a moment on the lawn quite alone. Her graceful figure was as rigid as a statue, her eyes were fixed, her hands were tightly clasped across her breast; her lips moved as they murmured with pathetic heart-breaking persistence,—

"What's to be done? What's to be done? Where to find him?—Oh, God! grant me light."

But this was not the moment for remorse and despair. She had done—unwittingly—an awful and terrible thing— the very worst crime, in her eyes, that woman ever committed—she saw it in all its horror. Her very blindness in not having guessed her husband's secret seemed now to her another deadly sin. She ought to have known! she ought to have known!

How could she imagine that a man who could love with so much intensity as Percy Blakeney had loved her from the first?—how could such a man be the brainless idiot he chose to appear? She, at least, ought to have known that he was wearing a mask, and having found that out, she should have torn it from his face, whenever they were alone together.

Her love for him had been paltry and weak, easily crushed by her own pride; and she, too, had worn a mask in assuming a contempt for him, whilst, as a matter of fact, she completely misunderstood him.

But there was no time now to go over the past. By her own blindness she had sinned; now she must repay, not by empty remorse, but by prompt and useful action.

Percy had started for Calais, utterly unconscious of the fact that his most relentless enemy was on his heels. He had set sail early that morning from London Bridge. Provided he had a favourable wind, he would no doubt be in France within twenty-four hours; no doubt he had reckoned on the wind and chosen this route.

Chauvelin, on the other hand, would post to Dover, charter a vessel there, and undoubtedly reach Calais much about the same time. Once in Calais, Percy would meet all those who were eagerly waiting for the noble and brave Scarlet Pimpernel, who had come to rescue them from horrible and unmerited death. With Chauvelin's eyes now fixed upon his every movement, Percy would thus not only be endangering his own life, but that of Suzanne's father, the old Comte de Tournay, and of those other fugitives who were waiting for him and trusting in him. There was also Armand, who had gone to meet de Tournay, secure in the knowledge that the Scarlet Pimpernel was watching over his safety.

All these lives and that of her husband, lay in Marguerite's hands; these she must save, if human pluck and ingenuity were equal to the task.

Unfortunately, she could not do all this quite alone. Once in Calais she would not know where to find her husband, whilst Chauvelin, in stealing the papers at Dover, had obtained the whole itinerary. Above every thing, she wished to warn Percy.

She knew enough about him by now to understand that he would never abandon those who trusted in him, that he would not turn back from danger, and leave the Comte de Tournay to fall into the bloodthirsty hands that knew of no mercy. But if he were warned, he might form new plans, be more wary, more prudent. Unconsciously, he might fall into a cunning trap, but—once warned—he might yet succeed.

And if he failed—if indeed Fate, and Chauvelin, with all the resources at his command, proved too strong for the daring plotter after all—then at least she would be there by his side, to comfort, love and cherish, to cheat death perhaps at the last by making it seem sweet, if they died both together, locked in each other's arms, with the supreme happiness of knowing that passion had responded to passion, and that all misunderstandings were at an end.

Her whole body stiffened as with a great and firm resolution. This she meant to do, if God gave her wits and strength. Her eyes lost their fixed look, they glowed with inward fire at the thought of meeting him again so soon, in the very midst of most deadly perils; they sparkled with the joy of sharing these dangers with him—of helping him perhaps—of being with him at the last—if she failed.

The childlike sweet face had become hard and set, the curved mouth was closed tightly over her clenched teeth. She meant to do or die, with him and for his sake. A frown, which spoke of an iron will and unbending resolution, appeared between the two straight brows; already her plans were formed. She would go and find Sir Andrew Ffoulkes first; he was Percy's best friend, and Marguerite remembered with a thrill, with what blind enthusiasm the young man always spoke of his mysterious leader.

He would help her where she needed help; her coach was ready. A change of raiment, and a farewell to little Suzanne, and she could be on her way.

Without haste, but without hesitation, she walked quietly into the house.

Chapter 20

The Friend

*L*ess than half an hour later, Marguerite, buried in thoughts, sat inside her coach, which was bearing her swiftly to London.

She had taken an affectionate farewell of little Suzanne, and seen the child safely started with her maid, and in her own coach, back to town. She had sent one courier with a respectful letter of excuse to His Royal Highness, begging for a postponement of the august visit on account of pressing and urgent business, and another on ahead to bespeak a fresh relay of horses at Faversham.

Then she had changed her muslin frock for a dark traveling costume and mantle, had provided herself with money—which her husband's lavishness always placed fully at her disposal—and had started on her way.

She did not attempt to delude herself with any vain and futile hopes; the safety of her brother Armand was to have been conditional on the imminent capture of the Scarlet Pimpernel. As Chauvelin had sent her back Armand's compromising letter, there was no doubt that he was quite satisfied in his own mind that Percy Blakeney was the man whose death he had sworn to bring about.

No! there was no room for any fond delusions! Percy, the husband whom she loved with all the ardour which her admiration for his bravery had kindled, was in immediate, deadly peril, through her hand. She had betrayed him to his enemy—unwittingly, 'tis true—but she *had* betrayed him, and if Chauvelin succeeded in trapping him, who so far was unaware of his danger, then his death would be at her door. His death! when with her very heart's blood, she would have defended him and given willingly her life for his.

She had ordered her coach to drive her to the "Crown" inn; once there, she told her coachman to give the horses food and rest. Then she ordered a chair, and had herself carried to the house in Pall Mall where Sir Andrew Ffoulkes lived.

Among all Percy's friends, who were enrolled under his daring banner, she felt that she would prefer to confide in Sir Andrew Ffoulkes. He had always been her friend, and now his love for little Suzanne had brought him closer to her still. Had he been away from home, gone on the mad errand with Percy, perhaps, then she would have called on Lord Hastings or Lord Tony—for she wanted the help of one of these young men, or she would be indeed powerless to save her husband.

Sir Andrew Ffoulkes, however, was at home, and his servant introduced her ladyship immediately. She went upstairs to the young man's comfortable bachelor's chambers, and was shown into a small, though luxuriously furnished, dining-room. A moment or two later Sir Andrew himself appeared.

He had evidently been much startled when he heard who his lady visitor was, for he looked anxiously—even suspiciously—at Marguerite, whilst performing the elaborate bows before her, which the rigid etiquette of the time demanded.

Marguerite had laid aside every vestige of nervousness; she was perfectly calm, and having returned the young man's elaborate salute, she began very calmly—

"Sir Andrew, I have no desire to waste valuable time in much talk. You must take certain things I am going to tell you for granted. These will be of no importance. What is important is, that your leader and comrade, the Scarlet Pimpernal . . . my husband . . . Percy Blakeney . . . is in deadly peril."

Had she had the remotest doubt of the correctness of her deductions, she would have had them confirmed now, for Sir Andrew, completely taken by surprise, had grown very pale, and was quite incapable of making the slightest attempt at clever parrying.

"No matter how I know this, Sir Andrew," she continued quietly, "thank God that I do, and that perhaps it is not too late to save him. Unfortunately, I cannot do this quite alone, and therefore have come to you for help."

"Lady Blakeney," said the young man, trying to recover himself, "I . . ."

"Will you hear me first?" she interrupted. "This is how the matter stands. When the agent of the French Government stole your papers that night in Dover, he found amongst them certain plans, which you or your leader meant to carry out for the rescue of the Comte de Tournay and others. The Scarlet Pimpernel—Percy, my husband— has gone on this errand himself to-day. Chauvelin knows that the Scarlet Pimpernel and Percy Blakeney are one and the same person. He will follow him to Calais, and there will lay hands on him. You know as well as I do the fate that awaits him at the hands of the Revolutionary Government of France. No interference from England— from King George himself—would save him. Robespierre and his gang would see to it that the interference came too late. But not only that, the much-trusted leader will also have been unconsciously the means of revealing the hiding place of the Comte de Tournay and of all those who, even now, are placing their hopes in him."

She had spoken quietly, dispassionately, and with firm, unbending resolution. Her purpose was to make that young man trust and help her, for she could do nothing without him.

"I do not understand," he repeated, trying to gain time, to think what was best to be done.

"Aye! but I think you do, Sir Andrew. You must know that I am speaking the truth. Look these facts straight in the face. Percy has sailed for Calais, I presume for some lonely part of the coast, and Chauvelin is on his track. *He* has posted for Dover, and will cross the Channel probably to-night. What do you think will happen?"

The young man was silent.

"Percy will arrive at his destination: unconscious of being followed he will seek out de Tournay and the others—

among these is Armand St. Just, my brother—he will seek them out, one after another, probably, not knowing that the sharpest eyes in the world are watching his every movement. When he has thus unconsciously betrayed those who blindly trust in him, when nothing can be gained from him, and he is ready to come back to England, with those whom he has gone so bravely to save, the doors of the trap will close upon him, and he will be sent to end his noble life upon the guillotine."

Still Sir Andrew was silent.

"You do not trust me," she said passionately. "Oh God! cannot you see that I am in deadly earnest? Man, man," she added, while, with her tiny hands she seized the young man suddenly by the shoulders, forcing him to look straight at her, "tell me, do I look like that vilest thing on earth—a woman who would betray her own husband?"

"God forbid, Lady Blakeney," said the young man at last, "that I should attribute such evil motives to you, but . . ."

"But what? . . . tell me. . . . Quick, man! . . . the very seconds are precious!"

"Will you tell me," he asked resolutely, and looking searchingly into her blue eyes, "whose hand helped to guide M. Chauvelin to the knowledge which you say he possesses?"

"Mine," she said quietly, "I own it—I will not lie to you, for I wish you to trust me absolutely. But I had no idea—how *could* I have?—of the identity of the Scarlet Pimpernel . . . and my brother's safety was to be my prize if I succeeded."

"In helping Chauvelin to track the Scarlet Pimpernel?"
She nodded.

"It is no use telling you how he forced my hand.
Armand is more than a brother to me, and . . . and . . .
how *could* I guess? . . . But we waste time, Sir Andrew
. . . every second is precious . . . in the name of God! . . .
my husband is in peril . . . your friend!—your comrade!
—Help me to save him."

Sir Andrew felt his position to be a very awkward one.
The oath he had taken before his leader and comrade was
one of obedience and secrecy; and yet the beautiful woman,
who was asking him to trust her, was undoubtedly in
earnest; his friend and leader was equally undoubtedly in
imminent danger and . . .

"Lady Blakeney," he said at last, "God knows you have
perplexed me, so that I do not know which way my duty
lies. Tell me what you wish me to do. There are nineteen
of us ready to lay down our lives for the Scarlet Pimpernel
if he is in danger."

"There is no need for lives just now, my friend," she
said drily; "my wits and four swift horses will serve the
necessary purpose. But I must know where to find him.
See," she added, while her eyes filled with tears, "I have
humbled myself before you, I have owned my fault to you;
shall I also confess my weakness?—My husband and I have
been estranged, because he did not trust me, and because I
was too blind to understand. You must confess that the
bandage which he put over my eyes was a very thick one.
Is it small wonder that I did not see through it? But last
night, after I led him unwittingly into such deadly peril, it
suddenly fell from my eyes. If you will not help me, Sir

Andrew, I would still strive to save my husband, I would still exert every faculty I possess for his sake; but I might be powerless, for I might arrive too late, and nothing would be left for you but lifelong remorse, and . . . and . . . for me, a broken heart."

"But, Lady Blakeney," said the young man, touched by the gentle earnestness of this exquisitely beautiful woman, "do you know that what you propose doing is man's work?—you cannot possibly journey to Calais alone. You would be running the greatest possible risks to yourself, and your chances of finding your husband now—were I to direct you ever so carefully—are infinitely remote."

"Oh, I hope there are risks!" she murmured softly. "I hope there are dangers, too!—I have so much to atone for. But I fear you are mistaken. Chauvelin's eyes are fixed upon you all, he will scarce notice me. Quick, Sir Andrew! —the coach is ready, and there is not a moment to be lost. . . . I *must* get to him! I *must!*" she repeated with almost savage energy, "to warn him that that man is on his track. . . . Can't you see—can't you see, that I *must* get to him . . . even . . . even if it be too late to save him . . . at least . . . to be by his side . . . at the last."

"Faith, Madame, you must command me. Gladly would I or any of my comrades lay down our lives for your husband. If you *will* go yourself . . . "

"Nay, friend, do you not see that I would go mad if I let you go without me." She stretched out her hand to him. "You *will* trust me?"

"I await your orders," he said simply.

"Listen, then. My coach is ready to take me to Dover. Do you follow me, as swiftly as horses will take you. We meet at nightfall at 'The Fisherman's Rest.' Chauvelin would avoid it, as he is known there, and I think it would be the safest. I will gladly accept your escort to Calais . . . as you say, I might miss Sir Percy were you to direct me ever so carefully. We'll charter a schooner at Dover and cross over during the night. Disguised, if you will agree to it, as my lacquey, you will, I think, escape detection."

"I am entirely at your service, Madame," rejoined the young man earnestly. "I trust to God that you will sight the *Day Dream* before we reach Calais. With Chauvelin at his heels, every step the Scarlet Pimpernel takes on French soil is fraught with danger."

"God grant it, Sir Andrew. But now, farewell. We meet to-night at Dover! It will be a race between Chauvelin and me across the Channel tonight—and the prize—the life of the Scarlet Pimpernel."

He kissed her hand, and then escorted her to her chair. A quarter of an hour later she was back at the "Crown" inn, where her coach and horses were ready and waiting for her. The next moment they thundered along the London streets, and then straight on to the Dover road at maddening speed.

She had no time for despair now. She was up and doing and had no leisure to think. With Sir Andrew Ffoulkes as her companion and ally, hope had once again revived in her heart.

God would be merciful. He would not allow so appalling a crime to be committed, as the death of a brave man through the hand of a woman who loved him, and worshipped him, and who would gladly have died for his sake.

Marguerite's thoughts flew back to him, the mysterious

hero, whom she had always unconsciously loved, when his identity was still unknown to her. Laughingly, in the olden days, she used to call him the shadowy king of her heart, and now she had suddenly found that this enigmatic personality whom she had worshipped, and the man who loved her so passionately, were one and the same: what wonder that one or two happier Visions began to force their way before her mind? She vaguely wondered what she would say to him when first they would stand face to face.

She had had so many anxieties, so much excitement during the past few hours, that she allowed herself the luxury of nursing these few more hopeful, brighter thoughts. Gradually the rumble of the coach wheels, with its incessant monotony, acted soothingly on her nerves: her eyes, aching with fatigue and many shed and unshed tears, closed involuntarily, and she fell into a troubled sleep.

Chapter 21

Suspense

*I*t was late into the night when she at last reached "The Fisherman's Rest." She had done the whole journey in less than eight hours, thanks to innumerable changes of horses at the various coaching stations, for which she always paid lavishly, thus obtaining the very best and swiftest that could be had.

Her coachman, too, had been indefatigable; the promise of special and rich reward had no doubt helped to keep him up, and he had literally burned the ground beneath his mistress' coach wheels.

The arrival of Lady Blakeney in the middle of the night caused a considerable flutter at "The Fisherman's Rest." Sally jumped hastily out of bed, and Mr. Jellyband was at great pains how to make his important guest comfortable.

Both these good folk were far too well drilled in the manners appertaining to innkeepers, to exhibit the slightest surprise at Lady Blakeney's arrival, alone, at this extraordinary hour. No doubt they thought all the more, but Marguerite was far too absorbed in the importance—the deadly earnestness—of her journey, to stop and ponder over trifles of that sort.

The coffee-room—the scene lately of the dastardly outrage on two English gentlemen—was quite deserted. Mr. Jellyband hastily relit the lamp, rekindled a cheerful bit of fire in the great hearth, and then wheeled a comfortable chair by it, into which Marguerite gratefully sank.

"Will your ladyship stay the night?" asked pretty Miss Sally, who was already busy laying a snow-white cloth on the table, preparatory to providing a simple supper for her ladyship.

"No! not the whole night," replied Marguerite. "At any rate, I shall not want any room but this, if I can have it to myself for an hour or two."

"It is at your ladyship's service," said honest Jellyband, whose rubicund face was set in its tightest folds, lest it should betray before "the quality" that boundless astonishment which the worthy fellow had begun to feel.

"I shall be crossing over at the first turn of the tide," said Marguerite, and in the first schooner I can get. But my coachman and men will stay the night, and probably several days longer, so I hope you will make them comfortable."

"Yes, my lady; I'll look after them. Shall Sally bring your ladyship some supper?"

"Yes, please. Put something cold on the table, and as soon as Sir Andrew Ffoulkes comes, show him in here."

"Yes, my lady."

Honest Jellyband's face now expressed distress in spite
of himself. He had great regard for Sir Percy Blakeney,
and did not like to see his lady running away with young
Sir Andrew. Of course, it was no business of his, and Mr.
Jellyband was no gossip. Still, in his heart, he recollected
that her ladyship was after all only one of them "furriners";
what wonder that she was immoral like the rest of them?

"Don't sit up, honest Jellyband," continued Marguerite, kindly, "nor you either, Mistress Sally. Sir Andrew
may be late."

Jellyband was only too willing that Sally should go to
bed. He was beginning not to like these goings-on at all.
Still, Lady Blakeney would pay handsomely for the
accommodation, and it certainly was no business of his.

Sally arranged a simple supper of cold meat, wine, and
fruit, on the table, then with a respectful curtsey, she
retired, wondering in her little mind why her ladyship
looked so serious, when she was about to elope with her
gallant.

Then commenced a period of weary waiting for Marguerite. She knew that Sir Andrew—who would have to
provide himself with clothes befitting a lacquey—could not
possibly reach Dover for at least a couple of hours. He was
a splendid horseman of course, and would make light in
such an emergency of the seventy-odd miles between London and Dover. He would, too, literally burn the ground
beneath his horse's hoofs, but he might not always get
very good remounts, and in any case, he could not have
started from London until at least an hour after she did.

She had seen nothing of Chauvelin on the road. Her
coachman, whom she questioned, had not seen anyone

answering the description his mistress gave him, of the
wizened figure of the little Frenchman.

Evidently, therefore, he had been ahead of her all the
time. She had not dared to question the people at the
various inns, where they had stopped to change horses.
She feared that Chauvelin had spies all along the route,
who might overhear her questions, then outdistance her
and warn her enemy of her approach.

Now she wondered at what inn he might be stopping,
or whether he had had the good luck of chartering a vessel
already, and was now himself on the way to France. That
thought gripped her at the heart as with an iron vise. If
indeed she should be too late already!

The loneliness of the room overwhelmed her; everything within was so horribly still; the ticking of the grandfather's clock—dreadfully slow and measured—was the
only sound which broke this awful loneliness.

Marguerite had need of all her energy, all her steadfast-
ness of purpose, to keep up her courage through this weary
midnight waiting.

Everyone else in the house but herself must have been
asleep. She had heard Sally go upstairs. Mr. Jellyband had
gone to see to her coachman and men, and then had
returned and taken up a position under the porch outside,
just where Marguerite had first met Chauvelin about a
week ago. He evidently meant to wait up for Sir Andrew
Ffoulkes, but was soon overcome by sweet slumbers, for
presently—in addition to the slow ticking of the clock—
Marguerite could hear the monotonous and dulcet tones of
the worthy fellow's breathing.

For some time now, she had realised that the beautiful

warm October's day, so happily begun, had turned into a
rough and cold night. She had felt very chilly, and was
glad of the cheerful blaze in the hearth: but gradually, as
time wore on, the weather became more rough, and the
sound of the great breakers against the Admiralty Pier,
though some distance from the inn, came to her as the
noise of muffled thunder.

The wind was becoming boisterous, rattling the leaded
windows and the massive doors of the old-fashioned house:
it shook the trees outside and roared down the vast chimney. Marguerite wondered if the wind would be favorable
for her journey. She had no fear of the storm, and would
have braved worse risks sooner than delay the crossing by
an hour.

A sudden commotion outside roused her from her meditations. Evidently it was Sir Andrew Ffoulkes, just arrived in
mad haste, for she heard his horse's hoofs thundering on
the flag-stones outside, then Mr. Jellyband's sleepy, yet
cheerful tones bidding him welcome.

For a moment, then, the awkwardness of her position
struck Marguerite; alone at this hour, in a place where she
was well known, and having made an assignation with a
young cavalier equally well known, and who arrives in
disguise! What food for gossip to those mischievously
inclined.

The idea struck Marguerite chiefly from its humorous
side: there was such quaint contrast between the serious-
ness of her errand, and the construction which would
naturally be put on her actions by honest Mr. Jellyband,
that for the first time since many hours, a little smile began
playing round the corners of her childlike mouth, and

when, presently, Sir Andrew, almost unrecognisable in his lacquey-like garb, entered the coffee-room, she was able to greet him with quite a merry laugh.

"Faith! Monsieur, my lacquey," she said, "I am satisfied with your appearance!"

Mr. Jellyband had followed Sir Andrew, looking strangely perplexed. The young gallant's disguise had confirmed his worst suspicions. Without a smile upon his jovial face, he drew the cork from the bottle of wine, set the chairs ready, and prepared to wait.

"Thanks, honest friend," said Marguerite, who was still smiling at the thought of what the worthy fellow must be thinking at that very moment, "we shall require nothing more; and here's for all the trouble you have been put to on our account."

She handed two or three gold pieces to Jellyband, who took them respectfully, and with becoming gratitude.

"Stay, Lady Blakeney," interposed Sir Andrew, as Jellyband was about to retire, "I am afraid we shall require something more of my friend Jelly's hospitality. I am sorry to say we cannot cross over to-night."

"Not cross over to-night?" she repeated in amazement. "But we must, Sir Andrew, we must! There can be no question of cannot, and whatever it may cost, we must get a vessel to-night."

But the young man shook his head sadly.

"I am afraid it is not a question of cost, Lady Blakeney. There is a nasty storm blowing from France, the wind is dead against us, we cannot possibly sail until it has changed."

Marguerite became deadly pale. She had not foreseen

this. Nature herself was playing her a horrible, cruel trick. Percy was in danger, and she could not go to him, because the wind happened to blow from the coast of France.

"But we must go!—we must!" she repeated with strange, persistent energy, "you know, we must go!—can't you find a way?"

"I have been down to the shore already," he said, "and had a talk to one or two skippers. It is quite impossible to set sail to-night, so every sailor assured me. No one," he added, looking significantly at Marguerite, "*no one* could possibly put out of Dover to-night."

Marguerite at once understood what he meant. *No one* included Chauvelin as well as herself. She nodded pleasantly to Jellyband.

"Well, then, I must resign myself," she said to him. "Have you a room for me?"

"Oh, yes, your ladyship. A nice, bright, airy room. I'll see to it at once. . . . And there is another one for Sir Andrew—both quite ready."

"That's brave now, mine honest Jelly," said Sir Andrew, gaily, and clapping his worthy host vigorously on the back. "You unlock both those rooms, and leave our candles here on the dresser. I vow you are dead with sleep, and her ladyship must have some supper before she retires. There, have no fear, friend of the rueful countenance, her ladyship's visit, though at this unusual hour, is a great honour to thy house, and Sir Percy Blakeney will reward thee doubly, if thou seest well to her privacy and comfort."

Sir Andrew had no doubt guessed the many conflicting doubts and fears which raged in honest Jellyband's head; and, as he was a gallant gentleman, he tried by this brave hint to allay some of the worthy innkeeper's suspicions. He had the satisfaction of seeing that he had partially succeeded. Jellyband's rubicund countenance brightened somewhat, at mention of Sir Percy's name.

"I'll go and see to it at once, sir," he said with alacrity, and with less frigidity in his manner. "Has her ladyship everything she wants for supper?"

"Everything, thanks, honest friend, and as I am famished and dead with fatigue, I pray you see to the rooms."

"Now tell me," she said eagerly, as soon as Jellyband had gone from the room, "tell me all your news."

"There is nothing else much to tell you, Lady Blakeney," replied the young man. "The storm makes it quite impossible for any vessel to put out of Dover this tide. But, what seemed to you at first a terrible calamity, is really a blessing in disguise. If we cannot cross over to France to-night, Chauvelin is in the same quandary."

"He may have left before the storm broke out."

"God grant he may," said Sir Andrew, merrily, "for very likely then he'll have been driven out of his course! Who knows? He may now even be lying at the bottom of the sea, for there is a furious storm raging, and it will fare ill with all small craft which happen to be out. But I fear me we cannot build our hopes upon the ship-wreck of that cunning devil, and of all his murderous plans. The sailors I spoke to, all assured me that no schooner had put out of Dover for several hours: on the other hand, I ascertained that a stranger had arrived by coach this afternoon, and had, like myself, made some inquiries about crossing over to France."

"Then Chauvelin is still in Dover?"

"Undoubtedly. Shall I go waylay him and run my sword through him? That were indeed the quickest way out of the difficulty."

"Nay! Sir Andrew, do not jest! Alas! I have often since last night caught myself wishing for that fiend's death. But what you suggest is impossible! The laws of this country do not permit of murder! It is only in our beautiful France that wholesale slaughter is done lawfully, in the name of Liberty and of brotherly love."

Sir Andrew had persuaded her to sit down to the table, to partake of some supper and to drink a little wine. This enforced rest of at least twelve hours, until the next tide, was sure to be terribly difficult to bear in the state of intense excitement in which she was. Obedient in these small matters like a child, Marguerite tried to eat and drink.

Sir Andrew, with that profound sympathy born in all those who are in love, made her almost happy by talking to her about her husband. He recounted to her some of the daring escapes the brave Scarlet Pimpernel had contrived for the poor French fugitives, whom a relentless and bloody revolution was driving out of their country. He made her eyes glow with enthusiasm by telling her of his bravery, his ingenuity, his resourcefulness, when it meant snatching the lives of men, women, and even children from beneath the very edge of that murderous, ever-ready guillotine.

He even made her smile quite merrily by telling her of the Scarlet Pimpernel's quaint and many disguises, through which he had baffled the strictest watch set against him at the barricades of Paris. This last time, the escape of the

Comtesse de Tournay and her children had been a veritable masterpiece—Blakeney disguised as a hideous old market-woman, in filthy cap and straggling grey locks, was a sight fit to make the gods laugh.

Marguerite laughed heartily as Sir Andrew tried to describe Blakeney's appearance, whose gravest difficulty always consisted in his great height, which in France made disguise doubly difficult.

Thus an hour wore on. There were many more to spend in enforced inactivity in Dover. Marguerite rose from the table with an impatient sigh. She looked forward with dread to the night in the bed upstairs, with terribly anxious thoughts to keep her company, and the howling of the storm to help chase sleep away.

She wondered where Percy was now. The *Day Dream* was a strong, well-built, sea-going yacht. Sir Andrew had expressed the opinion that no doubt she had got in the lee of the wind before the storm broke out, or else perhaps had not ventured into the open at all, but was lying quietly at Gravesend.

Briggs was an expert skipper, and Sir Percy handled a schooner as well as any master mariner. There was no danger for them from the storm.

It was long past midnight when at last Marguerite retired to rest. As she had feared, sleep sedulously avoided her eyes. Her thoughts were of the blackest during these long, weary hours, whilst that incessant storm raged which was keeping her away from Percy. The sound of the distant breakers made her heart ache with melancholy. She was in the mood when the sea has a saddening effect upon the nerves. It is only when we are very happy, that we can bear to gaze merrily upon the vast and limitless expanse of water, rolling on and on with such persistent, irritating monotony, to the accompaniment of our thoughts, whether grave or gay. When they are gay, the waves echo their gaiety; but when they are sad, then every breaker, as it rolls, seems to bring additional sadness, and to speak to us of hopelessness and of the pettiness of all our joys.

Chapter 22

Calais

*T*he weariest nights, the longest days, sooner or later must perforce come to an end.

Marguerite had spent over fifteen hours in such acute mental torture as well-nigh drove her crazy. After a sleepless night, she rose early, wild with excitement, dying to start on her journey, terrified lest further obstacles lay in her way. She rose before anyone else in the house was astir, so frightened was she, lest she should miss the one golden opportunity of making a start.

When she came downstairs, she found Sir Andrew Ffoulkes sitting in the coffee-room. He had been out half an hour earlier, and had gone to the Admiralty Pier, only to find that neither the French packet nor any privately chartered vessel could put out of Dover yet. The storm was then at its fullest, and the tide was on the turn. If the wind did not abate or change, they would perforce have to wait another ten or twelve hours until the next tide, before a start could be made. And the storm had not abated, the wind had not changed, and the tide was rapidly drawing out.

Marguerite felt the sickness of despair when she heard this melancholy news. Only the most firm resolution kept her from totally breaking down, and thus adding to the young man's anxiety, which evidently had become very keen.

Though he tried to disguise it, Marguerite could see that Sir Andrew was just as anxious as she was to reach his comrade and friend. This enforced inactivity was terrible to them both.

How they spent that wearisome day at Dover, Marguerite could never afterwards say. She was in terror of showing herself, lest Chauvelin's spies happened to be about, so she had a private sitting-room, and she and Sir Andrew sat there hour after hour, trying to take, at long intervals, some perfunctory meals, which little Sally would bring them, with nothing to do but to think, to conjecture, and only occasionally to hope.

The storm had abated just too late; the tide was by then too far out to allow a vessel to put off to sea. The wind had changed, and was settling down to a comfortable north-westerly breeze—a veritable godsend for a speedy passage across to France.

And there those two waited, wondering if the hour would ever come when they could finally make a start. There had been one happy interval in this long weary day, and that was when Sir Andrew went down once again to the pier, and presently came back to tell Marguerite that he had chartered a quick schooner, whose skipper was ready to put to sea the moment the tide was favourable.

From that moment the hours seemed less wearisome; there was less hopelessness in the waiting; and at last, at five o'clock in the afternoon, Marguerite, closely veiled and followed by Sir Andrew Ffoulkes, who, in the guise of her lacquey, was carrying a number of impedimenta, found her way down to the pier.

Once on board, the keen, fresh sea air revived her, the breeze was just strong enough to nicely swell the sails of the *Foam Crest*, as she cut her way merrily towards the open.

The sunset was glorious after the storm, and Marguerite, as she watched the white cliffs of Dover gradually disappearing from view, felt more at peace, and once more almost hopeful.

Sir Andrew was full of kind attentions, and she felt how lucky she had been to have him by her side in this, her great trouble.

Gradually the grey coast of France began to emerge from the fast-gathering evening mists. One or two lights could be seen flickering, and the spires of several churches to rise out of the surrounding haze.

Half an hour later Marguerite had landed upon French shore. She was back in that country where at this very moment men slaughtered their fellow-creatures by the hundreds, and sent innocent women and children in thousands to the block.

The very aspect of the country and its people, even in this remote sea-coast town, spoke of that seething revolution, three hundred miles away, in beautiful Paris, now

rendered hideous by the constant flow of the blood of her
noblest sons, by the wailing of the widows, and the cries
of fatherless children.

The men all wore red caps—in various stages of cleanliness—but all with the tricolor cockade pinned on the
left-hand side. Marguerite noticed with a shudder that,
instead of the laughing, merry countenance habitual to
her own countrymen, their faces now invariably wore a
look of sly distrust.

Every man nowadays was a spy upon his fellows: the
most innocent word uttered in jest might at any time be
brought up as a proof of aristocratic tendencies, or of
treachery against the people. Even the women went about
with a curious look of fear and of hate lurking in their
brown eyes; and all watched Marguerite as she stepped on
shore, followed by Sir Andrew, and murmured as she
passed along: *"Sacrés aristos!"* or else *"Sacrés Anglais!"*

Otherwise their presence excited no further comment.
Calais, even in those days, was in constant business com-
munication with England, and English merchants were
often to be seen on this coast. It was well known that in
view of the heavy duties in England, a vast deal of French
wines and brandies were smuggled across. This pleased the
French *bourgeois* immensely; he liked to see the English
Government and the English king, both of whom he
hated, cheated out of their revenues; and an English
smuggler was always a welcome guest at the tumble-down
taverns of Calais and Boulogne.

So, perhaps, as Sir Andrew gradually directed Marguerite through the tortuous streets of Calais, many of the
population, who turned with an oath to look at the strang-

ers clad in the English fashion, thought that they were bent on purchasing dutiable articles for their own fog-ridden country, and gave them no more than a passing thought.

Marguerite, however, wondered how her husband's tall, massive figure could have passed through Calais unobserved: she marvelled what disguise he assumed to do his noble work without exciting too much attention.

Without exchanging more than a few words, Sir Andrew was leading her right across the town, to the other side from that where they had landed, and on the way towards Cap Gris Nez. The streets were narrow, tortuous, and mostly evil-smelling, with a mixture of stale fish and damp cellar odours. There had been heavy rain here during the storm last night, and sometimes Marguerite sank ankle-deep in the mud, for the roads were not lighted save by the occasional glimmer from a lamp inside a house.

But she did not heed any of these petty discomforts: "We may meet Blakeney at the 'Chat Gris.' " Sir Andrew had said, when they landed, and she was walking as if on a carpet of rose-leaves, for she was going to meet him almost at once.

At last they reached their destination. Sir Andrew evidently knew the road, for he had walked unerringly in the dark, and had not asked his way from anyone. It was too dark then for Marguerite to notice the outside aspect of this house. The "Chat Gris," as Sir Andrew had called it, was evidently a small wayside inn on the outskirts of Calais, and on the way to Gris Nez. It lay some little distance from the coast, for the sound of the sea seemed to come from afar.

Sir Andrew knocked at the door with the knob of his
cane, and from within Marguerite heard a sort of grunt
and the muttering of a number of oaths. Sir Andrew
knocked again, this time more peremptorily: more oaths
were heard, and then shuffling steps seemed to draw near
the door. Presently this was throw open, and Marguerite
found herself on the threshold of the most dilapidated,
most squalid room she had ever seen in all her life.

The paper, such as it was, was hanging from the walls
in strips; there did not seem to be a single piece of
furniture in the room that could, by the wildest stretch of
imagination, be called "whole." Most of the chairs had
broken backs, others had no seats to them, one corner of
the table was propped up with a bundle of faggots, there
where the fourth leg had been broken.

In one corner of the room there was a huge hearth, over
which hung a stock-pot, with a not altogether unpalatable
odour of hot soup emanating therefrom. On one side of the
room, high up in the wall, there was a species of loft,
before which hung a tattered blue-and-white checked curtain. A rickety set of steps led up to this loft.

On the great bare walls, with their colourless paper, all
stained with varied filth, there were chalked up at intervals in great bold characters, the words: "Liberté—Egalité
—Fraternité."

The whole of this sordid abode was dimly lighted by an
evil-smelling oil-lamp, which hung from the rickety rafters
of the ceiling. It all looked so horribly squalid, so dirty
and uninviting, that Marguerite hardly dared to cross the
threshold.

Sir Andrew, however, had stepped unhesitatingly forward.

"English travellers, citoyen!" he said boldly, and speaking in French.

The individual who had come to the door in response to Sir Andrew's knock, and who, presumably, was the owner of this squalid abode, was an elderly, heavily-built peasant, dressed in a dirty blue blouse, heavy sabots, from which wisps of straw protruded all round, shabby blue trousers, and the inevitable red cap with the tricolour cockade, that proclaimed his momentary political views. He carried a short wooden pipe, from which the odour of rank tobacco emanated. He looked with some suspicion and a great deal of contempt at the two travellers, muttered "Sacrrrés Anglais!" and spat upon the ground to further show his independence of spirit, but, nevertheless, he stood aside to let them enter, no doubt well aware that these same Sacrrrés Anglais always had well-filled purses.

"Oh, lud!" said Marguerite, as she advanced into the room, holding her handkerchief to her dainty nose, "what a dreadful hole! Are you sure this is the place?"

"Aye! 'tis the place, sure enough," replied the young man as, with his lace-edged, fashionable handkerchief, he dusted a chair for Marguerite to sit on; "but I vow I never saw a more villainous hole."

"Faith!" she said, looking round with some curiosity and a great deal of horror at the dilapidated walls, the broken chairs, the rickety table, "it certainly does not look inviting."

The landlord of the "Chat Gris"—by name, Brogard—had taken no further notice of his guests; he concluded that presently they would order supper, and in the meanwhile it was not for a free citizen to show deference, or

even courtesy, to anyone, however smartly they might be
dressed.

By the hearth sat a huddled-up figure clad, seemingly,
mostly in rags: that figure was apparently a woman, although even that would have been hard to distinguish,
except for the cap, which had once been white, and for
what looked like the semblance of a petticoat. She was
sitting mumbling to herself, and from time to time stirring
the brew in her stock-pot.

"Hey, my friend!" said Sir Andrew at last, "we should
like some supper. . . . The citoyenne there," he added,
pointing to the huddled-up bundle of rags by the hearth,
"is concocting some delicious soup, I'll warrant, and my
mistress has not tasted food for several hours."

It took Brogard some few moments to consider the
question. A free citizen does not respond too readily to
the wishes of those who happen to require something of
him.

"Sacrrrés aristos!" he murmured, and once more spat
upon the ground.

Then he went very slowly up to a dresser which stood in
a corner of the room; from this he took an old pewter soup-
tureen and slowly, and without a word, he handed it to
his better-half, who, in the same silence, began filling the
tureen with the soup out of her stock-pot.

Marguerite had watched all these preparations with absolute horror; were it not for the earnestness of her purpose, she would incontinently have fled from this abode of
dirt and evil smells.

"Faith! our host and hostess are not cheerful people,"
said Sir Andrew, seeing the look of horror on Marguerite's

face. "I would I could offer you a more hearty and more appetising meal . . . but I think you will find the soup eatable and the wine good; these people wallow in dirt, but live well as a rule."

"Nay! I pray you, Sir Andrew," she said gently, "be not anxious about me. My mind is scarce inclined to dwell on thoughts of supper."

Brogard was slowly pursuing his gruesome preparations; he had placed a couple of spoons, also two glasses on the table, both of which Sir Andrew took the precaution of wiping carefully.

Brogard had also produced a bottle of wine and some bread, and Marguerite made an effort to draw her chair to the table and to make some pretence at eating. Sir Andrew, as befitting his *rôle* of lacquey, stood behind her chair.

"Nay, Madame, I pray you," he said, seeing that Marguerite seemed quite unable to eat, "I beg of you to try and swallow some food—remember you have need of all your strength."

The soup certainly was not bad; it smelt and tasted good. Marguerite might have enjoyed it, but for the horrible surroundings. She broke the bread, however, and drank some of the wine.

"Nay, Sir Andrew," she said, "I do not like to see you standing. You have need of food just as much as I have. This creature will only think that I am an eccentric Englishwoman eloping with her lacquey, if you'll sit down and partake of this semblance of supper beside me."

Indeed, Brogard, having placed what was strictly necessary upon the table, seemed not to trouble himself any further about his guests. The Mère Brogard had quietly shuffled out of the room, and the man stood and lounged about, smoking his evil-smelling pipe, sometimes under Marguerite's very nose, as any free-born citizen who was anybody's equal should do.

"Confound the brute!" said Sir Andrew, with native British wrath, as Brogard leant up against the table, smoking and looking down superciliously at these two *sacrrrés Anglais*.

"In Heaven's name, man," admonished Marguerite, hurriedly, seeing that Sir Andrew, with British-born instinct, was ominously clenching his fist, "remember that you are in France, and that in this year of grace this is the temper of the people."

"I'd like to scrag the brute!" muttered Sir Andrew, savagely.

He had taken Marguerite's advice and sat next to her at table, and they were both making noble efforts to deceive one another, by pretending to eat and drink.

"I pray you," said Marguerite, "keep the creature in a good temper, so that he may answer the questions we must put to him."

"I'll do my best, but, begad! I'd sooner scrag him than question him. Hey! my friend," he said pleasantly in French, and tapping Brogard lightly on the shoulder, "do you see many of our quality along these parts? Many English travellers, I mean?"

Brogard looked round at him, over his near shoulder, puffed away at his pipe for a moment or two as he was in no hurry, then muttered,—

"Heu!—sometimes!"

"Ah!" said Sir Andrew, carelessly, "English travellers always know where they can get good wine, eh! my friend? —Now, tell me, my lady was desiring to know if by any chance you happen to have seen a great friend of hers, an English gentleman, who often comes to Calais on business; he is tall, and recently was on his way to Paris—my lady hoped to have met him in Calais."

Marguerite tried not to look at Brogard, lest she should betray before him the burning anxiety with which she waited for his reply. But a free-born French citizen is never in any hurry to answer questions: Brogard took his time, then he said very slowly,—

"Tall Englishman?—To-day!—Yes."

"You have seen him? asked Sir Andrew, carelessly.

"Yes, to-day," muttered Brogard, sullenly. Then he quietly took Sir Andrew's hat from a chair close by, put it on his own head, tugged at his dirty blouse, and generally tried to express in pantomime that the individual in question wore very fine clothes. "*Sacrré aristo!*" he muttered, "that tall Englishman!"

Marguerite could scarce repress a scream.

"It's Sir Percy right enough," she murmured, "and not even in disguise!"

She smiled, in the midst of all her anxiety and through her gathering tears, at thought of "the ruling passion strong in death"; of Percy running into the wildest, maddest dangers, with the latest-cut coat upon his back, and the laces of his jabot unruffled.

"Oh! the foolhardiness of it!" she sighed. "Quick, Sir Andrew! ask the man when he went."

"Ah, yes, my friend," said Sir Andrew, addressing

Brogard, with the same assumption of carelessness, "my lord always wears beautiful clothes; the tall Englishman you saw, was certainly my lady's friend. And he has gone, you say?"

"He went . . . yes . . . but he's coming back . . . here—he ordered supper . . ."

Sir Andrew put his hand with a quick gesture of warning upon Marguerite's arm; it came none too soon, for the next moment her wild, mad joy would have betrayed her. He was safe and well, was coming back here presently, she would see him in a few moments perhaps. . . . Oh! the wildness of her joy seemed almost more than she could bear.

"Here!" she said to Brogard, who seemed suddenly to have been transformed in her eyes into some heaven-born messenger of bliss. "Here!—did you say the English gentleman was coming back here?"

The heaven-born messenger of bliss spat upon the floor, to express his contempt for all and sundry *aristos*, who chose to haunt the "Chat Gris."

"Heu!" he muttered, "he ordered supper—he will come back. . . . *Sacrré Anglais!*" he added, by way of protest against all this fuss for a mere Englishman.

"But where is he now?—Do you know?" she asked eagerly, placing her dainty white hand upon the dirty sleeve of his blue blouse.

"He went to get a horse and cart," said Brogard, laconically, as, with a surly gesture, he shook off from his arm that pretty hand which princes had been proud to kiss.

"At what time did he go?"

But Brogard had evidently had enough of these question-

ings. He did not think that it was fitting for a citizen—
who was the equal of anybody—to be thus catechised by
these *sacrés aristos*, even though they were rich English
ones. It was distinctly more fitting to his new-born dignity
to be as rude as possible; it was a sure sign of servility to
meekly reply to civil questions.

"I don't know," he said, surlily. "I have said enough,
voyons, les aristos! . . . He came to-day. He ordered supper.
He went out. —He'll come back. *Voilà!*"

And with this parting assertion of his rights as a citizen
and a free man, to be as rude as he well pleased, Brogard
shuffled out of the room, banging the door after him.

Chapter 23

Hope

"Faith, Madame!" said Sir Andrew, seeing that Marguerite seemed desirous to call her surly host back again, "I think we'd better leave him alone. We shall not get anything more out of him, and we might arouse his suspicions. One never knows what spies may be lurking around these God-forsaken places."

"What care I?" she replied lightly, "now I know that my husband is safe, and that I shall see him almost directly!"

"Hush!" he said in genuine alarm, for she had talked quite loudly, in the fulness of her glee, "the very walls have ears in France, these days."

He rose quickly from the table, and walked round the bare, squalid room, listening attentively at the door, through which Brogard had just disappeared, and whence only muttered oaths and shuffling footsteps could be heard. He also ran up the rickety steps that led to the attic, to assure himself that there were no spies of Chauvelin's about the place.

"Are we alone, Monsieur, my lacquey?" said Marguerite, gaily, as the young man once more sat down beside her. "May we talk?"

"As cautiously as possible!" he entreated.

"Faith, man! but you wear a glum face! As for me, I could dance with joy! Surely there is no longer any cause for fear. Our boat is on the beach, the *Foam Crest* not two miles out at sea, and my husband will be here, under this very roof, within the next half hour perhaps. Sure! there is naught to hinder us. Chauvelin and his gang have not yet arrived."

"Nay, madam! that I fear we do not know."

"What do you mean?"

"He was at Dover at the same time that we were."

"Held up by the same storm, which kept us from starting."

"Exactly. But—I did not speak of it before, for I feared to alarm you—I saw him on the beach not five minutes before we embarked. At least, I swore to myself at the time that it was himself; he was disguised as a *curé*, so that Satan, his own guardian, would scarce have known him. But I heard him then, bargaining for a vessel to take him swiftly to Calais; and he must have set sail less than an hour after we did."

Marguerite's face had quickly lost its look of joy. The terrible danger in which Percy stood, now that he was actually on French soil, became suddenly and horribly clear to her. Chauvelin was close upon his heels; here in Calais, the astute diplomatist was all-powerful; a word from him and Percy could be tracked and arrested and . . .

Every drop of blood seemed to freeze in her veins; not
even during the moments of her wildest anguish in England had she so completely realised the imminence of the
peril in which her husband stood. Chauvelin had sworn to
bring the Scarlet Pimpernel to the guillotine, and now the
daring plotter, whose anonymity hitherto had been his
safeguard, stood revealed through her own hand, to his
most bitter, most relentless enemy.

Chauvelin when he waylaid Lord Tony and Sir Andrew Ffoulkes in the coffee-room of "The Fisherman's
Rest"—had obtained possession of all the plans of this
latest expedition. Armand St. Just, the Comte de Tournay
and other fugitive royalists were to have met the Scarlet
Pimpernel—or rather, as it had been originally arranged,
two of his emissaries—on this day, the 2nd of October,
at a place evidently known to the league, and vaguely
alluded to as the "Père Blanchard's hut."

Armand, whose connection with the Scarlet Pimpernel
and disavowal of the brutal policy of the Reign of Terror
was still unknown to his countrymen, had left England a
little more than a week ago, carrying with him the necessary instructions, which would enable him to meet the
other fugitives and to convey them to this place of safety.

This much Marguerite had fully understood from the
first, and Sir Andrew Ffoulkes had confirmed her surmises.
She knew, too, that when Sir Percy realized that his own
plans and his directions to his lieutenants had been stolen
by Chauvelin, it was too late to communicate with Armand, or to send fresh instructions to the fugitives.

They would, of necessity, be at the appointed time and
place, not knowing how grave was the danger which now
awaited their brave rescuer.

Blakeney, who as usual had planned and organised the whole expedition, would not allow any of his younger comrades to run the risk of almost certain capture. Hence his hurried note to them at Lord Grenville's ball—"Start myself to-morrow—alone."

And now with his identity known to his most bitter enemy, his every step would be dogged, the moment he set foot in France. He would be tracked by Chauvelin's emissaries, followed until he reached that mysterious hut where the fugitives were waiting for him, and there the trap would be closed on him and on them.

There was but one hour—the hour's start which Marguerite and Sir Andrew had of their enemy—in which to warn Percy of the imminence of his danger, and to persuade him to give up the foolhardy expedition, which could only end in his own death.

But there *was* that one hour.

"Chauvelin knows of this inn, from the papers he stole," said Sir Andrew, earnestly, "and on landing will make straight for it."

"He has not landed yet," she said, "we have an hour's start of him, and Percy will be here directly. We shall be mid-Channel ere Chauvelin has realised that we have slipped through his fingers."

She spoke excitedly and eagerly, wishing to infuse into her young friend some of that buoyant hope, which still clung to her heart. But he shook his head sadly.

"Silent again, Sir Andrew?" she said with some impatience. "Why do you shake your head and look so glum?"

"Faith, Madame," he replied, " 'tis only because in making your rose-coloured plans, you are forgetting the most important factor."

"What in the world do you mean?—I am forgetting nothing. . . . What factor do you mean?" she added with more impatience.

"It stands six foot odd high," replied Sir Andrew, quietly, "and hath name Percy Blakeney."

"I don't understand," she murmured.

"Do you think that Blakeney would leave Calais without having accomplished what he set out to do?"

"You mean . . . ?"

"There's the old Comte de Tournay . . ."

"The Comte . . . ?" she murmured.

"And St. Just . . . and others . . ."

"My brother!" she said with a heart-broken sob of anguish. "Heaven help me, but I fear I had forgotten."

"Fugitives as they are, these men at this moment await with perfect confidence and unshaken faith the arrival of the Scarlet Pimpernel, who has pledged his honour to take them safely across the Channel."

Indeed, she had forgotten! With the sublime selfishness of a woman who loves with her whole heart, she had in the last twenty-four hours had no thought save for him. His precious, noble life, his danger—he, the loved one, the brave hero, he alone dwelt in her mind.

"My brother!" she murmured, as one by one the heavy tears gathered in her eyes, as memory came back to her of Armand, the companion and darling of her childhood, the man for whom she had committed the deadly sin, which had so hopelessly imperilled her brave husband's life.

"Sir Percy Blakeney would not be the trusted, honoured leader of a score of English gentlemen," said Sir Andrew, proudly, "if he abandoned those who placed their trust in him. As for breaking his word, the very thought is preposterous!"

There was silence for a moment or two. Marguerite had buried her face in her hands, and was letting the tears slowly trickle through her trembling fingers. The young man said nothing; his heart ached for this beautiful woman in her awful grief. All along he had felt the terrible *impasse* in which her own rash act had plunged them all. He knew his friend and leader so well, with his reckless daring, his mad bravery, his worship of his own word of honour. Sir Andrew knew that Blakeney would brave any danger, run the wildest risks sooner than break it, and with Chauvelin at his very heels, would make a final attempt, however desperate, to rescue those who trusted in him.

"Faith, Sir Andrew," said Marguerite at last, making brave efforts to dry her tears, "you are right, and I would not now shame myself by trying to dissuade him from doing his duty. As you say, I should plead in vain. God grant him strength and ability," she added fervently and resolutely, "to outwit his pursuers. He will not refuse to take you with him, perhaps, when he starts on his noble work; between you, you will have cunning as well as valour! God guard you both! In the meanwhile I think we should lose no time. I still believe that his safety depends upon his knowing that Chauvelin is on his track."

"Undoubtedly. He has wonderful resources at his command. As soon as he is aware of his danger he will exercise more caution: his ingenuity is a veritable miracle."

"Then, what say you to a voyage of reconnaissance in

the village whilst I wait here against his coming!—You
might come across Percy's track and thus save valuable
time. If you find him, tell him to beware!—his bitterest
enemy is on his heels!"

"But this is such a villainous hole for you to wait in."

"Nay, that I do not mind!—But you might ask our surly
host if he could let me wait in another room, where I
could be safer from the prying eyes of any chance traveller.
Offer him some ready money, so that he should not fail to
give me word the moment the tall Englishman returns."

She spoke quite calmly, even cheerfully now, thinking
out her plans, ready for the worst if need be; she would
show no more weakness, she would prove herself worthy
of him, who was about to give his life for the sake of his
fellow-men.

Sir Andrew obeyed her without further comment. Instinctively he felt that hers now was the stronger mind; he was
willing to give himself over to her guidance, to become
the hand, whilst she was the directing head.

He went to the door of the inner room, through which
Brogard and his wife had disappeared before, and knocked;
as usual, he was answered by a salvo of muttered oaths.

"Hey! friend Brogard!" said the young man peremrpto-
rily, "my lady would wish to rest here awhile. Could you
give her the use of another room? She would wish to be
alone."

He took some money out of his pocket, and allowed it
to jingle significantly in his hand. Brogard had opened the
door, and listened, with his usual surly apathy, to the
young man's request. At the sight of the gold, however, his
lazy attitude relaxed slightly; he took his pipe from his
mouth and shuffled into the room.

He then pointed over his shoulder at the attic up in the wall.

"She can wait up there!" he said with a grunt. "It's comfortable, and I have no other room."

"Nothing could be better," said Marguerite in English; she at once realised the advantages such a position hidden from view would give her. "Give him the money, Sir Andrew; I shall be quite happy up there, and can see everything without being seen."

She nodded to Brogard, who condescended to go up to the attic, and to shake up the straw that lay on the floor.

"May I entreat you, madam, to do nothing rash," said Sir Andrew, as Marguerite prepared in her turn to ascend the rickety flight of steps. "Remember this place is infested with spies. Do not, I beg of you, reveal yourself to Sir Percy, unless you are absolutely certain that you are alone with him."

Even as he spoke, he felt how unnecessary was this caution: Marguerite was as calm, as clear-headed as any man. There was no fear of her doing anything that was rash.

"Nay," she said, with a slight attempt at cheerfulness, "that can I faithfully promise you. I would not jeopardise my husband's life, nor yet his plans, by speaking to him before strangers. Have no fear, I will watch my opportunity, and serve him in the manner I think he needs it most."

Brogard had come down the steps again, and Marguerite was ready to go up to her safe retreat.

"I dare not kiss your hand, madam," said Sir Andrew, as she began to mount the steps, "since I am your lacquey, but I pray you be of good cheer. If I do not come across Blakeney in half an hour, I shall return, expecting to find him here."

"Yes, that will be best. We can afford to wait for half an hour. Chauvelin cannot possibly be here before that. God grant that either you or I may have seen Percy by then. Good luck to you, friend! Have no fear for me."

Lightly she mounted the rickety wooden steps that led to the attic. Brogard was taking no further heed of her. She could make herself comfortable there or not as she chose. Sir Andrew watched her until she had reached the loft and sat down upon the straw. She pulled the tattered curtains across, and the young man noted that she was singularly well placed there, for seeing and hearing, whilst remaining unobserved.

He had paid Brogard well; the surly old innkeeper would have no object in betraying her. Then Sir Andrew prepared to go. At the door he turned once again and looked up at the loft. Through the ragged curtains Marguerite's sweet face was peeping down at him, and the young man rejoiced to see that it looked serene, and even gently smiling. With a final nod of farewell to her, he walked out into the night.

Chapter 24

The Death-Trap

*T*he next quarter of an hour went by swiftly and noiselessly. In the room downstairs, Brogard had for a while busied himself with clearing the table and re-arranging it for another guest.

It was because she watched these preparations, that Marguerite found the time slipping by more pleasantly. It was for Percy that this semblance of supper was being got ready. Evidently Brogard had a certain amount of respect for the tall Englishman, as he seemed to take some trouble in making the place look a trifle less uninviting than it had done before.

He even produced, from some hidden recess in the old dresser, what actually looked like a table-cloth; and when he spread it out, and saw it was full of holes, he shook his head dubiously for a while, then was at much pains so to spread it over the table, as to hide most of its blemishes.

247

Then he got out a serviette, also old and ragged, but possessing some measure of cleanliness, and with this he carefully wiped the glasses, spoons and plates, which he put on the table.

Marguerite could not help smiling to herself as she watched all these preparations, which Brogard accomplished to an accompaniment of muttered oaths. Clearly the great height and bulk of the Englishman, or perhaps the weight of his fist, had overawed this free-born citizen of France, or he would never have been at such trouble for any *sacrré aristo*.

When the table was set—such as it was—Brogard surveyed it with evident satisfaction. He then dusted one of the chairs with the corner of his blouse, gave a stir to the stock-pot, threw a fresh bundle of faggots on to the fire, and slouched out of the room.

Marguerite was left alone with her reflections. She had spread her travelling cloak over the straw, and was sitting fairly comfortably, as the straw was fresh, and the evil odours from below came up to her only in a modified form.

But, momentarily, she was almost happy; happy because, when she peeped through the tattered curtains, she could see a rickety chair, a torn table-cloth, a glass, a plate and a spoon; that was all. But those mute and ugly things seemed to say to her, that they were waiting for Percy; that soon, very soon, he would be here, that the squalid room being still empty, they would be alone together.

That thought was so heavenly, that Marguerite closed her eyes in order to shut out everything but that. In a few minutes she would be alone with him; she would run

down the ladder, and let him see her; then he would take
her in his arms, and she would let him see that, after that,
she would gladly die for him, and with him, for earth
could hold no greater happiness than that.

And then what would happen? She could not even
remotely conjecture. She knew, of course, that Sir Andrew was right, that Percy would do everything he had set
out to accomplish; that she—now she was here—could do
nothing, beyond warning him to be cautious, since
Chauvelin himself was on his track. After having cau-
tioned him, she would perforce have to see him go off
upon his terrible and daring mission; she could not even
with a word or look, attempt to keep him back. She would
have to obey, whatever he told her to do, even perhaps
have to efface herself, and wait, in indescribable agony,
whilst he, perhaps, went to his death.

But even that seemed less terrible to bear than the
thought that he should never know how much she loved
him—that at any rate would be spared her; the squalid
room itself, which seemed to be waiting for him, told her
that he would be here soon.

Suddenly her over-sensitive ears caught the sound of
distant footsteps drawing near; her heart gave a wild leap
of joy! Was it Percy at last? No! the step did not seem
quite as long, nor quite as firm as his; she also thought
that she could hear two distinct sets of footsteps. Yes! that
was it! two men were coming this way. Two strangers
perhaps, to get a drink, or . . .

But she had not time to conjecture, for presently there
was a peremptory call at the door, and the next moment it
was violently thrown open from the outside, whilst a
rough, commanding voice shouted,—

"Hey! Citoyen Brogard! Holà!"

Marguerite could not see the newcomers, but, through a hole in one of the curtains, she could observe one portion of the room below.

She heard Brogard's shuffling footsteps, as he came out of the inner room, muttering his usual string of oaths. On seeing the strangers, however, he paused in the middle of the room, well within range of Marguerite's vision, looked at them, with even more withering contempt than he had bestowed upon his former guests, and muttered, *"Sacrrrée soutane!"*

Marguerite's heart seemed all at once to stop beating; her eyes, large and dilated, had fastened on one of the newcomers, who, at this point, had taken a quick step forward towards Brogard. He was dressed in the soutane, broad-brimmed hat and buckled shoes, habitual to the French *curé*, but as he stood opposite the innkeeper, he threw open his soutane for a moment, displaying the tricolour scarf of officialism, which sight immediately had the effect of transforming Brogard's attitude of contempt, into one of cringing obsequiousness.

It was the sight of this French *curé*, which seemed to freeze the very blood in Marguerite's veins. She could not see his face, which was shaded by his broad-brimmed hat, but she recognized the thin, bony hands, the slight stoop, the whole gait of the man! It was Chauvelin!

The horror of the situation struck her as with a physical blow; the awful disappointment, the dread of what was to come, made her very senses reel, and she needed almost superhuman effort, not to fall senseless beneath it all.

"A plate of soup and a bottle of wine," said Chauvelin

imperiously to Brogard, "then clear out of here—understand? I want to be alone."

Silently, and without any muttering this time, Brogard obeyed. Chauvelin sat down at the table, which had been prepared for the tall Englishman, and the innkeeper busied himself obsequiously round him, dishing up the soup and pouring out the wine. The man who had entered with Chauvelin and whom Marguerite could not see, stood waiting close by the door.

At a brusque sign from Chauvelin, Brogard had hurried back to the inner room, and the former now beckoned to the man who had accompanied him.

In him Marguerite at once recognised Desgas, Chauvelin's secretary and confidential factotum, whom she had often seen in Paris, in the days gone by. He crossed the room, and for a moment or two listened attentively at the Brogards' door.

"Not listening?" asked Chauvelin, curtly.

"No, citoyen."

For a second Marguerite dreaded lest Chauvelin should order Desgas to search the place; what would happen if she were to be discovered, she hardly dared to imagine. Fortunately, however, Chauvelin seemed more impatient to talk to his secretary than afraid of spies, for he called Desgas quickly back to his side.

"The English schooner?" he asked.

"She was lost sight of at sundown, citoyen," replied Desgas, "but was then making west, towards Cap Gris Nez."

"Ah!—good!—" muttered Chauvelin, "and now, about Captain Jutley?—what did he say?"

"He assured me that all the orders you sent him last week have been implicitly obeyed. All the roads which converge to this place have been patrolled night and day ever since: and the beach and cliffs have been most rigorously searched and guarded."

"Does he know where this 'Père Blanchard's' hut is?"

"No, citoyen, nobody seems to know of it by that name. There are any amount of fishermen's huts all along the coast, of course . . . but . . ."

"That'll do. Now about tonight?" interrupted Chauvelin, impatiently.

"The roads and the beach are patrolled as usual, citoyen, and Captain Jutley awaits further orders."

"Go back to him at once, then. Tell him to send reinforcements to the various patrols; and especially to those along the beach—you understand?"

Chauvelin spoke curtly and to the point, and every word he uttered struck at Marguerite's heart like the death-knell of her fondest hopes.

"The men," he continued, "are to keep the sharpest possible look-out for any stranger who may be walking, riding, or driving, along the road or the beach, more especially for a tall stranger, whom I need not describe further, as probably he will be disguised; but he cannot very well conceal his height, except by stooping. You understand?"

"Perfectly, citoyen," replied Desgas.

"As soon as any of the men have sighted a stranger, two of them are to keep him in view. The man who loses sight of the tall stranger, after he is once seen, will pay for his negligence with his life; but one man is to ride straight back here and report to me. Is that clear?"

"Absolutely clear, citoyen."

"Very well, then. Go and see Jutley at once. See the reinforcements start off for the patrol duty, then ask the captain to let you have half-a-dozen more men and bring them here with you. You can be back in ten minutes. Go—"

Desgas saluted and went to the door.

As Marguerite, sick with horror, listened to Chauvelin's directions to his underling, the whole of the plan for the capture of the Scarlet Pimpernel became appallingly clear to her. Chauvelin wished that the fugitives should be left in false security waiting in their hidden retreat until Percy joined them. Then the daring plotter was to be surrounded and caught red-handed, in the very act of aiding and abetting royalists, who were traitors to the republic. Thus, if his capture were noised abroad, even the British Government could not legally protest in his favour; having plotted with the enemies of the French Government, France had the right to put him to death.

Escape for him and them would be impossible. All the roads patrolled and watched, the trap well set, the net, wide at present, but drawing together tighter and tighter, until it closed upon the daring plotter, whose superhuman cunning even could not rescue him from its meshes now.

Desgas was about to go, but Chauvelin once more called him back. Marguerite vaguely wondered what further devilish plans he could have formed, in order to entrap one brave man, alone, against two-score of others. She looked at him as he turned to speak to Desgas; she could just see his face beneath the broad-brimmed curé's hat. There was at that moment so much deadly hatred, such fiendish malice in the thin face and pale, small eyes, that Marguerite's last hope died in her heart, for she felt that from this man she could expect no mercy.

"I had forgotten," repeated Chauvelin, with a weird chuckle, as he rubbed his bony, talon-like hands one against the other, with a gesture of fiendish satisfaction. "The tall stranger may show fight. In any case no shooting, remember, except as a last resort. I want that tall stranger alive . . . if possible."

He laughed, as Dante has told us that the devils laugh at sight of the torture of the damned. Marguerite had thought that by now she had lived through the whole gamut of horror and anguish that human heart could bear; yet now, when Desgas left the house, and she remained alone in this lonely, squalid room, with that fiend for company, she felt as if all that she had suffered was nothing compared with this. He continued to laugh and chuckle to himself for a while, rubbing his hands together in anticipation of his triumph.

His plans were well laid, and he might well triumph! Not a loophole was left, through which the bravest, the most cunning man might escape. Every road guarded, every corner watched, and in that lonely hut somewhere on the coast, a small band of fugitives waiting for their rescuer, and leading him to his death—nay! to worse than death. That fiend there, in a holy man's garb, was too much of a devil to allow a brave man to die the quick, sudden death of a soldier at the post of duty.

He, above all, longed to have the cunning enemy, who had so long baffled him, helpless in his power; he wished to gloat over him, to enjoy his downfall, to inflict upon him what moral and mental torture a deadly hatred alone can devise. The brave eagle, captured, and with noble wings clipped, was doomed to endure the gnawing of the rat. And she, his wife, who loved him, and who had brought him to this, could do nothing to help him.

Nothing, save to hope for death by his side, and for one brief moment in which to tell him that her love—whole, true and passionate—was entirely his.

Chauvelin was now sitting close to the table; he had taken off his hat, and Marguerite could just see the outline of his thin profile and pointed chin, as he bent over his meagre supper. He was evidently quite contented, and awaited events with perfect calm; he even seemed to enjoy Brogard's unsavoury fare. Marguerite wondered how so much hatred could lurk in one human being against another.

Suddenly, as she watched Chauvelin, a sound caught her ear, which turned her very heart to stone. And yet that sound was not calculated to inspire anyone with horror, for it was merely the cheerful sound of a gay, fresh voice singing lustily, "God save the King!"

Chapter 25

The Eagle and the Fox

*M*arguerite's breath stopped short; she seemed to feel her very life standing still momentarily whilst she listened to that voice and to that song. In the singer she had recognised her husband. Chauvelin, too, had heard it, for he darted a quick glance towards the door, then hurriedly took up his broad-brimmed hat and clapped it over his head.

The voice drew nearer; for one brief second the wild desire seized Marguerite to rush down the steps and fly across the room, to stop that song at any cost, to beg the cheerful singer to fly—fly for his life, before it be too late. She checked the impulse just in time. Chauvelin would stop her before she reached the door, and, moreover, she had no idea if he had any soldiers posted within his call. Her impetuous act might prove the death-signal of the man she would have died to save.

"Long to reign over us, God save the King!"

sang the voice more lustily than ever. The next moment
the door was thrown open and there was dead silence for a
second or so.

Marguerite could not see the door: she held her breath,
trying to imagine what was happening.

Percy Blakeney on entering had, of course, at once
caught sight of the *curé* at the table; his hesitation lasted
less than five seconds, the next moment Marguerite saw
his tall figure crossing the room, whilst he called in a
loud, cheerful voice,—

"Hello, there! no one about? Where's that fool Brogard?"

He wore the magnificent coat and riding-suit which he
had on when Marguerite last saw him at Richmond, so
many hours ago. As usual, his get-up was absolutely irreproachable, the fine Mechlin lace at his neck and wrists
was immaculate in its gossamer daintiness, his hands looked
slender and white, his fair hair was carefully brushed, and
he carried his eyeglass with his usual affected gesture. In
fact, at this moment, Sir Percy Blakeney, Bart., might
have been on his way to a garden-party at the Prince of
Wales', instead of deliberately, cold-bloodedly running his
head in a trap, set for him by his deadliest enemy.

He stood for a moment in the middle of the room,
whilst Marguerite, absolutely paralysed with horror, seemed
unable even to breathe.

Every moment she expected that Chauvelin would give
a signal, that the place would fill with soldiers, that she
would rush down and help Percy to sell his life dearly. As

he stood there, suavely unconscious, she very nearly
screamed out to him,—

"Fly, Percy!—'tis your deadly enemy!—fly before it be
too late!"

But she had not time even to do that, for the next
moment Blakeney quietly walked to the table, and, jovially clapping the *curé* on the back, said in his own drawly,
affected way,—

"Odds fish! . . . er . . . M. Chauvelin. . . . I vow I
never thought of meeting you here."

Chauvelin, who had been in the very act of conveying
soup to his mouth, fairly choked. His thin face became
absolutely purple, and a violent fit of coughing saved this
cunning representative of France from betraying the most
boundless surprise he had ever experienced. There was no
doubt that this bold move on the part of the enemy had
been wholly unexpected, as far as he was concerned: and
the daring impudence of it completely nonplussed him for
the moment.

Obviously he had not taken the precaution of having
the inn surrounded with soldiers. Blakeney had evidently
guessed that much, and no doubt his resourceful brain had
already formed some plan by which he could turn this
unexpected interview to account.

Marguerite up in the loft had not moved. She had made
a solemn promise to Sir Andrew not to speak to her
husband before strangers, and she had sufficient self-control
not to throw herself unreasoningly and impulsively across
his plans. To sit still and watch these two men together
was a terrible trial of fortitude. Marguerite had heard
Chauvelin give the orders for the patrolling of all the

roads. She knew that if Percy now left the "Chat Gris"—in whichever direction he happened to go—he could not go far without being sighted by some of Captain Jutley's men on patrol. On the other hand, if he stayed, then Desgas would have time to come back with the half-dozen men Chauvelin had specially ordered.

The trap was closing in, and Marguerite could do nothing but watch and wonder. The two men looked such a strange contrast, and of the two it was Chauvelin who exhibited a slight touch of fear. Marguerite knew him well enough to guess what was passing in his mind. He had no fear for his own person, although he certainly was alone in a lonely inn with a man who was powerfully built, and who was daring and reckless beyond the bounds of probability. She knew that Chauvelin would willingly have braved perilous encounters for the sake of the cause he had at heart, but what he did fear was that this impudent Englishman would, by knocking him down, double his own chances of escape; his underlings might not succeed so well in capturing the Scarlet Pimpernel, when not directed by the cunning hand and the shrewd brain, which had deadly hate for an incentive.

Evidently, however, the representative of the French Government had nothing to fear for the moment, at the hands of his powerful adversary. Blakeney, with his most inane laugh and pleasant good-nature, was solemnly patting him on the back.

"I am so demmed sorry . . ." he was saying cheerfully, "so very sorry . . . I seem to have upset you . . . eating soup, too . . . nasty, awkward thing, soup . . . er . .

Begad!—a friend of mine died once . . . er . . . choked
. . . just like you . . . with a spoonful of soup."

And he smiled shyly, good-humouredly, down at
Chauvelin.

"Odd's life!" he continued, as soon as the latter had
somewhat recovered himself, "beastly hole this . . . ain't
it now? La! you don't mind?" he added, apologetically, as
he sat down on a chair close to the table and drew the
soup tureen towards him. "That fool Brogard seems to be
asleep or something."

There was a second plate on the table, and he calmly
helped himself to soup, then poured himself out a glass of
wine.

For a moment Marguerite wondered what Chauvelin
would do. His disguise was so good that perhaps he meant,
on recovering himself, to deny his identity: but Chauvelin
was too astute to make such an obviously false and childish move, and already he too had stretched out his hand
and said pleasantly,—

"I am indeed charmed to see you, Sir Percy. You must
excuse me—h'm—I thought you the other side of the
Channel. Sudden surprise almost took my breath away."

"La!" said Sir Percy, with a good-humored grin, "it did
that quite, didn't it—er—M.—er—Chaubertin?"

"Pardon me—Chauvelin."

"I beg pardon—a thousand times. Yes—Chauvelin of
course. . . . Er . . . I never could cotton to foreign
names. . . ."

He was calmly eating his soup, laughing with pleasant
good-humour, as if he had come all the way to Calais for

the express purpose of enjoying supper at this filthy inn, in the company of his arch-enemy.

For the moment Marguerite wondered why Percy did not knock the little Frenchman down then and there— and no doubt something of the sort must have darted through his mind, for every now and then his lazy eyes seemed to flash ominously, as they rested on the slight figure of Chauvelin, who had now quite recovered himself and was also calmly eating his soup.

But the keen brain, which had planned and carried through so many daring plots, was too far-seeing to take unnecessary risks. This place, after all, might be infested with spies; the innkeeper might be in Chauvelin's pay. One call on Chauvelin's part might bring twenty men about Blakeney's ears for aught he knew, and he might be caught and trapped before he could help or, at least, warn the fugitives. This he would not risk; he meant to help the others, to get *them* safely away; for he had pledged his word to them, and his word he *would* keep. And whilst he ate and chatted, he thought and planned, whilst, up in the loft, the poor, anxious woman racked her brain as to what she should do, and endured agonies of longing to rush down to him, yet not daring to move for fear of upsetting his plans.

"I didn't know," Blakeney was saying jovially, "that you . . . er . . . were in holy orders."

"I . . . er . . . hem . . ." stammered Chauvelin. The calm impudence of his antagonist had evidently thrown him off his usual balance.

"But, la! I should have known you anywhere," contin- ued Sir Percy, placidly, as he poured himself out another glass of wine, "although the wig and hat have changed you a bit."

"Do you think so?"

"Lud! they alter a man so . . . but . . . begad! I hope you don't mind my having made the remark? . . . Demmed bad form making remarks. . . . I hope you don't mind?"

"No, no, not at all—hem! I hope Lady Blakeney is well," said Chauvelin, hurriedly changing the topic of conversation.

Blakeney, with much deliberation, finished his plate of soup, drank his glass of wine, and, momentarily, it seemed to Marguerite as if he glanced quickly all round the room.

"Quite well, thank you," he said at last, drily. There was a pause, during which Marguerite could watch these two antagonists who, evidently in their minds, were measuring themselves against one another. She could see Percy almost full face where he sat at the table not ten yards from where she herself was crouching, puzzled, not knowing what to do, or what she should think. She had quite controlled her impulse by now of rushing down and disclosing herself to her husband. A man capable of acting a part, in the way he was doing at the present moment, did not need a woman's word to warn him to be cautious.

Marguerite indulged in the luxury, dear to every tender woman's heart, of looking at the man she loved. She looked through the tattered curtain, across at the handsome face of her husband, in whose lazy blue eyes, and behind whose inane smile, she could now so plainly see the strength, energy, and resourcefulness which had caused the Scarlet Pimpernel to be reverenced and trusted by his followers. "There are nineteen of us ready to lay down our

lives for your husband, Lady Blakeney," Sir Andrew had
said to her; and as she looked at the forehead, low, but
square and broad, the eyes, blue, yet deep-set and intense,
the whole aspect of the man, of indomitable energy,
hiding, behind a perfectly acted comedy, his almost superhuman strength of will and marvellous ingenuity, she understood the fascination which he exercised over his
followers, for had he not also cast his spells over her heart
and her imagination?

Chauvelin, who was trying to conceal his impatience
beneath his usual urbane manner, took a quick look at his
watch. Desgas should not be long: another two or three
minutes, and this impudent Englishman would be secure
in the keeping of half a dozen of Captain Jutley's most
trusted men.

"You are on your way to Paris, Sir Percy?" he asked
carelessly.

"Odd's life, no," replied Blakeney, with a laugh. "Only
as far as Lille—not Paris for me . . . beastly uncomfortable
place Paris, just now . . . eh, Monsieur Chaubertin . . .
beg pardon . . . Chauvelin!"

"Not for an English gentleman like yourself, Sir Percy,"
rejoined Chauvelin, sarcastically, "who takes no interest in
the conflict that is raging there."

"La! you see it's no business of mine, and our demmed
government is all on your side of the business. Old Pitt
daren't say 'Bo' to a goose. You are in a hurry, sir," he
added, as Chauvelin once again took out his watch; "an
appointment, perhaps. . . . I pray you take no heed of
me. . . . My time's my own."

He rose from the table and dragged a chair to the

hearth. Once more Marguerite was terribly tempted to go to him, for time was getting on; Desgas might be back at any moment with his men. Percy did not know that and . . . oh! how horrible it all was—and how helpless she felt.

"I am in no hurry," continued Percy, pleasantly, "but, la! I don't want to spend any more time than I can help in this God-forsaken hole! But, begad! sir," he added, as Chauvelin had surreptitiously looked at his watch for the third time, "that watch of yours won't go any faster for all the looking you give it. You are expecting a friend, maybe?"

"Aye—a friend!"

"Not a lady—I trust, Monsieur l'Abbé," laughed Blakeney; "surely the holy Church does not allow? . . . eh? . . . what! But, I say, come by the fire . . . it's getting demmed cold."

He kicked the fire with the heel of his boot, making the logs blaze in the old hearth. He seemed in no hurry to go, and apparently was quite unconscious of his immediate danger. He dragged another chair to the fire, and Chauvelin, whose impatience was by now quite beyond control, sat down beside the hearth, in such a way as to command a view of the door. Desgas had been gone nearly a quarter of an hour. It was quite plain to Marguerite's aching senses, that as soon as he arrived, Chauvelin would abandon all his other plans with regard to the fugitives, and capture this impudent Scarlet Pimpernel at once.

"Hey, M. Chauvelin," the latter was saying airily, "tell me, I pray you, is your friend pretty? Demmed smart these little French women sometimes—what? But I protest I need not ask," he added, as he carelessly strode back towards the supper-table. "In matters of taste the Church has never been backward. . . . Eh?"

But Chauvelin was not listening. His every faculty was now concentrated on that door through which presently Desgas would enter. Marguerite's thoughts, too, were centered there, for her ears had suddenly caught, through the stillness of the night, the sound of numerous and measured treads some distance away.

It was Desgas and his men. Another three minutes and they would be here! Another three minutes and the awful thing would have occurred: the brave eagle will have fallen in the ferret's trap! She would have moved now and screamed, but she dared not; for whilst she heard the soldiers approaching, she was looking at Percy and watching his every movement. He was standing by the table whereon the remnants of the supper, plates, glasses, spoons, salt and pepper-pots were scattered pell-mell. His back was turned to Chauvelin and he was still prattling along in his own affected and inane way, but from his pocket he had taken his snuff-box, and quickly and suddenly he emptied the contents of the pepper-pot into it.

Then he again turned with an inane laugh to Chauvelin,—

"Eh? Did you speak, sir?"

Chauvelin had been too intent on listening to the sound of those approaching footsteps, to notice what his cunning adversary had been doing. He now pulled himself together, trying to look unconcerned in the very midst of his anticipated triumph.

"No," he said presently, "that is—as you were saying, Sir Percy—?"

"I was saying," said Blakeney, going up to Chauvelin,

by the fire, "that the Jew in Piccadilly has sold me better snuff this time than I have ever tasted. Will you honour me, Monsieur l'Abbé?"

He stood close to Chauvelin in his own careless, *débonnair* way, holding out his snuff-box to his arch-enemy.

Chauvelin, who, as he told Marguerite once, had seen a trick or two in his day, had never dreamed of this one. With one ear fixed on those fast-approaching footsteps, one eye turned to the door where Desgas and his men would presently appear, lulled into false security by the impudent Englishman's airy manner, he never even remotely guessed the trick which was being played upon him.

He took a pinch of snuff.

Only he, who has ever by accident sniffed vigorously a dose of pepper, can have the faintest conception of the hopeless condition in which such a sniff would reduce any human being.

Chauvelin felt as if his head would burst—sneeze after sneeze seemed nearly to choke him; he was blind, deaf, and dumb for the moment, and during that moment Blakeney quietly, without the slightest haste, took up his hat, took some money out of his pocket, which he left on the table, then calmly stalked out of the room!

Chapter 26

The Jew

*I*t took Marguerite some time to collect her scattered senses; the whole of this last short episode had taken place in less than a minute, and Desgas and the soldiers were still about two hundred yards away from the "Chat Gris."

When she realised what had happened, a curious mixture of joy and wonder filled her heart. It all was so neat, so ingenious. Chauvelin was still absolutely helpless, far more so than he could even have been under a blow from the fist, for now he could neither see, nor hear, nor speak, whilst his cunning adversary had quietly slipped through his fingers.

Blakeney was gone, obviously to try and join the fugitives at the Père Blanchard's hut. For the moment, true, Chauvelin was helpless; for the moment the daring Scarlet Pimpernel had not been caught by Desgas and his men. But all the roads and the beach were patrolled. Every place was watched, and every stranger kept in sight. How far could Percy go, thus arrayed in his gorgeous clothes, without being sighted and followed?

Now she blamed herself terribly for not having gone down to him sooner, and given him that word of warning and of love which, perhaps, after all, he needed. He could not know of the orders which Chauvelin had given for his capture, and even now, perhaps . . .

But before all these horrible thoughts had taken concrete form in her brain, she heard the grounding of arms outside, close to the door, and Desgas' voice shouting "Halt!" to his men.

Chauvelin had partially recovered; his sneezing had become less violent, and he had struggled to his feet. He managed to reach the door just as Desgas' knock was heard on the outside.

Chauvelin threw open the door, and before his secretary could say a word, he had managed to stammer between two sneezes—

"The tall stranger—quick!—did any of you see him?"

"Where, citoyen?" asked Desgas, in surprise.

"Here, man! through that door! not five minutes ago."

"We saw nothing, citoyen! The moon is not yet up, and . . ."

"And you are just five minutes too late, my friend," said Chauvelin, with concentrated fury.

"Citoyen . . . I . . ."

"You did what I ordered you to do," said Chauvelin, with impatience. "I know that, but you were a precious long time about it. Fortunately, there's not much harm done, or it had fared ill with you, Citoyen Desgas."

Desgas turned a little pale. There was so much rage and hatred in his superior's whole attitude.

"The tall stranger, citoyen—" he stammered.

"Was here, in this room, five minutes ago, having supper at that table. Damn his impudence! For obvious reasons, I dared not tackle him alone. Brogard is too big a fool, and that cursed Englishman appears to have the strength of a bullock, and so he slipped away under your very nose."

"He cannot go far without being sighted, citoyen."

"Ah?"

Captain Jutley sent forty men as reinforcements for the patrol duty: twenty went down to the beach. He again assured me that the watch has been constant all day, and that no stranger could possibly get to the beach, or reach a boat, without being sighted."

"That's good.—Do the men know their work?"

"They have had very clear orders, citoyen: and I myself spoke to those who were about to start. They are to shadow—as secretly as possible—any stranger they may see, especially if he be tall, or stoop as if he would disguise his height."

"In no case to detain such a person, of course," said Chauvelin, eagerly. "That impudent Scarlet Pimpernel would slip through clumsy fingers. We must let him get to the Père Blanchard's hut now; there surround and capture him."

"The men understand that, citoyen, and also that, as soon as a tall stranger has been sighted, he must be shadowed, whilst one man is to turn straight back and report to you."

"That is right," said Chauvelin, rubbing his hands, well pleased.

"I have further news for you, citoyen."

"What is it?"

"A tall Englishman had a long conversation about three-quarters of an hour ago with a Jew, Reuben by name, who lives not ten paces from here."

"Yes—and?" queried Chauvelin, impatiently.

"The conversation was all about a horse and cart, which the tall Englishman wished to hire, and which was to have been ready for him by eleven o'clock."

"It is past that now. Where does that Reuben live?"

"A few minutes' walk from this door."

"Send one of the men to find out if the stranger has driven off in Reuben's cart."

"Yes, citoyen."

Desgas went to give the necessary orders to one of the men. Not a word of this conversation between him and Chauvelin had escaped Marguerite, and every word they had spoken seemed to strike at her heart, with terrible hopelessness and dark foreboding.

She had come all this way, and with such high hopes and firm determination to help her husband, and so far she had been able to do nothing, but to watch, with a heart breaking with anguish, the meshes of the deadly net closing round the daring Scarlet Pimpernel.

He could not now advance many steps, without spying eyes to track and denounce him. Her own helplessness struck her with the terrible sense of utter disappointment. The possibility of being of the slightest use to her husband had become almost *nil*, and her only hope rested in being allowed to share his fate, whatever it might ultimately be.

For the moment, even her chance of ever seeing the man she loved again, had become a remote one. Still, she was determined to keep a close watch over his enemy, and a vague hope filled her heart, that whilst she kept Chauvelin in sight, Percy's fate might still be hanging in the balance.

Desgas had left Chauvelin moodily pacing up and down the room, whilst he himself waited outside for the return of the man, whom he had sent in search of Reuben. Thus several minutes went by. Chauvelin was evidently devoured with impatience. Apparently he trusted no one: this last trick played upon him by the daring Scarlet Pimpernel had made him suddenly doubtful of success, unless he himself was there to watch, direct and superintend the capture of this impudent Englishman.

About five minutes later, Desgas returned, followed by an elderly Jew, in a dirty, threadbare gaberdine, worn greasy across the shoulders. His red hair, which he wore after the fashion of the Polish Jews, with the corkscrew curls each side of his face, was plentifully sprinkled with grey—a general coating of grime, about his cheeks and his chin, gave him a peculiarly dirty and loathsome appearance. He had the habitual stoop, those of his race affected in mock humility in past centuries, before the dawn of equality and freedom in matters of faith, and he walked behind Desgas with the peculiar shuffling gait, which has remained the characteristic of the Jew trader in continental Europe to this day.

Chauvelin, who had all the Frenchman's prejudice against the despised race, motioned to the fellow to keep at a respectful distance. The group of the three men were standing just underneath the hanging oil-lamp, and Marguerite had a clear view of them all.

"Is this the man?" asked Chauvelin.

"No, citoyen," replied Desgas, "Reuben could not be found, so presumably his cart has gone with the stranger; but this man here seems to know something, which he is willing to sell for a consideration."

"Ah!" said Chauvelin turning away with disgust from the loathsome specimen of humanity before him.

The Jew, with characteristic patience, stood humbly on one side, leaning on a thick knotted staff, his greasy, broad-brimmed hat casting a deep shadow over his grimy face, waiting for the noble Excellency to deign to put some questions to him.

"The citoyen tells me," said Chauvelin peremptorily to him, "that you know something of my friend, the tall Englishman, whom I desire to meet. . . . *Morbleu!* keep your distance, man," he added hurriedly, as the Jew took a quick and eager step forward.

"Yes, your Excellency," replied the Jew, who spoke the language with that peculiar lisp, which denotes Eastern origin, "I and Reuben Goldstein met a tall Englishman, on the road, close by here this evening."

"Did you speak to him?"

"He spoke to us, your Excellency. He wanted to know if he could hire a horse and cart to go down along the St. Martin Road, to a place he wanted to reach to-night."

"What did you say?"

"I did not say anything," said the Jew in an injured tone, "Reuben Goldstein, that accursed traitor, that son of Belial . . ."

"Cut that short, man," interrupted Chauvelin, roughly, "and go on with your story."

"He took the words out of my mouth, your Excellency: when I was about to offer the wealthy Englishman my horse and cart, to take him wheresoever he chose, Reuben had already spoken, and offered his half-starved nag, and his broken-down cart."

"And what did the Englishman do?"

"He listened to Reuben Goldstein, your Excellency, and put his hand in his pocket then and there, and took out a handful of gold, which he showed to that descendant of Beelzebub, telling him that all that would be his, if the horse and cart were ready for him by eleven o'clock."

"And, of course, the horse and cart were ready?"

"Well! they were ready in a manner, so to speak, your Excellency. Reuben's nag was lame as usual; she refused to budge at first. It was only after a time and with plenty of kicks, that she at last could be made to move," said the Jew with a malicious chuckle.

"Then they started?"

"Yes, they started about five minutes ago. I was disgusted with that stranger's folly. An Englishman too!—He ought to have known Reuben's nag was not fit to drive."

"But if he had no choice?"

"No choice, your Excellency?" protested the Jew, in a rasping voice, "did I not repeat to him a dozen times, that my horse and cart would take him quicker, and more comfortably than Reuben's bag of bones. He would not listen. Reuben is such a liar, and has such insinuating ways. The stranger was deceived. If he was in a hurry, he would have had better value for his money by taking my cart."

"You have a horse and cart too, then?" asked Chauvelin, peremptorily.

"Aye! that I have, your Excellency, and if your Excellency wants to drive . . ."

"Do you happen to know which way my friend went in Reuben Goldstein's cart?"

Thoughtfully the Jew rubbed his dirty chin. Marguerite's heart was beating well-nigh to bursting. She had heard the peremptory question; she looked anxiously at the Jew, but could not read his face beneath the shadow of his broad-brimmed hat. Vaguely she felt somehow as if he held Percy's fate in his long, dirty hands.

There was a long pause, whilst Chauvelin frowned impatiently at the stooping figure before him: at last the Jew slowly put his hand in his breast pocket, and drew out from its capacious depths a number of silver coins. He gazed at them thoughtfully, then remarked, in a quiet tone of voice,—

"This is what the tall stranger gave me, when he drove away with Reuben, for holding my tongue about him, and his doings."

Chauvelin shrugged his shoulders impatiently.

"How much is there there?" he asked.

"Twenty francs, your Excellency," replied the Jew, "and I have been an honest man all my life."

Chauvelin without further comment took a few pieces of gold out of his own pocket, and leaving them in the palm of his hand, he allowed them to jingle as he held them out towards the Jew.

"How many gold pieces are there in the palm of my hand?" he asked quietly.

Evidently he had no desire to terrorize the man, but to conciliate him, for his own purposes, for his manner was pleasant and suave. No doubt he feared that threats of the guillotine, and various other persuasive methods of that type, might addle the old man's brains, and that he would be more likely to be useful through greed of gain, than through terror of death.

The eyes of the Jew shot a quick, keen glance at the gold in his interlocutor's hand.

"At least five, I should say, your Excellency," he replied obsequiously.

"Enough, do you think, to loosen that honest tongue of yours?"

"What does your Excellency wish to know?"

"Whether your horse and cart can take me to where I can find my friend the tall stranger, who has driven off in Reuben Goldstein's cart?"

"My horse and cart can take your Honour there, where you please."

"To a place called the Père Blanchard's hut?"

"Your Honour has guessed?" said the Jew in astonishment.

"You know the place?"

"I know it, your Honour."

"Which road leads to it?"

"The St. Martin Road, your Honour, then a footpath from there to the cliffs."

"You know the road?" repeated Chauvelin, roughly.

"Every stone, every blade of grass, your Honour," replied the Jew quietly.

Chauvelin without another word threw the five pieces of gold one by one before the Jew, who knelt down, and on his hands and knees struggled to collect them. One rolled away, and he had some trouble to get it, for it had lodged underneath the dresser. Chauvelin quietly waited while the old man scrambled on the floor, to find the piece of gold.

When the Jew was again on his feet, Chauvelin said,—

"How soon can your horse and cart be ready?"

"They are ready now, your Honour."

"Where?"

"Not ten meters from this door. Will your Excellency deign to look?"

"I don't want to see it. How far can you drive me in it?"

"As far as the Père Blanchard's hut, your Honour, and further than Reuben's nag took your friend. I am sure that, not two leagues from here, we shall come across that wily Reuben, his nag, his cart and the tall stranger all in a heap in the middle of the road."

"How far is the nearest village from here?"

"On the road which the Englishman took, Miquelon is the nearest village, not two leagues from here."

"There he could get fresh conveyance, if he wanted to go further?"

"He could—if he ever got so far."

"Can you?"

"Will your Excellency try?" said the Jew simply.

"That is my intention," said Chauvelin very quietly, "but remember, if you have deceived me, I shall tell off two of my most stalwart soldiers to give you such a beating, that your breath will perhaps leave your ugly body for ever. But if we find my friend the tall Englishman, either on the road or at the Père Blanchard's hut, there will be ten more gold pieces for you. Do you accept the bargain?"

The Jew again thoughtfully rubbed his chin. He looked at the money in his hand, then at his stern interlocutor, and at Desgas, who had stood silently behind him all this while. After a moment's pause, he said deliberately,—

"I accept."

"Go and wait outside then," said Chauvelin, "and remember to stick to your bargain, or by Heaven, I will keep to mine."

With a final, most abject and cringing bow, the old Jew shuffled out of the room. Chauvelin seemed pleased with his interview, for he rubbed his hands together, with that usual gesture of his, of malignant satisfaction.

"My coat and boots," he said to Desgas at last.

Desgas went to the door, and apparently gave the necessary orders, for presently a soldier entered, carrying Chauvelin's coat, boots, and hat.

He took off his soutane, beneath which he was wearing close-fitting breeches and a cloth waistcoat, and began changing his attire.

"You, citoyen, in the meanwhile," he said to Desgas, "go back to Captain Jutley as fast as you can, and tell him to let you have another dozen men, and bring them with you along the St. Martin Road, where I daresay you will soon overtake the Jew's cart with myself in it. There will be hot work presently, if I mistake not, in the Père Blanchard's hut. We shall corner our game there, I'll warrant, for this impudent Scarlet Pimpernel has had the audacity—or the stupidity, I hardly know which—to adhere to his original plans. He has gone to meet de Tournay, St. Just and the other traitors, which for the moment, I thought, perhaps, he did not intend to do. When we find them, there will be a band of desperate men at bay. Some of our men will, I presume, be put *hors de combat*. These royalists are good swordsmen, and the Englishman is devilish cunning, and looks very powerful. Still, we shall be five against one at least. You can follow the cart closely with your men, all along the St. Martin Road, through Miquelon. The Englishman is ahead of us, and not likely to look behind him."

Whilst he gave these curt and concise orders, he had completed his change of attire. The priest's costume had been laid aside, and he was once more dressed in his usual dark, tight-fitting clothes. At last he took up his hat.

"I shall have an interesting prisoner to deliver into your hands," he said with a chuckle, as with unwonted familiarity he took Desgas' arm, and led him towards the door. "We won't kill him outright, eh, friend Desgas? The Père Blanchard's hut is—an I mistake not—a lonely spot upon the beach, and our men will enjoy a bit of rough sport there with the wounded fox. Choose your men well, friend Desgas . . . of the sort who would enjoy that type of sport—eh? We must see that Scarlet Pimpernel wither a bit—what?—shrink and tremble, eh? . . . before we finally . . ."—he made an expressive gesture, whilst he laughed a low, evil laugh, which filled Marguerite's soul with sickening horror.

"Choose your men well, Citoyen Desgas," he said once more, as he led his secretary finally out of the room.

Chapter 27

On the Track

*N*ever for a moment did Marguerite Blakeney hesitate.
The last sounds outside the "Chat Gris" had died away in
the night. She had heard Desgas giving orders to his men,
and then starting off towards the fort, to get a reinforce-
ment of a dozen more men: six were not thought sufficient
to capture the cunning Englishman, whose resourceful
brain was even more dangerous than his valor and his
strength.

Then a few minutes later, she heard the Jew's husky
voice again, evidently shouting to his nag, then the
rumble of wheels, and noise of a rickety cart bumping over
the rough road.

Inside the inn, everything was still. Brogard and his
wife, terrified of Chauvelin, had given no sign of life; they
hoped to be forgotten, and at any rate to remain unper-

ceived: Marguerite could not even hear their usual volleys
of muttered oaths.

She waited a moment or two longer, then she quietly
slipped down the broken stairs, wrapped her dark cloak
closely round her and slipped out of the inn.

The night was fairly dark, sufficiently so at any rate to
hide her dark figure from view, whilst her keen ears kept
count of the sound of the cart going on ahead. She hoped
by keeping well within the shadow of the ditches which
lined the road, that she would not be seen by Desgas'
men, when they approached, or by the patrols, which she
concluded were still on duty.

Thus she started to do this, the last stage of her weary
journey, alone, at night, and on foot. Nearly three leagues
to Miquelon, and then on to the Père Blanchard's hut,
wherever that fatal spot might be, probably over rough
roads: she cared not.

The Jew's nag could not get on very fast, and though
she was weary with mental fatigue and nerve strain, she
knew that she could easily keep up with it, on a hilly
road, where the poor beast, who was sure to be half-
starved, would have to be allowed long and frequent rests.
The road lay some distance from the sea, bordered on
either side by shrubs and stunted trees, sparsely covered
with meagre foliage, all turning away from the North,
with their branches looking in the semi-darkness, like
stiff, ghostly hair, blown by a perpetual wind.

Fortunately, the moon showed no desire to peep between the clouds, and Marguerite hugging the edge of the
road, and keeping close to the low line of shrubs, was
fairly safe from view. Everything around her was so still:

only from far, very far away, there came like a long soft moan, the sound of the distant sea.

The air was keen and full of brine; after that enforced period of inactivity, inside the evil-smelling, squalid inn, Marguerite would have enjoyed the sweet scent of this autumnal night, and the distant melancholy rumble of the waves; she would have revelled in the calm and stillness of this lonely spot, a calm, broken only at intervals by the strident and mournful cry of some distant gull, and by the creaking of the wheels, some way down the road: she would have loved the cool atmosphere, the peaceful immensity of Nature, in this lonely part of the coast: but her heart was too full of cruel foreboding, of a great ache and longing for a being, who had become infinitely dear to her.

Her feet slipped on the grassy bank, for she thought it safest not to walk near the centre of the road, and she found it difficult to keep up a sharp pace along the muddy incline. She even thought it best not to keep too near to the cart; everything was so still, that the rumble of the wheels could not fail to be a safe guide.

The loneliness was absolute. Already the few dim lights of Calais lay far behind, and on this road there was not a sign of human habitation, not even the hut of a fisherman or of a woodcutter anywhere near; far away on her right was the edge of the cliff, below it the rough beach, against which the incoming tide was dashing itself with its constant, distant murmur. And ahead the rumble of the wheels, bearing an implacable enemy to his triumph.

Marguerite wondered at what particular spot, on this lonely coast, Percy could be at this moment. Not very far surely, for he had had less than a quarter of an hour's start of Chauvelin. She wondered if he knew, that in this cool, ocean-scented bit of France, there lurked many spies, all eager to sight his tall figure, to track him to where his unsuspecting friends waited for him, and then, to close the net over him and them.

Chauvelin, on ahead, jolted and jostled in the Jew's vehicle, was nursing comfortable thoughts. He rubbed his hands together, with content, as he thought of the web which he had woven, and through which that ubiquitous and daring Englishman could not hope to escape. As the time went on, and the old Jew drove him leisurely but surely along the dark road, he felt more and more eager for the grand finale of this exciting chase after the mysterious Scarlet Pimpernel.

The capture of the audacious plotter would be the finest leaf in Citoyen Chauvelin's wreath of glory. Caught, red-handed, on the spot, in the very act of aiding and abetting the traitors against the Republic of France, the Englishman could claim no protection from his own country. Chauvelin had, in any case, fully made up his mind that all intervention should come too late.

Never for a moment, did the slightest remorse enter his heart, as to the terrible position in which he had placed the unfortunate wife, who had unconsciously betrayed her husband. As a matter of fact, Chauvelin had ceased even to think of her: she had been a useful tool, that was all.

The Jew's lean nag did little more than walk. She was going along at a slow jog trot, and her driver had to give her long and frequent halts.

"Are we a long way yet from Miquelon?" asked Chauvelin from time to time.

"Not very far, your Honour," was the uniform placid reply.

"We have not yet come across your friend and mine, lying in a heap in the roadway," was Chauvelin's sarcastic comment.

"Patience, noble Excellency," rejoined the son of Moses, "they are ahead of us. I can see the imprint of the cart wheels, driven by that traitor, that son of the Amalekite."

"You are sure of the road?"

"As sure as I am of the presence of those ten gold pieces in the noble Excellency's pockets, which I trust will presently be mine."

"As soon as I have shaken hands with my friend the tall stranger, they will certainly be yours."

"Hark, what was that?" said the Jew suddenly.

Through the stillness, which had been absolute, there could now be heard distinctly the sound of horses' hoofs on the muddy road.

"They are soldiers," he added in an awed whisper.

"Stop a moment, I want to hear," said Chauvelin.

Marguerite had also heard the sound of galloping hoofs, coming towards the cart, and towards herself. For some time she had been on the alert thinking that Desgas and his squad would soon overtake them, but these came from the opposite direction, presumably from Miquelon. The darkness lent her sufficient cover. She had perceived that the cart had stopped, and with utmost caution, treading noiselessly on the soft road, she crept a little nearer.

Her heart was beating fast, she was trembling in every limb; already she had guessed what news these mounted men would bring. "Every stranger on these roads or on the

beach must be shadowed, especially if he be tall or stoops
as if he would disguise his height; when sighted a mounted
messenger must at once ride back and report." Those had
been Chauvelin's orders. Had then the tall stranger been
sighted, and was this the mounted messenger, come to
bring the great news, that the hunted hare had run its
head into the noose at last?

Marguerite, realizing that the cart had come to a standstill, managed to slip nearer to it in the darkness; she crept
close up, hoping to get within earshot, to hear what the
messenger had to say.

She heard the quick words of challenge—

"Liberté, Fraternité, Egalité!" then Chauvelin's quick
query:—

"What news?"

Two men on horseback had halted beside the vehicle.

Marguerite could see them silhouetted against the midnight sky. She could hear their voices, and the snorting of
their horses, and now, behind her, some little distance
off, the regular and measured tread of a body of advancing
men: Desgas and his soldiers.

There had been a long pause, during which, no doubt,
Chauvelin satisfied the men as to his identity, for presently, questions and answers followed each other in quick
succession.

"You have seen the stranger?" asked Chauvelin, eagerly.

"No, citoyen, we have seen no tall stranger; we came
by the edge of the cliff."

"Then?"

"Less than a quarter of a league beyond Miquelon, we
came across a rough construction of wood, which looked

like the hut of a fisherman, where he might keep his tools
and nets. When we first sighted it, it seemed to be empty,
and, at first we thought that there was nothing suspicious
about it, until we saw some smoke issuing through an
aperture at the side. I dismounted and crept close to it. It
was then empty, but in one corner of the hut, there was a
charcoal fire, and a couple of stools were also in the hut. I
consulted with my comrades, and we decided that they
should take cover with the horses, well out of sight, and
that I should remain on the watch, which I did."

"Well! and did you see anything?"

"About half an hour later, I heard voices, citoyen, and
presently, two men came along towards the edge of the
cliff; they seemed to me to have come from the Lille
Road. One was young, the other quite old. They were
talking in a whisper, to one another, and I could not hear
what they said."

One was young, the other quite old. Marguerite's aching heart almost stopped beating as she listened: was the
young one Armand?—her brother?—and the old one de
Tournay—were they the two fugitives who, unconsciously,
were used as a decoy, to entrap their fearless and noble
rescuer.

"The two men presently went into the hut," continued
the soldier, whilst Marguerite's aching nerves seemed to
catch the sound of Chauvelin's triumphant chuckle, "and
I crept nearer to it then. The hut is very roughly built,
and I caught snatches of their conversation."

"Yes?—Quick!—What did you hear?"

"The old man asked the young one, if he were sure that
was the right place. 'Oh, yes,' he replied, ''tis the place

sure enough,' and by the light of the charcoal fire he showed to his companion a paper, which he carried. 'Here is the plan,' he said, 'which he gave me before I left London. We were to adhere strictly to that plan, unless I had contrary orders, and I have had none. Here is the road we followed, see . . . here the fork . . . here we cut across the St. Martin Road . . . and here is the footpath which brought us to the edge of the cliff.' I must have made a slight noise then, for the young man came to the door of the hut, and peered anxiously all round him. When he again joined his companion, they whispered so low that I could no longer hear them."

"Well?—and?" asked Chauvelin, impatiently.

"There were six of us altogether, patrolling that part of the beach, so we consulted together, and thought it best that four should remain behind and keep the hut in sight, and I and my comrade rode back at once to make report of what we had seen."

"You saw nothing of the tall stranger?"

"Nothing, citoyen."

"If your comrades see him, what would they do?"

"Not lose sight of him for a moment, and if he showed signs of escape, or any boat came in sight, they would close in on him, and, if necessary, they would shoot: the firing would bring the rest of the patrol to the spot. In any case they would not let the stranger go."

"Aye! but I did not want the stranger hurt—not just yet," murmured Chauvelin, savagely, "but there, you've done your best. The Fates grant that I may not be too late . . ."

"We met half a dozen men just now, who have been patrolling this road for several hours."

"Well?"

"They have seen no stranger either."

"Yet he is on ahead somewhere, in a cart or else . . . Here! there is not a moment to lose. How far is that hut from here?"

"About a couple of leagues, citoyen."

"You can find it again?—at once?—without hesitation?"

"I have absolutely no doubt, citoyen."

"The footpath, to the edge of the cliff?—Even in the dark?"

"It is not a dark night, citoyen, and I know I can find my way," repeated the soldier firmly.

"Fall in behind then. Let your comrade take both your horses back to Calais. You won't want them. Keep beside the cart, and direct the Jew to drive straight ahead; then stop him, within a quarter of a league of the footpath; see that he takes the most direct road."

Whilst Chauvelin spoke, Desgas and his men were fast approaching, and Marguerite could hear their footsteps within a hundred yards behind her now. She thought it unsafe to stay where she was, and unnecessary too, as she had heard enough. She seemed suddenly to have lost all faculty even for suffering: her heart, her nerves, her brain seemed to have become numb after all these hours of ceaseless anguish, culminating in this awful despair.

For now there was absolutely not the faintest hope. Within two short leagues of this spot, the fugitives were waiting for their brave deliverer. He was on his way, somewhere on this lonely road, and presently he would join them; then the well-laid trap would close, two dozen men, led by one, whose hatred was as deadly as his cunning was malicious, would close round the small band of fugitives, and their daring leader. They would all be captured. Armand, according to Chauvelin's pledged word would be restored to her, but her husband, Percy, whom with every breath she drew she seemed to love and worship more and more, he would fall into the hands of a remorseless enemy, who had no pity for a brave heart, no admiration for the courage of a noble soul, who would show nothing but hatred for the cunning antagonist, who had baffled him so long.

She heard the soldier giving a few brief directions to the Jew, then she retired quickly to the edge of the road, and cowered behind some low shrubs, whilst Desgas and his men came up.

All fell in noiselessly behind the cart, and slowly they all started down the dark road. Marguerite waited until she reckoned that they were well outside the range of earshot, then, she too in the darkness, which suddenly seemed to have become more intense, crept noiselessly along.

Chapter 28

The
Père Blanchard's
Hut

As in a dream, Marguerite followed on; the web was drawing more and more tightly every moment round the beloved life, which had become dearer than all. To see her husband once again, to tell him how she had suffered, how much she had wronged, and how little understood him, had become now her only aim. She had abandoned all hope of saving him: she saw him gradually hemmed in on all sides, and, in despair, she gazed round her into the darkness, and wondered whence he would presently come, to fall into the death-trap which his relentless enemy had prepared for him.

The distant roar of the waves now made her shudder; the occasional dismal cry of an owl, or a sea-gull, filled her with unspeakable horror. She thought of the ravenous beasts—in human shape—who lay in wait for their prey,

and destroyed them, as mercilessly as any hungry wolf, for
the satisfaction of their own appetite of hate. Marguerite
was not afraid of the darkness, she only feared that man,
on ahead, who was sitting at the bottom of a rough
wooden cart, nursing thoughts of vengeance, which would
have made the very demons in hell chuckle with delight.

Her feet were sore. Her knees shook under her, from
sheer bodily fatigue. For days now she had lived in a wild
turmoil of excitement; she had not had a quiet rest for
three nights; now she had walked on a slippery road for
nearly two hours, and yet her determination never swerved
for a moment. She would see her husband, tell him all,
and, if he was ready to forgive the crime, which she had
committed in her blind ignorance, she would yet have the
happiness of dying by his side.

She must have walked on almost in a trance, instinct
alone keeping her up, and guiding her in the wake of the
enemy, when suddenly her ears, attuned to the slightest
sound, by that same blind instinct, told her that the cart
had stopped, and that the soldiers had halted. They had
come to their destination. No doubt on the right, somewhere close ahead, was the footpath that led to the edge
of the cliff and to the hut.

Heedless of any risks, she crept quite close up to where
Chauvelin stood, surrounded by his little troop: he had
descended from the cart, and was giving some orders to
the men. These she wanted to hear: what little chance she
yet had, of being useful to Percy, consisted in hearing
absolutely every word of his enemy's plans.

The spot where all the party had halted must have lain
some eight hundred meters from the coast; the sound of

the sea came only very faintly, as from a distance. Chauvelin and Desgas, followed by the soldiers, had turned off sharply to the right of the road, apparently on to the footpath, which led to the cliffs. The Jew had remained on the road, with his cart and nag.

Marguerite, with infinite caution, and literally crawling on her hands and knees, had also turned off to the right: to accomplish this she had to creep through the rough, low shrubs, trying to make as little noise as possible as she went along, tearing her face and hands against the dry twigs, intent only upon hearing without being seen or heard. Fortunately—as is usual in this part of France—the footpath was bordered by a low, rough hedge, beyond which was a dry ditch, filled with coarse grass. In this Marguerite managed to find shelter; she was quite hidden from view, yet could contrive to get within three yards of where Chanvelin stood, giving orders to his men.

"Now," he was saying in a low and peremptory whisper, "where is the Père Blanchard's hut?"

"About eight hundred metres from here, along the footpath," said the soldier who had lately been directing the party, "and halfway down the cliff."

"Very good. You shall lead us. Before we begin to descend the cliff, you shall creep down to the hut, as noiselessly as possible, and ascertain if the traitor royalists are there? Do you understand?"

"I understand, citoyen."

"Now listen very attentively, all of you," continued Chauvelin, impressively, and addressing the soldiers collectively, "for after this we may not be able to exchange another word, so remember every syllable I utter, as if your very lives depended on your memory. Perhaps they do," he added drily.

"We listen, citoyen," said Desgas, "and a soldier of the Republic never forgets an order."

"You, who have crept up to the hut, will try to peep inside. If an Englishman is there with those traitors, a man who is tall above the average, or who stoops as if he would disguise his height, then give a sharp, quick whistle as a signal to your comrades. All of you," he added, once more speaking to the soldiers collectively, "then quickly surround and rush into the hut, and each seize one of the men there, before they have time to draw their firearms; if any of them struggle, shoot at their legs or arms, but on no account kill the tall man. Do you understand?"

"We understand, citoyen."

"The man who is tall above the average, is probably also strong above the average; it will take four or five of you at least to overpower him."

There was a little pause, then Chauvelin continued,—

"If the royalist traitors are still alone, which is more than likely to be the case, then warn your comrades who are lying in wait there, and all of you creep and take cover behind the rocks and boulders round the hut, and wait there, in dead silence, until the tall Englishman arrives; then only rush the hut, when he is safely within its doors. But remember, that you must be as silent as the wolf is at night, when he prowls around the pens. I do not wish those royalists to be on the alert—the firing of a pistol, a shriek or call on their part would be sufficient, perhaps, to warn the tall personage to keep clear of the cliffs, and of the hut, and," he added emphatically, "it is the tall Englishman whom it is your duty to capture to-night."

"You shall be implicitly obeyed, citoyen."

"Then get along as noiselessly as possible, and I will follow you."

"What about the Jew, citoyen?" asked Desgas, as silently like noiseless shadows, one by one the soldiers began to creep along the rough and narrow footpath.

"Ah, yes; I had forgotten the Jew," said Chauvelin, and, turning towards the Jew, he called him peremptorily.

"Here, you . . . Aaron, Moses, Abraham, or whatever your confounded name may be," he said to the old man, who had quietly stood beside his lean nag, as far away from the soldiers as possible.

"Benjamin Rosenbaum, so it please your Honor," he replied humbly.

"It does not please me to hear your voice, but it does please me to give you certain orders, which you will find it wise to obey."

"So please your Honour . . ."

"Hold your confounded tongue. You shall stay here, do you hear? with your horse and cart until our return. You are on no account to utter the faintest sound, or to breathe even louder than you can help; nor are you, on any consideration whatever, to leave your post, until I give you orders to do so. Do you understand?"

"But your Honour—" protested the Jew pitiably.

"There is no question of 'but' or of any argument," said Chauvelin, in a tone that made the timid old man tremble from head to foot. "If, when I return, I do not find you here, I most solemnly assure you that, wherever you may try and hide yourself, I can find you, and that punishment swift, sure and terrible, will sooner or later overtake you. Do you hear me?"

"But your Excellency . . ."

"I said, do you hear me?"

The soldiers had all crept away; the three men stood alone together in the dark and lonely road, with Marguerite there, behind the hedge, listening to Chauvelin's orders, as she would to her own death sentence.

"I heard your Honour," protested the Jew again, while he tried to draw nearer to Chauvelin, "and I swear by Abraham, Isaac and Jacob that I would obey your Honour most absolutely, and that I would not move from this place until your Honour once more deigned to shed the light of your countenance upon your humble servant; but remember, your Honour, I am a poor old man; my nerves are not as strong as those of a young soldier. If midnight marauders should come prowling round this lonely road, I might scream or run in my fright! And is my life to be forfeit, is some terrible punishment to come on my poor old head for that which I cannot help?"

The Jew seemed in real distress; he was shaking from head to foot. Clearly he was not the man to be left by himself on this lonely road. The man spoke truly; he might unwittingly, in sheer terror, utter the shriek that might prove a warning to the wily Scarlet Pimpernel.

Chauvelin reflected for a moment.

"Will your horse and cart be safe alone, here, do you think?" he asked roughly.

"I fancy, citoyen," here interposed Desgas, "that they will be safer, without that dirty, cowardly Jew, as with him. There seems no doubt that, if he gets scared, he will either make a bolt of it, or shriek his head off."

"But what am I to do with the brute?"

"Will you send him back to Calais, citoyen?"

"No, for we shall want him to drive back the wounded presently," said Chauvelin, with grim significance.

There was a pause again—Desgas, waiting for the decision of his chief, and the old Jew whining beside his nag.

"Well, you lazy, lumbering old coward," said Chauvelin at last, "you had better shuffle along behind us. Here, Citoyen Desgas, tie this handkerchief tightly round the fellow's mouth."

Chauvelin handed a scarf to Desgas, who solemnly began winding it round the Jew's mouth. Meekly Benjamin Rosenbaum allowed himself to be gagged; he, evidently, preferred this uncomfortable state to that of being left alone, on the dark St. Martin Road. Then the three men fell in line.

"Quick!" said Chauvelin, impatiently, "we have already wasted much valuable time."

And the firm footsteps of Chauvelin and Desgas, the shuffling gait of the old Jew, soon died away along the footpath.

Marguerite had not lost a single one of Chauvelin's words of command. Her every nerve was strained to completely grasp the situation first, then to make a final appeal to those wits which had so often been called the sharpest in Europe, and which alone might be of service now.

Certainly the situation was desperate enough; a tiny band of unsuspecting men, quietly awaiting the arrival of their rescuer, who was equally unconscious of the trap laid for them all. It seemed so horrible, this net, as it were drawn in a circle, at dead of night, on a lonely beach, round a few defenceless men, defenceless because they were tricked and unsuspecting; of these one was the husband she idolised, another the brother she loved. She vaguely wondered who the others were, who were also calmly waiting for the Scarlet Pimpernel, while death lurked behind every boulder of the cliffs.

For the moment she could do nothing but follow the soldiers and Chauvelin. She feared to lose her way, or she would have rushed forward and found that wooden hut, and perhaps been in time to warn the fugitives and their brave deliverer yet.

For a sccond, the thought flashed through her mind of uttering the piercing shrieks, which Chauvelin seemed to dread, as a possible warning to the Scarlet Pimpernel and his friends—in the wild hope that they would hear, and have yet time to escape before it was too late. But she did not know how far from the edge of the cliff she was; she did not know if her shrieks would reach the ears of the doomed men. Her effort might be premature, and she would never be allowed to make another. Her mouth would be securely gagged, like that of the Jew, and she, a helpless prisoner in the hands of Chauvelin's men.

Like a ghost she flitted noiselessly behind that hedge: she had taken her shoes off, and her stockings were by now torn off her feet. She felt neither soreness nor weariness; indomitable will to reach her husband in spite of adverse Fate, and of a cunning enemy, killed all sense of bodily pain within her, and rendered her instincts doubly acute.

She heard nothing save the soft and measured footsteps of Percy's enemies on in front; she saw nothing but—in her mind's eye—that wooden hut, and he, her husband, walking blindly to his doom.

Suddenly, those same keen instincts within her made her pause in her mad haste, and cower still further within the shadow of the hedge. The moon, which had proved a friend to her by remaining hidden behind a bank of clouds, now emerged in all the glory of an early autumn night, and in a moment flooded the weird and lonely landscape with a rush of brilliant light.

There, not two hundred metres ahead, was the edge of the cliff, and below, stretching far away to free and happy England, the sea rolled on smoothly and peaceably. Marguerite's gaze rested for an instant on the brilliant, silvery waters, and as she gazed her heart, which had been numb with pain for all these hours, seemed to soften and distend, and her eyes filled with hot tears: not three miles away, with white sails set, a graceful schooner lay in wait.

Marguerite had guessed rather than recognized her. It was the *Day Dream*, Percy's favorite yacht, with old Briggs, that prince of skippers, aboard, and all her crew of British sailors: her white sails, glistening in the moonlight, seemed to convey a message to Marguerite of joy and hope, which yet she feared could never be. She waited there, out at sea, waited for her master, like a beautiful white bird all ready to take flight, and he would never reach her, never see her smooth deck again, never gaze any more on the white cliffs of England, the land of liberty and of hope.

The sight of the schooner seemed to infuse into the poor, wearied woman the superhuman strength of despair. There was the edge of the cliff, and some way below was the hut, where presently her husband would meet his death. But the moon was out: she could see her way now: she would see the hut from a distance, run to it, rouse them all, warn them at any rate to be prepared and to sell their lives dearly, rather than be caught like so many rats in a hole.

She stumbled on behind the hedge in the low, thick grass of the ditch. She must have run on very fast, and had outdistanced Chauvelin and Desgas, for presently she reached the edge of the cliff, and heard their footsteps distinctly behind her. But only a very few yards away, and now the moonlight was full upon her, her figure must have been distinctly silhouetted against the silvery background of the sea.

Only for a moment, though; the next she had cowered, like some animal doubled up within itself. She peeped down the great rugged cliffs—the descent would be easy enough, as they were not precipitous, and the great boulders afforded plenty of foothold. Suddenly, as she gazed, she saw at some little distance on her left, and about midway down the cliffs, a rough wooden construction, through the walls of which a tiny red light glimmered like a beacon. Her very heart seemed to stand still, the eagerness of joy was so great, that it felt like an awful pain.

She could not gauge how distant the hut was, but without hesitation she began the steep descent, creeping from boulder to boulder, caring nothing for the enemy behind, or for the soldiers, who evidently had all taken cover since the tall Englishman had not yet appeared.

On she pressed, forgetting the deadly foe on her track, running, stumbling, footsore, half-dazed, but still on . . . When, suddenly, a crevice, or stone, or slippery bit of rock, threw her violently to the ground. She struggled again to her feet, and started running forward once more to give them that timely warning, to beg them to flee before he came, and to tell him to keep away—away from this death-trap—away from this awful doom. But now she realised that other steps, quicker than her own, were already close at her heels. The next instant a hand dragged at her skirt, and she was down on her knees again, whilst something was wound round her mouth to prevent her uttering a scream.

Bewildered, half frantic with the bitterness of disappointment, she looked round her helplessly, and, bending down quite close to her, she saw through the mist, which seemed to gather round her, a pair of keen, malicious eyes, which appeared to her excited brain to have a weird, supernatural green light in them.

She lay in the shadow of a great boulder; Chauvelin could not see her features, but he passed his thin, white fingers over her face.

"A woman!" he whispered, "by all the Saints in the calendar."

"We cannot let her loose, that's certain," he muttered to himself. "I wonder now . . ."

Suddenly he paused, and after a few seconds of deadly silence, he gave forth a long, low, curious chuckle, while once again Marguerite felt, with a horrible shudder his thin fingers wandering over her face.

"Dear me! dear me!" he whispered, with affected gallantry, "this is indeed a charming surprise," and Marguerite felt her resistless hand raised to Chauvelin's thin, mocking lips.

The situation was indeed grotesque, had it not been at the same time so fearfully tragic: the poor, weary woman, broken in spirit, and half frantic with the bitterness of her disappointment, receiving on her knees the *banal* gallantries of her deadly enemy.

Her senses were leaving her; half choked with the tight grip round her mouth, she had no strength to move or to utter the faintest sound. The excitement which all along had kept up her delicate body, seemed at once to have subsided, and the feeling of blank despair to have completely paralysed her brain and nerves.

Chauvelin must have given some directions, which she was too dazed to hear, for she felt herself lifted from off her feet: the bandage round her mouth was made more secure, and a pair of strong arms carried her towards that tiny, red light, on ahead, which she had looked upon as a beacon and the last faint glimmer of hope.

Chapter 29

Trapped

She did not know how long she was thus carried along, she had lost all notion of time and space, and for a few seconds tired nature, mercifully, deprived her of consciousness.

When she once more realised her state, she felt that she was placed with some degree of comfort upon a man's coat, with her back resting against a fragment of rock. The moon was hidden again behind some clouds, and the darkness seemed in comparison more intense. The sea was roaring some two hundred feet below her, and on looking all round she could no longer see any vestige of the tiny glimmer of red light.

That the end of the journey had been reached, she gathered from the fact that she heard rapid questions and answers spoken in a whisper quite close to her.

"There are four men in there, citoyen; they are sitting by the fire, and seem to be waiting quietly."

"The hour?"

"Nearly two o'clock."

"The tide?"

"Coming in quickly."

"The schooner?"

"Obviously an English one, lying some three kilometres out. But we cannot see her boat."

"Have the men taken cover?"

"Yes, citoyen."

"They will not blunder?"

"They will not stir until the tall Englishman comes, then they will surround and overpower the five men."

"Right. And the lady?"

"Still dazed, I fancy. She's close behind you, citoyen."

"And the Jew?"

"He's gagged, and his legs strapped together. He cannot move or scream."

"Good. Then have your gun ready, in case you want it. Get close to the hut and leave me to look after the lady."

Desgas evidently obeyed, for Marguerite heard him creeping away along the stony cliff, then she felt that a pair of warm, thin, talon-like hands took hold of both her own, and held them in a grip of steel.

"Before that handkerchief is removed from your pretty mouth, fair lady," whispered Chauvelin close to her ear, "I think it right to give you one small word of warning. What has procured me the honour of being followed across the Channel by so charming a companion, I cannot, of course, conceive, but, if I mistake not, the purpose of this flattering attention is not one that would commend itself to my vanity and I think that I am right in surmising,

moreover, that the first sound which your pretty lips
would utter, as soon as the cruel gag is removed, would be
one that would perhaps prove a warning to the cunning
fox, which I have been at such pains to track to his lair."

He paused a moment, while the steel-like grasp seemed
to tighten round her wrist; then he resumed in the same
hurried whisper—

"Inside that hut, if again I am not mistaken, your
brother, Armand St. Just, waits with that traitor de
Tournay, and two other men unknown to you, for the
arrival of the mysterious rescuer, whose identity has for so
long puzzled our Committee of Public Safety—the audacious Scarlet Pimpernel. No doubt if you scream, if there
is a scuffle here, if shots are fired, it is more than likely
that the same long legs that brought this scarlet enigma
here, will as quickly take him to some place of safety. The
purpose then, for which I have travelled all these miles, will
remain unaccomplished. On the other hand it only rests
with yourself that your brother—Armand—shall be free to
go off with you tonight if you like, to England, or any
other place of safety."

Marguerite could not utter a sound, as the handkerchief
was wound very tightly round her mouth, but Chauvelin
was peering through the darkness very closely into her
face; no doubt too her hand gave a responsive appeal to
his last suggestion, for presently he continued:—

"What I want you to do to ensure Armand's safety is a
very simple thing, dear lady."

"What is it?" Marguerite's hand seemed to convey to
his, in response.

"To remain—on this spot, without uttering a sound,

until I give you leave to speak. Ah! but I think you will
obey," he added, with that funny dry chuckle of his as
Marguerite's whole figure seemed to stiffen, in defiance of
this order, "for let me tell you that if you scream, nay! if
you utter one sound, or attempt to move from here, my
men—there are thirty of them about—will seize St. Just,
de Tournay, and their two friends, and shoot them here—by
my orders—before your eyes."

Marguerite had listened to her implacable enemy's speech
with ever-increasing terror. Numbed with physical pain,
she yet had sufficient mental vitality in her, to realize the
full horror of this terrible "either—or" he was once more
putting before her; an "either—or" ten thousand times
more appalling and horrible, than the one he had suggested to her that fatal night at the ball.

This time it meant that she should keep still, and allow
the husband she worshipped to walk unconsciously to his
death, or that she should, by trying to give him a word of
warning, which perhaps might even be unavailing, actually give the signal for her own brother's death, and that
of three other unsuspecting men.

She could not see Chauvelin, but she could almost feel
those keen, pale eyes of his fixed maliciously upon her
helpless form, and his hurried, whispered words reached
her ear, as the death-knell of her last faint, lingering
hope.

"Nay, fair lady," he added urbanely, "you can have no
interest in anyone save St. Just, and all you need do for
his safety is to remain where you are, and to keep silent.
My men have strict orders to spare him in every way. As
for that enigmatic Scarlet Pimpernel, what is he to you?

Believe me, no warning from you could possibly save him. And now dear lady, let me remove this unpleasant coercion, which has been placed before your pretty mouth. You see I wish you to be perfectly free, in the choice which you are about to make."

Her thoughts in a whirl, her temples aching, her nerves paralysed, her body numb with pain, Marguerite sat there, in the darkness which surrounded her as with a pall. From where she sat she could not see the sea, but she heard the incessant mournful murmur of the incoming tide, which spoke of her dead hopes, her lost love, the husband she had with her own hand betrayed, and sent to his death.

Chauvelin removed the handkerchief from her mouth. She certainly did not scream: at that moment, she had no strength to do anything but barely to hold herself upright, and to force herself to think.

Oh! think! think! think! of what she should do. The minutes flew on; in this awful stillness she could not tell how fast or how slowly; she heard nothing, she saw nothing: she did not feel the sweet-smelling autumn air, scented with the briny odour of the sea, she no longer heard the murmur of the waves, the occasional rattling of a pebble, as it rolled down some steep incline. More and more unreal did the whole situation seem. It was impossible that she, Marguerite Blakeney, the queen of London society, should actually be sitting here on this bit of lonely coast, in the middle of the night, side by side with a most bitter enemy: and oh! it was not possible that somewhere, not many hundred feet away perhaps, from where she stood, the being she had once despised, but who now, in every moment of this weird, dreamlike life, became more and more dear—it was not possible that *he* was unconsciously, even now walking to his doom, whilst she did nothing to save him.

Why did she not with unearthly screams, that would re-echo from one end of the lonely beach to the other, send out a warning to him to desist, to retrace his steps, for death lurked here whilst he advanced? Once or twice the screams rose to her throat—as if by instinct: then, before her eyes there stood the awful alternative: her brother and those three men shot before her eyes, practically by her orders: she their murderer.

Oh! that fiend in human shape, next to her, knew human—female—nature well. He had played upon her feelings as a skilful musician plays upon an instrument. He had gauged her very thoughts to a nicety.

She could not give that signal—for she was weak, and she was a woman. How could she deliberately order Armand to be shot before her eyes, to have his dear blood upon her head, he dying perhaps with a curse on her, upon his lips. And little Suzanne's father, too! he, an old man; and the others!—oh! it was all too, too horrible.

Wait! wait! wait! how long? The early morning hours sped on, and yet it was not dawn: the sea continued its incessant mournful murmur, the autumnal breeze sighed gently in the night: the lonely beach was silent, even as the grave.

Suddenly from somewhere, not very far away, a cheerful, strong voice was heard singing "God save the King!"

Chapter 30

The Schooner

*M*arguerite's aching heart stood still. She felt, more than she heard, the men on the watch preparing for the fight. Her senses told her that each, with sword in hand, was crouching, ready for the spring.

The voice came nearer and nearer; in the vast immensity of these lonely cliffs, with the loud murmur of the sea below, it was impossible to say how near, or how far, nor yet from which direction came that cheerful singer, who sang to God to save his King, whilst he himself was in such deadly danger. Faint at first, the voice grew louder and louder; from time to time a small pebble detached itself apparently from beneath the firm tread of the singer, and went rolling down the rocky cliffs to the beach below.

Marguerite as she heard, felt that her very life was slipping away, as if when that voice drew nearer, when that singer became entrapped . . .

She distinctly heard the click of Desgas' gun close to her. . . .

No! no! no! no! Oh, God in heaven! this cannot be! let Armand's blood then be upon her own head! let her be branded as his murderer! let even he, whom she loved, despise and loathe her for this, but God! oh God! save him at any cost!

With a wild shriek, she sprang to her feet, and darted round the rock, against which she had been cowering; she saw the little red gleam through the chinks of the hut; she ran up to it and fell against its wooden walls, which she began to hammer with clenched fists in an almost maniacal frenzy, while she shouted,—

"Armand! Armand! for God's sake fire! your leader is near! he is coming! he is betrayed! Armand! Armand! fire in Heaven's name!"

She was seized and thrown to the ground. She lay there moaning, bruised, not caring, but still half-sobbing, half-shrieking,—

"Percy, my husband, for God's sake fly! Armand! Armand! why don't you fire?"

"One of you stop that woman screaming," hissed Chauvelin, who hardly could refrain from striking her.

Something was thrown over her face; she could not breathe, and perforce she was silent.

The bold singer, too, had become silent, warned, no doubt, of his impending danger by Marguerite's frantic shrieks. The men had sprung to their feet, there was no need for further silence on their part; the very cliffs echoed the poor, heart-broken woman's screams.

Chauvelin, with a muttered oath, which boded no good

to her, who had dared to upset his most cherished plans, had hastily shouted the word of command,—

"Into it, my men, and let no one escape from that hut alive!"

The moon had once more emerged from between the clouds: the darkness on the cliffs had gone, giving place once more to brilliant, silvery light. Some of the soldiers had rushed to the rough wooden door of the hut, whilst one of them kept guard over Marguerite.

The door was partially open; one of the soldiers pushed it further, but within all was darkness, the charcoal fire only lighting with a dim, red light the furthest corner of the hut. The soldiers paused automatically at the door, like machines waiting for further orders.

Chauvelin, who was prepared for a violent onslaught from within, and for a vigorous resistance from the four fugitives, under cover of the darkness, was for the moment paralysed with astonishment when he saw the soldiers standing there at attention, like sentries on guard, whilst not a sound proceeded from the hut.

Filled with strange, anxious foreboding, he, too, went to the door of the hut, and peering into the gloom, he asked quickly,—

"What is the meaning of this?"

"I think, citoyen, that there is no one there now," replied one of the soldiers imperturbably.

"You have not let those four men go?" thundered Chauvelin, menacingly. "I ordered you to let no man escape alive!—Quick, after them, all of you! Quick, in every direction!"

The men, obedient as machines, rushed down the rocky

incline towards the beach, some going off to right and left, as fast as their feet could carry them.

"You and your men will pay with your lives for this blunder, citoyen sergeant," said Chauvelin viciously to the sergeant who had been in charge of the men; "and you, too, citoyen," he added, turning with a snarl to Desgas, "for disobeying my orders."

"You ordered us to wait, citoyen, until the tall Englishman arrived and joined the four men in the hut. No one came," said the sergeant sullenly.

"But I ordered you just now, when the woman screamed, to rush in and let no one escape."

"But, citoyen, the four men who were there before had been gone some time, I think . . ."

"You think?—You? . . ." said Chauvelin, almost choking with fury, "and you let them go . . ."

"You ordered us to wait, citoyen," protested the sergeant, "and to implicitly obey your commands on pain of death. We waited."

"I heard the men creep out of the hut, not many minutes after we took cover, and long before the woman screamed," he added, as Chauvelin seemed still quite speechless with rage.

"Hark!" said Desgas suddenly.

In the distance the sound of repeated firing was heard. Chauvelin tried to peer along the beach below, but as luck would have it, the fitful moon once more hid her light behind a bank of clouds, and he could see nothing.

"One of you go into the hut and strike a light," he stammered at last.

Stolidly the sergeant obeyed: he went up to the charcoal fire and lit the small lantern he carried in his belt; it was evident that the hut was quite empty.

"Which way did they go?" asked Chauvelin.

"I could not tell, citoyen," said the sergeant; "they went straight down the cliff first, then disappeared behind some boulders."

"Hush! what was that?"

All three men listened attentively. In the far, very far distance, could be heard faintly echoing and already dying away, the quick, sharp splash of half a dozen oars. Chauvelin took out his handkerchief and wiped the perspiration from his forehead.

"The schooner's boat!" was all he gasped.

Evidently Armand St. Just and his three companions had managed to creep along the side of the cliffs, whilst the men, like true soldiers of the well-drilled Republican army, had with blind obedience, and in fear of their lives, implicitly obeyed Chauvelin's orders—to wait for the tall Englishman, who was the important capture.

They had no doubt reached one of the creeks which jut far out to sea on this coast at intervals; behind this, the boat of the *Day Dream* must have been on the look-out for them, and they were by now safely on board the British schooner.

As if to confirm this last supposition, the dull boom of a gun was heard from out at sea.

"The schooner, citoyen," said Desgas, quietly; "she's off."

It needed all Chauvelin's nerve and presence of mind not to give way to a useless and undignified access of rage. There was no doubt now, that once again, that accursed

British head had completely outwitted him. How he had contrived to reach the hut, without being seen by one of the thirty soldiers who guarded the spot, was more than Chauvelin could conceive. That he had done so before the thirty men had arrived on the cliff was, of course, fairly clear, but how he had come over in Reuben Goldstein's cart, all the way from Calais, without being sighted by the various patrols on duty was impossible of explanation. It really seemed as if some potent Fate watched over that daring Scarlet Pimpernel, and his astute enemy almost felt a superstitious shudder pass through him, as he looked round at the towering cliffs, and the loneliness of this outlying coast.

But surely this was reality! and the year of grace 1792: there were no fairies and hobgoblins about. Chauvelin and his thirty men had all heard with their own ears that accursed voice singing "God save the King," full twenty minutes *after* they had all taken cover around the hut; by that time the four fugitives must have reached the creek, and got into the boat, and the nearest creek was more than a mile from the hut.

Where had that daring singer got to? Unless Satan himself had lent him wings, he could not have covered that mile on a rocky cliff in the space of two minutes; and only two minutes had elapsed between his song and the sound of the boat's oars away at sea. He must have remained behind, and was even now hiding somewhere about the cliffs; the patrols were still about, he would still be sighted, no doubt. Chauvelin felt hopeful once again.

One or two of the men, who had run after the fugitives, were now slowly working their way up the cliff: one of them reached Chauvelin's side, at the very moment that this hope arose in the astute diplomatist's heart.

"We were too late, citoyen," the soldier said, "we reached the beach just before the moon was hidden by that bank of clouds. The boat had undoubtedly been on the look-out behind that first creek, a mile off, but she had shoved off some time ago, when we got to the beach, and was already some way out to sea. We fired after her, but of course, it was no good. She was making straight and quickly for the schooner. We saw her very clearly in the moonlight."

"Yes," said Chauvelin, with eager impatience, "she had shoved off some time ago, you said, and the nearest creek is a mile further on."

"Yes, citoyen! I ran all the way, straight to the beach, though I guessed the boat would have waited somewhere near the creek, as the tide would reach there earliest. The boat must have shoved off some minutes before the woman began to scream."

Some minutes before the woman began to scream! Then Chauvelin's hopes had not deceived him. The Scarlet Pimpernel may have contrived to send the fugitives on ahead by the boat, but he himself had not had time to reach it; he was still on shore, and all the roads were well patrolled. At any rate, all was not yet lost, and would not be, whilst that impudent Britisher was still on French soil.

"Bring the light in here!" he commanded eagerly, as he once more entered the hut.

The sergeant brought his lantern, and together the two men explored the little place: with a rapid glance Chauvelin noted its contents: the cauldron placed close under an aperture in the wall, and containing the last few dying embers of burned charcoal, a couple of stools, overturned as if in the haste of sudden departure, then the fisherman's tools and his nets lying in one corner, and beside them, something small and white.

"Pick that up," said Chauvelin to the sergeant, pointing to this white scrap, "and bring it to me."

It was a crumpled piece of paper, evidently forgotten there by the fugitives, in their hurry to get away. The sergeant, much awed by the citoyen's obvious rage and impatience, picked the paper up and handed it respectfully to Chauvelin.

"Read it, sergeant," said the latter curtly.

"It is almost illegible, citoyen . . . a fearful scrawl. . . ."

"I ordered you to read it," repeated Chauvelin, viciously.

The sergeant, by the light of his lantern, began deciphering the few hastily scrawled words.

"I cannot quite reach you, without risking your lives and endangering the success of your rescue. When you receive this, wait two minutes, then creep out of the hut one by one, turn to your left sharply, and creep cautiously down the cliff; keep to the left all the time, till you reach the first rock, which you see jutting far out to sea—behind it in the creek the boat is on the look-out for you—give a long, sharp whistle—she will come up—get into her—my men will row you to the schooner, and thence to England and safety—once on board the *Day Dream* send the boat back for me, tell my men that I shall be at the creek, which is in a direct line opposite the 'Chat Gris' near Calais. They know it. I shall be there as

soon as possible— they must wait for me at a safe
distance out at sea, till they hear the usual signal. Do
not delay—and obey these instructions implicitly."

"Then there is the signature, citoyen," added the sergeant, as he handed the paper back to Chauvelin.

But the latter had not waited an instant. One phrase of
the momentous scrawl had caught his ear. "I shall be at
the creek which is in a direct line opposite the 'Chat Gris'
near Calais": that phrase might yet mean victory for
him.

"Which of you knows this coast well?" he shouted to his
men who now one by one had all returned from their
fruitless run, and were all assembled once more round the
hut.

"I do, citoyen," said one of them, "I was born in Calais,
and know every stone of these cliffs."

"There is a creek in a direct line from the 'Chat Gris'?"

"There is, citoyen. I know it well."

"The Englishman is hoping to reach that creek. He
does *not* know every stone of these cliffs, he may go there
by the longest way round, and in any case he will proceed
cautiously for fear of the patrols. At any rate, there is a
chance to get him yet. A thousand francs to each man
who gets to that creek before that long-legged Englishman."

"I know a short cut across the cliffs," said the soldier,
and with an enthusiastic shout, he rushed forward, followed closely by his comrades.

Within a few minutes their running footsteps had died
away in the distance. Chauvelin listened to them for a
moment; the promise of the reward was lending spurs to

the soldiers of the Republic. The gleam of hate and anticipated triumph was once more apparent on his face.

Close to him Desgas still stood mute and impassive,
waiting for further orders, whilst two soldiers were kneel-
ing beside the prostrate form of Marguerite. Chauvelin
gave his secretary a vicious look. His well-laid plan had
failed, its sequel was problematical; there was still a great
chance now that the Scarlet Pimpernel might yet escape,
and Chauvelin, with that unreasoning fury, which sometimes assails a strong nature, was longing to vent his rage
on somebody.

The soldiers were holding Marguerite pinioned to the
ground, though she, poor soul, was not making the faintest
struggle. Overwrought nature had at last peremptorily asserted herself, and she lay there in a dead swoon: her eyes
circled by deep purple lines, that told of long, sleepless
nights, her hair matted and damp round her forehead, her
lips parted in a sharp curve that spoke of physical pain.

The cleverest woman in Europe, the elegant and fashionable Lady Blakeney, who had dazzled London society with
her beauty, her wit and her extravagances, presented a
very pathetic picture of tired-out, suffering womanhood,
which would have appealed to any but the hard, vengeful
heart of her baffled enemy.

"It is no use mounting guard over a woman who is half
dead," he said spitefully to the soldiers, "when you have
allowed five men who were very much alive to escape."

Obediently the soldiers rose to their feet.

"You'd better try and find that footpath again for me,
and that broken-down cart we left on the road."

Then suddenly a bright idea seemed to strike him.

"Ah! by-the-bye! where is the Jew?'"

"Close by here, citoyen," said Desgas; "I gagged him and tied his legs together as you commanded."

From the immediate vicinity, a plaintive moan reached Chauvelin's ears. He followed his secretary, who led the way to the other side of the hut, where, fallen into an absolute heap of dejection, with his legs tightly pinioned together, and his mouth gagged, lay the unfortunate descendant of Israel.

His face in the silvery light of the moon, looked positively ghastly with terror: his eyes were wide open and almost glassy, and his whole body was trembling, as if with ague, while a piteous wail escaped his bloodless lips. The rope which had originally been wound round his shoulders and arms had evidently given way, for it lay in a tangle about his body, but he seemed quite unconscious of this, for he had not made the slightest attempt to move from the place where Desgas had originally put him: like a terrified chicken which looks upon a line of white chalk, drawn on a table, as on a string which paralyses its movements.

"Bring the cowardly brute here," commanded Chauvelin.

He certainly felt exceedingly vicious, and since he had no reasonable grounds for venting his ill-humour on the soldiers who had but too punctually obeyed his orders, he felt that the son of the despised race would prove an excellent butt. With true French contempt of the Jew, which has survived the lapse of centuries even to this day, he would not go too near him, but said with biting sarcasm, as the wretched old man was brought in full light of the moon by the two soldiers,—

"I suppose now, that being a Jew, you have a good memory for bargains?

"Answer!" he again commanded, as the Jew with trembling lips seemed too frightened to speak.

"Yes, your Honour," stammered the poor wretch.

"You remember, then, the one you and I made together in Calais, when you undertook to overtake Reuben Goldstein, his nag and my friend the tall stranger? Eh?"

"B . . . b . . . but . . . your Honour . . ."

"There is no 'but.' I said, do you remember?"

"Y . . . y . . . y . . . yes . . . your Honour!"

"What was the bargain?"

There was dead silence. The unfortunate man looked round at the great cliffs, the moon above, the stolid faces of the soldiers, and even at the poor, prostrate, inanimate woman close by, but said nothing.

"Will you speak?" thundered Chauvelin, menacingly.

He did try, poor wretch, but, obviously, he could not. There was no doubt, however, that he knew what to expect from the stern man before him.

"Your Honour . . ." he ventured imploringly.

"Since your terror seems to have paralysed your tongue, said Chauvelin, sarcastically, "I must needs refresh your memory. It was agreed between us, that if we overtook my friend the tall stranger, before he reached this place, you were to have ten pieces of gold."

A low moan escaped from the Jew's trembling lips.

"But," added Chauvelin, with slow emphasis, "if you deceived me in your promise, you were to have a sound beating, one that would teach you not to tell lies."

"I did not, your Honour; I swear it by Abraham . . ."

"And by all the other patriarchs, I know. Unfortunately, they are still in Hades, I believe, according to your creed, and cannot help you much in your present trouble. Now, you did not fulfil your share of the bargain, but I am ready to fulfil mine. Here," he added, turning to the soldiers, "the buckle-end of your two belts to this confounded Jew."

As the soldiers obediently unbuckled their heavy leather belts, the Jew set up a howl that surely would have been enough to bring all the patriarchs out of Hades and elsewhere, to defend their descendant from the brutality of this French official.

"I think I can rely on you, citoyen soldiers," laughed Chauvelin, maliciously, "to give this old liar the best and soundest beating he has ever experienced. But don't kill him," he added drily.

"We will obey, citoyen," replied the soldiers as imperturbably as ever.

He did not wait to see his orders carried out: he knew that he could trust these soldiers—who were still smarting under his rebuke—not to mince matters, when given a free hand to belabour a third party.

"When that lumbering coward has had his punishment," he said to Desgas, "the men can guide us as far as the cart, and one of them can drive us in it back to Calais. The Jew and the woman can look after each other," he added roughly, "until we can send somebody for them in the morning. They can't run away very far, in their present condition, and we cannot be troubled with them just now."

Chauvelin had not given up all hope. His men, he

knew, were spurred on by the hope of the reward. That enigmatic and audacious Scarlet Pimpernel, alone and with thirty men at his heels, could not reasonably be expected to escape a second time.

But he felt less sure now: the Englishman's audacity had baffled him once, whilst the wooden-headed stupidity of the soldiers, and the interference of a woman had turned his hand, which held all the trumps, into a losing one. If Marguerite had not taken up his time, if the soldiers had had a grain of intelligence, if . . . it was a long "if," and Chauvelin stood for a moment quite still, and enrolled thirty odd people in one long, overwhelming anathema. Nature, poetic, silent, balmy, the bright moon, the calm, silvery sea spoke of beauty and of rest, and Chauvelin cursed nature, cursed man and woman, and above all, he cursed all long-legged, meddlesome British enigmas with one gigantic curse.

The howls of the Jew behind him, undergoing his punishment sent a balm through his heart, overburdened as it was with revengeful malice. He smiled. It eased his mind to think that some human being at least was, like himself, not altogether at peace with mankind.

He turned and took a last look at the lonely bit of coast, where stood the wooden hut, now bathed in moonlight, the scene of the greatest discomfiture ever experienced by a leading member of the Committee of Public Safety.

Against a rock, on a hard bed of stone, lay the unconscious figure of Marguerite Blakeney, while some few paces further on, the unfortunate Jew was receiving on his broad back the blows of two stout leather belts, wielded by the stolid arms of two sturdy soldiers of the Republic. The howls of Benjamin Rosenbaum were fit to make the dead rise from their graves. They must have wakened all the gulls from sleep, and made them look down with great interest at the doings of the lords of the creation.

"That will do," commanded Chauvelin, as the Jew's moans became more feeble, and the poor wretch seemed to have fainted away, "we don't want to kill him."

Obediently the soldiers buckled on their belts, one of them viciously kicking the Jew to one side.

"Leave him there," said Chauvelin, "and lead the way now quickly to the cart. I'll follow."

He walked up to where Marguerite lay, and looked down into her face. She had evidently recovered consciousness, and was making feeble efforts to raise herself. Her large, blue eyes were looking at the moonlit scene round her with a scared and terrified look; they rested with a mixture of horror and pity on the Jew, whose luckless fate and wild howls had been the first signs that struck her, with her returning senses; then she caught sight of Chauvelin, in his neat, dark clothes, which seemed hardly crumpled after the stirring events of the last few hours. He was smiling sarcastically, and his pale eyes peered down at her with a look of intense malice.

With mock gallantry, he stooped and raised her icy-cold hand to his lips, which sent a thrill of indescribable loathing through Marguerite's weary frame.

"I much regret, fair lady," he said in his most suave tones, "that circumstances, over which I have no control, compel me to leave you here for the moment. But I go away, secure in the knowledge that I do not leave you unprotected. Our friend Benjamin here, though a trifle the worse for wear at the present moment, will prove a gallant defender of your fair person, I have no doubt. At dawn I will send an escort for you; until then, I feel sure that you will find him devoted, though perhaps a trifle slow."

Marguerite only had the strength to turn her head away. Her heart was broken with cruel anguish. One awful thought had returned to her mind, together with gathering consciousness: "What had become of Percy?—What of Armand?"

She knew nothing of what had happened after she heard the cheerful song, "God save the King," which she believed to be the signal of death.

"I, myself," concluded Chauvelin, "must now very reluctantly leave you. *Au revoir*, fair lady. We meet, I hope, soon in London. Shall I see you at the Prince of Wales' garden party?—No?—Ah, well, *au revoir!*—Remember me, I pray, to Sir Percy Blakeney."

And, with a last ironical smile and bow, he once more kissed her hand, and disappeared down the footpath in the wake of the soldiers, and followed by the imperturbable Desgas.

Chapter 31

The Escape

Marguerite listened—half-dazed as she was—to the fast-retreating, firm footsteps of the four men.

All nature was so still that she, lying with her ear close to the ground, could distinctly trace the sound of their tread, as they ultimately turned into the road, and presently the faint echo of the old cart-wheels, the halting gait of the lean nag, told her that her enemy was a quarter of a league away. How long she lay there she knew not. She had lost count of time; dreamily she looked up at the moonlit sky, and listened to the monotonous roll of the waves.

The invigorating scent of the sea was nectar to her wearied body, the immensity of the lonely cliffs was silent and dreamlike. Her brain only remained conscious of its ceaseless, its intolerable torture of uncertainty.

She did not know!—

324

She did not know whether Percy was even now, at this moment, in the hands of the soldiers of the Republic, enduring—as she had done herself—the gibes and jeers of his malicious enemy. She did not know, on the other hand, whether Armand's lifeless body did not lie there, in the hut, whilst Percy had escaped, only to hear that his wife's hands had guided the human bloodhounds to the murder of Armand and his friends.

The physical pain of utter weariness was so great, that she hoped confidently her tired body could rest here for-ever, after all the turmoil, the passion, and the intrigues of the last few days—here, beneath that clear sky, within sound of the sea, and with this balmy autumn breeze whispering to her a last lullaby. All was so solitary, so silent, like unto dreamland. Even the last faint echo of the distant cart had long ago died away, afar.

Suddenly . . . a sound . . . the strangest, undoubtedly, that these lonely cliffs of France had ever heard, broke the silent solemnity of the shore.

So strange a sound was it that the gentle breeze ceased to murmur, the tiny pebbles to roll down the steep incline! So strange, that Marguerite, wearied, overwrought as she was, thought that the beneficial unconsciousness of the approach of death was playing her half-sleeping senses a weird and elusive trick.

It was the sound of a good, solid, absolutely British "Damn!"

The sea-gulls in their nest awoke and looked round in astonishment; a distant and solitary owl set up a midnight hoot, the tall cliffs frowned down majestically at the strange, unheard-of sacrilege.

Marguerite did not trust her ears. Half-raising herself on her hands, she strained every sense to see or hear, to know the meaning of this very earthly sound.

All was still again for the space of a few seconds; the same silence once more fell upon the great and lonely vastness.

Then Marguerite, who listened as in a trance, who felt she must be dreaming with that cool, magnetic moonlight overhead, heard again; and this time her heart stood still, her eyes large and dilated, looked round her, not daring to trust to her other sense.

"Odd's life! but I wish those demmed fellows had not hit quite so hard!"

This time it was quite unmistakable, only one particular pair of essentially British lips could have uttered those words, in sleepy, drawly, affected tones.

"Damn!" repeated those same British lips, emphatically. "Zounds! but I'm as weak as a rat!"

In a moment Marguerite was on her feet.

Was she dreaming? Were those great, stony cliffs the gates of paradise? Was the fragrant breath of the breeze suddenly caused by the flutter of angels' wings, bringing tidings of unearthly joys to her, after all her suffering, or—faint and ill—was she the prey of delirium?

She listened again, and once again she heard the same very earthly sounds of good, honest British language, not the least akin to whisperings from paradise or flutter of angels' wings.

She looked round her eagerly at the tall cliffs, the lonely hut, the great stretch of rocky beach. Somewhere there, above or below her, behind a boulder or inside a crevice, but still hidden from her longing, feverish eyes, must be the owner of that voice, which once used to irritate her, but which now would make her the happiest woman in Europe, if only she could locate it.

"Percy! Percy!" she shrieked hysterically, tortured between doubt and hope, "I am here! Come to me! Where are you? Percy! Percy! . . ."

"It's all very well calling me, m'dear!" said the same sleepy, drawly voice, "but odd's my life, I cannot come to you: those demmed frog-eaters have trussed me like a goose on a spit, and I am as weak as a mouse . . . I cannot get away."

And still Marguerite did not understand. She did not realise for at least another ten seconds whence came that voice, so drawly, so dear, but alas! with a strange accent of weakness and of suffering. There was no one within sight . . . except by that rock . . . Great God! . . . the Jew! . . . Was she mad or dreaming? . . .

His back was against the pale moonlight, he was half-crouching, trying vainly to raise himself with his arms tightly pinioned. Marguerite ran up to him, took his head in both her hands . . . and looked straight into a pair of blue eyes, good-natured, even a trifle amused—shining out of the weird and distorted mask of the Jew.

"Percy! . . . Percy! . . . my husband!" she gasped, faint with the fulness of her joy. "Thank God! Thank God!"

"La! m'dear," he rejoined good-humoredly, "we will both do that anon, an you think you can loosen these demmed ropes, and release me from my inelegant attitude."

She had no knife, her fingers were numb and weak, but she worked away with her teeth, while great welcome tears poured from her eyes, onto those poor, pinioned hands.

"Odd's life!" he said, when at last, after frantic efforts on her part, the ropes seemed at last to be giving way, "but I marvel whether it has ever happened before, that an English gentleman allowed himself to be licked by a demmed foreigner, and made no attempt to give as good as he got."

It was very obvious that he was exhausted from sheer physical pain, and when at last the rope gave way, he fell in a heap against the rock.

Marguerite looked helplessly round her.

"Oh! for a drop of water on this awful beach!" she cried in agony, seeing that he was ready to faint again.

"Nay, m'dear," he murmured with his good-humoured smile, "personally I should prefer a drop of good French brandy! an you'll dive in the pocket of this dirty old garment, you'll find my flask. . . . I am demmed if I can move."

When he had drunk some brandy, he forced Marguerite to do likewise.

"La! that's better now! Eh! little woman?" he said, with a sigh of satisfaction. "Heigh-ho! but this is a queer rig-up for Sir Percy Blakeney, Bart., to be found in by his lady, and no mistake. Begad!" he added, passing his hand over his chin, "I haven't been shaved for nearly twenty hours: I must look a disgusting object. As for these curls . . ."

And laughingly he took off the disfiguring wig and curls, and stretched out his long limbs, which were cramped from many hours' stooping. Then he bent forward and looked long and searchingly into his wife's blue eyes.

"Percy," she whispered, while a deep blush suffused her delicate cheeks and neck, "if you only knew . . ."

"I do know, dear . . . everything," he said with infinite gentleness.

"And can you ever forgive?"

"I have naught to forgive, sweetheart; your heroism, your devotion, which I, alas! so little deserved, have more than atoned for that unfortunate episode at the ball."

"Then you knew? . . . " she whispered, "all the time . . ."

"Yes!" he replied tenderly, "I knew . . . all the time. . . . But, begad! had I but known what a noble heart yours was, my Margot, I should have trusted you, as you deserved to be trusted, and you would not have had to undergo the terrible sufferings of the past few hours, in order to run after a husband, who has done so much that needs forgiveness."

They were sitting side by side, leaning up against a rock, and he had rested his aching head on her shoulder. She certainly now deserved the name of "the happiest woman in Europe."

"It is a case of the blind leading the lame, sweetheart, is it not?" he said with his good-natured smile of old. "Odd's life! but I do not know which are the more sore, my shoulders or your little feet."

He bent forward to kiss them, for they peeped out through her torn stockings, and bore pathetic witness to her endurance and devotion.

"But, Armand . . . " she said, with sudden terror and remorse, as in the midst of her happiness the image of the beloved brother, for whose sake she had so deeply sinned, rose now before her mind.

"Oh! have no fear for Armand, sweetheart," he said tenderly, "did I not pledge you my word that he should be safe? He with de Tournay and the others are even now on board the *Day Dream.*"

"But how?" she gasped, "I do not understand."

"Yet, 'tis simple enough, m'dear," he said with that funny, half-shy, half-inane laugh of his, "you see! when I found that that brute Chauvelin meant to stick to me like a leech, I thought the best thing I could do, as I could not shake him off, was to take him along with me. I had to get to Armand and the others somehow, and all the roads were patrolled, and every one on the look-out for your humble servant. I knew that when I slipped through Chauvelin's fingers at the 'Chat Gris,' that he would lie in wait for me here, whichever way I took. I wanted to keep an eye on him and his doings, and a British head is as good as a French one any day."

Indeed it had proved to be infinitely better, and Marguerite's heart was filled with joy and marvel, as he continued to recount to her the daring manner in which he had snatched the fugitives away, right from under Chauvelin's very nose.

"Dressed as the dirty old Jew," he said gaily, "I knew I should not be recognized. I had met Reuben Goldstein in Calais earlier in the evening. For a few gold pieces he supplied me with this rig-out, and undertook to bury himself out of sight of everybody, whilst he lent me his cart and nag."

"But if Chauvelin had discovered you," she gasped excitedly, "your disguise was good . . . but he is so sharp."

"Odd's fish!" he rejoined quietly, "then certainly the

game would have been up. I could but take the risk. I know human nature pretty well by now," he added, with a note of sadness in his cheery, young voice, "and I know these Frenchmen out and out. They so loathe a Jew, that they never come nearer than a couple of yards of him, and begad! I fancy that I contrived to make myself look about as loathsome an object as it is possible to conceive."

"Yes!—and then?" she asked eagerly.

"Zooks!—then I carried out my little plan: that is to say, at first I only determined to leave everything to chance, but when I heard Chauvelin giving his orders to the soldiers, I thought that Fate and I were going to work together after all. I reckoned on the blind obedience of the soldiers. Chauvelin had ordered them on pain of death, not to stir until the tall Englishman came. Desgas had thrown me down in a heap quite close to the hut; the soldiers took no notice of the Jew, who had driven Citoyen Chauvelin to this spot. I managed to free my hands from the ropes, with which the brute had trussed me; I always carry pencil and paper with me wherever I go, and I hastily scrawled a few important instructions on a scrap of paper; then I looked about me. I crawled up to the hut, under the very noses of the soldiers, who lay under cover without stirring, just as Chauvelin had ordered them to do, then I dropped my little note into the hut, through a chink in the wall, and waited. In this note I told the fugitives to walk noiselessly out of the hut, creep down the cliffs, keep to the left until they came to the first creek, to give a certain signal, when the boat of the *Day Dream*, which lay in wait not far out to sea, would pick them up. They obeyed implicitly, fortunately for them and for me.

The soldiers who saw them were equally obedient to Chauvelin's orders. They did not stir! I waited for nearly half an hour; when I knew that the fugitives were safe I gave the signal, which caused so much stir."

And that was the whole story. It seemed so simple! and Marguerite could but marvel at the wonderful ingenuity, the boundless pluck and audacity which had evolved and helped to carry out this daring plan.

"But those brutes struck you!" she gasped in horror, at the bare recollection of the fearful indignity.

"Well! that could not be helped," he said gently, "whilst my little wife's fate was so uncertain, I had to remain here by her side. Odd's life!" he added merrily, "never fear! Chauvelin will lose nothing by waiting, I warrant! Wait till I get him back to England!—La! he shall pay for the thrashing he gave me with compound interest, I promise you."

Marguerite laughed. It was so good to be beside him, to hear his cheery voice, to watch that good-humoured twinkle in his blue eyes, as he stretched out his strong arms, in longing for that foe, and anticipation of his well-deserved punishment.

Suddenly, however, she started: the happy blush left her cheek, the light of joy died out of her eyes: she had heard a stealthy footfall overhead, and a stone had rolled down from the top of the cliffs right down to the beach below.

"What's that?" she whispered in horror and alarm.

"Oh! nothing, m'dear," he muttered with a pleasant laugh, "only a trifle you happened to have forgotten . . . my friend, Ffoulkes . . ."

"Sir Andrew!" she gasped.

Indeed, she had wholly forgotten the devoted friend and companion, who had trusted and stood by her during all these hours of anxiety and suffering. She remembered him now, tardily and with a pang of remorse.

"Aye! you had forgotten him, hadn't you, m'dear?" said Sir Percy, merrily. "Fortunately, I met him, not far from the 'Chat Gris,' before I had that interesting supper party, with my friend Chauvelin. . . . Odd's life! but I have a score to settle with that young reprobate!—but in the meanwhile, I told him of a very long, very roundabout road, that would bring him here by a very circuitous road which Chauvelin's men would never suspect, just about the time when we are ready for him, eh, little woman?"

"And he obeyed?" asked Marguerite, in utter astonishment.

"Without word or question. See, here he comes. He was not in the way when I did not want him, and now he arrives in the nick of time. Ah! he will make pretty little Suzanne a most admirable and methodical husband."

In the meanwhile Sir Andrew Ffoulkes had cautiously worked his way down the cliffs: he stopped once or twice, pausing to listen for the whispered words, which would guide him to Blakeney's hiding-place.

"Blakeney!" he ventured to say at last cautiously, "Blakeney! are you there?"

The next moment he rounded the rock against which Sir Percy and Marguerite were leaning, and seeing the weird figure still clad in the long Jew's gaberdine, he paused in sudden, complete bewilderment.

But already Blakeney had struggled to his feet.

"Here I am, friend," he said with his funny, inane

laugh, "all alive! though I do look a begad scarecrow in these demmed things."

"Zooks!" ejaculated Sir Andrew in boundless astonishment as he recognized his leader, "of all the . . ."

The young man had seen Marguerite, and happily checked the forcible language that rose to his lips, at sight of the exquisite Sir Percy in this weird and dirty garb.

"Yes!" said Blakeney, calmly, "of all the . . . hem! . . . My friend!—I have not yet had time to ask you what you were doing in France, when I ordered you to remain in London? Insubordination? What? Wait till my shoulders are less sore, and, by Gad, see the punishment you'll get."

"Odd's fish! I'll bear it," said Sir Andrew, with a merry laugh, "seeing that you are alive to give it. . . . Would you have had me allow Lady Blakeney to do the journey alone? But, in the name of heaven, man, where did you get these extraordinary clothes?"

"Lud! they are a bit quaint, ain't they?" laughed Sir Percy, jovially. "But, odd's fish!" he added, with sudden earnestness and authority, "now you are here, Ffoulkes, we must lose no more time: that brute Chauvelin may send someone to look after us."

Marguerite was so happy, she could have stayed here for ever, hearing his voice, asking a hundred questions. But at mention of Chauvelin's name she started in quick alarm, afraid for the dear life she would have died to save.

"But how can we get back?" she gasped; "the roads are full of soldiers between here and Calais, and . . ."

"We are not going back to Calais, sweetheart," he said, "but just the other side of Gris Nez, not half a league from here. The boat of the *Day Dream* will meet us there."

"The boat of the *Day Dream?*"

"Yes!" he said, with a merry laugh; "another little trick of mine. I should have told you before that when I slipped that note into the hut, I also added another for Armand, which I directed him to leave behind, and which has sent Chauvelin and his men running full tilt back to the 'Chat Gris' after me; but the first little note contained my real instructions, including those to old Briggs. He had my orders to go out further to sea, and then towards the west. When well out of sight of Calais, he will send the galley to a little creek he and I know of, just beyond Gris Nez. The men will look out for me—we have a preconcerted signal, and we will all be safely aboard, whilst Chauvelin and his men solemnly sit and watch the creek which is 'just opposite the "Chat Gris." ' "

"The other side of Gris Nez? But I . . . I cannot walk, Percy," she moaned helplessly as, trying to struggle to her tired feet, she found herself unable even to stand.

"I will carry you, dear," he said simply; "the blind leading the lame, you know."

Sir Andrew was ready, too, to help with the precious burden, but Sir Percy would not entrust his beloved to any arms but his own.

"When you and she are both safely on board the *Day Dream,*" he said to his young comrade, "and I feel that Mlle. Suzanne's eyes will not greet me in England with reproachful looks, then it will be my turn to rest."

And his arms, still vigorous in spite of fatigue and suffering, closed round Marguerite's poor, weary body, and lifted her as gently as if she had been a feather.

Then, as Sir Andrew discreetly kept out of earshot,

there were many things said—or rather whispered—which even the autumn breeze did not catch, for it had gone to rest.

All his fatigue was forgotten; his shoulders must have been very sore, for the soldiers had hit hard, but the man's muscles seemed made of steel, and his energy was almost supernatural. It was a weary tramp, half a league along the stony side of the cliffs, but never for a moment did his courage give way or his muscles yield to fatigue. On he tramped, with firm footstep, his vigorous arms encircling the precious burden, and . . . no doubt, as she lay, quiet and happy, at times lulled to momentary drowsiness, at others watching, through the slowly gathering morning light, the pleasant face with the lazy, drooping blue eyes, ever cheerful, ever illumined with a good-humoured smile, she whispered many things, which helped to shorten the weary road, and acted as a soothing balsam to his aching sinews.

The many-hued light of dawn was breaking in the east, when at last they reached the creek beyond Gris Nez. The galley lay in wait: in answer to a signal from Sir Percy, she drew near, and two sturdy British sailors had the honor of carrying my lady into the boat.

Half an hour later, they were on board the *Day Dream*. The crew, who of necessity were in their master's secrets, and who were devoted to him heart and soul, were not surprised to see him arriving in so extraordinary a disguise.

Armand St. Just and the other fugitives were eagerly awaiting the advent of their brave rescuer; he would not stay to hear the expressions of their gratitude, but found the way to his private cabin as quickly as he could, leaving Marguerite quite happy in the arms of her brother.

Everything on board the *Day Dream* was fitted with that exquisite luxury, so dear to Sir Percy Blakeney's heart, and by the time they all landed at Dover he had found time to get into some of the sumptuous clothes which he loved, and of which he always kept a supply on board his yacht.

The difficulty was to provide Marguerite with a pair of shoes, and great was the little middy's joy when my lady found that she could put foot on English shore in his best pair.

The rest is silence!—silence and joy for those who had endured so much suffering, yet found at last a great and lasting happiness.

But it is on record that at the brilliant wedding of Sir Andrew Ffoulkes, Bart., with Mlle. Suzanne de Tournay de Basserive, a function at which H.R.H. the Prince of Wales and all the *élite* of fashionable society were present, the most beautiful woman there was unquestionably Lady Blakeney, whilst the clothes Sir Percy Blakeney wore were the talk of the *jeunesse dorée* of London for many days.

It is also a fact that M. Chauvelin, the accredited agent of the French Republican Government, was not present at that or any other social function in London, after that memorable evening at Lord Grenville's ball.

Afterword

Kathryn Lasky

*I*t was a November day many years ago when I first read *The Scarlet Pimpernel*. It had to be November because that was when we did France. England had been dispatched in September and October of my ninth-grade European history course. It was probably late November when I read the novel. We had already rammed through the era when France was not France at all but just a bubbling cauldron of Gallic states waiting to be pulled together by Charlemagne. That must have taken at least three weeks. We were now at the Revolution. We had memorized the reasons behind the revolution. (There were three as I recall.) We had learned the dates of the Reign of Terror, the names of the main players, studied diagrams of the guillotine, even made mini models of it and sliced apples (that was what was considered a hands-on learning experience in those days).

Although such a curriculum might sound like a press march through history, there was one very significant feature in this course—the absence of textbooks. Instead, we were required to read historical novels and biographies. The teacher, a certain Sarah Lois Haber, served as a kind of textbook incarnate. Her large head with its voluminous pompadour was stuffed with historical facts and figures. Maps of every battle or skirmish were etched on her brain. She gave us the data, and from that point on we were to take it and read with passion the historical novels that lined the floor-to-ceiling shelves of her classroom. This was how we slammed our way across continents, through centuries, revolutions, annihilations, wars, plagues, and the crumblings and resurrections of empires.

It wasn't a bad teaching strategy. Beneath it all was the basic conviction that facts can only take a person so far. And "so far" was not far enough for Miss Haber. Her students must understand not simply the facts, but the fabric of history. They must be smuggled into the very heart of the time, the events, and the place. Historical novels were the vehicle. What better way could there be to cut to the center of the drama of the year 1789 than on the satin coattails of the daring, the impudent, the elusive Scarlet Pimpernel?

Has ever a spy been so marvelously packaged as Sir Percy Blakeney? Trussed up in his exquisite lace jabots and embroidered waistcoats, the perfect eighteenth-century fop with his lazy eyes, idiotic laugh, and seemingly slow wit, he was devoted to fashion, fast horses, and silly jokes. He was the embodiment of frivolity and material excess.

Yet, behind the lace and satin was a blend of cunning, courage, impudence, and brains. To have deliberately chosen to appear as a brainless idiot makes the character of Sir Percy infinitely enigmatic and one of the most intriguing in spy fiction. Can one ever imagine James Bond subjecting himself to such compromising transformations, ones that could possibly impugn his masculinity as well as his intelligence? The patriotism of 007 definitely had its limitations and stopped well short of lace jabots and wrist flounces, not to mention a falsetto laugh! Such is not the case with the Scarlet Pimpernel.

The Baroness Orczy, however, knew that it was not enough to simply invent a fabulous character. She needed to use him well, and smart lady that she was, she seemed to realize first of all that battlegrounds thoughout history— despite changes in costume, weapons and combatants— have a dreary monotony. She chose instead to set her action, for the most part, away from the smoke and fire of combat and the bloody platform of Madame la Guillotine. She used as her stage the balls of the aristocracy and the humble wayside inns of small coastal English and French villages. In effect these settings were the true battlefields of the Scarlet Pimpernel and it is in these places that the readers' sensibilities are awakened to the very texture of the period and its conflicts. When Marguerite Blakeney from her attic perch in the squalid inn of Chat Gris peeps through the tattered curtains, we are drawn into that spellbound horror she is experiencing as she watches the surly innkeeper cursing the aristocracy while he prepares the table for the *sacrré aristo*. Marguerite's own husband is about to arrive and become entrapped. We hear the burr of that elongated roughened r sound as the innkeeper mutters and wipes the cutlery with his dirty rag. Every detail from the torn tablecloth to the spoon and the wineglass looms with cinematic intensity. Time has been bridged and a vanished world has reappeared with every atom in place.

Only pages before, we had been caught in a crossfire of the elaborate bows and curtsies required by the rigid etiquette of the period. We had seen the powdered wigs, the lavish gowns, and the be-ribboned walking sticks carried by the ladies of fashion. These scenes far from the fusillade of the Bastille or the blood of the guillotine have astounding revelatory powers. It is as if the Baroness has provided the reader with a periscope to see the profound futility, emptiness, and moral bankruptcy of the period.

The real tension that underlies the book comes from the Scarlet Pimpernel himself and the elaborate masks he has chosen to wear to disguise his true nature. It is the acts of masking and unmasking that give the story its driving energy. Sir Percy is more than clever in his disguises. They not only cover up his identity but reveal and exploit the inherent stupidities and weaknesses of his adversaries. By disguising himself as an old Jew he exposes the rampant anti-semitism of France as well as makes use of it for his own gain. For how else can an immensely tall man disguise his stature than to slouch in a manner thought to be congenitally Jewish! When an entire nation has so thoroughly deluded itself it makes easy work for one clever spy.

It was my contention as a young reader, and remains so

as a middle-aged reader now, that Baroness Orczy was not merely serving up a literary device when she conceived the notion of the fop-as-spy. The Scarlet Pimpernel is much more than a device. We as readers become mesmerized by Sir Percy Blakeney not merely because of his courage and wit but because he represents to us what we all dream of doing—trying on another life and daring to play a high-stakes game. This in fact is the one demand that all truly great literature makes of us: It proposes a new measure or a new identity and then attempts to lure the reader into believing that he or she can perhaps do it too. Play this high-stakes game. In this instance the game is in a time and place that may seem distant to young readers and yet through the Baroness's consummate narrative skill the story crackles with life and inexorably we are drawn to its very center. We have in fact been smuggled through time to become stowaways in history.